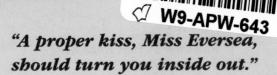

"A proper kiss, Miss Eversea, should turn you inside out."

⁓∞⁓

"It should . . . touch places in you that you didn't know existed, set them ablaze, until your entire being is hungry and wild. It should . . . hold a moment, I want to explain this as clearly as possible."

He tipped his head back and paused to consider, as though he were envisioning this and wanted to relate every detail correctly. "It should slice right down through you like a cutlass with a pleasure so devastating it's very nearly pain."

He waited, watching her face, allowing her to accommodate the potent words.

Her mouth was parted. Her breathing short. She couldn't look away. His eyes and voice held her as fast as if he'd cradled her face with his hands.

And as he said them, an echo of sensation sounded in her, like a remembered dream, an instinct awakened.

She thought about Mars getting ready to give Venus a good pleasuring.

Stop, she should say.

"And . . . ?" she whispered.

Romances by Julie Anne Long

Julie Anne Long

What I Did For A Duke

AVON

An Imprint of HarperCollinsPublishers

This is a work of fiction. Names, characters, places, and incidents are products of the author's imagination or are used fictitiously and are not to be construed as real. Any resemblance to actual events, locales, organizations, or persons, living or dead, is entirely coincidental.

AVON BOOKS
An Imprint of HarperCollins*Publishers*
10 East 53rd Street
New York, New York 10022-5299

Copyright © 2011 by Julie Anne Long
ISBN 978-0-06-188568-6
www.avonromance.com

First Avon Books paperback printing: March 2011

Avon Trademark Reg. U.S. Pat. Off. and in Other Countries, Marca Registrada, Hecho en U.S.A.
HarperCollins® is a registered trademark of HarperCollins Publishers.

Printed in the U.S.A.

10 9 8 7 6 5 4 3 2 1

For Steve Axelrod, brilliant agent and friend—
it's been an honor, pleasure, and adventure so
far, and I have a hunch it will continue to be.

Acknowledgments

My sincere appreciation to my splendid editor, May Chen, for her enthusiasm, support and insight; to all the gifted, hard-working people at Avon who helped make this book possible, especially Tom Egner for the beautiful cover design; to my fabulous agent, Steve Axelrod, for the wisdom and humor that make him such a pleasure to work with; and to Melisa, Karen, Toni, Josh, and all my friends and loved ones for inspiration, support, laughter, and sanity.

What I Did For A Duke

Chapter 1

From a deucedly awkward crouch between a birdbath and a shrubbery in the back garden of a Sussex manor house, Ian Eversea watched the silhouette of a woman pass tantalizingly once . . . twice . . . *Hallelujah!* Three times!—before the upper story window.

The window went black. The lamp had been doused.

A signal and a confirmation.

He launched to a stand. His knees cracked like gunshots. He froze. Yet he was alone but for a sky full of stars; naught a soul would witness his furtive journey to the tree.

The road to this tree—and to the last three nights of coyly escalating sensual games in her bedroom—began during a conversation at a ball in honor of Abigail's engagement to the Duke of Falconbridge one week earlier. At this very house.

Introductions were made; attraction was instant; conversation was brief, every word of it a veritable pearl of innuendo in a lengthening strand of indiscretion. From the beginning, for Ian, all of it was excellent, *excellent*: her lush burnished beauty, the veneer of innocence over a delightful if startling moral recklessness, all of *that* wrapped in one particularly titillating danger: she was engaged to Alexander Moncrieffe, the Duke of Falconbridge, who'd allegedly poisoned his first wife a decade earlier (naught had ever been *proven*, of course, nor had any formal accusation ever been made, but the *ton* knew better than to let such delicious gossip die). He'd fought more than one duel. So they said. He was a cold, elegant, staggeringly wealthy man. He gambled, both at cards and with investments, and he never, ever lost. One trifled with him at one's peril.

Or so gossip had it.

Before drifting away, Lady Abigail had tapped Ian lightly on the arm with her fan and laconically added there was an oak tree *right* outside her bedchamber window.

He knew the tree. He'd seen it as they'd arrived for the ball through the opportunistic eyes of the typical Eversea male: it leaned conspiratorially against the red brick of the house; its trunk was solid and there were low sturdy branches a grown man could easily scale without damaging essential parts of his anatomy. But its most compelling feature was the branch that stretched yearningly—one might (*he* might) even say insistently—toward a particular window.

And he'd wondered who'd slept in that room.

It was no cause for wonderment for either Ian or Lady Abigail that they were in such accord.

Perhaps I'll see you after midnight tomorrow.

There had never been a "perhaps" about it.

For three nights he'd made this journey, from the crouch by the fountain to her bed. For three nights he'd progressed from a kiss to getting her nearly undressed. Tonight she'd promised to be entirely unwrapped when he slid into the bed, and urged him to be, too.

So his heart was thumping hard when he jumped up to get a grip on a lower branch, shinned up the trunk to the one that led to her window and swung up. She'd left the window open an inch or two. He curled his fingers beneath and slid it up gingerly, as too eagerly grabbing at the weathering frame the night before was how he'd come by his splinter. He hooked both legs over the sill, then ducked to slide his long body through. The drop into her bedroom was short; a thick Savonnerie carpet swirled in lights and darks muffled his landing.

He tore off his clothes with the urgency of a man fighting off fire ants.

He propped a hand on a table near the window, yanked off his boots, and lined them up side by side on the carpet. His fingers flew over buttons as he rid himself of his coat and shirt and trousers; he wadded all of them together and stacked them next to the bed.

Oh, God. And it was all *very* good, from the crouch to the splinter to the tree. Every sound, every sensation, amplified his desire and was now familiar and erotic and all of a piece, all part of the act itself: The rustle of the sheets as he lifted them to slide into the bed next to her, the first sweet shock of their smooth coolness on his skin, the ghost of lavender scent they released, the first skim of his fingers over the warm skin of the woman waiting in bed, herself little more than a shadow made of fragrant and silky flesh in which he would soon bury himself as she'd promised, her sigh of welcome, the unmistakable gut-chilling metallic *click* of a pistol being cocked—

Holy Mother of—!

Perhaps not that.

That was new.

Ian and Abigail scrambled away from each other and sat bolt upright in the bed. Heart thudding against his breastbone, Ian fumbled futilely for his pistol—he was *nude* and his pistol was in his boot. He surreptitiously slid one bare foot out of the bed and laid it flat on the floor, preparing to launch as appropriate—out the window or at the wielder of the pistol. His eyes frantically raked the dark.

"Oh, you won't want to move another hair."

The voice was low, dark, and almost offhandedly, lightheartedly menacing.

Mother of God. It was like the night itself had spoken.

Ian was not a coward. But all the little hairs on the back of his neck and arms went erect when one of the shadows detached itself from the corner chair in which it had been slumping and grew taller and taller . . . and began to drift toward them.

Not a spectre. A man, of course. Dressed strategically in dark clothing. The better to hide, to corner, to trap.

Abigail's breathing was audible, tattered by terror.

The man moved toward the bed with the languid loose-limbed purpose of a stalking leopard. Errant moonlight allowed in through the window glanced off the barrel of his pistol. And off something else, something metal, in his other hand. . . . A lamp.

He settled it gently, precisely down on the small table next to the window, and then took what seemed like an insufferable amount of time to light it, but then fear did rather play havoc with one's sense of time. The flame shuddered fitfully and at last took hold. And at last a man's face flickered in and out of light and shadow. It was a bit like watching Lucifer sitting at a campfire.

"Moncrieffe."

Ian's voice was hoarse with shock. Unfortunately, Abigail gasped the word at the same time, lending the flavor of a bad pantomime to the whole thing.

It all would have been quite funny had this been someone else's grave, grave dilemma.

The Duke of Falconbridge pondered them. He was already unusually tall, and the lamplight threw an even taller shadow of him against the wall. Two spectral dukes hovering over the bed, and both of them had pistols.

Ian couldn't decide whether to fix his eyes upon Moncrieffe's face or the weapon. One was aimed precisely at the center of Ian's chest, which was covered now in a cold film of sweat. Both were identically gleaming, impassive, and deadly.

He had no doubts about whether Moncrieffe was capable of shooting. His reputation rather preceded him.

"Eversea." The duke nodded in an ironic parody of a social greeting.

It contained nothing of surprise. As though he had expected him.

Had in fact, stalked him, watched him, and lain in wait— . . . God . . . for how many nights?

"How did y-you . . . ?" Ian stammered.

Perhaps this wasn't the time to ask questions, but he truly was curious.

His hands were perspiring now, too.

"As I never sleep before midnight, Eversea, and I'm a guest here, I saw your horse tethered in the road for three nights now. Honestly, knowing you as I do, it wasn't difficult to draw conclusions. I set the horse free, by the way."

Christ! He loved that horse.

Well, they were in Sussex, and the horse would find its way back to Eversea House, of that he was certain. Or into the hands of the Gypsies who camped in Sussex, who would know better than attempt to sell a horse that belonged to an Eversea.

But as for whether *Ian* would ever make it back to the house . . .

Abigail's hand found his and gripped. As if he could offer comfort! He might need that hand to do battle with the duke.

Perhaps if he attempted to placate. "I never . . ." he began. "We never *quite* . . ."

The duke's eyebrows flicked upward, daring Ian to finish that thought.

Which he regretted doing the moment he did.

". . . It's not what it seems."

The ensuing silence was palpably incredulous. Even Abigail turned to look at him in gap-mouthed astonishment that anyone would actually say that outside of a bad pantomime.

But bloody hell—and more's the pity—it was true. More accurately, it wasn't *yet* what it seemed.

"I might be more moved by that assertion if it didn't sound so *regretful*, Eversea."

The duke almost sounded amused. But then irony, when delivered cold and shaved very, very fine, could sound like amusement.

There was nothing at all amusing about the un-wavering aim of that pistol.

Abigail and Ian flinched when the duke broke from the circle of lamplight and strode slowly over to Abigail's side of the bed. All this *slinking* was very unnerving, because Ian knew the man usually moved as though he resented gravity. With long, im-patient strides and focus and purpose. He wasn't a *stroller.*

He stood over her.

Abigail audibly swallowed.

Down, down, down. The duke lowered the pistol. They watched it with the avidity with which they would an indecisive cobra. Perhaps . . . perhaps he meant to lock it? To tuck it away? To—

He stopped lowering it when the muzzle was aimed precisely at Abigail's throat.

She squeezed her eyes closed and hoarse prayers rushed between her lips.

Ian's rib cage stopped moving. His breathing had arrested. Abigail's hand was like ice in his, and for an ungentlemanly moment he wanted to fling it back to her, to reject their mutual idiocy, to ask her how on earth she thought *he* could comfort her or resolve the circumstance. The two of them were only involved for the pleasure of it. He assessed his chances of flying at the duke and knocking him to the floor before he could shoot. After all, he was naked and coated in terror sweat and would therefore theoretically be dif-ficult to grip. The duke was tall but wiry and *might* topple should he be struck by a hurtling Eversea.

But Ian didn't like his chances. He'd seen the man shoot at Manton's.

He'd no choice. He'd talked his way into this; he'd talk his way out of it.

"For God's sake, Moncrieffe." His voice was still frayed but he was proud that it didn't tremble. "Do you have to torment *her*? Call me out or shoot *me* and have done with it. The fault is entirely mine."

This wasn't at all true, as Abigail had in fact set the whole thing in motion, but it was perhaps the most gallant thing Ian had yet said in his life. Then again, centuries of splendid breeding and battle-tempering were difficult to combat. They rose inconveniently to the surface in moments of greatest peril, it would seem.

"Just . . . for the love of God, do whatever it is you intend to do."

Silence as the duke considered—or pretended to consider—this entreaty.

"Very well," the duke said with equanimity. "As you make an excellent point, Eversea, I'll do what I intended to do all along. And what I *intend* to do . . ."

Ian was so focused on the pistol he hadn't noticed the man was unbuttoning his trousers as he spoke.

". . . is share her with you. Slide over, Eversea."

Their gasps nearly sucked the air out of the room.

Satisfied he'd shocked a few years from their lives, Alexander Moncrieffe, the sixth Duke of Falconbridge, paused his hand on his trouser buttons and contemplated all the whiteness: bulging white eyes, the naked white shoulders, the white sheet his fiancée had yanked modestly up beneath her chin to disguise from him all that pale nudity she was willingly sharing with Eversea.

He knew him, of course, and his brothers and

father, from White's, from entirely noncommittal encounters over cigars and brandies in libraries after balls. They were a close-knit, legendarily charming, legendarily wealthy lot.

He mulled the notion of toying with them a little more and rejected it as pointless. And perhaps more to the point, boring.

Perhaps it was because he was, as was whispered, getting old.

He was nearly *forty*.

Instead he moved—so quickly Abigail stifled another shriek and Ian flung his arms up over their heads in defensive alarm—across the room and yanked the window up high, then bent and seized Eversea's boots—it had been all he could do not to shoot the scoundrel as he'd watched him *neatly line them up*—and hurled them like spears—*One! Two!*—out the window. Next he hurled out the wadded bundle of clothes. For one thrilling moment Ian's coat caught a passing breeze and flapped like a bat sideways through the night before disappearing.

But the shirt didn't get far. It caught in the branches of the tree and dangled by the cuffs and swung gaily, as though inhabited by an invisible trapeze artist.

They were all mesmerized by it for half a second.

Then Moncrieffe spun on his heel and aimed the pistol precisely at Ian's sweating white forehead.

"Leave the way you came, Eversea. Now." The words were etched in menace.

He could sense that Ian's muscles were bunched in preparation to fend off an attack or perhaps launch one. He was younger, but Moncrieffe was certain the fight would be fair even if he didn't have a pistol. He'd had years of experience in which to perfect all manner and methods of fighting, dirty included. Perhaps especially.

"Do you need me to define 'now' for you as well as 'honor,' Eversea? Test me." He took an infinitesimal step forward.

This propelled the boy. Ian slid swiftly from the bed, attempting to drag the sheet with him. He was yanked backward abruptly. He shot a glance over his shoulder. Abigail had a stubborn grip on it.

He tugged desperately, eyebrows raised pleadingly.

She held on to it tenaciously, frowned, and gave her head a frantic little shake.

Oh, for God's sake.

The duke ripped the sheet from Eversea's hand.

Ian Eversea was stark naked in the lamplight, long white feet and hairy shins and all. To his credit, though he didn't quite plant his hands nonchalantly on his hips, he didn't uselessly overlap his hands over his penis. After all, everyone in the room knew he possessed one.

"Moncrieffe. We can settle this like men over the weapon of your choice. I welcome it. I deserve it. You've every right. Choose your weapon."

Touching speech. Everseas were unfailingly polite.

Bastards and *rogues*, but polite.

A number of glib retorts occurred to Moncrieffe. *Well,* you *obviously fancy yourself a swordsman, Eversea,* sprang to mind. But he didn't suffer fools or knaves. Ever. He was nearly forty years old, and the sands in his hourglass of patience were ever-dwindling.

He was sardonic even in his thoughts these days.

"Your punishment will fit the crime." He stood back to allow Eversea a path to the window.

And Ian walked like a condemned prisoner to the guillotine.

The duke and Abigail silently watched Ian squeeze himself out. It wasn't at all pretty, involving bending and contorting and the exposing of places Moncrieffe deeply regretted seeing even by lamplight. At last came what amounted to watching a moonset as his white hindquarters vanished, and then Ian shinnied back out onto that once-inviting, now perfidious branch.

They heard a grunt and a ripping sound as Ian yanked free his shirt from the branch, and came away with only half of it. Moncrieffe shut the window emphatically on Ian's muttered heartfelt epithet and yanked the curtains closed.

When he yanked the curtains Abigail jumped a little and turned regretful, startled eyes on him, as though he'd just prematurely concluded a puppet show.

He weakened. Just a little. Somewhere in the icy clarity of his rage was an echo of what he'd once felt when he looked at her. Her hair was down, and she'd luscious piles of it, like doubloons spilled from a pirate chest. He *could* have had it down long before now. He could have had his hands tangling through it. He could have had her on her back, writhing beneath him. He knew very well how to seduce a woman, to persuade her she wanted him even if she wasn't entirely convinced. Most of them wanted him.

Well, he supposed he should have known.

"Why?" he said finally.

"Why do you want to know?" she rejoindered.

Excellent point. He'd probably regret hearing it.

"Answer me," he said anyway. Beneath the quiet words thrummed a threat that would have had a stalwart man taking a step backward.

She swallowed again. She licked her fear-parched lips. He watched her pink tongue running over their fine outline with a certain detached appreciation that swelled again into rage, like a tide.

"He's delightful," she said simply, faintly, plucking nervously at the sheet she clung to in one fist. Her voice was still weak from shock, but she shrugged, an attempt at arrogance. "And handsome. And young. And popular." She paused. "And nobody likes you," she couldn't resist concluding with faint acid petulance.

Well. Succinct, he would give her that.

Women often *wanted* him. More than one man wanted to *be* him.

But it was true: nobody liked him.

Nobody that mattered to Lady Abigail Beasley, anyhow. And that meant most of the *ton*.

He gave a short laugh. "You think my armor impenetrable, Abigail? That I'm unwoundable? Not *all* of the rumors regarding my character are true."

More of them than were decent *were* true, however. Nevertheless.

It wasn't as though she hadn't known what she was getting into when she'd agreed to marry him, and it wasn't as though she'd objected.

"That *is* your armor, Moncrieffe—the notion that nobody likes you. I do believe you revel in it."

Well, of course he did. But it was such a remarkably astute thing to say, the first honest and true and genuinely intelligent thing she'd ever said directly to him, and he hated her for saying it with her beautiful shoulders bare and the blankets clutched up to her breasts and likely the scent of Ian Eversea lingering on the sheets next to her.

He *ought* to shoot her in principle.

He ought to care enough to do it.

He'd tried to care. He'd in fact intended to try very hard once they were married, which had been the whole point of proposing. Because she'd fired his imagination more than any other woman had in so long. He liked her easy laugh, her rough-velvet voice, the shape of her lips, the color of her hair, the promising lushness of her body, her . . . simplicity. She wasn't stupid; wasn't complex. He'd enjoyed her company the way he did spring days and fine meals. She flirted effortlessly, sometimes provocatively, but never crassly. And he wasn't a fool. He'd made a decision that she would be his next wife, knowing the conclusion of the courtship was as good as foregone, as he was a wealthy duke and she was the daughter of a titled but nearly penniless baron.

Still, he'd courted her like the gentleman he'd been raised to be, astounding everyone. But he didn't want to know whether his future wife could be easily had, so he'd kissed her only once. But oh, he'd made it a thorough one. Thorough enough to know her lips could fire sparks along his nerve endings, and that he wanted her in his bed, and that she hadn't at all minded kissing him. Marriages were made on much less promising starts all the time.

And what was love if not a certain pleasantly deluded familiarity built up over years? If not a set of personal attributes set fire by imagination, the way, for an instance, one can look up at a night sky and see not just a random scattering of bright stars, but an enormous Starry Plough?

Well, wasn't it?

He was certain he'd known once what love meant. He didn't know anymore.

But he *had* meant to try.

And this loss was the thing that fueled his rage. Among other things. *Cuckold* was a ridiculous word. It sounded like precisely what it was. He couldn't pull from the mix of things he felt in the moment which was the truest emotion.

But she'd made a fool of him. As had Eversea.

Nobody ever did that twice. Nobody did it without suffering a consequence.

And revenge he understood.

"Like Mr. Eversea, I'm leaving the way I entered your house, Abigail. Through the front door, past your very alarmed footman, whose loyalty to your family proved no match for a duke with a pistol. Given your predilection for midnight visitors, you may consider hiring a servant with more intestinal fortitude. We shall both put it about that the end of our engagement was a mutual parting of the ways. You will inform your father he will need to see to another way to pay his debts. I will have nothing more to do with either of you. A timely trip to the Continent might be in order to allow things time to settle."

It was more an order than a suggestion, and she knew this well.

And likely rumors about the reasons for her hasty departure would find fertile ground in her absence, and none of them would be charitable. She would likely be unmarriageable in the wake of them. At least to anyone of quality and rank.

It was only what she'd earned.

He watched in silence as the ramifications sank in.

"Alex . . . Ian and I didn't actually . . ." Her voice was trembling now. Gone was arrogance. In its place was entreaty. "I never meant to . . . *I've* never actually . . ."

Even now her sensual rasp of a voice stealthily slipped past his sense and brushed against his senses, and even now they responded like a cat stroked awake from sleep. *We're simple creatures, men*, he thought, with a bitter disdain for himself and Eversea and all other men who were used to taking what they wanted. *We think we're so clever. And yet we're always surprised to find ourselves entrapped or made fools of.*

She'd been a . . . hope. If she were anything else, then his loss was greater, and he'd had enough of loss. His soul fair echoed with it.

She must have sensed the chink in his armor. And slowly, slowly she lowered the sheet, and he watched as a pair of lovely breasts came into view.

God.

He had a good look, as he was a man, after all. He could admire and be repelled at the same time. She would *sell* herself in this moment? He wasn't *that* simple.

"I don't care whether you *actually*. Cover yourself."

He calmly locked his pistol and slid it into the band of his trousers, and with that motion he became aware of exhaustion. His hands felt weighted; his shoulders felt weighted, and now that the rage had ebbed he felt hollow and cold, as though a fever had broken.

Her shoulders dropped with an exhale. Had she really thought he might shoot her? Another man might have. He might have in fact been that other man . . . . ten years ago.

He turned to leave her. But she spoke again.

"What *do* you intend to do to him?"

Her question was excellent. He'd ruined more than one man who had crossed him or betrayed him or had otherwise dealt other than honestly with him. He would destroy a man's fortune with the cold, subtle, thorough determination of a plague of termites in order to make a point. He'd done things of which he was not proud but which he did not regret, and rumor and reputation comprised what was known about him now. It had made him outrageously wealthy and feared.

He was not a kind man. He did not forgive.

And it was true: nobody liked him.

"What makes you think I intend to do anything?" he said softly.

He left her to ponder that as he slipped back down the stairs.

Chapter 2

here's just the one left up there. Wonder why it won't just give up and join its brothers here on the ground? Such *fortitude!*"

Genevieve dutifully peered in the direction Lord Harry Osborne was pointing, which was up. They were standing on the long, tree-flanked lane that led to the Eversea house. Above them the sky was an eye-searing rain-washed blue. Below them the ground was a mosaic of picturesquely dying leaves, red and gold and brown and noisy as they shuffled through them. It was autumn, and all of the trees now looked stripped and vulnerable.

All save one. And trust Harry to notice it.

That single dangling leaf either epitomized suspense or fortitude, depending upon whether one was Genevieve or Harry.

Take the plunge, for God's sake, she willed it.

She stared up at it with all the concentrated force of her deep blue Eversea eyes. But she'd never been able to will things into being with silence, or by wishing upon blown dandelions or stars, and goodness knows she'd tried.

Lord Harry Osborne would be Viscount Garland once his father cocked up his toes. Now he was just a young lord with splendid hair—a dozen shades of gold, artfully waving, pushed away from his high pale forehead—and a profile Genevieve Eversea could have sculpted in marble in the dark from memory and installed atop the pianoforte, if she hadn't feared her brothers would choke to death on their mirth.

Perhaps it was for the best that she didn't know how to sculpt.

She did draw and paint and did both diligently, but possessed modest talent. She didn't mind. Her gift and passion lay in the observation and recognition of talent and beauty, whether it was found in the work of an Italian master or the profile of a viscount-to-be.

Three years ago they'd met. He was the cousin of a cousin of her friend Lady Millicent Blenkenship, and he'd been invited to a house party. Harry was clever, sunny, confident, often gregarious to the point of obliviousness and prone to impassioned expression, for the whole world was a safe and welcoming delight to a handsome young aristocrat. Genevieve was quick, precise, and quiet; she always swiftly sieved her own thoughts through layers of care and propriety before they left her mouth. *Her* proverbial still waters ran very deep. And while Harry's cheery obliviousness often mortified him, not to mention other people, it charmed her to her toes and she excelled at smoothing ruffled feathers. They were both enchanted by beauty; they were both aficionados of art and poetry and fiction; they found each other immeasurably witty. For three years, the two of them, along with the cheerful and open and lovely Lady Millicent, who Genevieve adored but secretly viewed as something of their pet, had been so nearly inseparable that they practically shared a name in the mouths of their other acquaintances: *HarryGenevieveMillicent*.

They'd never spoken of their attachment. But surely it was obvious. Surely everything she felt for Harry pulsed around her, visible as those halos painted around saints in medieval paintings.

And she had waited for three years for Harry to muster nerve to say the words that would make her his wife. The only impediment she could see to their marriage was his lack of funds. Harry would inherit a title—but everybody knew he was in want of an heiress to keep the ancestral lands flourishing. Her father had been indulgent when it came to her brothers' wives; her mother had put her foot down when it came to her girls. She wanted her daughters to marry money and titles.

But they loved Harry. *Everybody* loved Harry. She would win them around to the idea, she knew it.

The guests for the Eversea house party would arrive over several days, on horseback and carriages; Harry yesterday evening. Millicent late last night. Rubbing fists into sleepy eyes, she had promptly tumbled into the bed assigned her and was likely still snoring upstairs or pushing her dark blond mop out of her face in order to get at her sipping chocolate. Millicent was not an early riser. She liked to be among the last to leave a ball at night and the last to leave her bed in the morning. But Genevieve usually sprang out of bed with the sun, helpless not to, as if she were part bird. Harry was another early riser, as he possessed an excess of vigor and needed long days in which to expend it, as he hadn't yet developed a fondness for gaming hells or climbing up the trellises of married countesses or all of those other things that kept a young man out late and in bed all morning snoring and hurling boots or any other available objects at anyone who dared tap at their bedchamber doors before noon.

And so he'd found her this morning, and he'd eaten his eggs with a distracted air. After breakfast, he'd been so diffident he was nearly toeing the ground. She'd never seen him diffident.

After much throat clearing he'd said, "I've something I wish to discuss with you, Genevieve. Will you go for a stroll with me?"

He hadn't made mention at all of Millicent.

Normally such strolls would have waited until Millicent was awake.

And Genevieve had *known*.

Oh, *at last, at last, at last.*

Thump. Thump. Thump. Her heart beat in time with their footsteps, until one seemed like an echo of the other. Anticipation was a shard in her chest. Eversea land stretched all around them, beloved, vast, familiar in all its seasonal incarnations, bit by bit going dormant for the autumn, waiting for winter to have its way with it.

They talked a little of general things. But the farther from the house the quieter Harry grew, until there were more silences than sentences.

And then they'd stopped beneath the tree.

It seemed he couldn't yet speak. He bent to pluck up a leaf. A crimson one. He laid it gently in his palm and studied it as though it were alive.

He looked at her. His eyes were pale blue. Full of glints like sun on the sea when he was contemplating some mischief, clear as a spring sky when he was solemn. She knew his eyes in every emotional weather.

He cleared his throat. "Genevieve, I've something important to say."

Thump, thump, thump. "Yes, Harry?"

I love you, too, Harry.

It seemed as though a fine layer of crystal suddenly enclosed the day. Everything glowed with supernatural brilliance. Even her nerves were spun glass. She would *ping* if he touched her.

Would he touch her after he proposed? Would he . . . kiss her?

Because she had imagined that kiss from the moment he'd first kissed her hand, just the once, in a garden at a ball. She'd memorized the shape of his lips long ago and imagined how they would fit against hers. And over and over she'd relived the brush of his lips against her skin, and knew, she *knew*, that if an impulsively given kiss like that could set fire to her blood, then a proper kiss . . . a proper kiss . . .

Dear God, she was *more* than ready for a proper kiss.

Heat rushed her limbs, flooded her cheeks. *Please, please, please, please.*

"Yes?" The word was barely more than a breath.

"Genevieve, I would very much like to . . ."

He swallowed hard. Beads of sweat appeared at his hairline.

"Yes, Harry?" she coaxed on a whisper. She leaned in. She wanted to remember every detail to include in the story she would tell their grandchildren. He was so close she could see a few largeish pores she hadn't known he'd possessed, and the golden-fair tips of his eyelashes, and the hairs in his nose, though it hardly seemed romantic to think of the hairs in his nose at a moment like this. But there they were and they were part of him and therefore beloved.

And then he filled his lungs with a long, long breath, like a man drawing back a bow, and his words rode out on an exhale that nearly blew back her hair. "I-should-very-much-like-to-marry—"

"*Yes!*"

"—Millicent."

He smiled at her, relieved to have finally said it.

"Whew," he added softly. And fished out a handkerchief from his pocket and mopped his brow.

Genevieve didn't precisely stagger. But her lips parted on an *oh* of breath, as though he'd jammed his walking stick hard between her ribs.

Silence of the howling sort ensued.

"My father thinks it's time I take a wife, and so do I. I intend to propose to her during the house party. I wanted you to know first."

Surely . . . surely she'd heard him incorrectly. Surely he was jesting. But he was blushing in that blotchy, shamed way men blushed. He looked desperately uncomfortable and as vulnerable as those stripped trees. He looked shy and full of entreaty.

And suddenly she couldn't feel her limbs.

"Ah, Millicent . . ." He paused and smiled fondly, and his eyes warmed. Suddenly she hated *everything* about his smile, and wished she didn't know so much about what made him smile. "Well, she's so unlike the two of us, who are so *sensible*, and she needs a husband like me."

Sensible! *Sensible?* Surely not. She was an Eversea.

Apparently he wasn't finished rhapsodizing. "No. She's so lighthearted and *spontaneous*—"

His words felt like an indictment. It wasn't as though Genevieve's heart was encased in *lead*. Though she considered it would be in better condition at the moment if it had been.

"And she's lively and unafraid and forthright and good company—"

He made it sound as though Millicent was a spaniel.

"Where the two of us, well, we're wiser and more mature, yes?"

She was just past twenty years old! Mature? *Wise?*

"And as I know you love her, too—"

Clearly not the way you do.

"—I needed to tell you, as I couldn't keep it inside any longer. And I couldn't bear the thought of keeping a secret from *you,* the dearest of all my friends."

Friend. At the moment she would rather have been called anything else. A wolverine.

He twirled the leaf between his fingers. It throbbed before her eyes, as though he'd plucked her heart bleeding from her chest and was now toying with it.

"I wanted you to know first, Genevieve. And to hear your opinion of it. If you would be so kind," he added awkwardly. "You are so kind. You're *always* . . . so kind."

If you would be so *kind?* He'd never been . . . *polite* to her. Or formal. Everything was terribly, terribly, hideously wrong. Up was down, black was white, rivers ran backward, all the Everseas deeply loved the Redmonds . . .

"And I wanted your blessing, as we are all such good friends."

He stopped talking.

Apparently she was expected to say something now.

"Friends," she parroted faintly. As if she could use only words he dealt out to her. She'd forgotten all of her own words. She scarcely knew who she was anymore. Harry had irrevocably just altered the physics of her life. For three years, her love for him had been . . . her own personal gravity. It gave shape to her days and momentum to her dreams of the future. She could envision no world without him.

"Yes!" He seized upon this as though it were actual conversation. "The *dearest* of friends."

She was sinking, sinking, sinking. She knew very clearly somehow that she would forever go on falling. Her brother Chase had told her that some men who came home from the war lived with a constant ringing in their ears caused by cannon fire. *She* would just have to live forever with the vertigo of heartbreak.

She stared at him for so long without blinking that her eyes began to burn and he began to look just a trifle uneasy.

He wanted her blessing?

Blessing, her arse.

The pain was a late arrival—the numbness had to finish its turn with her first—but it was nasty. She wanted to buckle, lie on her side and gasp like an eviscerated fish. She held her breath against it, but her mouth parted. *She* cared naught for living in the moment, but apparently her body was *sensible*. It wanted to breathe.

And when she did, she breathed in wood smoke.

She gagged. She never wanted to smell wood smoke again. It was the smell of heartbreak.

Harry, her . . . her . . . . *murderer* . . . was fussing idly with one of the silver buttons on his coat, but peering at her intently. And for the first time since she'd known him, she couldn't read his thoughts.

"Will you . . . will you be happy for me, Genevieve?"

Was he peering at her as intently as she thought? Perhaps it was just that shock had turned the world convex. He looked almost distorted, preserved under glass, already untouchable and forever out of reach.

"Happy," she parroted after a moment. She had trouble with the *P*s. Her lips were rubbery and incompetent. But somehow she got the corners of her mouth up. Because when one was *happy*, one smiled.

This response seemed to satisfy him. He turned slowly away from her and thrust his hands deep into his pockets, hunching his shoulders self-consciously, and then sighed, looking back toward the house, perhaps pondering the wonderment of impending matrimony.

"And once Millicent and I are wed, should I be so fortunate as to be accepted by her, we shall all of course *continue* to be such great friends. There will be parties and picnics and children and—"

That's when Genevieve spun on her heel abruptly.

She didn't precisely run. She wanted to. Still, she made good time for a woman with legs of lead. The distance back to the house stretched like taffy. Her eyes were burning, burning, and she wasn't certain whether it was anguish or blazing fury or some nasty combination that was causing it. *I'll never reach it. I'll never outrace this feeling, because it'll be every-where I go from now on, Harry on my heels, yammering on about his future without me.*

Up ahead a tiny human figure was walking toward them. A moment later she realized it was her sister, Olivia. And for one wildly disorienting second she recalled that one's loved ones purport-edly greet the freshly dead at the gates of Heaven. Perhaps when one's heart is irrevocably broken one is welcomed into the Land of the Heartbroken by others who share the condition.

Although Olivia, of course, stoutly denied her heart was anything other than sound and unaf-fected by the disappearance of Lyon Redmond.

Harry was talking, though she could barely hear him through the cyclone of misery in her heart and mind.

"I don't know quite when I'll propose. But I expect I'll know when the right moment arises. *Definitely* during the days of the house party. I can't think of a lovelier place to do it than Eversea House, sur-rounded by friends."

He might as well have been speaking a different language.

Who *was* he? How *could* he? How could he con-template a life without her?

Funny how his obliviousness had lost its charm.

Her anguish wrestled with fury and shock, and the result was silence. It was her defense and her punishment and her refuge and her revenge, always. Quiet Genevieve Eversea.

Olivia called out to them.

"Oh, excellent, Genevieve, Harry. I thought I would find the two of you early birds out walking.

I have the most extraordinary news. Mother sent me to tell you and to fetch you back to the house straightaway. No one has died," she hastened to clarify.

Just me, Genevieve thought violently.

Oh, but Harry was eager to hear. "Well, let's have it then, Olivia!"

"*Wait* until you hear who Papa has invited to the house party."

And wouldn't you know, behind them that leaf at last came down, spiraling like a graceful suicide.

"You climbed out the window *bare* arsed? Down a *tree*?"

Ian had found an excellent audience in his brother Colin. He couldn't keep the story to himself any longer, and in the comfort of the Pig & Thistle in Pennyroyal Green it seemed safe to tell it.

"I could only find my shirt. Flapping from the tree. Tore it when I attempted to free it and wore it home like a damned skirt, tied 'round my waist. Found one boot by stumbling over it. My pistol was in the other one! Would be a bloody miracle if it didn't fire through the toe. I want it back! Practically part of me, that boot, and I miss it like a limb. Lost skin from my shin climbing down that damn tree naked. Nearly unmanned myself. Limped for miles in the dark."

He refrained from describing the splinter he'd acquired in an unmentionable place during his exit, as that splinter would become as ubiquitous in Eversea lore as the bloody song about Colin that was still, to this day, sung in pubs and musicales all over England. They would never, never let him forget it.

"In one boot." Colin marveled over this.

"In one boot."

Here in the safe warmth and noise of the Pig & Thistle the tables were crowded, the fire was leaping, a group, including Jonathan Redmond, was clustered about the dartboard and damned Redmond was winning again, which reminded him that he could have sworn he'd seen *Violet* Redmond, of all people, arguing with what appeared to be a sailor down by the docks just the other night, after a ball for the Earl of Ardmay. Obviously he'd been drinking too much; rumor had it she was attending a house party in the country, nowhere near London. He hadn't mentioned a word of it to anyone. Culpepper and Cooke were hunched over the chessboard and Cooke's eyebrows as usual looked as frisky and alert as pets. Ian couldn't help but look around and around, drinking in blessed familiarity, laying his hand flat against the scarred wood table. The previous week's events seemed like a hellish dream, the sort one had after a heavy dinner and too much bad liquor. It was even possible to laugh about it now.

"Christ. And you're still alive?"

Colin was both clearly impressed and tamping what appeared to be something like envy. It was an exploit worthy of *him* at his best. Or at his worst. However one viewed it.

"Why did you do it?"

"If you mean scale a tree to get to Lady Abigail, I'm shocked you need to ask. Shocked. *You've* seen her!" He waited for Colin to nod in masculine comprehension. "It was the challenge of the thing, you see. And I'd gotten away with it for three nights. And the fourth . . ." He slumped into despair and sighed, and his sigh evolved into a theatrical groan and he dropped his face into his palms. "The fourth would have been a *magical* thing," he croaked through his fingers. "You should have felt her skin . . . her bare shoulders . . . oh, God, Colin. So soft."

Colin shifted restlessly. He was a married man now. Not a dead man.

"But the fiancée of the bloody Duke of Falconbridge! Ian, for the love of . . ."

Ian lifted his head up slowly, suspiciously. His eyes widened when it occurred to him that Colin—of all people!—was actually about to give him a *scolding*.

And off he went:

"*I* might be invincible, Ian, but that doesn't mean *you* are. You ought to marry and stop all this nonsense."

If Ian's feet hadn't still been sore he might have succumbed to the urge to kick Colin's shin under the table. Colin had decided that marriage was his cure for everything, since *he* was so delighted with the condition. He drove everyone mad with this theory.

"You can speak of invincibility *now*, Colin," is what he said aloud. "You should have liked to have been me, or any of us, that morning, as we waited in London for the news of your . . . of your . . ."

Death by hanging was how that sentence should have been completed, but they still didn't speak of it easily. None of them liked to remember a moment in which they'd confronted the notion that Everseas might be something other than invincible after all, since they'd seemed to have gotten away with everything since 1066 or thereabouts.

Of course they *were*, as it turned out. Invincible, that was. But this had only been reestablished after a few years had been shaved from everyone's lives.

Colin had never shared with his family the *whole* story of how he'd been rescued from the gallows. He'd rather glossed it over. In truth the woman who was now his wife had been paid to do it for reasons *far* from noble, but now they were married and happily raising cows and sheep, and he saw no need to invoke hoots and mirth from his brothers, which is precisely what would happen when they discovered he'd been rescued by a girl. And the fact that he'd been a hairsbreadth away from an ignominious death—though they'd been accused of numerous things over the centuries, but not one Eversea had been *caught* until Colin—was still a slightly sensitive topic.

Ian said, "Given the opportunity, you'd have done something very like it if you hadn't married, and you know it. The bit with the countess and trellis—"

Colin interjected hurriedly. "Well, you got away with your life if not your clothes, so why do you still look so bloody enervated? Did he call you out?"

Ian opened his mouth. He hesitated.

Colin flung himself back in his chair and stared at his brother balefully. "He called you out, didn't he? Oh, God. You'll die of a certainty. And yes, I'll be your second."

"Oh, ye of little faith. The bastard makes a lovely large target. I'd hardly be likely to miss."

Colin snorted. "So you'd cuckold the man and then shoot him dead. I've never been prouder of you." He drained his ale and waved futilely for another one. Polly Hawthorne, Ned Hawthorne's

daughter, still hadn't forgiven him for marrying
Madeline Greenway, crushing dreams she'd harbored—well, that she and nearly every female in
Pennyroyal Green between the ages of twelve and
eighty had harbored—since she was eight. She was
just sixteen or seventeen years old now and she'd
perfected pretending he was invisible. "Ian, if you
would . . ." he said desperately.

Ian sighed and beckoned to Polly with a flap of a
hand. She flounced over. To Ian she gave a radiant
smile. To Colin she gave a view of her back.

"A light and a dark, Polly, my sweetness."

Her smile broadened, her dimples deepened. "Of
course, Mr. Eversea."

And off she went.

"Truth be told, Colin, and I would only say this
to you, as you've spent nearly your entire life in the
pursuit of absolutely the wrong women—"

"All *excellent* women," Colin hastened to defend.

"I'm sure they seemed so at the time," Ian humored. "And all *very* wrong. I mean, dangling
from that trellis outside of Countess Malmsey's
window—"

"Your point?" Colin interjected darkly.

"Well, you see, regardless of what I've done, of
course I'd attempt to shoot him. I won't stand there
and be shot by the duke for the nobility of the thing.
But do consider that I may have done him a favor. I
shall never tell a soul beyond you, but Lady Abigail
Beasley is . . . no lady. Good heavens, she is as bold
as either you or I and she knows one or two things
she cannot have come by at the knee of her gov-
erness. And oh, what I would have learned on the
fourth night . . ." He shook his head. "Anyhow, you'd

think she'd have the sense to stay true to a man like the duke. His reputation is hardly a secret. Better he should know of her faithlessness now, aye?"

"Yes. It was all altruism on your part, I'm certain. You deserve a medal. And I'm certain one day you'll share a good laugh about it with Moncrieffe next time your paths cross in White's if you don't kill each other first."

Ian froze. Somehow it hadn't yet occurred to him that of course he'd be seeing the duke about town, and an encounter in White's wasn't only possible, it was entirely likely. He was feeling bolder, however, and as though he could survive the ignominy of an incidental meeting.

"I've heard the engagement has been ended. Upon 'mutual agreement of both parties,'" Colin added. "And that she departed the country."

He had no doubt the duke had ordered her to leave the country.

"And where should the likes of you get gossip like that?"

"Adam. Someone in the village told him, as it had filtered into the village from London. Women tell him *everything.*"

His tone said everything about why this was both a marvelous advantage and a terrible curse. Adam Sylvaine was their cousin on their mother's side, and since the Everseas owned the living they'd installed him as a vicar and the little church in Pennyroyal Green had never been more crowded on Sundays, owing to Adam's . . . appeal.

Polly Hawthorne wove through the crowd and pointedly settled both ales down in front of Ian. She cut Colin dead with an admirable flick of her long, black braid as she departed with coins jingling in her hand.

Ian grinned. He was beginning to feel a little more like himself, despite his barked shin and raw feet and hands and the damned souvenir splinter in his thumb, which was working itself out only slowly, surely a form of penance.

"And besides, the duke *didn't* call me out. He just sent me out the window."

Colin leaned back slowly against his chair. He pressed his lips together pensively.

And then he began drumming his fingers rhythmically against his tankard of ale. And said nothing.

"What?" Ian demanded irritably.

"Ah, but here is what troubles me, Ian. They say the duke's heart is so hard and black that musket balls glance right off. And that he *always* gets his revenge in some fashion."

"Rumor and conjecture and pure bloody balderdash." The rumors were easier to dismiss, anyway, after that first sip of the dark. Courage in a tankard.

"If he didn't call you out, then what *did* he say? Anything?"

Ian hesitated to say it aloud. "Something about the punishment fitting the crime," he admitted.

Colin took this in.

"Chhh*rrrrist*," he finally said grimly.

Ian didn't have time to retort. Olivia and Genevieve had just pushed through the door of the Pig & Thistle, letting in a gust of autumn air, and when they didn't immediately begin divesting themselves of cloaks and gloves—the warmth of the place was like donning a second coat—he correctly imagined they were to collect him to greet guests at home.

The Everseas were holding an autumn house party. Another blessedly normal event.

He gestured with his chin in their direction, and held a finger to his lips, which was unnecessary. It was a tacit understanding that not a word of his exploit would be breathed to anyone else in the family.

Their sisters immediately spotted their tall brothers slouched over ales and wended their way through the tables, nodding and smiling to friends and acquaintances in the pub.

"I wonder what's wrong with Genevieve," Ian murmured. "She looks a bit pale."

They didn't mention Olivia. She looked lovely, as usual, but they both almost unconsciously glanced toward the dartboard, where Jonathan Redmond was handily winning and looking more and more like his brother Lyon, the eldest Redmond, every day, which did nothing to endear him to the Everseas. The Redmonds maintained Olivia was the heartless siren who had caused their heir to mysteriously disappear. Olivia steadfastly denied anything of the sort, insisted, sometimes with a yawn, sometimes with a tinkly incredulous laugh, that her heart was whole and hale, all the while skillfully shaking off suitors with the grace with which a duck shakes water from its feathers.

And Ian would have strangled Lyon Redmond if he could, because despite everything, not a one of them could bear to see anyone hurt their sisters.

"Darling brothers, we've been sent to fetch you. Father is expecting an important guest in a few hours and he wants you to be present when he arrives."

"Who could possibly warrant my presence so urgently?"

Olivia presented the name with as much ceremony as she would a scepter.

"The Duke of Falconbridge."

To their astonishment, their brothers greeted this news with resounding silence.

Olivia murmured in Genevieve's ear, "I wonder what's wrong with Ian. He looks pale."

Chapter 3

The duke stood in the Everseas' echoing marble foyer, his feet planted on the north end of an enormous inlaid marble compass star, a mosaic in shades of gold. A team of efficient liveried footmen had borne away his hat and coat and walking stick and trunk, a groom and several excited stable boys had taken breathless custody of his carriage and team. A cluster of housemaids stood peering 'round the landing down at him. He gained an impression of bright eyes, knuckles stuffed in mouths to stifle giggles, mob caps quivering as they whispered excitedly.

He was always watched. He was accustomed to it.

"Pardon, Your Grace!"

He dodged another pair of footmen staggering under armloads of incongruously dazzling flowers. Brilliant hothouse blooms in oranges and crimsons, like a Tahitian sunset on stalks.

"Try the green salon," Jacob Eversea called after them as he bustled into the foyer. "Ask Mrs. Eversea where you ought to put it."

"Olivia," Mr. Eversea explained cryptically, turning back to the duke. "Delighted, honored to have you with us, Moncrieffe. You couldn't have written ahead at a more opportune time. We're having a ball! A modest affair, of course, compared to the London occasions, but we do have a suitable room for it and enthusiastic company expected. I do hope you'll be comfortable while you're with us. And we can most certainly get up a card game from all the neighbor men on Saturday. Couldn't be happier you suggested it. They'll all be honored to lose their blunt to you. I'll send word 'round the ballroom."

"Thank you, Eversea. I couldn't hope for more satisfactory accommodations."

He'd been up the stairs and down again swiftly. His chamber was large and primarily brown and comfortable indeed, softness everywhere in the carpets and curtains and counterpane, but he'd merely brushed the dust off before he'd inquired of a housemaid as to where Ian Eversea slept.

And then he'd slipped in the room and deposited Ian's other boot on the end of the bed. The boot pistol had blown a ragged hole through the toe of it when it landed a good thirty or so feet outside of Abigail's window.

Jacob Eversea and the duke looked up then when they heard footsteps on the marble stairs.

"Where the devil did this come from?" Ian's voice preceded him down the stairs. He was holding the boot.

He halted so quickly on the bottom stair when he saw the duke he nearly toppled off.

"I believe you're acquainted with my son Ian?" Jacob turned to the duke.

Ian thrust the boot behind his back and froze, motionless as any pointing hunting spaniel. He stared.

At last he came down from the step and walked across the cold marble as gingerly as if it were hot coals. And then he bowed low. The instinct was a reflex in Everseas, anyway, and doubtless bought him time to think. When he was upright his complexion was nearly indistinguishable in color from the marble.

Whatever he'd thought on the way down hadn't comforted him in the least.

"Our paths have crossed." The duke addressed this to Jacob and bowed low, too, but his bow was a parody. "How is your horse, Ian?"

"Present," Ian said faintly after a moment. His horse had found its way home, from Lady Abigail's house, in other words.

"Clever horse," the duke acknowledged.

Unlike his master, were the unspoken words.

"What brings you to Eversea House, Moncrieffe?"

Very polite the question, but strain pitched it nearly an octave higher than Ian's usual voice. His nostrils had flared; white lines made dents on either side of them.

"Opportunity," Moncrieffe said simply.

And smiled the sort of smile that wolves do, when they have their prey neatly cornered.

While the duke was upstairs brushing off the dust and planting a boot at the foot of Ian's bed, Genevieve had made a futile dash for her bedroom. Colin had slipped away to his home, Ian had made it up the stairs, Olivia had slipped away . . .

But her mother was lying in wait, and Genevieve had been captured in the foyer just before the duke arrived.

What did the Everseas know about the Duke of Falconbridge? If you asked Jacob, he would say the man had a knack for brilliantly choosing investments and had not yet thrown in his lot with Isaiah Redmond's Mercury Club, which meant he might very well make an excellent partner in business endeavors for Jacob. He approved of his cattle—six matched bays—and of his new barouche, and even of his reputation, as the Eversea family closet rattled with skeletons and rumors swirled smokelike around how they'd acquired their undeniably immense fortune. He approved of the duke's gambling skills and was looking forward to plying his own against him.

If one would have asked *Genevieve* about the duke, she would have said she knew that he was very tall. Fair-skinned. Dark haired. Exuded an impatience and importance so thoroughly intimidating it preceded him into rooms like a gust of strong wind. Even when he was motionless for long periods of time—she'd seen him standing at balls, hands folded behind his back, like Wellington surveying a battlefield, the crowds eddying around him at a polite and careful distance as surely as if he were surrounded by a moat, he somehow always looked poised to dash. He had overlooked her, both literally (she was petite) and figuratively, at the two balls at which they'd been mutually present, and she had known only relief. She didn't know whether he was handsome, though certainly women thought his aura of danger had its appeal and no one shielded their eyes in horror in his presence. She simply never intended to look at him long enough to decide for herself.

She knew, of course, it was said that he'd poisoned his wife when she mysteriously died and he'd inherited all of her money, that he'd allegedly dueled with swords, that he'd once shot a man for pleasure, that he'd ruined more than one man who'd dared deal dishonestly with him, sometimes *years* later, which meant he'd undertaken it with cold-blooded thoroughness and planning. He'd been engaged for a time to Lady Abigail Beasley and now he wasn't.

And he was standing in the foyer.

He was talking to her father and . . . well, he *appeared* to be smiling. Her father did make people smile; her brothers didn't come by their roguish charm accidentally. Likely they were discussing barouches or horses or the other sorts of things that bonded men the world over.

And she could see, leaning over on the second landing of the stairs, a cluster of housemaids avidly staring and whispering, like mice watching a cat. As though safety could be had in numbers.

When they heard Isolde Eversea's slippers clacking over the marble they scattered.

Her pretty mother bore down upon Genevieve, looking bright and purposeful, which could not bode well.

"A word, Genevieve, love, if you will."

She was steered into the green sitting room, called as such because it was . . . primarily green. Shades of it were everywhere in the delicate curving furniture, a hearty plump settee, long velvet curtains roped in silver tasseled cord. A soothing room. Apart from the explosion of color provided by a bouquet of exotic blooms in the corner.

"Good grief. It looks like a blessed jungle in here. But the young men will continue to send flowers," her mother said, and gingerly touched a spiky leaf on the bouquet.

Olivia's admirers were legion and persistent, primarily because Olivia was beautiful and indifferent.

It wasn't as though Genevieve never received flowers. They were generally of the sentimental sort, however, or of the pale and delicate sort, rather than the . . . *magnificent* sort. Her suitors assumed Genevieve Eversea would prefer flowers pulled up out of the ground in meadows. Seasonal. Infinitely more practical and sweet and *quiet*.

And then Isolde peered at Genevieve. "What's wrong?" she demanded sharply.

"Naught, Mama."

"You look ill. White as a sheet and green 'round the gills. We'll have Harriet make you a simple."

So she was to be savagely heartbroken and then poisoned by one of their cook's noxious herbal brews in the space of a few hours? Dante would find inspiration in this day.

"Then I truly *will* be ill, Mama," she pointed out with quiet desperation.

There was no hope for it; her mother had decided upon her course and that was that.

"It's a wonderful day for a walk, don't you think, Genevieve?" she said with suspicious brightness.

"No," she said quickly.

As far as Genevieve was concerned, horrible things happened on walks. She would consent to take a walk only if it ended at the Cliffs of Dover. Far, far away from here.

"I know you've been out, but another dose of fresh air would do you a world of good." Her mother was deaf only to her own objective. "I think it would be lovely if you young people take the duke"—meaning the duke of course *wasn't*, strictly speaking, young—"out to see the folly and perhaps the ruins. Before the rains arrive and turn that hill just before it into mud."

Genevieve was aghast. Oh. Please, please, *please* no. She was fit only for shutting the door of her room, lying sideways on her bed, and holding herself tightly to muffle the pain of loss. She didn't think she would cry. Not yet. Perhaps later she would.

Now every sound, every sight, every sensation, landed on her and stung. She was raw. Speaking to the Duke of Falconbridge seemed inconceivable.

Honestly, she should visit her cousin Adam, the vicar, to review with him her sins—surely if she'd committed any they were modest?—to see which of them might have resulted in her sudden plunge into purgatory. Perhaps it was a cumulative sort of thing. Perhaps if the little sins went too long un-repented the punishment could only be dramatic and sudden.

"Mama, the duke can hardly wish to see the folly and the ruins. Doubtless a dozen follies and ruins feature on his properties, and all of them are greater follies and more ruinous than ours. I'm certain he'd rather spend time with Papa."

And do things men nearer to that age do. Smoke cigars. Complain of gout.

This last thought was mere indulgence in petulance. Papa was actually quite fit unless one quibbled over a slight thickening at the middle. He hadn't any gout. His sons were tall and lanky, and every last one of them was taller than he, and Colin was the tallest by an inch.

And the duke was hardly Papa's age. Yet.

But they'd taken the duke's hat, the footmen. She could see from where she stood a frost of gray at each temple. He wore his hair a little longer than was strictly fashionable, though he had plenty of it, and most of it was black. Perhaps when one reached his age one simply stopped caring about fashion. Though his clothes were impeccably tailored, emphasizing his lean grace.

And she knew he did have a folly. At *least* one, given how much of England he was alleged to own. Genevieve was familiar with one of the duke's properties—Rosemont—as she'd gone to tour it once when he was away at one of his other vast tracts of lands. It was surprisingly modest by duke terms, a redbrick manor in West Sussex presiding over a collection of softly swelling hills, which surrounded a lake populated by enormous, irritable swans and overhung with willows. The garden had been brilliant with its namesake blooms and the fountain in the courtyard featured a lasciviously grinning stone satyr performing an arabesque and spitting water high into the air.

She'd found it delightful. It's pocket-sized, whimsical beauty hardly seemed to suit him, but then he normally spent his time in London and likely had all but forgotten he owned it.

Her mother lowered her voice. "He is lately . . . *disengaged*, as you know."

And then Genevieve fully understood what her mother was contemplating.

And it was much, much worse than a stroll.

"Mama . . . I feel *terrible*," she modified rapidly. "I feel . . ." What would convince her mother? ". . . I feel faint." It wasn't entirely a lie, so it wasn't another sin. How did one feign a swoon? She placed the back of her hand on her forehead. Swoons seemed to begin that way. She fumbled for the arm of the settee with her other hand, and sank slowly into it.

She was petite, but she had the constitution of a plow horse. She'd never fainted in her life.

Her mother narrowed her eyes, eyes so very similar to her own. She missed almost nothing, Mama, but she was immovable.

"I'll own you are not yourself, Genevieve, but I'm inclined to blame whatever it is you did or didn't eat for breakfast. You are fit enough to walk with a duke, and you are always lovely, even when pale."

"But Mama—I do have a terrible—" What part of her ought to ache cripplingly enough to excuse her from the walk but not require a frantic messenger sent to fetch the doctor? She could hardly say *soul*. "—headache."

"Unless you can demonstrate to me that you're missing a limb necessary for performing a *stroll*, you will go, Genevieve. You will be kind to the man, as he may have suffered a loss and perhaps be . . . consolable. Inclined to remedy his loss."

"But Mama, he's . . . I can't . . . but he . . ."

". . . is a man who can keep you in the manner to which you've become accustomed and do honor to this family. I know you are a bit. . . . well, a bit *shy* . . . my dear . . . but this will do you good."

Her mother gave her back an implacable I-know-what's-good-for-you-better-than-you-do gaze.

It was disorienting. How was it that she hadn't noticed this before? *Nobody* knew. Nobody knew what was best for her and what she wanted. And why did anyone believe she was shy? She wasn't the *least* shy. *Quiet* was *not* synonymous with *shy*.

She must have looked stricken, for her mother sighed.

"For heaven's sake, my love, we aren't speaking of indenturing you to the man. It's one walk. It needn't dictate the course of forever and I'm not one of those mamas who orchestrate their children's lives, though I'm of a mind to change. After all, every woman needs an avocation," she added darkly.

"Where is Olivia?" Genevieve tried mulishly.

Olivia was slippery, that's what Olivia was. She might very well be hiding behind a flower arrangement and snickering at Genevieve.

Out of the corner of her eye she could see yet another one being brought through the door. Mrs. Mullin, the housekeeper, stood scratching her head in the foyer, clearly wondering where to direct the footmen.

Her father and Ian and the duke had vanished from the foyer. To look at horses or some such, no doubt.

Isolde sighed. "My dear, *please* just . . ."

And then Genevieve watched in horror as her mother actually . . .

. . . *wrung her hands*.

This was a dirty trick, indeed. Not for the first time, or even the thousandth, Genevieve wished that she had her sister's fortitude. For despite her battered emotional condition she of course took pity on her mother, who worried so over all of them, had stal-

wartly and with humor survived sending sons off
to war and to the gallows, and had truly despaired
that Olivia would ever be married.

For her mother's sake, she would go on the walk.

She hadn't any conversation or charm or any of
herself to spare. But she would go and walk alongside
the duke.

When her mother saw her softening she placed a
hand on her knee and offered a concession.

"My dear, you're certain to enjoy yourself. After
all, Harry and Millicent will go along, too."

Chapter 4

Moncrieffe's first look at the girl he meant to seduce and abandon was hardly promising, though this in itself suggested his task might be easier than he'd dreamed. She was petite and colorless and lightless. Her complexion was fair and unblemished, but it was difficult to know her age, for the bloom was most certainly off of her. Her walking dress was white muslin striped in gray, and she'd thrown a shawl around it, and was clutching it defensively in one pale fist. Her presence was in fact so subdued he would not have been surprised to hear she was mute.

Her friend, on the other hand—introduced as Lady Millicent Blenkenship—was a place a man could comfortably rest his eyes. A lush round girl. Lord Harry Osborne and an almost comically wary Ian Eversea were to come along on this walk, too, and Jacob Eversea, as host, was to lead the way.

Moncrieffe was not one for walks that led nowhere in particular to places of minimal interest. He could have demurred. He possessed rank; the Everseas were polite. In all likelihood they would do anything he suggested, perhaps even launch into a rousing version of that everlasting pub song about

Colin Eversea's ignominious rescue from the gallows, though they might be a trifle sensitive about that for all he knew.

But he had an objective, and so he assented, and they all mounted an expedition to see the Everseas' folly.

"Breathe that in, eh, Moncrieffe! Nothing like a hint of sea in the Sussex autumn air." This was Jacob Eversea, heartily striding forward.

Despite the fact that he ... *owned* so much of the fresh air and open spaces of England, Moncrieffe spent most of his time in the coal-smut-thickened skies of London.

Which could be why he was promptly wracked by a fit of coughing the moment he dutifully inhaled.

He stopped. His concerned hosts ringed him. Through watering eyes he gained an impression of sympathetic watching eyes. Out of the corner of his eye he noticed Ian Eversea trying not to look hopeful about his impending demise.

He put up one finger: *Momentarily.*

"That'll clear a man's lungs, by God, won't it, Moncrieffe." Jacob Eversea was waiting patiently. "We're not going to lose you, are we?"

"By God," Moncrieffe croaked, when he could speak again. "I'm well. Naught to be concerned about. 'Tis nothing a good snort of dirty London air wouldn't cure."

Jacob Eversea snorted at that. "I've some cigars that come a close substitute. I'll share them later as a cure once we've endured this trip. Five-card loo tonight, eh, Your Grace? And come Saturday ... spread the word, lads!" he directed to Ian and Harry.

Who smiled politely.

"I would tolerate no other diversion at night," the duke said somberly, and the elder Eversea laughed.

For five-card loo was the game the duke was known for winning the most. And it was hardly considered a reputable game.

"Do you need a walking staff?"

What a quiet voice.

The duke turned slowly, incredulously toward it, then looked down. This was Miss Genevieve Eversea asking. So very politely and *solicitously*. As though she expected him to tip over should his boot encounter a rut and they would have to rush to fetch a plow horse to tow him up out of it.

"Oh, for heaven's sake, Genevieve. The duke is in excellent health," Eversea called back to her irritably as they trundled up the lane.

Genevieve didn't seem at all nonplussed by her father's tone. She was doubtless used to him.

He may as well begin charming her now.

"He's correct, Miss Eversea. But your concern is kind, indeed," the duke said softly.

"Harry! Do look at that funny squirrel! He's so fat!"

Lady Millicent was all but skipping up the lane, but she'd paused to point at a small round beast that glowered and made those gulping squirrel noises at them from on high. It flicked its tale irritably. "I should like to draw it!"

"Plenty more squirrels where that one came from, Millicent," Jacob said with infinitely dry patience.

And so with Jacob's pace, and Ian's eagerness to keep his distance from Moncrieffe, and Millicent pointing out squirrels to Harry, Genevieve and the duke were in due time left behind. He wondered if she was doing it out of solicitousness, the way one might humor an invalid.

She seemed to be comfortable saying absolutely nothing.

They walked for a few moments down that lane lined with stripped trees. Leaves crunched underfoot.

"I love this part of England. I've an estate but a few hours from here."

That he hadn't seen in several months because . . . well, why would he? He'd a larger one even closer; he preferred his St. James Square town house. Rosemont held memories that gave him no comfort.

"Rosemont," she said softly.

Which surprised him.

He considered whether he liked her voice. It was low, a soft alto; very refined. But the word had been all but uninflected. He'd learned over the years that one can quickly ascertain whether someone possessed intelligence from a mere syllable or two. It was something about the confidence with which they spoke.

He was instantly certain she was not a simpleton.

"Do you know it, Miss Eversea? Rosemont?"

"Yes."

He looked around. Naught but trees and a long drive; beyond them were soft rolling hills. This was Sussex, all right. He waited.

And waited.

"This is the place in the conversation where one might forgive me for thinking you'd expound a bit."

It was admirably dry, that sentence. She *ought* to smile. She ought to be attempting to charm *him*, after all. At least a little. He was a bloody duke.

"It's lovely," was all she said. Dutifully. Perhaps interpreting him literally.

Or *perhaps* as a means of discouraging any other such witticisms.

"Did you like the dolphin pool?" he asked, knowing full well there was no such thing at Rosemont.

"Satyr pool," she corrected him.

"You recall the satyr?"

"Yes."

"The one urinating in the fountain in the circular drive?"

"It's spitting," she corrected.

Dear God, this was discouraging. She wasn't even *blushing*, and he'd most definitely been offensive. She possessed not a shred of whimsy.

"Ah, of course. I hadn't visited it in some time but I recollect it was performing one or another of a man's favorite pastimes. Spitting, smoking, wagering . . ."

She didn't quite sigh. But he had the most peculiar impression that she was stifling one.

He began to wonder if he'd been wrong and if she was dim, after all.

Or insufferably prim.

It *might* be satisfying to undo all of that.

Then again, it might be an onerous chore.

Up ahead he saw the long figure of Ian Eversea walking alongside his father. He glanced behind him, from him to Genevieve, a flicker of concern over his pale face.

The duke intercepted the glance and returned it with black inscrutability.

Ian whipped his head back around immediately, and absently felt his back, as though he expected to find a dagger plunged there any minute.

"It was very thoughtful of you, Miss Eversea, to consider whether I might need assistance walking. Kindness is a very appealing quality. It is everything I hope for in a wife."

There. He'd gone and said the word every girl considered the grail of conversation.

"My sister, Olivia, is very kind," she said almost too quickly. "She would make a splendid wife."

He blinked. It was the liveliest she'd sounded yet. "Oh?"

"Olivia deserves to make a splendid match. She was thwarted in love once before. A grand title would be perfect."

"As a *consolation* prize?" She'd succeeded in startling him.

"I'm terribly sorry. I didn't mean to make you squeak."

What a word! "I've never *squeaked* in my entire life."

"You achieved a special octave then, if you prefer," she allowed calmly. "And you just did it again."

And now he was determined to ruffle the calm, calm surface that was Genevieve Eversea's composure, if only to ascertain she was human. The girl was either void of social skills—which seemed unlikely, given her upbringing—or she was a minx and she was trying to deflect him for some unfathomable reason. Regardless, she'd seized control of their conversation.

He wanted it back.

"A special octave . . ." He pretended to muse this. "Are you suggesting I sound like a castrato?"

Ah! At last! An agreeable tide of pink slowly flooded those pale cheeks. A second passed during which he'd thought she was speechless.

"If the shoe fits," she finally agreed absently.

He turned sharply to look at her. He narrowed his eyes.

But her eyes were fixed on the lane ahead and then she dropped them to her feet just as Lord Harry turned and began walking backward, waving gaily at her.

She lifted her head slightly, with an obvious effort raised a hand back at him, produced a strained smile, and dropped her eyes.

And then she breathed in so deeply her shoulders lifted. As though bracing herself. And when she looked up again, the tops of her ears were pink, he noticed. From cold, or was some other suppressed emotion heating them up?

"It's only that . . . well, if Olivia cannot be with the man she loves, as he has vanished like a bloody *cowardly* . . ."

She stopped talking abruptly. Yanking herself back like a dog on a lead.

Which was a pity, as the words had acquired a fascinating whiff of venom and had begun to escalate in volume. She would have done some squeaking of her own.

Genevieve Eversea was beginning to interest him.

"If she cannot be with the man she loves . . ." he prompted.

"I do believe she can only to be with someone . . . impressive."

"Impressive . . ." He pretended to ponder this. "I hope you do not think I presume, but I cannot help but wonder if you're referring to me. Given my rank and fortune, some might describe me as such. And I'm flattered indeed, given that there really are so many other words you could have chosen to describe me."

A pause followed. The girl was most definitely a *thinker*.

"We have only just become acquainted, Lord Moncrieffe. I might elect to use other words to describe you should I come to know you better."

Exquisite and refined as convent lace, her manners, her delivery.

And still he could have sworn she was having one over on him.

She seemed to be watching her feet now. The scenery didn't interest her, or it caused her discomfort.

And as he watched her, something unfamiliar stirred.

He was . . . *genuinely* interested in what she might say next.

And as for Genevieve Eversea, she gave him only her profile. One would have thought she'd never been so bored. No frisking about for her, like her friend up ahead.

"Look at *that* squirrel! It has a stripe!" he heard faintly. Followed by a delighted squeal from the lush Lady Millicent.

Jacob Eversea, Ian, Lord Harry, and Lady Millicent had momentarily disappeared over the swell of a small hill.

And on they strode for a few more silent moments.

"Do you ever gamble, Miss Eversea?"

"No," she said shortly.

"A pity. Because I suspect you have an excellent game face. You'd make a *fortune*."

Her head swiveled quickly toward him, her eyes

wide. She quickly looked away again, and just as quickly recomposed herself.

He studied her profile. Quite ordinary, sadly. She'd lovely skin. Pity there was no color in it, in her cheeks *or* lips. The lashes were thick and black. It was difficult to know much about her figure, given that she'd draped a shawl over the dress. Her hair was dark and shiny and from the looks of how it was pinned up, plentiful. He tried to find something in all of this to inspire enthusiasm for the seduction. He found nothing.

"And the best part about gambling, Miss Eversea, is that sometimes . . . you *win*. I nearly always win."

She couldn't disguise but instantly doused that flicker of wary comprehension in her eyes. Ah. She suspected he was onto her. But she was determined to pretend she didn't understand him.

This was . . . well, there was no other word for it. This was *interesting*.

What was a girl of twenty or so doing possessed of such control? Why was she . . . *deploying* it around him? Considering that most of the members of her family were hardly known for theirs. And for heaven's sake, he was a *duke* and hardly a gargoyle. His presence and reputation never failed to elicit some sort of reaction, but not once, not once had he witnessed indifference. She was an anomaly.

"I thank you for your suggestion, Your Grace, but my family is possessed of a substantial fortune—"

"Indeed?" he said, as if this was news to him. Because it amused him to say it.

"And I don't approve of gambling."

"And of course one must only engage in pastimes one approves of."

She was silent. Her lips compressed. More disapproval? Or could it be she was actually suppressing a smile?

She continued steadfastly refusing to look at him. She sighed.

After a few more steps, when she spoke again, it was with bemusement he began to suspect that he wasn't the only one with an objective today. But what was *hers*?

"It is just that Olivia's happiness is so important to me. I cannot imagine any man who came to know her wouldn't come to love her, for everyone does," she said earnestly.

He narrowed his eyes in suspicion again. And he said absolutely nothing.

Miss Eversea wasn't the only thinker.

"Selflessness is such an appealing quality," he volleyed with quiet passion. "It's perhaps my favorite of all qualities in any female. And when someone puts the happiness of a loved one before her own . . . why, it's *irresistibly* appealing," he added meaningfully.

She went grimly silent.

And as he walked and stared at the backs of her friends and Jacob and Ian, something peculiar happened to him. Could that twinge somewhere in his solar plexus be . . . enjoyment? Could that tension around his mouth be . . . a smile struggling to form?

She walked on. Her eyes flicked toward him, flicked away. He could sense her furious concentration. She watched the backs of the heads of her friends, one bright gold, the other burnished gold.

She gave a short unconscious little huff of breath.

Sounding like an impatient horse.

He stifled a laugh. He *was*! He was, despite himself, genuinely, officially if perversely . . . enjoying himself. She could never win, of course. She possessed admirable control but that impatient huff gave her game away. He would find a niche in her defenses; he would parry expertly; he *would* charm her. He always inevitably got what he wanted. Still, it was an unusual pleasure to be matched with a worthy opponent.

She cleared her throat. "Yes. Well. Olivia is selfless as well, as she is *devoted* to causes. She is very active in the abolitionist society."

"Do you suppose she'd be equally devoted to the comfort and pleasure of her husband?"

Her eyes widened in surprise. Amusingly, this question actually gave her pause.

Her head tipped, considering it.

"She is considered a great beauty," is what she finally said instead.

He brushed a knuckle against his lips to keep the laugh from escaping.

"And she of course *is*," he agreed. "I have had the pleasure of seeing her in a ballroom. I am tempted to believe the very name Eversea is all but synonymous with"—*treachery, debauchery*—"beauty."

Her brows were straight and dark and slim as hyphens in that pale, ordinary face. They twitched as though she was desperate to frown. He found himself looking forward almost breathlessly to what she might say next.

But she said nothing.

So he spoke. "Why did everyone assume the bouquets were for Olivia? I imagine you receive your share."

He doubted this.

"They generally are for Olivia," she said with equanimity. "They generally arrive by the bushel after a ball."

"Surely *your* admirers must be legion, too."

A twitch of the brows again. He'd noticed she grew restive when subjected to overt compliments. He would calibrate accordingly.

"Oh, they are." She seized upon this, perhaps as a way to deter him. "One can scarcely see me for the hordes of young men at balls. You would need a cricket bat to fight them off."

That won't work, either, Miss Eversea.

"But don't the hordes shower you with blooms? They ought to."

"I am a frequent recipient of white lilies," she said evenly. "And daisies and daffodils. White roses. Narcissus. And bunches of wildflowers."

A passionless recitation.

"A virtuous selection, indeed. And do you like those kinds of flowers?"

"I like all flowers," she allowed noncommittally, after a moment.

"How very democratic of you."

She seemed to be biting the inside of her lip against a smile.

He would make her smile if it *killed* him.

"But it's understood Olivia in particular is so vivid and vivacious, and she has such strong passions. I believe the flowers are meant to convey admiration for this," she explained.

"And while those are indeed admirable qualities

in a woman, I also appreciate subtleties of character," he parried.

"And yet so very little is subtle about Lady Abigail Beasley," Miss Eversea pointed out peevishly, quickly.

God.

He nearly grunted with the force of her thrust home. And she'd demonstrated a willingness to play dirty.

Silence plunked like an anvil between them.

Lady Abigail Beasley. The name oddly deflated him. He found for a moment he had nothing, nothing at all, to say.

He wondered what Miss Eversea was thinking when she thought of Abigail Beasley. The word *Abigail* still meant to him curls ambered by firelight, a laugh just shy of bawdy, a body, he supposed, that hadn't a prayer of remaining shy. A body very like the one possessed by that laughing girl Millicent Blenkenship.

And then he saw white shoulders and a blanket drawn up to her chest and the naked white arse of Ian Eversea squeezing out the window in the dark.

Up ahead of him, that lanky worthless brother of this colorless girl walked free. If he had a spear now, he could skewer him with one jerk of his arm.

Alex was suddenly aware of the oppressive grayness of the day, tacked down around them like a tent. The fury and shame of his cuckolding, the sheer ridiculousness of it, washed over him again.

He glanced up at Ian.

I will shame you, he thought. *I will take from her what you took from me.*

"I always imagined that's the expression men

wore as they were about to shoot each other in a duel," Genevieve offered conversationally.

So she'd been watching him. She was observant and clever and it suddenly irritated him. Plain girls who were also clever were a ha'pence a dozen and he didn't want or need to be scrutinized.

Without saying anything, he composed his face into what he hoped were neutral planes, rather than bloodthirsty ones. But still he said nothing.

"Were you in love with her?"

Oh, for *God's* sake. Love. Women lobbed that bloody word as gaily as a shuttlecock. Someone ought to teach them it was a bloody *grenade*. And she'd said it so insufferably *gently*, too. The same way she'd asked him if he'd needed a walking staff.

"It's not a *toy*, that word, Miss Eversea," he muttered under his breath.

"I beg your pardon?" So politely said after a moment he wondered if she was bored. She likely didn't actually care whether he was in love.

Her thoughts had distantly drifted in the span of only a few seconds. She in truth couldn't be less interested in his answer, he thought.

Have a care, Miss Eversea, he thought. *I'm learning more and more about you.*

Soon enough he'd ensure her thoughts were entirely for him.

He'd never yet failed when he'd set out to seduce a woman, and this girl, regardless, was human. Likely she hadn't many suitors and very little experience with romance. Where there was a temper passion generally lurked. He would find a way to unleash it and take advantage of it.

He watched the mirror-bright, valet-shined toes

of his boots kick up fallen leaves. Gold, brown, russet sprayed up, came down. He looked up. The autumn-stripped trees clawed at the sky, and he was aware that despite his own fine looks and robust health he would soon be staring down his own autumn years.

"To address your question fairly, Miss Eversea . . . while I understand my broken engagement is a popular topic of conversation among the fashionable set, one must consider the possibility that the end of it was serendipitous for both Lady Abigail and I. And that thus freed our hearts might now love more appropriately and happily."

Take *that*, Miss Eversea. He was rather proud of *that*.

That epic, steaming mound of balderdash.

It also contained the word *love*, which was to women the way shiny things were to magpies. She would seize upon it. She would probably speak *gently* again. He would find a way beneath her ramparts yet.

Miss Eversea drew in a long, thoughtful breath, and slowly, slowly tilted her head back. A faint hint of line shadowed that smooth white forehead. The beginnings of a frown.

"Hearts?" she finally repeated pensively.

He laughed.

He couldn't help it. He managed to turn it into a cough into his fist when she turned abruptly toward him, but it was genuine, and she'd surprised it from him. Bloody hell, it sounded as though she doubted he'd ever possessed a beating heart but was prepared to humor his delusion.

The trouble was he wasn't even certain whether he did, either. Or that he knew any longer how to use it for anything other than a fancy bellows for pumping blood through his body.

She was quiet again. She was leaning forward a bit into the wind, her hands tightly clasped to hold her shawl over her. She was too cold, or perhaps she simply wanted to create a more streamlined profile in order to plow more efficiently through an increasingly frisky fall wind and get closer to her friends and her brother and away from him.

To get this walk over with, for he sensed she'd embarked upon it on sufferance.

It was like watching a pony stalwartly traverse the moors. God, but that wasn't at all a sensual thought, and he'd need to muster a certain amount of pleasure in the prospect of ruining her or he'd never get the job done.

Oh, very well: a delicate pony, then.

"Millicent, do have a look at this squirrel!" Far up ahead of them, Harry was pointing up.

"What are your pleasures and pursuits, Lord Moncrieffe?" Miss Eversea asked too brightly, when the silence had gone on for more than was strictly comfortable or polite.

That creaky conversation lubricant. It irritated him again that she was humoring him.

"Well, I'm partial to whores."

Her head whipped toward him like a weathervane in a hurricane. Her eyes, he noted, were enormous, and such a dark blue they were nearly purple. Her mouth dropped, and the lower lip was quivering with shock or . . . or . . .

"Whor . . . *whores* . . . ?" She choked out the word as if she'd just inhaled it like bad cigar smoke.

He widened his own eyes with alarm, recoiling slightly.

"I . . . I *beg* your pardon—*Horses*. Honestly, Miss Eversea," he stammered. "I do wonder what you *think* of me if that's what you heard." He shook his head ruefully. "*Horses.* Those hooved beasts a man can race, wager upon, plow a field with, harness to a phaeton, and drive at deliciously reckless speeds."

She stared at him now as he walked. Those wide eyes went narrow, bringing him into focus, isolating him in a very potent, too intelligent beam of blue.

"And one cannot do any of that with whores?" she asked softly.

His turn to drop his jaw. He clapped it shut again.

She'd pointed that neat profile away from him again. But when the corners of her pale mouth had tightened, he saw—yes, he saw—a dimple. And now he was *certain*, he was certain she was doing combat with a smile.

His heart picked up a beat or two. "It's a frustrating truism," he allowed resignedly, "but it's a rare whore who'll consent to be harnessed to a plow."

And with awe he saw her lose her battle with that smile.

It fought first with one corner of her mouth, then the other, and then it broke all over her like a sunrise. The very shape of her face changed. Or rather, she came into focus at last in that moment; she'd simply been awaiting illumination from within.

There were dimples, and a pointed chin, and elegant cheekbones. Her face was heart-shaped, sweetly drawn, very *alive*. She was *incandescent* with wicked amusement.

In that moment was an entirely different girl.

He stared, stunned.

And then the smile was gone, fading too quickly the way sunrises inevitably do, and she was quiet again.

Which is when he realized something important: Something or someone had *made* the light go out of Genevieve Eversea. And what he'd been seeing and walking with and talking with, up until the moment of that smile, was a shell.

Fascinating realization.

And possibly very useful.

Harry turned and came back to her, trailed by Millicent. "Genevieve, you ought to see the sunlight coming down on the folly. It reminds me of the Canaletto we love so!"

Harry and Millicent glanced toward the duke and smiled politely. Canaletto was an Italian painter, he knew that much, and cared less.

"The folly is up ahead," Harry reassured him, and Millicent nodded in eager encouragement. As though he might think it a great chore to walk such a distance.

The folly is up ahead. He couldn't help but wonder if those words were prescient as they all crested the hill.

And it was the last he spoke alone to Genevieve Eversea for the rest of the afternoon.

Chapter 5

~~~OO~~~

The duke took a light supper in his room. He attended to some correspondence related to his various estates, filling sheets of foolscap with succinct and rote instructions for his bailiffs, his banker, his man of affairs at Rosemont. He sealed them; they could be delivered by mail coach.

But one message was urgent. He dashed off a specifically worded request, sprinkled it with sand, sealed it with wax and a press of his ring, then rang for a footman.

"If you would kindly find a messenger to take this to Rosemont posthaste, I will reward handsomely."

The footman had no doubt such a messenger could easily be found.

He arrived early for the reception the Everseas were holding for a few guests prior to the ball, a "modest" (as described by Mrs. Eversea) affair attended by local aristocracy and close friends from Pennyroyal Green, a few friends from outlying villages, a few in from London. He was greeted by Jacob and brought from guest to guest for introductions. A few people he was already acquainted with; neighbors in Sussex and fellow members of White's.

Others, particularly the locals, were strangers. He'd seldom seen curtsies so deep or eyes so wide. He was polite; he was cool; he was enigmatic. He was every bit what they expected and wanted the storied Duke of Falconbridge to be, because it amused him to be so.

In truth, his eyes were on the stairs. He waited with the patience of a cat near a mouse hole for Genevieve Eversea to arrive.

He almost didn't recognize her when she did appear.

Her dress was a glossy silk of midnight blue, cut very low, and the "sleeves"—really scraps of net—clung to her pale, flawless shoulders, as though she'd tumbled down through clouds to get here and brought a few shreds of sky with her.

Her neck was long. Her collarbone had that smooth pristine temptation of a bank of new-fallen snow. It was interrupted only by a drop of a blue stone on a chain that pointed directly at quite confident cleavage, as if the owner knew full well it was splendid and was accustomed to exposing it. Her sleek dark hair was dressed up high and away from her face, and tiny diamanté sparks were scattered through it. Her face beneath it was revealed in delicate simplicity. A smooth, pale, high forehead, etched cheekbones. Elegant as Wedgwood, set off by that dark, dark hair and those vivid eyes.

He stared.

He wasn't precisely . . . nonplussed. Still, this particular vision of Genevieve Eversea required reconciling with the quiet girl in the morning dress, the moor pony with the determined gait. As though they were not quite the same thing, or were perhaps *variations* of the same thing, like verb tenses. He felt a bit like a boy who needed to erase his morning lessons and begin again.

She saw him and composed her face in resignation. Oh, there would come a day when she would do more than tolerate him, he'd decided.

"Oh. Good evening, Your Grace." She curtsied.

"Good evening, Miss Eversea. You've stars in your hair."

Why had he said that? He was startled. Out it had come. She had on dark blue gloves that hugged her arms up just past her elbows. She touched one to her hair.

"If you wish. But it wasn't what my maid called them." Sconces on the walls and chandeliers overhead lit everyone flatteringly, including him, no doubt, and when she moved her dress shifted like water under moonlight. He very much liked her serious slim brows, he decided then.

She surreptitiously swept a glance around the buzzing salon and flicked open her fan, rather like a bird rustling flight feathers. She was preparing to flee him.

"They're lovely." He said this because they were, and because he couldn't simply leave it at "You've stars in your hair," which sounded more like a puzzled accusation than a compliment.

He found he had nothing else to say. Which was very unlike him.

As usual, she wasn't assisting him, either. She was scanning the room, planning her escape strategy, and trying not to appear as though she was.

"It won't curl," she muttered finally. "I wish it would."

She brought her hand down from her hair abruptly. She looked abashed, as though she regretted saying it the moment it left her mouth. She bit her bottom lip.

"Why should you want it to curl?" He was genuinely baffled. He recalled his wife and her maid conferring before balls about how her hair should be done, their eyes locked with great intensity in the mirror, the two of them passionately gesticulating. One would have thought they were negotiating a treaty.

Genevieve paused, surprised by the question. "Primarily because it *won't* curl, I suppose." She looked just as surprised by her answer, and gave a little laugh, enjoying the absurdity of it.

He was struck by the peculiar philosophical profundity of this.

"I suppose we all tend to want the impossible. And sometimes in attempting it we achieve something near enough to the impossible to elicit satisfaction."

Her eyes didn't glaze over, to her credit. But at the word "impossible" all the light fled her face. The dimming was so instant and complete it was exactly like watching theater lights doused. Her eyes darted to some point across the room, lingered for an infinitesimal hungry second, came back to him and settled upon his face again with a certain stoic resignation.

Intrigued, he followed the direction of the eye dart. The salon was crowded already with exquisitely dressed sherry-clutching adults, but his eyes lingered on the lovely, glowing young woman, Lady Millicent Blenkenship. He'd admired the back of her at length today. The front of her, particularly in that gown, had much to recommend it, too. Beneath the lamplight her skin had the warmth of a ripe peach and hair shone the color of old gold, and her eloquently curved body was hugged by expertly tailored russet silk. Her cleavage was a thing of majesty. She'd enormous brandy-colored eyes and a very nice, warm laugh, and she was laughing now. A woman a man could bask in, who would probably be a lush joy in bed and not much of a challenge in any other way, which seemed very peaceful to him.

Next to her was Lord Harry Osborne. He was the one who'd just made Lady Millicent laugh.

Osborne, he knew, wasn't a bad sort, and his opinion of him hadn't changed at all during their walk today. Handsome but not too full of himself, polite to his elders and betters, didn't leave his accounts with his creditors in arrears, managed not to be dull despite all of these qualities, and the only blot thus far on his reputation involved the organization of phaeton races during which quite a few lordlings lost outrageous amounts of blunt. But of this Moncrieffe secretly approved. Fools and their money *ought* to be parted. He'd also heard Osborne needed more of it. As a gentleman, he could scarcely engage in a profession. He needed an heiress to keep the modest land he was inheriting thriving.

Osborne. *This* was the person who had stolen the light from Genevieve Eversea.

He would have laid a wager upon it.

Genevieve couldn't seem to disentangle her manners from whatever had sent her on a bleak Harry-related reverie. She waved her fan beneath her chin instead, as if movement was a substitution for speech. It was also a warning to him that she was about to take flight. She looked about yearningly as more guests arrived, drifted into the room, took note of the dangerous duke, widened their eyes in amazement, moved on, stared, muttered, and finally relaxed with people of their own rank (moderate) and reputation (benign). It became almost rhythmic, the eye-widening. He nodded, smiled, tried to look as benevolent as he was capable of appearing. Which was even less so than he realized.

They stood before a painting of a white horse. And Osborne had mentioned Canaletto today. He suspected Miss Eversea was a lover of art.

And so he said, in order to give a rudder of sorts to this conversation, "I'm delighted to find so many fine paintings in your home. We didn't have an opportunity to discuss it today, but I find that art moves me."

She examined him. "I suspect it moves you in the opposite direction."

He bit back a smile. "Oh, now, consider that you might underestimate me, Miss Eversea," he cajoled. "For example, this very fine painting of a horse by . . . by . . ."

Damn.

He did know the name of the artist. He'd had portraits of his horses done, too. A man must commemorate his loved ones, after all.

"Ward," she completed dryly. "James Ward." But he had her attention now. Perhaps she hoped to be entertained by whatever inanity he would next produce.

He glanced again toward Lord Harry, who was now entertaining and being entertained by a number of young people. He imagined it was where Genevieve preferred to be . . . and yet not to be, to paraphrase the Bard. Hmm. He couldn't detect any particular devotion to Harry in Millicent. Or of him to her. She seemed to be enjoying *all* of the young men.

A few of whom were aiming calf-eyed gazes at Miss Genevieve Eversea.

Who took no note. It was either that, or she took the calf-eyed admiration as much for granted as the chandelier light. Always present. Nothing to remark upon. Rather like the types of flowers routinely sent to her.

"Of course. The name of the painter simply eluded me in the moment, as I was lost in admiration of your gown." He added that simply so she could enjoy an inanity, and the corner of her mouth did tip sardonically. "But I recognized it as a Ward."

She didn't snort. Her eyes did go skeptically wide. If her manners were any less fine she would have rolled them.

"Very well, then. I knew it was *fine*, and not, for instance, painted by your six-year-old niece," he revised.

This won him a genuine, albeit reluctant, smile. Swiftly there and gone.

Her mouth was the palest pink, he noticed then. As neat and promising as a rose about to bloom. Dimples appeared when she smiled.

He tried not to frown. But it was still a bit disorienting. She'd possessed the same mouth this afternoon. It wasn't something she'd donned along with the gown.

"You knew it was a *horse*, which is generally all a

painting needs in order for a man to admire it and declare it fine. A horse or a dog. And I haven't a niece. Yet."

He seized the opportunity to steer the conversation toward his objective.

"But perhaps you will, soon enough. Your brother Colin has wed, I understand. An enviable condition, matrimony. I do still hope one day very soon to enter into it."

"He *has* wed." She said this gingerly, with something akin to bemusement, as though she still couldn't believe it herself, and as though the subject was a spiny one. "So has my oldest brother, Marcus, as well. And another of my brothers, Charles, is engaged to marry the widow of a colonel. Ian, on the other hand, shows no sign of *shackling* himself, as they . . ."

She trailed off. She was staring at the duke as if she'd seen something multi-legged crawl over his face.

"As they?" He'd needed to ease his jaw in order to prompt her. It was inordinately tight.

". . . as they say," she completed distantly, on an odd note. A faint puzzled dent took up residence between her brows as she regarded him.

"It's a pleasure to hear of the men in your family enjoying matrimony."

"Is it?" She said this almost sharply.

He knew an unfamiliar sensation. Uneasiness. He could imagine her peering at a painted canvas with those sharp eyes, mercilessly scanning it for authenticity, the same way she was examining him now.

Back to art, then. More comfortable, apparently, for both of them.

"Who is your favorite painter, Miss Eversea?"

"I might have to say Titian." She said this almost reluctantly, as if Titian was something precious she kept to herself. "It's the luminous quality of the tones of skin, the incomparable reds, the affection with which he paints his . . ."

She stopped and gave her head a little shake, and a small smile and a half shrug, as though she scarcely qualified to describe the wonder of Titian.

And because she suspected she was boring him.

Luminous quality. Titian didn't particularly interest him. But what he did to Miss Genevieve's face when she'd described him, in fact, fascinated him.

"Miss Eversea, it may interest you to know I've a marvelous collection of paintings at Falconbridge Hall, all in want of an expert to admire it and teach me more about it. And there are some beautiful works at Rosemont, too." One in particular he didn't want to mention, necessarily. Not yet.

Canvases covered in ancestors, for the most part, was what he had at Falconbridge Hall, row upon row of them with eyes and noses and airs of entitlement all very similar to his. It was like strolling through a gallery of mirrors.

"Do you?" she said, clearly more alarmed than enthusiastic. Her fan flicked nervously in her fingers. Her eyes darted toward the stream of guests. She was calculating where and when she could dive into it.

"Oh yes. And many of the paintings are by Italian masters acquired by my father. Perhaps one day you'd like to see—"

With astonishing speed, Genevieve's arm shot out, seized the arm of a young lady and plucked her from the crowd the way a bear plucks a trout from a stream.

"Miss *Oversham*!" she gushed. "Allow me to introduce you to our very esteemed guest, the Duke of Falconbridge."

Miss Oversham's eyes bulged in astonishment at the name. The plume atop her head quivered like a captured bird. "That won't be necess—that is, I was just—"

But Genevieve was surprisingly strong for her size, and she had a good grip on the tall Miss Oversham's elbow. She didn't even relinquish it when the woman curtsied.

"We were discussing art," Genevieve volunteered brightly. "And I know you're a lover of art as I am. I'm certain the duke will enjoy telling you about his family's collection of portraits. I didn't wish to leave him without a delightful conversational partner while I attend to a small pressing matter."

And with that, Genevieve Eversea released Miss Oversham, sidled through the crowd, through a doorway, and disappeared, every bit as graceful and purposeful as an otter navigating a bend in the river.

Wiley minx.

And so he was left alone with Miss Oversham, who wore yellow but managed not to look jaundiced in it, thanks to a fine head of shiny dark hair and a warm complexion. She was very pretty, he supposed, in that she had even features and all of her teeth, all of which she was showing to him now. She was tall enough to nearly look him in the eye, and the plume, he decided, was a poor choice, as it would be visible through the crowd no matter where one stood. She might as well have planted a flag atop her head.

She continued beaming fulsomely at him.

"A pleasure to meet a fellow art lover. What do you think of James Ward, Miss Oversham? Is there a finer painter of horses in all the land?"

He waited.

Her smile radiated at him.

Perhaps she was poor of hearing? He raised his voice and leaned forward. *"What do you think of James Ward, Miss Oversham?"*

She fingered the silk of her fan nervously and her smile expanded.

He grew acerbic. "My apologies, Miss Oversham, but has something I said amused you? Has Ward suddenly become passé? Are horses objects of mirth? Do allow me to share the joke."

She cleared her throat. She wasn't mute. Excellent. "You needn't shout, Lord Moncrieffe. It's just . . ." He leaned forward as it seemed she was about to confide something. "It's just I cannot seem to stop smiling."

It was his turn to go silent.

"You do it very well," he offered cautiously, finally.

"Thank you." She beamed queasily.

Out of the corner of his eye he saw Genevieve Eversea slip back into the room, a sleek little blue shadow. She was now carrying a cup of punch. Pressing business, indeed! He watched her locate a spot the size of her bum on a nearby tufted settee and wedge herself in behind a large-rumped denizen of the Pennyroyal Green community, he suspected, as he hadn't yet been introduced, and Eversea had seen to it that everyone of any rank had been introduced to him. It was an excellent location in which to moon over Harry, he thought, without being spotted by any of her other admirers.

He wondered if she was within earshot of his conversation with Lady Oversham.

To whom he returned his attention. He gave a start when he discovered her splendid teeth were still bared.

"*I've* a painting of a horse by Ward," he volunteered. "Comet, my stallion's name is. I've another horse, too. Named Nimbus."

Genevieve's fan slipped from her grasp. Perhaps she'd been having a quiet laugh at his expense and it had jostled from her grip. When she bent over to retrieve it, her bodice gapped, affording him a startling view of almost *all* of two deliciously round, pale breasts.

It was such a sensual shock the breath went out of him.

It was all the more erotic because he knew he was the only one who could see it, and because she didn't know that he could, and because they were both in the midst of a crowd.

He was a man. He gulped down the view for the duration of its offering, which was cruelly brief. And then Genevieve was upright again, and regret washed him.

Miss Oversham didn't seem to notice his infinitesimal distraction.

When he returned his attention to her, his composure ruffled, his mind's eye filled with breasts, Miss Oversham was plucking at a bracelet on her wrist. And smiling.

"I think I understand, Miss Oversham. Do I make you . . . well, do I make you nervous?" His tone was gently cajoling, the way a favorite uncle might speak to her.

Genevieve Eversea assumed a position so alert he was *certain* she was listening. If she'd been an insect her antennae would have been waving about.

"Yes!" Miss Oversham admitted with some relief. The smile snapped neatly back into place. "It's nerves! I'm terribly sorry, sir, and not proud to admit it, but that's the truth of it. It's just . . . the things that are *said* about you. The . . . duels. The . . ." She stopped. Her fingers worried over the stones in her bracelet.

The rest was clearly unspeakable.

She'd acquired a mortified flush. She was now a beaming red and yellow and brown, like some exotic bird. A toucan.

"Ah, now," he soothed in his low, easy voice, the way he would a spooked horse or a woman whose bodice he was about to slip lower. It worked a treat. Her pupils dilated in sudden interest, for it was *that* kind of voice and she was a woman after all. She'd decided he was attractive and pleasant and she visibly softened. When he bothered to use that tone on women they generally did.

"When one is a duke, one often forgets the effect the title has on others, but I am just a man, I assure you, albeit one with a title. The stories that abound are mostly apocryphal. Shall we address some of them?"

Genevieve took a genteel sip of the punch she'd retrieved. And then studied her lap as assiduously as if she'd had a book open there. The better to concentrate on what he was saying, he supposed.

He'd never seen more vigilant shoulder blades.

Miss Oversham nodded cautiously. "You are too kind, sir." Her smile was tremulous.

"I am nothing of the sort," he said quite sincerely, but she took it quite another way, and he could see she found his modesty affecting.

He shifted his weight onto one leg, the picture of casual elegance, the picture of someone settling in for a long chat.

"Well, let's explore which of them makes you the most nervous. Might it be the rumor that I shot a man in a Brighton pub simply for the pleasure of watching him die?"

She blanched so instantly it was like watching a curtain come down over her face.

"Oh. I see you hadn't heard that one."

"D-did you? Sh-shoot . . . ?"

"Shoot a man for pleasure?" he helpfully completed. "Oh, no, no, no. Dear me, no," he soothed.

Color made a tentative foray into her cheeks. "Thank goodness!"

"I shot him because he'd bumped against me and caused me to spill my ale. No pleasure in it at all."

The line of Miss Eversea's spine seemed positively *alive* with . . . something. Outrage? Horror? Hilarity? He noticed the very fine line of hair traveling up the fragile nape of her neck, and something about that intimate little trail made the back of his own neck tingle as though she'd brushed her fingers there.

Something entirely unexpected was happening in the region of his solar plexus.

"I see," Miss Oversham said faintly. She was very

still, but her eyes darted nervously, as if they hoped to escape without her.

"He lived," he hastened to reassure her. " 'Twas just a flesh wound."

"Excellent," she tried, after he waited a patient moment. But her lips were still peeled back from her teeth and the word sounded parched and entirely insincere.

"Perhaps you've heard the rumor that I fought a duel with pistols with the Marquis of Cordry?"

She nodded helplessly.

He put a hand over his heart. "I can assure you the two of us never aimed a single pistol at one another."

"None?" She sounded skeptical. She wasn't completely stupid, Miss Oversham.

"None. We fought with swords and he stabbed me and then I stabbed him and disarmed him, and the doctor only treated the both of us for flesh wounds and the law never once interfered. I won. And I've only a wee scar."

This last was meant to reassure her.

She was stricken silent.

"Soooo . . . ." He tapped a finger thoughtfully against his chin. "Those are the rumors I hear most often about myself. Are there any others you'd like addressed?"

He knew the one she would be incapable of not broaching. It took a moment for her to get the word out.

"W-wife?" The way she croaked it called to mind someone sitting bolt upright in bed in the middle of the night and wheezing *"Ghost!"* at an apparition.

"You are perhaps referring to the rumor that

implies I poisoned my wife for her money?" he requested clarification brightly.

At last she nodded, and the plume waved like wheat in a rainstorm.

"Well, firstly, it's true I'm staggeringly wealthy, but it's family money," he assured her.

"Staggeringly wealthy?" She sounded very sober and alert. For a blessed second, her teeth disappeared.

"Well *most* of it is family money," he revised self-deprecatingly. "I've won a good deal in gaming hells. I'm a deep and lucky player, and you may have heard among the rumors that I seldom lose—though I always seem to have the best luck in the very worst of the hells, as fate would have it." He shook his head ruefully. "But my sword skills are quite useful there, let me tell *you*, ha-ha! One is generally set upon late at night in Seven Dials or Covent Garden, but I make short work of thugs."

He waited.

"Excellent," she finally whispered, sounding horrified.

"And some of the money I earned from men who had the *unmitigated poor sense* to attempt to get the better of me in business. If you can believe it!" He all but nudged her conspiratorially in the ribs with his elbow. "Ha-ha! I ask you!"

"I imagine that wouldn't be at all sensible." Her smile was rigid now.

"Not at *all*," he nearly purred, very softly. "And the *rest* of my money, and I assure you the amount was modest, became mine upon my wife's death as it was part of her settlement. But I of course didn't *poison* her . . ."

"Wonderful!" Miss Oversham enthused with great relief.

He paused eloquently.

". . . to get her money," he concluded softly.

Miss Oversham's smile congealed entirely. She'd gone waxen. She in fact looked near swooning.

He smiled slowly. "Feeling better about me now?" he asked gently.

Chapter 6

❦

And this was when Genevieve leaped up, abandoning her punch on the floor.

Alive with remorse, in seconds Genevieve rescued Miss Oversham in the same way she'd sent her to the Duke of Falconbridge purgatory, only in reverse: she took her gently by the elbow, produced the excuse required by etiquette for absconding with his conversational partner—"We mustn't monopolize Miss Oversham's time now, and I know Louisa will want to know more about the modiste Miss Oversham uses, as she has just admired her dress"—which was a lie—and steered her to a healing conversation with Louisa, Marcus's wife. Louisa was human balm in most circumstances. Lovely as a spring day but not the sort to make one envious, any more than one would envy the sun its ability to shine.

Relieved at having resolved the misery she'd inflicted upon poor Miss Oversham, she turned to dash from the room and almost ran headlong into a linen-covered wall.

The wall turned out to be Moncrieffe, who must have taken all of two entire steps in order to follow her.

She was now beginning to feel hunted. Though surely this wasn't the case.

"I imagine you're proud of the way you ingratiated yourself with Miss Oversham, Your Grace?"

"Ah, Miss Eversea. You'll excuse me if I confess that it gladdens my heart to know that you abandoned your manners in order to listen to my conversation. But do feel at liberty to ask me anything you wish to know. You needn't hover about like a lovely little bird to catch a morsel of information."

She did roll her eyes at the "lovely little bird."

And this made the devil *smile*.

Then again, doubtless it was almost a relief to speak to someone who was glowering rather than beaming at him. She almost took pity on him.

"What is the *matter* with you?" is what she came out with finally.

"What is the *matter* with me? *That's* what you wish to ask of me, when there are so many other interesting questions you could produce? Lady Oversham conducted a veritable *interview*. Surely you can best her."

"You terrified her! On purpose!"

"On the contrary," he objected, surprised. "I simply recited a list of facts. You're spluttering."

"I'm not spluttering." Genevieve took a step backward. The room was now her social chessboard and she was planning her moves with clever, grim determination.

He stepped forward.

"I do admire a woman of courage. And it takes courage to deflect a duke."

"I've no courage at all, then," she hastened to disparage herself. "I would never *dream* of deflecting a duke."

"Perhaps we can discuss this further during the

dancing portion of the evening. You'll enjoy waltzing with me later this evening, Miss Eversea. I dance very well, despite the height."

"Your modesty is as appealing as your sensitivity, Lord Moncrieffe. But perhaps a reel other than the waltz? We differ so in height I shall be speaking to your third button throughout the dance. Else you will need to look a great distance down and I will need to look a great distance *up*. I shouldn't like you to end the evening with an aching neck."

Inevitable at your creaky, advanced age, she left eloquently, palpably unspoken.

He looked down at her for a moment, head slightly cocked, as if he could hear that unworthy thought echoing in her mind.

"My third button is so often a wallflower during balls I doubt it will mind your conversation overmuch."

She blinked. This was so delightfully . . . *silly* . . . she forgot herself absolutely for a moment. She stole a glance at his third button. It was nacre, of course, as were the rest of them, and looked like an expensive and luminous tiny moon brought down from the sky specifically to button up the duke. A row of snobs, those buttons, all of them.

Lovely gown, it might say to her. *But can* you *trace your ancestry back to the Conqueror?*

Actually, her family could, and this was in fact when all the trouble with the Redmonds allegedly began. *That's* what she would tell the button.

He'd caught her looking at his button. He was smiling faintly, cryptically. He gave his head the slightest, slightest of to and fro shakes, as if once again he could read her thoughts.

"I very much enjoy the Sir Roger de Coverley," she tried with polite stubbornness. "I would enjoy dancing it with you."

This wasn't true. But it was always the last dance of the evening. And a reel, not a waltz, and quite energetic, which made conversation difficult. With any luck he would have tired of the dancing and gone off to bed or off to the pub or off to see whatever debaucheries could be had in Sussex by the time the Sir Roger de Coverley got under way. Surely her brothers would keep him informed of the wickedness a man could get up to in the neighborhood.

She was also almost afraid to touch him. He was so very much . . . a *man*. Solid. Loomingly tall and angular. He demanded too much from her. She wanted to be alone with the enormity of her heartbreak, to nurse it for a time, and to not have to think or deflect. She wanted peace. And it was *almost* achievable in a throng like this, for all she need do was move through the crowd, a smile pasted on, and never alight and never talk to anybody.

But as luck would have it, that's when she heard Harry laugh.

Her head turned toward it helplessly, the way it might celestial trumpets, and joy and misery thwacked her heart between them like a lawn tennis ball.

Harry noticed her looking, as he always did; he'd always seemed to know precisely where she was in a room. He threw her a quick smile, the smile that was mischievous and conspiratorial and intimate and had once meant everything to her, for they'd exchanged any number of these sorts of smiles across crowded rooms and each one had woven a net of shared understanding about just the two of them. Or so she'd thought. For all she knew he'd been flinging smiles just like that at Millicent the entire time she'd known the two of them, or compromising Millicent in the garden of some London town house the times he was out of view.

Maybe he'd even kissed more than Millicent's *hand*.

And that thought stabbed her clean through.

She would have to retrain her heart not to leap like an ecstatic pet every time she heard his voice.

Harry glanced at the duke, then back at her, and then with comic sly speed crossed his eyes dourly before returning his attention to her brother Marcus and his wife, Louisa.

He was teasing her and sympathizing with her about the duke. He might have the grace to feel jealous, she thought. But no, he clearly didn't see the duke as a rival. Why should he, when he didn't see her as a *woman*, really. When he saw her as a *friend*.

And when the duke was more a contemporary of her father than of Harry.

Back to the duke.

It was like looking from spring to winter.

"I greatly admire your exquisite manners, Miss Eversea, and your concern for my physical comfort during the waltz is touching, indeed. So I know you'll indulge me when I say I would very much prefer to dance the waltz, as I look less awkward during it than I do during any of the country dances. I am all arms and legs, as you can see."

What nonsense. He was all towering grace and she had no doubt he'd look as fit and appropriate hopping about during a reel as he would sailing through the room in a waltz.

But she began to believe the bit he'd told Miss Oversham about the duel. Because if there was anything the duke did expertly it was identify vulnerabilities, parry, and thrust home.

But she was not without her own resources. She'd at last backed up the appropriate number of steps to do what she'd been planning to do.

"Lord Moncrieffe, I'm certain you would enjoy speaking with my sister, Olivia, while I greet my cousin Adam, the vicar of Pennyroyal Green."

She stepped aside almost with a flourish to reveal Olivia standing near the ornate carved mantel. And before Olivia could get hold of Genevieve to stop her—and her hand did dart out in a valiant try—Genevieve had abandoned him once more.

And with something almost akin to a *whoosh* she disappeared into the crowd.

He looked after her. He was amused again. He intended to seduce and abandon her; he hadn't expected to *enjoy* himself so thoroughly. He was the Duke of Falconbridge, for God's sake. He didn't sport a hump or a wen, he possessed all of his teeth, a flat stomach, and considerable sexual confidence. He could objectively assess his reflection in the mirror and knew most women found it *far* from wanting, even if his reputation frightened them. But many of them enjoyed being frightened.

And yet Genevieve had just knocked him off onto her sister like mud from her shoe.

Olivia Eversea was indeed a beauty, no question. But a fearsome one. She fair glittered, as if she was made of brittle opaque glass and a candle burned inside her. Her skin was very fine, like her sister's. The elegant bones of her face were more pronounced because she was a bit too thin, and her eyes were fierce, a little cynical, and fringed with lashes so black and luxurious a man could be forgiven for believing she was one of those soft and gentle types. A trap, those lashes. Like an anemone. Her hair was naturally curly—ah, perhaps the source of Genevieve's envy—piled up in a way that was meant to appear sweetly haphazard but which he knew likely took a team of expert women with heated tongs and other exotic implements to erect and properly tame. A few strands fell in lively, calculated abandon to her collarbone, which was also a trifle too sharp. She wore green, a sea foam shade. It was still a reflex, noting the colors of gowns, because his wife had forever asked him which colors suited her. *All of them do*, he would have told her, would she have tolerated such democracy for a moment.

"Good evening, Your Grace. Have you been sent to court me?"

Well.

"No one sends me anywhere I do not wish to go," he replied easily. "I'm delighted to have an opportunity to speak with you."

"She's immeasurably kind, my sister." Her mouth was wry at the corner and the words ironic. She sounded as though she was making a mental note to pinch Genevieve by the ear for setting a duke upon her. For clearly she thought this was why the duke was here.

"She is indeed kind." He was certain there would be no disadvantage to flattering Genevieve to her sister. "She knew I would enjoy your company and conversation. And she assures me that you are kind, as well."

"I'm not," Olivia disagreed. "I'm committed. But not kind."

"She assured me of that, as well," he said smoothly. "Committed is an admirable thing to be sure. I've been accused of a similar quality."

He was certainly committed to a course of action, anyway, with regards to Genevieve Eversea. Though he doubted anyone would call it admirable.

Across the room he noted, the way a predator notes prey, the presence of Ian Eversea.

"You're committed to flattery, of a certainty." Acerbic, though one could tolerate an acid tongue for a time when the owner of it was so very pretty. Like being pecked by a songbird.

"On the contrary. I'm not merely committed to flattery. I'm a positive *acolyte* of flattery."

She smiled at that, and waved her fan thoughtfully beneath her chin, cocking her head, deciding whether he interested her.

Careful, Miss Eversea. You might slip up and flirt.

He considered whether he found Olivia's directness appealing. It certainly simplified conversation. But simplification wasn't necessarily always an *improvement*. Directness often disguised as much as it revealed, and was a marvelous defense. He could imagine suitors slinking away upon having frankness *batted* at them by the lovely Olivia Eversea.

Primarily he suspected Olivia Eversea quite simply didn't care what he thought of her, while Genevieve Eversea's impulses were . . . well, they *were* in truth . . . *kind*. She cared whether he was comfortable even when she was uncomfortable. She was, in her way, more of a challenge and less of one.

And her kindness was what he would inevitably be able to exploit to achieve his ends.

Wiley she might be. But he was building his strategy.

He looked for her again, as he was *indeed* committed. Genevieve was now in conversation with a Mr. Adam Sylvaine, Pennyroyal Green's vicar and a cousin on their mother's side. He was long-boned and easy of manner. A striking man, what with the height and silvery-fair hair. All of which darkly amused the duke. He was certain bums were packed tightly on the Pennyroyal Green's little pews every Sunday, and that most of them belonged to females. Clever decision on the part of the Everseas, taking such a cousin on as the vicar.

And knowing their proclivities, certain to result in a scandal involving some poor unwed village girl and that vicar being run out of Pennyroyal Green on a rail or tumbling out of some woman's window.

"Perhaps you'd be kind enough to share a dance with me later this evening, Miss Eversea?"

"Perhaps I *will* be just that kind." Olivia smiled.

He suspected he received precisely the same amount of attention and charm as every other man who approached her. She *appeared* indomitable. He suspected she was something like the opposite.

He, like everyone else, knew the story of Lyon Redmond's disappearance, and how she had allegedly *driven* him away.

The loss of love took everyone differently, he knew. Perhaps she'd spent all of the love she had, and was left with clever deflection to protect her wounds.

"Millicent!" Olivia said brightly, and sure enough, that lovely, laughing burnished girl, who was but a few feet away, turned, and then looked up, up, up, into his face.

"I wonder if you might tell Lord Moncrieffe about your interest in art."

"I do enjoy drawing and painting," Millicent agreed brightly.

"Are you a lover of Italian art then, Lady Blenkenship?"

He said this as Olivia Eversea slipped away. He almost laughed as he saw her vanish into the crowd.

Genevieve Eversea was nowhere to be seen.

"Ital . . . oh, you're thinking of Genevieve. Miss Eversea. She is a great lover of Italian art. Caravaggio and the like," Lady Millicent said with an airy wave of her hand.

"And the like" encompassed rather a lot of artists, he thought, all of whom were fairly distinctive. He knew *that* much about art.

She was staring at him somewhat nervously with those big sherry-colored eyes. Her eyes crept surreptitiously toward his hairline. Probably in search of horns or dueling scars or signs of creeping recession.

He stifled a sigh. He'd already played the game of "terrify the maiden" once this evening. It was much more entertaining when he was certain someone was eavesdropping, and he still saw Genevieve nowhere in the crowd.

"What manner of art do you enjoy, Lady Blenkenship?" He struggled to keep the impatience from his voice. Lord, but he was weary of pretending to enjoy art.

She hesitated. She bit her lip. And then Lady Blenkenship leaned forward and confided on a whisper, "Well, as it so happens, I can show you right now."

This was a bit startling. And a bit more . . . promising?

"Are you interested in the work of James Ward?" he asked carefully. He was proud of himself for remembering the name. He didn't, however, want to look at the damned horse again.

Lady Blenkenship looked this way and that, her big eyes assessing the crowd to see if anyone was looking directly at them at the moment.

"Would you like to see my . . . sketches?"

She asked it with her eyes downcast, peering flirtatiously up at him through her lashes.

Her *sketches*?

Was he being propositioned in a crowded salon? Did she intend to lure him up to her chamber? Did he *mind*? It was a complication, if Lady Blenkenship intended to seduce him, but he was no stranger to complications.

"Show me your sketches, Lady Blenkenship," he said softly, with the smile he reserved for innuendo.

She instantly reached down behind the settee behind her and produced, to his astonishment, a sketchbook and handed it to him.

"Go on," she urged on a whisper. "Tell me what you think."

She'd clasped her hands in front of her, then brought them nervously up to her mouth. Her big eyes liquid with nervous anticipation.

What on earth would he find in it? He looked

about the salon just as she had. This way and that, ensuring no one was looking directly at him. He hoped he'd find nudes and was at the same time rather worried he would.

He opened her sketchbook furtively. He turned the first page up by one corner, took a peek. And then he turned it all the way over.

He stared for a good long time at the first drawing.

She nearly bounced on her toes awaiting his verdict.

"Lady Blenkenship?"

"Yes?" she said breathlessly.

"This is a kitten. In a basket."

She nodded eagerly.

"This is a sketch of a kitten in a basket."

A fluffy, big-eyed kitten was sitting neatly in a round basket, paws draped over the edge.

"Do you like it?" Millicent was practically nibbling on her knuckles with nerves.

"It's a *kitten* in a *basket*," he pointed out slowly. As if this was answer enough.

"Look at the next one," she urged excitedly.

He gingerly turned the page. He stared.

"It's . . . kittens playing with a yarn ball." Something like hysteria tinged his voice.

"Ginger, Tom, and Molly!" she announced, stabbing a brown-gloved hand over their images as she announced their names. The amber stones on her bracelet clinked together. "Aren't they *precious*?"

He slowly turned the pages, one by one. One by one. Kittens playing with a string. Kittens lapping milk. Kittens sniffing flowers.

"Lady Blenkenship?"

"Yes?"

"Do you like kittens?"

"Oh, I *do*!" she confided breathlessly.

He sighed, handed the sketchbook back to her, and to her astonishment promptly abandoned her and wended his way through the crowd.

He didn't *dislike* kittens. But life was too short to continue this conversation.

He needed a brandy now. Jacob Eversea had invited him upstairs to discuss a potential investment in a gas lighting endeavor.

If he couldn't have a brandy he'd make do with three more cups of ratafia.

He turned the corner in search of the ratafia only to find Ian Eversea strolling in his direction. They froze in a passage before a small elegant marble table, over which an enormous mirror helpfully framed the two of them and reflected a goodly number of the people standing in the salon. Ian froze, darted a look at the mirror, and then seemed visibly relieved. Moncrieffe could almost read his thoughts. It meant the rest of the salon could see the two of them, and that someone was bound to notice if the duke inserted a stiletto into his torso, for instance.

The two men confronted each other silently. Fury and embarrassment and an all-too-vivid memory came at Moncrieffe in a swift wave before receding.

All Ian Eversea, all the rest of the salon would see reflected in the mirror, was cold, dangerous elegance.

"Mr. Eversea," he drawled. "We haven't yet had a chance to speak alone. I hardly recognize you . . . in clothing."

"What are you about, Moncrieffe?" Eversea did look decidedly ill.

"What am I about . . . ? Well, I'm *about* to enjoy, or at least drink, a cup of ratafia. Or brandy if I can get it. I'm about to join your father for a brief discussion of an investment opportunity in his study. I'm about to divest your neighbors and guests of their money in five-card loo. But that's later. More importantly, I'm about to dance with your sister."

It was the smile Moncrieffe offered here, and the way he said "sister," that had Ian reaching, in a reflex almost as old as time, for a sword he wasn't wearing.

He forced his hand to ease.

For Moncrieffe had seen it; he casually placed his own hand inside his coat. A pistol was never far from his person.

"Your grievance is with me, Moncrieffe, not my family. The offer to settle my offense against you stands. Feel free to choose your weapons, your time, and your seconds. If you would leave my father and sisters alone, I should be grateful."

Moncrieffe sighed, bored. "Grate—" He shook his head with exaggerated incredulity. "I've chosen my weapon, Eversea, and my time. A second won't be necessary for what I have in mind."

Ian stared at him with an expression uncannily similar to his sister's. Penetrating, fixed. His eyes were blue, his hair was long and waving in the way that Byron had made swooningly popular, and the sort of reddish dark brown that would go even more auburn in the sun.

So some of the Everseas ended up with curly locks, while Genvieve was saddled with the straight ones.

The thought came from nowhere, and almost, *almost* made Moncrieffe smile.

"You won't be able to *stare* my intent out of me, Eversea," he said mildly. "Now, doubtless you'll be missed at the party if you linger here. I want my drink before the dancing starts, and I hear the orchestra tuning even now. Quite looking forward to it. I've been promised a *waltz* by your sister Genevieve."

Ian went still as suspicion took hold. And then he seemed to reflect upon this, and something like relief passed over his face.

"Not Genevieve. I *know* her. She'll never look at you when she could be looking at Osborne or some other young blood. She'll see you as more a contemporary of Father's than of hers. And she's cleverer than a woman ought to be."

"Would you like to wager on that?"

"I know better than to wager with you."

"A pity. Second to revenge I enjoy building my fortune. And besides, you really don't know what I intend to do, Eversea. If you would step aside so I can pass?"

"I will be watching you, Moncrieffe."

"You ought to," Moncrieffe agreed. "But it won't do any good."

"I *am* sorry, you know."

For a moment Moncrieffe was almost convinced. He knew Ian had served with distinction in the war. And he knew some men returned from it filled with recklessness, feeling restless and incomplete in the absence of danger to deflect. In the absence of a purpose as large as war.

But this was philosophical rumination. He didn't care why Eversea had cuckolded him.

"I have to wonder that you haven't learned that actions have consequences, Eversea. You *did* serve in the war, did you not? An excellent place to learn such a thing."

Eversea said nothing. He touched the side of his face absently, where a slight powder burn showed beneath the skin of his handsome face.

"I keep waiting for you to be as original as the rest of your family, Eversea, and you continue to disappoint me. Of *course* you're sorry. The first words out of the mouths of men who are caught doing something they're only too happy to continue *until* they're caught. It's a . . . it's a dull old story. Now, if you will excuse me . . ."

"You could have defended her honor. Lady Abigail's."

A risky suggestion.

"She surrendered her honor rather willingly, didn't she? This is the last I will discuss it. Your father might be interested to know what you did. And I will tell him if you interfere in the . . . enjoyment of my stay. But do feel free to entertain the possibility that my presence here is entirely social in nature and that I'm simply here to torture you with uncertainty."

"I've considered it," Ian said in such a way that meant he'd considered and rejected it. "What precisely did you mean when you said the punishment will fit the crime?"

Moncrieffe sighed. "Honestly. What makes you think I'll answer the question?"

"A man has to *try*."

"I imagine that's written beneath the Eversea coat of arms," the duke drawled.

They were both surprised when something like a glimmer of humor sparked between them.

"If you ask the Redmonds what our coat of arms features . . . ." Ian began.

"Oh, I would wager they'd answer . . . A window, a gallows, a trellis, and the club with which you killed their ancestor in order to steal a cow."

Ian laughed shortly. It was a pained and surprised sound, but it was genuine.

And then the spark of understanding died, because Ian's transgression really was ignominious and they both knew it couldn't stand without the duke addressing it.

And both were faintly conscious of regret.

"Ask yourself this: . . . What do you think the nature of the crime was, Mr. Eversea the younger? Let that puzzle divert you until the answer is revealed to you."

He moved briskly around Ian, who stepped back to give him a wide berth, and toward the music and his goal.

Chapter 7

The ball had hardly begun and it seemed endless, but then one of heartbreak's chief qualities seemed to be its ability to distort time and distances. And it wasn't as though she was a stranger to anticipation. She understood now it came in an infinite variety. There was the good sort, as in the night before a birthday, and the awful sort, as in the morning they'd waited for news of Colin's death by hanging.

This sort had got its teeth into her nape.

Genevieve was almost tempted to seize Millicent by the arm, drag her up to Harry and snarl, "He has something he wishes to say to you."

And then stand there with her arms crossed, foot tapping, until Harry came out with the words.

She'd scarcely had time to speak alone with Millicent since the house party had got under way in earnest. But she watched Millicent through new eyes. Millicent, who enjoyed sketching kittens and who laughed at nearly everything, and who was so remarkably pretty that the London bloods routinely sent to her blooms that rivaled Olivia's for ostentation, if not originality. Had she missed minute clues indicating Millicent might harbor a particular passion for Harry? Had Genevieve, who was so startlingly observant when it came to assessing a painting, for instance, overlooked what was right beneath her nose?

But Millicent seemed no different than she ever had. She seemed to enjoy the banquet of male attention with the same equanimity with which she enjoyed the buffet of food. Millicent suffered no torments of emotion; Millicent had no need for control; Millicent floated on a sea of sunny contentment.

In an agony of suspicion, Genevieve watched Harry for signs of passionate devotion to Millicent, for yearning glances, in blushes or stammers, for signs of any symptoms specific to the lovestruck.

She saw . . . attention. Devotion would have been an exaggeration.

It was unbearable. It was *all* unbearable. The weight of the impending proposal sat on her chest like an anvil. She swung from miserably thwarted love to righteous fury and back again every time she looked at him, and it made her so dizzy and ill she'd cast accounts upstairs, discreetly.

And Harry, the Marquis de Sade of Sussex, had claimed a waltz, and she could hardly refuse him.

Nor, God help her, did she want to.

She *might* accidentally tread upon him, however. Hard.

But now she stood in the ballroom, a fraud in a ball gown, gaiety and music and color kaleidoscoping around her. It was intolerable that she should be expected to *dance* with *anyone* when she bore such a grievous wound. But everywhere she looked were members of her family, who acknowledged her with quick smiles or eyebrows raised. Apart from Ian, who looked, she noticed once more, nearly as ill as she felt. Decidedly pale and twitchy.

Her mother would most *definitely* notice if she'd gone missing. Her mother saw her now, blew her a subtle little kiss, and tipped her head in a signal with a smile that at first confused Genevieve. And then, oh God, she realized the Sussex Waltz was beginning which reminded her that . . .

She turned.

The other man she'd been unable to refuse earlier was standing before her.

He stretched out a hand.

She could not for the life of her understand what the Duke of Falconbridge wanted from her. She ascribed his presence and his attention to the week's general theme, which was "torture." He'd perhaps come to Sussex to shop for a wife, since he'd recently shed himself of the candidate he'd selected.

It wouldn't be her.

Regardless of how determined he might be. And the man personified determination. Regardless of the glimmer of temptation she'd felt to . . . well, allow herself to be charmed. To surrender to the sheer force of him. The notion that she'd ever thought she could entirely ignore someone of his reputation on her walk today she ascribed to naïveté and heartbreak. He'd skillfully found her unprotected flank again and again.

He'd even made her smile when she'd thought to never do it again.

And yet she recalled his eyes when she'd said the name "Abigail." She'd panicked; she'd played her trump. And she'd hurt him.

This was the impression that lingered.

It was as though everything else he'd said and done up until then had been steps in a dance, and he'd only dropped his mask when she tripped him.

So he was a clever man, a watchful man, a powerful man, but a man with unexpectedly human vulnerabilities. She wasn't certain she cared. She still didn't think he was a *nice* man.

She took his hand. She was immediately overwhelmingly conscious of its size; it enveloped hers with almost absurd masculine strength.

And they glided in to join the dancers.

She'd been right. She could stare his third shirt button in the eye, and likely they looked almost comical swirling together about the ballroom.

But he was brisk and graceful. Something of his strength communicated to her, and for a moment she felt as though she were sailing.

And, since the theme of the week was torture, he was intent on conversation.

"May I ask a question, Miss Eversea?"

"I can hardly prevent you."

She'd been trying to daunt him. The contrary man's eyes lit with humor instead. *What color are they?* she wondered idly. His eyes? She didn't care. They were dark.

"Well, let's see. . . . One of your brothers escaped the gallows . . ."

"He was innocent," she said shortly. "And that's a statement, not a question."

"Patience. And your sister is engaged in the pursuit of worthy causes . . ."

"We've established that, yes. I await the question . . ."

"Have patience. And another of your brothers is

a war hero, having been desperately wounded in battle . . ."

" 'Hero' is among the vast number of things we enjoy calling my brother Chase, yes. You are reciting to me things I know."

"Patience. I wonder, does it play havoc on your nerves, being part of such a, shall we say, *eventful* family?"

You *play havoc with my nerves.*

It was an odd question. She doubted it was an innocent one. "I love my family. All families are eventful."

He cocked an illustratively disbelieving brow.

He was right, of course. Few families were as eventful as the Everseas.

He regarded her thoughtfully for half a bar of music. *One, two, three. . . . One, two, three . . .*

"Well, I've given it some thought, Miss Eversea, and I've decided you haven't at all answered my question. And since I managed to at last *produce* a question, perhaps you would agree it is only fair to produce an answer for me."

She almost laughed. Her equilibrium *was* thrown. And for a merciful instant she forgot about the anvil on her chest.

"I think I prefer to speak to your third button after all."

"My third button is not at home to unannounced guests," he said sternly.

She did laugh then, delighted.

And he smiled down at her, and what she saw were excellent teeth and faint lines: at the corners of his eyes, one faint one bisecting his forehead, a cleanly drawn jaw. His nose was straight. His shirt was stunningly white. Everything about him was elegant and emphatically drawn.

His strength was such that she felt for a moment buoyed, relieved of the burden of staying upright under her own power. He was not one of those broad sturdy men that populated the Sussex countryside; he was quicksilver and sinewy.

And out of the corner of her eye, she thought she saw Harry's head turn her way, a familiar flash of gold. She craned her head sharply, briefly, the way someone might if they thought they'd stumbled across a guinea. But the ballroom was crowded and she didn't see him after all, and deflated, enervated, she returned her attention to the duke.

"I imagine paintings are very restful after the, shall we say, vigor and unpredictability surrounding anyone named Eversea. Paintings stay the same day after day, don't they?"

It *sounded* like an innocent question. Genevieve was immediately wary. She suspected everything this man said and did was fueled by strategy.

"But one can notice and feel new things about the same painting, depending upon how you feel on a certain day."

They swept in a turn and suddenly Genevieve's feet struck earth again with a thud and she panicked. The ballroom had once been Genevieve's favorite room in the house, with its glowing amber floor and that row of gaudy chandeliers on high and when it was empty it echoed with the promise of music and gaiety. But now it was the place where she could not see Harry or Millicent. Torment came at her in a fresh wave. Was he even now on bended knee behind that unconscionably bushy fern in the far corner? Had he herded her out to the back garden—where it was in fact far too cold to issue a proposal, in her opinion, but there were stars out and—

Oh, dear Heaven above thank *God* there he was. Dancing with Millicent. Were they yet engaged?

"Can you really see different things in a painting from day to day?" This seemed to genuinely interest the duke. She wasn't certain which part of it fascinated him most, the fact that a painting could change or that she thought it could.

"Well, it isn't like a crystal ball. Whereby you see shifting images and the like. But haven't you ever looked at a painting for a length of time, or on more than one occasion, and experienced it differently each time?"

Where to begin explaining art to someone who seemed to know nothing about it? Now, if she were dancing with Harry . . .

"Of course. As a young man touring the Continent, I once looked at *length* at a painting called *Venus and Mars* by an Italian painter called Veronese. Do you know it? Venus is nude as the day she was born, and Mars is entirely clothed and down on his knees in front of her, and it looks as though Mars is about to give her a pleasuring. And there are cherubs hanging about. I looked at it for quite some time."

A . . . pleasuring. *God above.*

He had her attention now.

She was speechless.

Everything was astonishing about what he'd just said. She stared up at him, her mind exploding with vivid images, her cheeks going increasingly hotter. She knew the painting. She knew *precisely* where Mars was kneeling in front of Venus.

The duke had said it purposely.

Suddenly she was acutely aware of her five senses, as though they were blinking on, one by one, like fireflies in the dark. Most particularly vivid was touch. She was potently aware of his hands: the one resting with firm assurance against her waist, warm there now through the fine silk of her gown, the other enfolding hers. She was acutely aware of his size, and everything that was masculine to her feminine.

Goodness. He could certainly look at her for a long time without blinking.

"Do you . . . know of a painter called Boticelli?" She sounded tentative.

"I do, in fact. But vaguely."

"I think he isn't rated highly enough. I enjoy his grace of line, the light infusing his subjects."

Moncrieffe knew a subtle thrill. He'd thrown out a temptation, a subtle invitation. She'd recognized it and taken it up. "And I have seen his *Venus and Mars*," he added. "Ironically, in it Venus is entirely clothed and Mars, the poor bastard, is sprawled looking as though she's just had her way with him and he's spent."

Somehow they'd drawn closer, closer, and he said this nearer to her ear than any man ought to be during a waltz.

"It's allegory." She murmured it, unconvincingly, in his ear.

"*Is* it," he murmured back. As though he didn't believe her. As though he was inviting her to consider that it was, in fact, a representation of what had just happened between Venus and Mars, of what could happen between any man and woman, between the two of them.

She'd gone quiet. What was she thinking? Had her own boldness, or his, overwhelmed her?

"I've an acquaintance by the name of Wyndham who paints. His paintings leave you in no question of what they're intended to represent. No viewers mistake them for anything other than what they are or read additional meanings into them."

Wyndham painted all the most lascivious paintings for The Velvet Glove, the bordello favored by any man who preferred his whores pretty. Everyone depicted in his paintings was naked, or mostly naked, and having a marvelous time.

"Did you make the acquaintance of this Mr. Wyndham in the process of pursuing your interest in . . . 'horses'?"

Well.

He was instantly riveted. His eyes focused intently, speculatively on her, and she looked back bravely enough, her eyes both glinting, and tentative and uncertain. It was clear to him that she was new to this sort of flirtation; she feinted and then fell back, as though with his questions he'd revealed a new path her nature was drawn to but hesitant to follow.

He smiled slowly. "I might have done."

She wasn't a coquette. But he would wager his life that what he'd sensed earlier in her was true: she kept her passions leashed, for reasons of her own.

Everything leashed could be unleashed. He would find a way.

She did battle with another of those wicked, delighted smiles; he saw it tugging at the corners of her mouth. He found himself waiting breathlessly for it to have its way with her; he wanted to see her smile beneath the chandelier light; he wanted to see her aglow again.

She did smile.

And when she did, he became all at once aware of small things, separate, all at once, the way a rising sun lights on objects one by one, illuminating them. The feel of her hand in his, how small, how fragile; her narrow waist supple beneath his hand and the frail layer of fabric between his hand and her skin; the light glinting from the jewel resting against her pale bosom, the scent of her, floral and womanly, a certain tightening in his gut. He lacked the precise vocabulary to describe what he felt. It was unexpected and he nearly stumbled; it was like inadvertently staring at his fingers during a pianoforte piece and losing his place.

He *could* truthfully say he'd lost his breath for a moment. He doubted she'd noticed.

He found it again in time to speak. "Do your feelings about paintings—and other things—change so very often then, Miss Eversea?"

"*Some* of my feelings about things never change. Including paintings."

It was a cryptic statement nevertheless meant to cover a multitude of things: how she felt about her family, about Harry, about the duke and whatever his motive might be for courting her, if that's what he was so determinedly doing.

"There are things the artist intends, and things the viewer sees, and what the viewer sees isn't always what the artist intends. Isn't always apparent upon first viewing. I suppose that was my original point," she added.

"Isn't it the same with people?" the duke asked.

Genevieve looked up warily. Was he actually implying she possessed *hidden depths*? Because of course she did, but it wasn't as though anyone else seemed to think so. Was he perhaps thinking of his erstwhile fiancée? She wondered why the engagement had ended, and if it had indeed been as mutual and friendly as gossip would have it.

She sincerely doubted it.

"I suppose it is," she decided to say carefully.

"But paintings are a good deal *safer* than people, aren't they, Miss Eversea?"

Safe. It was another word she found unflattering and yet strangely appealing. She had a terrible suspicion this was leading to another assessment of her character she wouldn't appreciate. She might be called "sensible" and "serene" and "mature" again and if he uttered those words she'd be unable to bear it. She would scream until the chandeliers shook.

"*Some* paintings are considered heretical," she said irritably.

"Ah, but that isn't the fault of the painting. It's the prejudice of the viewer. For instance, isn't the fault of your *dress* that when you turn it looks like a pond rippling beneath a full moon at midnight. Or that you resemble a naiad rising from the depths in it. It is the opinion of this particular viewer."

Her head went back in shock.

And instead of casting her eyes down bashfully again, or fluttering her lashes in coy confusion or responding with a mumbled thank-you . . . she locked her eyes with his.

Her eyes were so soft. Like the hearts of pansies. But they were also surprisingly intensely searching, and he thought he could feel them probing his soul. Sorting through impressions.

Hot color swept her cheekbones as she absorbed the impact of this observation. She was attempting to decode it.

So she wasn't immune to the compliment. She simply didn't trust it.

In truth, he hadn't fully expected to say it himself. Where on earth had it come from? This was what unnerved him.

And to think he'd once thought her face ordinary.

How could anyone think this was a *quiet* girl? Her stillness and calm were deceptive. She disturbed him the way the approach of a distant storm did; she enervated him. She felt like . . . portent. He wondered if she contained her passions because she instinctively knew they'd too rapidly run away from her if unleashed.

He sensed seducing her would neither be as impossible nor as tedious as he'd originally feared. And if he kept her off balance just often enough the event might happen sooner rather than later.

She finally ducked her head. She was frowning just a little, troubled.

"Do you see what you expect to see, Miss Eversea?" he said softly.

"Lines," she murmured.

"Lines?"

"I saw lines. The faint ones in your forehead. And

the ones at the corners of your eyes. Perhaps from frowning overmuch?"

She suggested this gently, as though he ought to give up the habit of glowering.

Why the . . . . little . . . *devil*.

He was perversely, wildly entertained.

"Are you insulting my appearance, Miss Eversea?" In all of his born days no woman had tried as hard not only to resist him but to actively *drive* him away.

"I didn't say they were unappealing. They add interest to your face. From an *artist's* perspective, anyhow," she added hurriedly, lest he mistake it for a compliment.

He'd been inwardly admiring her *eyes* and *she'd* been counting the lines 'round his as though they were the rings in the oak in Ashdown Forest and would reveal his true age to her.

Which was nearly, but not quite, twice hers.

Then again, she'd just shot another miserable, yearning glance toward Osborne, who hadn't yet any lines to speak of in his face. He probably scarcely even taxed the edge of his shaving razor with whiskers yet.

"So if they're not unappealing, perhaps they're *appealing*," he pressed, with mordant humor.

"Perhaps from an artist's perspective," she clarified firmly, and a little desperately. "They're not *un*appealing."

"And from a woman's perspective?"

"I suppose it would depend upon the woman."

He admired the dodging so thoroughly he laughed. Was she counting his gray hairs as well?

There were only a few. *Dashing,* he'd been assured. His mirror assured him of the same thing. He still had nearly all of his hair. Most of it was black.

"I believe women generally find other aspects of my character more diverting, as the lines have not yet been mentioned to me in casual conversation. It must take the eye of an artist to notice them. And point them out. Your attention to detail is astonishing."

He'd deftly complimented her into a corner yet again and she knew it.

He felt her ribs move in a sigh beneath his waltzing hand. He did smile.

She could try to discourage him. But he was luring her, a bit at a time, closer and closer to him. She was reluctantly intrigued and drawn to him and confused by why she was.

It's because I'm a grown man, Miss Eversea. Not a boy.

He felt her draw in a quick, sharp breath; her rib cage moved beneath his hand. Her mouth went tight and white at the corners of her mouth, as though she was suppressing some pain.

She glanced across the room. That handsome Lady Millicent Blenkenship was dancing with Lord Harry Osborne. They were nearly the same height, and swept in circles in pleasing unison, two bright golden heads.

He decided to test a theory.

"As I said earlier today, though it's unfortunate I've parted ways with Lady Abigail, I do hope to experience the same happiness in marriage your brother Colin knows."

"Please."

The pain in the word shocked him.

"Please," she repeated more reasonably and carefully, as though she were correcting herself on the pronunciation of the word. "I shouldn't like to discuss matrimony."

Even her distress was dignified and contained. But it was real. Two hot spots of color sat high on her cheeks. He sensed that for her this amounted to an outburst. She was suffering greatly.

What could it be? Why?

She didn't look directly at him. Breathing to settle herself. She looked at his third button, hidden beneath his cravat. He was peculiarly tempted to rest his cheek against her shiny head. To murmur things. He knew how to soothe. But the memory was distant and the instinct awkward from disuse.

"I understand," he said quietly.

He didn't. But it made her dart a suspicious, curious look up at him. And then widen her eyes in curious concern she quickly disguised.

Perhaps if he, too, implied he nursed a broken heart he'd garner sympathy. Because she was innately kind.

Suddenly he felt a bit like her gaoler. So be it. She was suffering the waltz with him when she'd rather fling herself into the arms of Harry Osborne or lurk in a corner, mooning about him and nursing whatever wound he'd inflicted upon her heart. Or her pride. Sometimes Moncrieffe wasn't certain they were different organs, particularly when it came to himself.

He'd warrant whatever misery was associated with Lord Harry Osborne had something to do with that deliciously lush Lady Blenkenship. Lady of the Kittens.

Genevieve had gone quiet and inward again, and he had the sense she was counting the steps of the waltz in her head, that she knew precisely how many more notes remained to be played, and that she was eager to have it over and done.

He allowed it. He didn't speak for the rest of it.

Oh, he'd warrant he could make the girl forget Lord Harry Osborne.

And after *that*, she'd need to spend the rest of her life forgetting the Duke of Falconbridge.

Chapter 8

The duke relinquished her with a bow when the waltz ended and Genevieve fled to the punch table. And thusly she managed to avoid a quadrille and a reel by availing herself of another cup of ratafia, sipping at it in an attempt to settle her nerves. But the inevitable could not be postponed.

For the first time in her life, she could find nothing to say to Harry when he came to claim his waltz with her.

"Shall we?" he said almost gently.

She couldn't bear to be touched by him. And at the same time it was a relief to be touched by him, because it was so familiar and safe. Safe—a word she was drawn to and shied from. Because of course Harry wasn't safe anymore. No one who rudely kicked the supports out from beneath her castles in the air could be considered safe.

Their hands settled in the familiar and correct places—hers nestled in his, his at her waist, and they began gliding in the familiar steps.

Speak to me, speak to me, speak to me.

She couldn't ask the question. For all she knew, she was now dancing with an engaged man. Harry may have impulsively burst out with a proposal midway through the Sussex Waltz and Millicent was simply waiting for Harry to get his cursory waltz with Genevieve over with so she could share the news.

She'd heard, also courtesy of her brother Chase, the former soldier who'd been badly wounded at Waterloo, that when one was stabbed deeply one ought to leave the knife in the wound, and not yank it out, lest one bleed to death.

She wasn't going to yank that question up out of the depths.

"So what do you think of the Duke of Falconbridge?" Harry began brightly.

"Ow," he said, as she trod on his foot and they stumbled a little.

"Sorry," she muttered insincerely. "He's an interesting man."

She was grateful for the invention of words like "interesting." It neutrally described such a diverse range of feelings and emotions. The human race *was* occasionally clever that way.

"Did he say anything scandalous?" Harry was amused with her choice of word. "Was he rude? He was rude to Millicent. He walked away from her without a word of excuse earlier this evening, she says."

It looks as though Mars is about to give her a pleasuring.

It probably qualified as both scandalous *and* rude.

"Not particularly. We discussed art." She wanted to answer monosyllabically. She did not want to engage in an actual conversation.

"Did you? I discussed art with Millicent, too. She's learned there's a nest of kittens in the barn and she aspires to sketch them in charcoal!"

That was it. The word "Millicent" had done it. She

was out of conversation. Harry would need to do all
of the talking. She would nod.

"I haven't yet asked her to marry me," he volunteered casually.

"Oh."

The relief was nauseating. Her knees nearly gave
way. Turning 'round and 'round in wide circles did
unpleasant things to her stomach, and once again
she couldn't wait until the music was over.

Don't talk anymore, Harry.

"But the moment is likely to present itself very
soon!" he reassured her cheerily.

She had long since ceased to be charmed by his
obliviousness.

"I'll be there to throw confetti," she said bitterly.

He didn't notice her tone. Or that she was now
staring daggers at him.

"I'm so happy you're happy with my decision."

What ought she to say to *that*? Nothing, she decided. No human being should be required to tolerate this.

"I say," he said suddenly, genuinely worried. "Are
you unwell, Genevieve?"

He sounded concerned, and his concern was an
affront that buffeted her again between tenderness
and fury. She *could* tell him how she felt, she supposed. But the notion of witnessing his pity . . . well,
she had very little faith that Harry would handle her
revelation with tact.

He would mean well; he would also be blunt.
And she was always the one who had salved over
his bluntness, who had rescued and soothed him.

And God help her, no matter what, she didn't
want anything to mar his happiness.

"I fear I've a *mal de tête*, as they say. I drank three cups of ratafia."

"Three whole *cups!*" Harry admonished with mock horror. "How very wicked! Genevieve Eversea, you know full well ratafia is the first step on the road to perdition."

She ought to have laughed. Normally she would have, but nothing was normal anymore. She'd instead been captivated by one of the words.

Wicked.

Mars, the poor bastard, is sprawled looking as though she's just had her way with him. What did that mean? What precisely did Venus *do* to Mars?

What did the *duke* know about those sorts of things?

Clearly the road to perdition intrigued her. If only Harry was the one standing there at the crossroads to it, beckoning and saying compelling things about Venus and Mars.

And what on earth constituted a good "pleasuring"?

Harry noticed she was distracted.

"Were you terribly surprised to find the Duke of Falconbridge beneath your roof?"

"Terribly."

"He seemed decent and pleasant enough today when we walked out to the ruins."

"That's because you talked of horses and barouches and Papa's investments."

"I suppose," Harry allowed cheerily.

After that, he was mercifully quiet.

She looked up at him, encountered those familiar blue eyes and looked away. Then she decided she would look at the hairs in his nose. Something tiny was clinging to one of them.

"The duke seems quite taken with you," he said suddenly.

Oh, no! Were others noticing, too? "Surely 'taken' is certainly an exaggeration. What makes you think so?"

Harry hesitated peculiarly. "I saw you smile when you danced with him."

So *he'd* been watching her, too. But of course he would look out for her. He was her *dearest friend*.

"I often smile, Harry," she said dismissively. *Or at least I did in days of yore.*

In other words, yesterday.

But she knew precisely what he meant. And yet he went on to explain it.

"But . . . I know the difference between your polite, I'm-dancing-with-you-because-I-must smile and . . . the other ones. The ones that are real."

Her breath caught. The revelation was astonishingly painful to hear. Of course he knew the difference, because Harry knew her and cared for her better than almost anyone in the world.

Or so she'd once thought.

She had given so many of her real smiles to him. Suddenly, absurdly, her supply of smiles seemed finite. She had only one or two left to give. She was exhausted.

"He came as a surprise, I'll admit. But he isn't terrible. The duke. He has lovely manners."

"'Lovely manners'!" Harry thought this was amusing. "What effusive praise. He was rude to Millicent. Walked away from her without a word! And he's your father's age! Perhaps he can scarcely tolerate company anymore, in the way the aged get."

"He's not, you know. Not quite Father's age."

Harry hesitated again. "How do you know?"

"A very good guess."

Harry let this lie. "I've heard he's seeking a wife," he confided. "Since he's parted ways with Lady Abigail. They say he's determined to get himself wed soon."

"People *would* say that."

The duke had said it again and again to her, of course, but he wasn't the type to say it to anyone else, she knew that instinctively.

She suddenly hated the word *wife*. She would never be Harry's *wife*. When he used the word, he would never refer to her.

It occurred to her that she had never considered the duke's first wife when he'd begun speaking of Abigail this morning. Then again, she was uncertain of the etiquette of bringing up a dead wife with someone newly met.

"Most men who lack a wife eventually do seek one." Speaking was exhausting and painful now.

"Yes," Harry agreed, after a peculiar pause. "And of course I'd know."

Her head *did* in truth hurt. All the shine—the gleaming floor, the sparkling chandeliers, the jewels winking on all of the people in the room—landed on her raw senses like hot sparks. She was dangerously close to crying. She hadn't yet. It was bound to happen soon, and it had better not happen in the ballroom.

She drew in a shuddering breath.

Harry, garrulous Harry, who could usually find something witty to say, was having difficulty building a conversation. But then she wasn't offering any conversational kindling.

Who would rescue *her*?

She allowed him to talk; she answered him mono-syllabically; and she decided it was the last dance of the evening for her.

She would rescue *herself*.

She unapologetically left the ballroom for her bedroom after the dance with Harry.

She did cry.

She did it in a practical way. She slipped out of her dress and hung it up first; didn't fling herself on the bed and crush the silk. She unpinned her hair. She lay down gingerly on her bed wearing just her shift, curled in on the pain in her gut, and waited.

The sobs came from somewhere shockingly deep. They wracked her. She choked as each one welled up, overtaking the one before. She let her pillow take her tears until it was hot and soaked. Her face was swollen and feverish feeling, her nose was running profusely. And suddenly she seemed to be done.

And then she turned her pillow over to the cool side and lay flat on it. Taking in shuddering breaths.

She felt a little better. But the moon was full, and because she hadn't closed her curtains firmly enough, a determined beam worked its way into her bedroom and landed across her bed.

She resented it profoundly. She was too weary to drag herself from the bed and walk the unthink-able distance between it and the window to close the curtains again. She tried flinging an arm over her eyes. It didn't work. She thrashed this way and that fitfully, as though she could dodge the beam.

She wondered whether Harry was fast asleep. She wondered whether Millicent had an inkling of what was about to happen to her.

She wondered whether Harry had lingered after the ball and lured Millicent out to the garden and knelt before her and . . .

She flung herself out of bed. She stopped to poke up the fire, stabbing at it with an excess of enthusiasm. Afraid to defy her, it blazed up eagerly.

And then she stalked across the room to the window to yank the curtains tightly closed. She gripped one of the soft curtains in her hand, and began to pull, and then froze.

Down below, pacing the garden . . . . was a man.

The short hairs stood up on the back of her neck.

She wouldn't be surprised if the horror of the day was capped by discovering that the phantom of some long-dead Eversea roamed the garden at night.

But it was no phantom. He wore a long, dark greatcoat; the wind whipped it out behind him. He was walking swiftly. He didn't seem to have a particular destination. But his stride was unnervingly familiar. And then he stopped and settled on the stone bench below and to the left of her bedroom window, his elbows resting on his knees. He turned his face up to the moon.

The moonlight glanced off silver at his temple and the perfect mirrored shine of a pair of Hessians.

It was the Duke of Falconbridge.

She stood motionless, breathless, watching through a parted inch of the curtains. Wondering if perhaps she was about to witness an assignation.

But after he'd drunk in the moonlight, he ducked his head. For quite some time. If he was another man, she might have thought he was praying. But his hands were thrust into his pockets for warmth. He was very still, but as usual his entire body seemed alert, ready to launch, defend, attack, move on.

And as if he was just as restless as she was, he stood again and continued walking, the wind whipping his coat out behind him. Eventually disappearing from view.

She glanced at the clock.

It was past midnight.

Chapter 9

Genevieve woke in a marvelous mood as usual to the music of three or four noisy birds perched in a tree outside her window. She lifted her hair away from her face where it seemed to have adhered during the night, smiled faintly, and—

Bloody hell.

Memory, as it would do, came crashing back into place, and along with the anvil of misery came to sit on her chest again. She accustomed herself to the weight of it, then slid out of bed and made her way to the window and rudely pushed aside the curtains. She was tempted to shoo the birds away.

She glanced down at the garden at the place the duke had stood just last night.

She must have imagined it, she decided.

Or dreamed it.

At breakfast, Moncrieffe was reminded why he disliked house parties so thoroughly. Something to do with all of the *people* to whom he was obligated to be civil. The fact that people grew considerably quieter around him helped matters, however. The conversation, a cheerful buzz, decidedly dropped in volume when he made his appearance, shaved, dressed expensively.

About a half dozen more servants appeared as well.

He spooned mounds of eggs onto his plate, and added kippers, selected a slice of ham, and then carried it to a table which had gone . . . well, not altogether silent. But he was reminded of letting a cat out into a garden when songbirds were in full voice. The chirps instantly became significantly less confident and frequent until the birds decided whether the cat was hungry and dangerous or elderly and toothless.

His was not an easy presence. He'd never minded. He was like the dam that redirected rivers. It was his role in life.

Still, breakfast wasn't entirely unpleasant. It smelled like a breakfast room ought. The air was thick with the strong dark scents of coffee and smoked meat and good bread, toasted. Filtered light came in through fine lace curtains. Silver and porcelain clinked together in a sort of music as hungry guests passed about jam pots and attacked their plates and slurped down beverages.

Housemaids buzzed about the room as excitedly as flies.

Genevieve Eversea was in a green wool walking dress, and she was such an island of stillness his eyes were drawn immediately and he rested them briefly.

She glanced up at him. Her eyes were suspiciously red-rimmed. But perhaps she'd had a very late night of it?

He didn't think so.

Jacob Eversea saw the duke and began to rise from his chair.

The duke gave his head a firm little shake. Eversea lifted his brows cheerfully and tipped his head in a gesture toward the empty chair next to him: *Sit here*. And the duke did.

Despite how he might feel about his son and what he intended to do to his daughter, he found himself liking Eversea the elder. He conveyed respect for Moncrieffe's station without obsequiousness. He was economical with words, the way men who'd lived through so much they cease to be impressed by overmuch are, and it was clear life in general amused him while very little unnerved him, but then his tolerance had been shaped by his offspring.

But the duke, despite himself, was curious about the Eversea marriage. His wife sat at his elbow and presided over breakfast with an air of detached amusement and the patience of a shepherd. Alex didn't mind her, either. She was very pretty, like her daughters. She didn't natter on the way some women did, filling the air with words for the sake of hearing their own voices, like a lonely bird hoping to attract other birds, the inevitable result of too many years married to a too-quiet man.

But he sensed a prevailing tension between the two Everseas. He didn't assume it had a thing to do with him, despite what he may have done with the youngest daughter. Marriages were mysteries, and well he knew. And tension could not set in where closeness hadn't once been.

"Good morning, Your Grace," Lady Millicent said bravely and cheerfully.

The duke reached for a knife in order to spread

butter on a thick piece of fried bread. When he lifted it, he went still. Frowned a little. Then arched his brows in, as though inspiration struck. And then he hefted it thoughtfully in his hand.

And then looked pointedly down the table toward Ian.

Ian's fork had been midway to his mouth when he intercepted the duke's black stare.

It missed his mouth by an inch, bounced off his chin, and a confetti of scrambled eggs showered Harry and Millicent and Olivia.

Everyone leaped from their chairs.

Harry was at a loss at whom to see to first. "Thank you, Ian, but I learned to feed myself years ago."

Much laughter ensued. Ian's sounded strained and his eyes weren't involved in it. They were fixed on the duke.

The duke eyed him in return until Ian at last looked down, becoming fascinated by his upside down reflection in a spoon.

Maidservants swarmed the table, curtsying like accordions for the benefit of the duke and all but wrestling over the opportunity to sweep up the eggs, jostling one another and nearly cracking their skulls at one point in a competition to clean.

"I've never seen you move so fast on my behalf before, Harriet," Ian declared.

"Beggin' yer pardon, Master Ian, but it ain't on yer behalf. Ye ain't a duke, are ye now?"

"No," he confirmed darkly.

"And we've one in t' 'ouse." This was unassailable logic as far as Harriet was concerned.

The duke, accepting the uproar as his due, calmly attended to cleaning his plate with the speed and efficiency with which he did nearly everything he considered necessary rather than a luxury.

He looked across the table at Genevieve, who had surgically incised what appeared to be a triangle on the top of her fried egg. With the tine of her fork, she delicately lifted off the limp white ceiling of it to expose runny yoke. Satisfied, she laid her fork down and dipped the corner of her toast into it.

She paused mid-bite when she noticed the duke watching her with rapt fascination.

And then she shrugged with one shoulder, smiled a little, and snipped off the corner of the toast with her teeth.

It was decided—no one knew where or when the idea originated, but it had been taken up with enthusiasm—that a walk would be undertaken to enjoy the weather while it lasted. The ladies would bring their sketchbooks and embroidery and the men would bring their cricket bats out to perfect their swings ahead of cricket season, and presumably to impress the women.

Since Genevieve could conceive of no place where she would be happy, outside was as good as inside, and it hardly seemed likely that Harry would propose to Millicent whilst surrounded by friends and holding a cricket bat.

And so walk out they did.

The day had remained insultingly bright and clear. It hardly seemed fair to her that autumn had divested the trees of their leaves and left them to stand embarrassingly nude in a relentlessly lemony sun, let alone the fact that made the world seem cheerfully indifferent to her internal chaos.

Everyone seemed to be oblivious. Chase, if he were here, might have noticed. Chase was seeing to business in London; he'd sent a brother and a sister he'd recently met, Liam and Meggy Plum, to live in Pennyroyal Green. And Colin could be very observant, but he was generally a rascal before he was sensitive, and he was at home with his wife a few miles away. Olivia assumed her head hurt. Louisa sent concerned glances and said nothing. Marcus didn't notice.

Ian *had* asked her if her head hurt, which seemed to be the extent of male knowledge of female complaints. She'd asked Ian if his head hurt, as he'd looked a little wobbly, too.

They both denied a thing was wrong.

She drifted away and found a place on the scrupulously barbered lawn far enough away from the cricket horseplay to spread out an old shawl. She sat down, tucked her dress neatly over her knees and leaned back on her hands and she watched the men, and ached, and thought.

Harry was all but glowing in the autumn sun. It was both soothing and bittersweet to watch him. A painter could create an entire palette and call it "Harry's Hair," and include in it gold and wheat and flaxen and—

A shadow blotted her view before she could add another color to the palette in her mind.

The shadow turned out to be the Duke of Falconbridge.

He settled down next to her on the grass. His pose almost mimicked hers. He stretched out his legs and leaned back on his hands. He plucked off his hat and gently laid it alongside him.

He said nothing at all for a time.

Merely shaded his eyes and followed the direction of hers.

She wondered again if she'd imagined him walking through the garden. So sodden and exhausted had she been she somehow doubted she'd actually seen him. And yet . . .

She wasn't going to trouble to be polite.

She was certain he would find something to say that she would object to or be uncomfortably fascinated by.

"He's handsome." The duke gestured with his chin toward Harry. "Osborne is. No *lines*."

She froze.

And then slowly, slowly turned toward him and fixed him with what she hoped was a subject-quelling incredulous stare.

"I suppose," she agreed warily. When one looked from Harry to the duke, the duke certainly suffered by comparison. And it wasn't as though sunlight wouldn't have anything to do with him. But he was certainly Harry's chiaroscuro opposite. He didn't *glow*. His hair was . . . his hair was black. Apart from that frost of gray at the temples, that was. And it was straight and just a bit too rakishly long, just in case anyone should forget his reputation for being dangerous. His skin was so fair that his dark eyes and brows were like punctuation on a page.

She turned away again, her body tensed against any further insights he might volunteer. Olivia and Millicent and Louisa looked like an autumn bouquet in their walking dresses. She focused on that soothing sight instead, deliberately blurring her vision until they were only color, rather than people, one of whom Harry wanted to marry.

"And you're in love with him?"

Holy—!

She actually yelped. It was as much his tone as the observation: conversational. She turned away again and looked straight ahead, her vision blurring in shock. *I am a glacier,* she told herself. *I am a slippery ice wall against which his insights can gain no purchase. He will stop talking. He will stop talking.*

"And he's . . . somehow broken your heart?"

He said this almost brightly, as though they'd set out to play a guessing game.

Oh God. *Pain.* She made a short involuntary sound. As though a wasp had sunk a stinger in.

She whirled furiously on him again, eyes burning with outrage.

So much for glacial control.

Oddly, he didn't look triumphant. He looked almost sympathetic.

"I'm afraid it's evident, Miss Eversea. To me, anyhow. If I'm not mistaken, no one else seems to have bothered to notice, if that's any comfort. Unless you've confided in anyone? Your sister, perhaps?"

Rather than claw him in fury, she curled her fingers into the grass, and would have yanked it up by the roots if she wouldn't have felt guilty about killing innocent plant life and creating more work for the groundskeeper.

And no. Olivia was the last person she would burden with the news of hopeless love.

"No," she said shortly. Thereby admitting her deepest, darkest secret.

"And has he kissed you?" he asked, lightly.

Each impertinent question shocked her anew and flayed fresh welts over raw and newly exposed secrets. All of her muscles contracted, as if colluding to shrink away from him.

Why was he doing this? How did he *know*?

"He's a *gentleman*," she said tightly.

How quickly could she spring up and bolt away? Could she pretend she was being chased by a wasp? If she ran screaming from the duke surely a scandal would ensue. If this was his idea of courtship then she had no doubt his fiancée had abandoned *him*.

"And has he *kissed* you?" he repeated in precisely the same inflection apart from a fresh and maddening hint of amusement.

Her heart rabbited away in her chest, kicking, kicking painfully. This kind of misery was entirely new, and she hadn't yet learned to accommodate it. Her stomach was roiling, her cheeks were flushed, and she wondered if she ought to go have a lengthy heartfelt chat with her handsome cousin, the vicar, to ask if there was any particular penance she could do to stop the unprecedented variety of suffering raining down upon her this week.

"He has kissed me," she confirmed coldly.

What made her say it? It wasn't entirely a lie. Perhaps pride had made her say it. Perhaps the very notion of another man kissing her would drive him away.

But Harry *had* kissed her hand once, lingeringly, as though her hand was a precious thing. It had surprised her; in her mind it had cemented their attachment.

"*Has* he?" Amused and clearly disbelieving.

"Point to the part of your body he kissed."

She stared rigidly across the expanse of green, eyeing her brother's cricket bat and contemplating other more satisfying uses for it. Ian was demonstrating a swing for Harry. And for Olivia and Millicent, of course, so Olivia and Millicent could admire his form.

As if they knew or cared anything about form. *The things we do for men*, Genevieve thought.

She was silent. She could simply refuse to say another word to the man.

"Was *this* the part?" The duke tapped the back of her hand with one long finger.

She snatched it away from him and cupped it in her other hand as though comforting it and glared daggers at him.

"If you *please*, Lord Moncrieffe."

The anguished embarrassment and her glare deterred him not at all. He raised his brows, waiting with infinite, infinite, downright *evil* patience, unruffled. His eyes were dark and deep, as reflective in the sunlight as the polished toes of his boots. Like a body of water, where one couldn't tell whether you could wade safely through or step in and be swallowed whole by depth. She had the strangest sense he could absorb anything with those eyes and reflect back the same irony: a glare, a smile, a tragedy, a comedy.

But there was something about him . . . She was tempted to wade in. Just a little. It was the same temptation she'd succumbed to when he'd discussed—just as deliberately—Venus and Mars. Because he wasn't wrong. Because he was honest, and she liked it. Because he was relentless, and she

admired it. Because she half hated him, but he didn't
bore her.

Because he spoke to her the way no one else had
ever spoken to her, which meant he saw her in a way
no one else saw her.

"Very well. He has kissed my hand, yes. Surely
there's nothing untoward about that."

"I suppose whether it was *untoward* depends on
his intent and the circumstances and how much you
enjoyed it."

"It was an excellent kiss," she all but whispered.

"Oh, I'm certain it was." The bloody man was
amused. "A real man would have kissed you on the
mouth, Miss Eversea. 'Gentleman' or no. And it's a
very good mouth you have." He volunteered this as
though offering advice on Harry's cricket form.

She stared at him, shock dropping open her
mouth.

Her *very good* mouth.

Damn him for inciting curiosity about what constituted a *good mouth*.

She nearly raised her hand to touch it. Stopped
herself. And then she did, surreptitiously, rest the
back of her hand against it.

They were soft, her lips, barely pink. Shaped
neatly and elegantly.

But what made it *good*?

She'd no vocabulary at all for this type of conversation. For the types of compliments he produced. They were very adult, and he presented
them to her as though she ought to know what to
do with them.

She didn't. But speaking with him reminded her
of the first time she'd taken a sip of coffee. A bitter,

foreign black brew, that grew more appealing, more rich and complex, the more necessary, the more she sipped.

He casually, deliberately removed his coat, folded it neatly, laid it next to him. The wind took the opportunity to play in his hair, lifting it a bit, tossing it about, letting it drop, satisfied at having mussed a duke.

He leaned back on his hands. And then idly turned to her. He inhaled, and exhaled an almost long-suffering sigh.

And he began in a patient, almost leisurely fashion, in a voice fashioned from dark velvet, a voice that stroked over her senses until they were lulled, to lecture directly to her as if she was a girl in the schoolroom.

"A proper kiss, Miss Eversea, should turn you inside out. It should . . . touch places in you that you didn't know existed, set them ablaze, until your entire being is hungry and wild. It should . . . hold a moment, I want to explain this as clearly as possible . . ." He tipped his head back and paused to consider, as though he were envisioning this and wanted to relate every detail correctly. "It should slice right down through you like a cutlass with a pleasure so devastating it's very nearly pain."

He waited, watching her face, allowing her to accommodate the potent words.

Her mouth was parted. Her breathing short. She couldn't look away. His eyes and voice held her as fast as if he'd cradled her face with his hands.

And as he said them, an echo of sensation sounded in her, like a remembered dream, an instinct awakened.

She thought about Mars getting ready to give Venus a good pleasuring.

Stop, she should say.

"And . . . ?" she whispered.

"It should make you do battle for control of your senses and your will. It should make you want to do things you'd never dreamed you'd want to do, and in that moment all of those things will make perfect sense. And it should herald, or at least promise, the most intense physical pleasure you've ever known, regardless of whether that promise is ever, ever fulfilled. It should, in fact . . ." he paused for effect ". . . haunt you for the rest of your life."

She sat wordlessly when he was done. As though waiting for the last notes of a stormy, discordant symphony to echo into silence.

The most intense physical pleasure.

His words reverberated in her. As if her body contained the ancient wisdom of what that meant, and now, having been reminded, craved it.

She should have gotten up to leave and not looked back.

"So you've had this kiss? Or is it something you aspire to?" Her voice was a low rasp.

For a moment he said nothing at all. And then he smiled a faint, slow, satisfied smile.

She had the oddest impression she'd passed a test. And that she'd surprised him yet again.

"I'll leave you to wonder about that, as well, Miss Eversea. I'm a man who cherishes my mystique."

She gave a little snort. But she was undoubtedly shaken.

She turned back to watch Harry, who was now

making a great show of balancing the cricket bat on his palm. It was jarringly the opposite of the conversation she was in the midst of.

Does Harry know about those sorts of kisses? Does he have those kinds of thoughts? Does he have any idea what one kiss of my hand would do to me? Of what dreams I would unfurl from it?

Is it only me, or do all women think this way?

Would a real man have kissed my mouth?

She was tempted to touch her mouth again, and to imagine.

She gripped the grass again, more tightly, needing to feel solid ground. She was dizzy, more confused than she'd been yesterday. As though the land around her was sea and she'd just been cast adrift in an ocean of sensual knowledge she would never now partake of if Harry married Millicent.

Damn the duke. She was devastatingly clever, but he'd just made it very, very clear that *she* knew nothing, nothing at all about . . . anything.

"Did he make you a promise on the heels of this 'kiss,' Miss Eversea?"

She was never going to enjoy the mocking way he referred to that *kiss*.

She said nothing.

But he seemed to take this as a confirmation.

"Are you spoken for? Did he back away from a promise?" he asked hurriedly. He sounded tense. Oddly as though he intended to deal unkindly with Harry if this was the case.

"Not . . . not as much. No. But everything was . . . implied. Or so I thought. We've been so close for so long, you see, and . . . there was no reason at all not to believe . . . especially not after yesterday . . ."

"And yet he is preparing to launch a proposal at your dear friend Millicent."

He might as well have shot an arrow straight into her solar plexus. Hearing those words spoken aloud by another human were just that pleasant.

She covered her eyes with her hand, sucked in a jagged breath. "Yes. He told me so. Yes."

She took her hand away and bravely looked back at him.

The duke took this in with raised eyebrows. And gave his head a little wondering shake, whether at Harry's or her expense, she could not be certain.

"Has *he* ever sent flowers to you?"

"He once presented me with a bouquet of wild-flowers he'd just picked," she confessed dismally.

The duke thought this was amusing, judging from what his eyebrows did.

"Has he kissed *her*? Any of her parts? Or sent flowers to her?"

Argh. The misery. "I don't know. She hasn't told me. *He* hasn't told me. And usually . . . well, Millicent and I tell each other everything. And I thought Harry told me everything, too."

"If you haven't told Millicent how you feel about Lord Harry, then you haven't told Millicent everything, have you?"

Well, then. She was generally assumed to be clever, but in that moment she felt a fool. He had an excellent point. She hadn't *dreamed* Harry harbored a tendre for Millicent; she'd floated along in the comfortable certainty of friendship.

"I'm afraid all of this is rather evident. To me. Otherwise, you are exceptionally inscrutable and

I'm certain not a soul suspects," he humored with suppressed laughter in his voice.

She scowled darkly at him. "And isn't that *just* my good fortune that *you* should notice and choose to torment me with it."

He laughed. Admittedly, he had a fine laugh, deep and genuine. She sensed he didn't do it easily. She liked the sense that she'd surprised it from him.

And therein lay his vulnerability. She could make him laugh.

She had another surprise for him. "Lord Moncrieffe, do tell me, since we're speaking so frankly. What is your game?"

Chapter 10

He didn't precisely . . . blink. But for an almost imperceptible second he went shockingly still.

"Game? I don't understand. What makes you feel there's a—"

She heaved a sigh that all but bent a furrow in the grass at their feet.

"Oh, *enough*," she said irritably. "Very clever people often assume no one else is as clever as they are. Which *isn't* very clever of them, when you think about it."

"After knowing you but a few short days, Miss Eversea, I would never make the mistake of assuming you aren't clever."

She would not be pacified, particularly in that ironic tone of voice. "I will be exceptionally clever now, then. You've made quite a show of courting me, which I can assure you, has been disconcerting for me and has caused mirth and discussion. But you're *not* interested in me. Not truly. I am naught like Lady Abigail. But Millicent is. Your eyes linger rather appreciatively on her whenever she's about, and she could not be more different from me and more like Lady Abigail in form and shape. I am quite aware I'm possessed of a few singular charms, as has been pointed out by other young men. But they're not of the sort *you* typically appreciate. You've a game. I want to know what it is. Surely you can't need my money."

He was . . . *lividly* . . . amused by this. Wicked, astounded delight was written all over his face.

"Charms, have you? Perhaps I enjoy a diversity of female charm—"

"Stop. Stop, stop, *stop*. And here is the other thing: Every time you look at my brother Ian or hear his name something brief and . . . *murderous* . . . flashes cross your face. It's there and then gone. Every. Time. *Not* very clever of you. And yes. I believe I'm the only one who notices."

Oh dear.

The silence was so absolute it was as though a dome had dropped over the two of them.

He wasn't at all amused now.

She'd never seen a man so still. It in and of itself was almost camouflage, like a wild creature blending into its environment, hoping to ward off attack or planning to mount one. She'd cornered him and he didn't like it. And all at once she was afraid, because she had no doubt this man was dangerous and resourceful and ruthless as a rule, but never more so than when cornered.

She doubted it happened very often.

He was clearly thinking rapidly.

Her heart battered away in her chest, but she was reckless from disappointment and possessed the courage of her temper and she frankly had stopped caring for perhaps the first time in her life.

She waited implacably for his answer. She didn't blink.

He drew in a breath. "Surely what you're noticing *flash cross my face* is merely a twinge of indigestion."

But he sounded peevish now. The amusement was back, but entwined with a note of warning. He would tolerate only so much prodding.

She lowered her voice to a hush. "What did Ian do? It has to do with Lady Abigail, doesn't it? I know my brothers, Lord Moncrieffe."

A silence. The wind took another frisky pass at his hair. His face was a strong one. He glanced at her, then glanced away, and his eyes settled on the man in question, and everything about him seemed made of implacable granite.

Genevieve was very glad she wasn't Ian at the moment.

"You presume too much," he said coldly.

"Presume! *I* presume? *I* presume? I believe you've set a precedent in presumption. What did Ian do? You may as well tell me. I shan't tell a soul."

He gave her his profile. A strong chin, not at all soft. Squared off. A downright elegant nose, straight as a blade. Every line of him precisely drawn.

"What Ian did isn't for the ears of ladies, Miss Eversea. Let's just say it was a killable offense. I might have been hanged for killing him, but few men would have blamed me for it."

Oh. The breath went out of her again.

His coldness *ought* to have deterred her. But now she understood he'd meant it to.

"Killable? I am not as innocent as you seem to believe. I know Colin nearly died tumbling from the trellis of a married countess. I am not naïve when it comes to the wildness of my brothers. But I assure you they do have good hearts—"

"Miss Eversea. Understand that I can tolerate no kind words about any of your brothers now."

His voice was dark and threatening as a newly dug grave. She ignored him and finished.

"—and unfortunately they occasionally make more than their share of mistakes. When the world seems to be your oyster one has a tendency to partake greedily and sometimes recklessly. But they have *good hearts* and are the most loyal of friends and Chase is even a war hero . . ."

She trailed off at the look he turned on her.

Almost . . . *hunted*. Furious. And resigned. She sensed he was about to tell her what Ian did, and he didn't want her to hear it, and now she wanted to stop him, and it was too late.

"I found him in bed with my fiancée. They were both nude. I found him there because I suspected I would. I in fact watched him make a daring climb up a tree and enter through a window three nights in a row before I stopped him."

Each vivid, potent word slapped at her. *Nude. Bed. Fiancée.*

She could envision the scene with shocking, sordid clarity. Her brother, disrobing, climbing into bed. The duke lying in wait to catch them, consumed by . . . anger? Grief? Had he felt numb? Was it pain or pride he felt or . . .

How in God's name had Ian gotten out *alive*?

She didn't like imagining this proud man watching this. It was in fact nearly unbearable to imagine.

"Did you love her?" She almost whispered it. And she regretted how lightly she'd asked him before.

The duke slowly shook his head to and fro, ruefully and wearily at the question, at some private amusement. Fortunately, he no longer looked murderous.

"I might have done," he said softly.

She was left to wonder what he meant.

She didn't press him. Because if he loved as strongly as he hated, he might have ultimately incinerated the girl.

Suddenly she was grateful only her hand had been kissed, and for her love for Harry, and for all she didn't know about love and sex.

They were both looking toward Ian now.

Ian, like Harry and Millicent, was entirely new. She realized he was doing his best to appear nonchalant, but she knew her brother very well. He laughed a bit too loud; his gestures were too emphatic. He was playacting devil-may-care for the duke. *That* would explain his twitchiness and the pallor he'd been sporting. It was almost funny.

Somehow she hadn't considered the cruelty behind such reckless, playful indulgence of whim and desire, of a man climbing through a window or up a trellis. That something or someone other than pride might be savaged, a heart broken, a life destroyed, hopes shattered. It seemed staggeringly selfish.

But then men, in all their charm, generally were, and the duke was hardly excluded.

"I'm sorry," she said sincerely, quietly. "It *was* shameful, what he did."

He lifted his hands on his knees, dropped them again. A sort of shrug. "Yes."

"Whereas you've never done anything shameful in your life."

He turned his head very, very slowly toward her. Then narrowed his eyes dangerously.

She met his gaze bravely. She tried and failed to get just one eyebrow up. Both went up. She really wished she had a signature sardonic gesture. She envied the duke his.

"It was done to *me*," he explained.

"Ah."

Something that may have been a smile came to haunt his mouth.

A firm, long, masculine, flexible mouth. She supposed it was good, too.

"And has he apologized to you? Ian?"

"I wouldn't allow it. I wouldn't have believed him, regardless. I believe he was sorry he was *caught*. I believe he was sorry I interrupted the two of them before it could proceed farther. But sorry for irrevocably altering the course of my life? For depriving me of my future happiness? I doubt he thought of it in those terms. I should *like* to make him sorry, however."

Dear God. Had his heart really been *broken*? Or his pride simply singed? All she knew was that legends had been made about the consequences of crossing this man.

She began tentatively. "Perhaps if you expressed it to him in those terms—"

He sighed exasperatedly. "Oh, for God's sake, Miss Eversea. I'm a *man*. I do not whinge on about my happiness. I shoot on the spot, or I take revenge later. I do both very well."

Take revenge later.

That's when it occurred to her. Her jaw dropped. Then she clapped it shut.

"And *I* was to be *revenge*?"

Another of those cornered silences from the duke.

He reassessed her. Deciding upon his strategy, no doubt.

"What did you plan to do, seduce and abandon me? 'Ha-ha, I showed you, Ian Eversea, I despoiled your sister because you despoiled my *fiancée*'?"

And then, bloody man, she would have sworn, she could have *sworn*, he was stifling a smile.

"'Despoiled'?"

She glared silent fury at him.

"Well, when you put it like that . . ." he said somberly.

Very risky to tease her now.

There were innumerable things she ought to be feeling. Shock and indignation and fury, among them. She ought to glower and storm away. She ought to lecture him.

She wavered instead on the brink of doing something tremendously subversive like . . . smiling.

He noticed her indecisiveness and took advantage.

"Would it have worked?"

She sighed. "Perhaps if I were in a more amenable frame of mind," she reassured him. "And less in love with Harry. You *are* a duke, after all."

"And that's *impressive*," he completed whimsically. "Of course, you were hardly cooperating. Flinging other young ladies into my path. Though I must say I was tempted by Olivia. You certainly paint a compelling picture and I was very nearly persuaded."

"You were nothing of the sort."

He laughed again, that rich masculine sound.

Across from them she noticed Harry's head turn. He shaded his eyes and watched them, then dropped the bat, and the girls laughed at him.

"Well, we've established that revenge of the sort

you were planning is now out of the question," she said firmly to her strange new friend. "Do you now plan to shoot Ian? Because I won't allow *that*."

"You won't allow it? You'll fling yourself bodily in front of him? Ah, now, that's a pity. And you're certain you shouldn't like me to compromise, ruin and abandon you?"

She could think of no other context and no other conversation in which such a statement would make her smile. Certainly her mother had raised her to be horrified by every one of those words, and every one of those words was potent with story and meaning.

But smile she did.

Thereby adding *herself* to the number of people who were new.

And the duke smiled, too, looking suspiciously very much like a man enjoying himself.

What a peculiar exchange. Then again, the two of them had both had their worlds upended recently. Whether *his* heart was broken or just his pride was another story. Nevertheless.

Something occurred to her.

"But would you really have done . . . all of that?" She didn't want to repeat words like "compromise," "seduce," and "abandon." "Not that it would have been at all possible. I simply ask."

His smile faded, and he turned away from her and plucked idly at the tiny daisies that had the ill fortune to be growing near where his restless hands were.

"You shouldn't ask questions when you know at heart you'd prefer not to hear the answers."

But then he looked at her directly. No smile in his face or eyes. Just a rueful admission about his mouth. A warning of sorts to not forget about the sort of man he really was.

"But you like me," she accused slowly.

"Nonsense. For one thing, you are far too clever. Which is not at all restful. I could never relax a single moment knowing you'll see right through me at all times."

She laughed, delighted, the sound musical and lilting.

Harry's head swiveled toward the sound at once. It was a sound he knew, of course, and he'd always been able to make her do it more than anyone else could. He shielded his eyes and straightened his spine.

And then stared very pointedly at Genevieve and the duke.

The duke spoke quickly, his voice quick and low and casual. "Don't flinch. Don't stare at him. Do what I say and watch what happens now."

"What—"

"*Hush.*"

He had such natural command she did exactly that.

And he reached over and lightly rested two fingers against her hand again. Gently pinned it to the grass, like a small pale butterfly.

As though his head were attached to the duke's fingers by a string, Harry's gaze followed it to the spot where they rested upon Genevieve's hand.

He froze.

He stared.

If he'd been a wild creature, his fur would have stood on end in objection.

And then, faintly but unmistakably . . . Harry frowned. Darkly.

Genevieve's breath caught sharply. She obediently stopped herself from staring at him. She looked down instead. Long enough to notice that the duke wore a gold signet ring, and that his hand was long and elegant and scrupulously groomed but sported emphatic veins, as though he'd used his hands to do difficult masculine things his entire life. Dark, crisp hair curled on his wrist, and that hair seemed almost embarrassingly intimate, because if she wanted to right now she could touch it. His finger looked very brown against her own white hand, which she normally took such care to keep from the sun. His hand could cover hers completely if he wanted, shelter it, vanquish it, comfort her or render her terrifyingly defenseless.

Funny how the spot where the duke's finger touched her was suddenly the locus of the universe for three people.

"Your hand is unconscionably soft, Miss Eversea," he murmured.

Oh.

And then he took his fingers away.

Her eyes widened. She couldn't lift her head just yet.

The shock of the stealthy compliment spread slowly through her, the way sherry did when bolted quickly. She flicked her eyes up at him. Made a quick frown of disapproval. Then inhaled to steady her nerves.

She could have sworn that spot where he'd touched her hummed with portent. Like he'd drawn the sword from the stone rather than lift his fingers.

She got her head up again at last and looked at him.

He was new, too.

"Now laugh again," the duke murmured. "Make it convincing. And for God's sake, don't look at *him* when you do it. Look at me. Laugh. *Laugh*," he hissed when it seemed her dumbstruck stare was permanent.

Genevieve gave her head a toss. "Ahhahahaha!"

He rolled his eyes. "Lovely molars," the duke murmured dryly. "Good thing you were born into money, for you would starve treading the boards. Now wait, and look at me while you do."

She did as commanded, caught up in the momentum of following his orders.

And he smiled.

It began lazily, and within seconds was as intimate and sensual and enveloping as a mink wrap. She felt that smile everywhere on the surface of her skin. All the little hairs on the back of her neck stood alertly, as though he'd brushed his fingers there, or as though they anticipated that he might. She felt . . . ensnared. And woefully . . . *thrilled*. And once again very, very out of her depth.

Until she reminded herself the smile was for effect. That sobered her.

Good God. For whom does he usually *produce this smile?*

Out of the corner of her eyes she saw Harry restively shift his feet. Like a horse nagged by flies. He leaned his weight on his cricket bat, twisting it into the ground thoughtfully. He was in fact watching Genevieve and the duke with a fixity of expression she could truthfully say she'd never before seen him wear.

His pale blue eyes were decidedly . . . flinty. His jaw, which was square, was set resolutely.

Well.

Was it jealousy? Protectiveness? Usually Harry found the world very accommodating. It provided him with joy and diversion and comfort and plenty of devoted, worshipful friends—like her—and very soon a *wife*. He'd always taken for granted Genevieve's regard, and why shouldn't he?

But how would Harry behave if his world behaved unexpectedly?

A diabolical possibility surged through Genevieve almost painfully, like blood rushing back into a sleeping limb.

"How did you know?" she whispered.

"He looks at you every time you laugh. Every. Time. He's been showing off this entire time, and I do believe it's on your behalf. And he noticed the last time I touched you," he said simply. "I noticed, even if you didn't. And right now it looks like two men would like to hurl cricket balls at me."

He meant Ian, too, who was watching the two of them with ill-disguised suspicion.

It *was* almost funny.

"It does rather, doesn't it?"

"You sound pleased, Miss Eversea. Oh, and by the way, if you stare at them now, it ruins everything you just accomplished. So look at me again, and try for something akin to fondness in your expression. Another of those fetching blushes wouldn't go amiss. Or if that's too distasteful, look off picturesquely into the middle distance."

But she was tired of taking direction from him. She rebelled and wrapped her arms around her knees, then rested her cheek upon them so she wouldn't have to look at anyone at all for a moment.

The muslin of her dress felt deliciously cool, which is when she realized her cheeks were almost feverishly hot. She'd been taking an unaccustomed emotional buffeting all afternoon. It was taking its toll upon her temperature. Blushes, flushes, and blanches.

Your hand is unconscionably soft.

You have an excellent mouth.

Compliments so specific, bold, and singular she scarcely held them in her thoughts for one second without blushing. She wanted to both savor and recoil from them.

She wished Harry had said them to her.

She contemplated whether she *was* in fact pleased to make Harry jealous. She breathed in, testing, and discovered instead of the jagged misery she'd inhaled for days she felt . . . *revived.*

The duke's voice came to her again. His voice was very like him, she thought, from the muslin safety of her knees where she could hear it without watching him. It had smoky edges and the resonance of a stringed instrument. It thrummed inside her. She wouldn't have minded at all listening to him recite poetry or something more pleasant than—

"So, Miss Eversea, are you just going to *allow* him to propose to your friend?"

—than that.

"I should do what instead? Confess my abiding love?" This was muffled and irritable, as she'd said it to her knee. Her tone said everything about the absurdity of *that* notion.

"*Doesn't* he love you? Didn't you just say it was always implied? If this is true, what then is the impediment? Certainly not your family or fortune. Perhaps the problem is *his* family or fortune?"

She was pensive. "I believe, though I'm not certain, he feels a certain . . . discomfiture over the fact that he hasn't an estate of his own yet, and won't until he inherits. And his income is considerably more modest than many other young men. He's hardly impoverished. And I don't mind at all that he isn't wealthy. I can't imagine that he believes that I do. Though my parents of a certainty do. But I'm simply guessing."

"Perhaps he doesn't know his own mind," the duke suggested. "Young men seldom do."

Was he trying to *comfort* her with that lofty bit of condescension?

"Do you speak from experience, Lord Moncrieffe?"

"It can only be from experience, given how long it's been since I was young."

She smiled then, albeit in a small way. If he was fishing for a compliment she wasn't going to deliver one. He *wasn't* young. He was nearly *forty*.

"Look at me again, Miss Eversea, if you would be so kind."

She sighed gustily again, and lifted her head up with theatrical reluctance. It was strangely not unpleasant to see him again. *What color* are *his eyes?* she wondered. She was a lover of detail but she'd been so determined to shed him that she hadn't wanted to collect details about him. His eyes were dark, but not brown. He'd taken off his hat and his hair lifted in the breeze, and she looked, really looked this time, and it was glossy, and well . . . very well, not only black. The sun struck sparks of bronze from it. The sun was behind him now, and his features were indistinct, and somehow this made it a little easier to speak to him. His miles of legs were folded up before him.

"I'm not suggesting you confess your undying love for him to his face. Quite the opposite. I'm suggesting you make him aware of his for *you*. He is a man, after all, and this will appeal to his pride and sense of the romantic. Young men like him are positively mad for romantic drama. Or perhaps you can make him *believe* his undying devotion is to you and not to your friend, which amounts to about the same thing. Young men are suggestible. I don't see that this one is exceptional."

She was instantly and passionately indignant. "Not *exceptional*? But you don't know him! He's kind and clever and his character is absolutely *unassailable* and he once gave me a hound pup for my birthday, though Papa made me give it back—"

He held up both hands defensively. "Do not *pelt* me with superlatives regarding Lord Harry, dear God, I beg of you. I'm certain he could walk from here to America upon the water. And kiss your *hand* all he likes." He thought this was very funny, clearly, and she scowled at him. "I meant, he's no different from other young men in that, no matter how clever he may be, he simply may not know his own mind and heart. Perhaps he simply needs someone to show his mind *to* him. It's not a character flaw to be *young*. Well, not usually, anyhow." He sent a dark and speaking look in the direction of Ian, lest she forget. "But perhaps you should set out to do something about it before he does something rash and irreversibly tragic like propose to your friend. Because, Miss Eversea, you are *kind*, and you would step away then and allow them their happiness at the expense of yours, regardless of whether or not it's *right*. St. Genevieve, the Martyr."

He'd managed to make "kind" sound like a character flaw. And St. Genevieve! Inwardly, she was anything but! Her body clenched with indignation.

Someone in her family needed to possess a modicum of restraint; it fell to her.

But he was correct. A choice faced her, a diabolical one. Where she liked life to be orderly and quiet, and she would do nothing rather than cause a stir.

"And why would *you* want to assist me?"

"Because now that the option of seducing and abandoning you no longer remains as you have caught me out—"

How easily he said the word "seducing." Here she was in danger of yet another temperature change.

"—I shall need some other way to amuse myself for the duration of the visit. And I would take great pleasure in tormenting your brother by leaving him wondering at how I intend to wreak vengeance upon him. Perhaps you'll be practical enough to agree with me that he would benefit from a little . . . humbling uncertainty."

"But you like vengeance so *very* much," she pointed out with mock solicitousness. "And I should hate to deprive you of it. You could give all of that up for me?"

This made him smile, slowly, with a pure, dazzling, wicked delight that strangely infected *her* with delight.

"You're so *thoughtful*," he said, with hushed fervor.

She gave a little shout of surprised laughter.

And then huffed out a breath to help her think.

She bit her lip. She tapped her foot. She stared at him.

He stared back. He gave a nonchalant shrug of one shoulder.

What do you have to lose, Miss Eversea?

Her eyes restlessly wandered the familiar lawn, which had always been the setting for play not tragicomedy, and her eyes lit upon Millicent and Olivia. She found no solace there, no clarity or simplicity. Her heart used to leap just a little when she saw either of them, like a dog giving a tail thump when a friend entered a room. But Millicent's complexion was flushed a golden peach from the walk and she was a little disheveled, her apron caught up in one hand, ringlets glued to her cheeks, all of which no doubt charmed Harry and made him feel *protective*. Her brown eyes were merry; her head was cocked in exaggerated interest. Olivia looked wryly amused by something Millicent was saying. But then Olivia rarely *lost* herself in merriment anymore. She had a marvelously abandoned laugh, her sister, and a wicked, wicked way with humor, but bloody Lyon Redmond had taken it with him when he'd disappeared. Left her to pour passion into causes.

And perhaps this was her fate if she simply *allowed* Harry to propose to Millicent. She'd turn into Olivia. Her whole life muffled, everything she saw and felt, covered over in a soft film of gray, like ash sprinkled over burned ruins.

Reflexively, she glanced toward Harry again, but Millicent was now blocking her view. She was striding over to her with her easy, graceful gait, her apron extended out before her, her bonnet bouncing on ribbons behind her.

She plumped cheerfully down next to Genevieve, and Genevieve instantly reached out and gently resettled her friend's bonnet atop her head and straightened it.

"Thank you," Millicent said absently, as though they'd done this a dozen times before—which they had, in fact, because Millicent's bonnet was forever slipping from her, something to do with laughing too hard and too often. And then she allowed Genevieve to help her pick out the knot before she drew out the ribbons and retied them neatly beneath her chin so she was shaded once again.

When they looked up the duke was watching all of this. Well, watching *her*. He was absolutely still again and his expression was disconcerting. Almost . . . well, she might have said "yearning," but that struck her as silly. It could have something to do with the slant of autumn light. And then he turned again, and shaded his eyes, surveying the Eversea land dispassionately. Perhaps calculating how many times over it would fit into *his* land.

Although between them, the Everseas and Redmonds owned a good portion of Sussex.

What haunted the duke besides being cuckolded? Was *no one* here at peace?

The thought momentarily darkly amused her: Harry was on pins and needles waiting to propose to Millicent, Ian was terrified of the unpredictable duke and pretending not to be, Olivia was Olivia, bereft of Lyon and filled with plans to save the world from itself, and as for herself, she was slowly dying of heartbreak and stretched on tenterhooks awaiting the death knell of her hope. And now being tormented by a duke.

And Millicent was oblivious to all of it and as happy as usual.

Genevieve could see again the unique appeal of that particular quality now. How very soothing it must be in its innocence and light. When one is satisfied with how the world *appears*, there is no need to look any deeper or farther. Peeking below the surface of things, one often discovers things one would rather not see, whether it is worms tilled up by the plow or wads of dust beneath a bed.

Millicent gestured to the daisies in her apron. "I thought we could make garlands for our hair. I've needle and thread in my pockets. I don't suppose I could persuade you to assist, Lord Moncrieffe?"

The duke snatched up his hat and coat and shot to his feet so quickly one would have thought Millicent had flung a scorpion into his lap.

"Er, I think I'll leave the weaving and braiding and whatnot to you ladies. Swinging bats is man's work."

He winked at Genevieve—winked!—and bowed to both of them, touched his hat, and strode off to join Ian and Harry.

She followed the line of him. He was so tall and lean, shoulders and spine meeting in clean, masculine angles, coat elegantly hanging from them, strides crisp and long as the swing of an ax. With the sky was a spotless blue, the grass a flat and brilliant green, he was an emphatic slash mark against the landscape.

She saw sunny Harry struggle to produce his usual smile as the duke approached. Hard speculation was, in fact, written all over his face for a discernible moment. Genevieve had never seen him look *hard* before. She ached a little bit for him, as she did whenever he suffered at all. She wanted the world to be every bit as kind as he expected it to be.

And yet . . . and yet . . . a perverse little song of hope started up in her heart.

Chapter 11

❦

I *thought* that would drive Moncrieffe away." Millicent was pleased with herself, as she shook her shawl out and settled herself more comfortably on it.

Genevieve laughed, but the laugh felt strangely weighted. Millicent still seemed new and faintly strange and superior, given that Harry had decided she was worth turning into a wife.

"Were you *trying* to drive him away, Mill?"

"Well, you didn't really want to sit there shadowed by the dour, dangerous duke, did you? Of course not. He was *terribly* rude to me last night. He walked away. You ought to be talking with me and Harry and Olivia."

Genevieve was so accustomed to sharing everything openly with Millicent. But she'd learned a good deal about strategy in just a few days—most of it in the last few minutes, in fact—thanks to the duke. So all she said was, "I talk to you and Harry all the time."

Even that was difficult to say. You and Harry. Harry and Millicent. Millicent and Harry. How would people refer to them when they were married? Which of their names would come first? Inextricably linked forever.

Her name would forever be excised from theirs.

The shock and pain and sheer disbelief came suddenly afresh and she was speechless.

Genevieve apparently waited too long to reply, because Millicent's mouth dropped open.

"*Never* say that you don't mind if that man is courting you!"

"I shan't," Genevieve said shortly. "Because it isn't true."

"It isn't what others were saying last night."

Splendid. Others *were* discussing them.

Off in the distance she saw the duke demonstrating what appeared to be a very fine cricket swing. She bit her lip against a laugh when she saw Ian flinch every time the duke swung the bat. A traitorous thought, but it really did serve him right.

What about you? Is Harry courting you, Millicent? Why is it she hadn't Olivia's talent for directness? Did it come with courage? Perhaps she hadn't any of that, either.

"But good heavens, Genevieve, he is a duke and if you marry him you'll be—"

"*Don't, don't, don't!*" Genevieve frantically prepared to cover her ears.

"—a duchess. Which wouldn't be *so* terrible, would it?"

Genevieve closed her eyes slowly. Did *no* one see? Had *no one* considered her a match for Harry? How was that even possible? *Everything* in her recoiled from the notion of being married to anyone but Harry. She could envision such a joyous, easy future with him. The duke's blood ran so cool he found everything faintly amusing and could calculate a revenge in which her life would be ruined in order to show the world he would not tolerate being crossed. *Ever.*

He was all too aware of the failings of his species and he knew how to use them to his advantage. A fascinating skill. A useful one. But hardly a loving one.

Your hand is unconscionably soft, Miss Eversea.

The words rushed back at her, and inwardly she shied from them again.

Millicent lowered her voice to an exaggerated hush. "Ah, but I heard he *poisoned* his first wife for her money. If you married him you mightn't be duchess for *long.*"

Genevieve rolled her eyes. "Everyone has heard that. How true do you think it likely is?"

She didn't believe it. But what if his *wife* had cuckolded him? What then?

"Not very," Millicent admitted. "That sort of murder is probably less common than pantomimes would have it. Not a thing was proved. Besides, I heard she was a rare beauty."

As if beauty precluded murder. Ian was quite lovely for a man, but he would have gotten himself murdered very neatly if he'd cuckolded a more hot-headed duke. As it was, he was hardly in a comfortable position.

The duke went to hand the bat to him. Ian dropped it. *His hands are probably sweating.*

"Dead wives are always rare beauties."

They both giggled wickedly at that. The three masculine heads swiveled, hoping and worrying that the girls were talking about them.

But she felt instantly guilty. What must his wife have been like?

She knew irony was a veil through which the

duke saw the entire world. And of course nothing could hurt him if everything amused him.

The realization struck her dumb for a moment.

"I do think he's in search of a wife since Lady Abigail threw him over," Millicent said, piercing a daisy stem, her tongue between her teeth to help her concentrate on her suture.

"She didn't throw him over. The end of their engagement was mutually decided," Genevieve said so shortly she realized she sounded very much like she was defending the duke.

She was even more surprised when she realized that she *was* defending the duke.

"Perhaps he's tired of sleeping alone."

"Millicent Emily Blenkenship!"

"Nevertheless." Millicent dimpled in a way she always had but which now made Genevieve wonder if Harry was enchanted by the dimple, too, and what Millicent knew about how men wished to *sleep*, and with whom. "So why on earth he could find fault with Abigail Beasley is beyond me, as she is considered a great beauty and she doesn't lack for charm. I like her well enough. Perhaps he was releasing her from her obligation to him because Abigail had fallen in love with someone else and he couldn't bear the notion. Still, it's difficult to imagine a man like him marrying for *loooooove*."

She drawled the word with exaggerated sentimentality. Because Millicent was funny and sunny and open, not careful and clever and watchful.

No wonder Harry wanted to marry her.

Correction: *thought* he wanted to marry her.

And *that* subversive thought was courtesy of the duke.

"Why are you staring at me so oddly?" Millicent said suddenly. Her needle and thread paused midair.

Genevieve blinked. "I think there's an ant crawling up your neck."

"Aaaaargh!" Millicent swiped at the nonexistent ant.

"Have you ever been kissed by a man, Millicent?"

"Genevieve!" Millicent's turn to gasp.

Her hand dropped to her lap, and her jaw all but swung down on its hinges.

Genevieve had surprised herself by blurting the question. Two days ago she would have asked it much more easily. No, that wasn't true: Two days ago it wouldn't have occurred to her to ask it, because she was certain Millicent would tell her if such a thing had ever happened.

"Well?" Her own daisy chain was about six inches in length now. About a third of the way to becoming a crown.

"Not . . . as such." Millicent wouldn't meet her eyes. "Why? Have *you* been kissed?"

"I asked you first."

They momentarily abandoned their daisies to their laps. And regarded each other in wary, stubborn, embarrassed silence.

"Have you thought of *marrying*?" Genevieve pressed. Why hadn't they discussed this before?

"I'm not on the shelf yet, Genevieve," she said reprovingly. "Nor are you. We can eke out a few more seasons before we live happily ever after and have broods of our own and set about marrying *them* off. Why do we need to talk of it at all? Perhaps I'd prefer to run off with the Gypsies."

Was Millicent really pragmatic as all that? Or was she dodging the question?

It didn't matter. Genevieve had lost her nerve. She hadn't the duke's ruthless patience for interviewing a clearly reluctant subject or Olivia's tenacity in pursuing an ends. What if Millicent was simply trying to spare her feelings? What would she do now if Millicent admitted she was passionately in love with Harry?

She didn't want to lose both friends.

She wanted to turn back time to the day before she knew Harry intended to propose to Millicent, or she wanted to turn the calendar ahead to the day when Harry and Millicent were married and she was done with her grief, or had at least come to an acceptance, had acquired four cats and settled into a wing of her parents' house with Olivia to grow old.

Suddenly the both of them were quiet, and their daisy wreaths were growing at an almost frenetic speed beneath their fingers. They both looked up at Harry. He smiled a smile that caught like the sweetest hook in her heart.

And lifted his hand in greeting.

Millicent and Genevieve lifted their hands in reply.

And behind Harry, Genevieve could have sworn the duke lifted an eyebrow.

Chapter 12

The evening passed uneventfully in terms of proposals being issued.

It didn't pass uneventfully for Harry, who lost
enough money to the duke in five-card loo to make
him perspire. Or for the ladies, who made significant
headway with their embroidery.

"There!" Millicent announced happily. She'd put
the finishing touches upon a sampler.

Genevieve leaned over and peered. It featured a
bundle of gray kittens tumbling about with a ball
of yarn.

"It's wonderful," Genevieve assured her warmly,
exchanging glances with Olivia from across the
room, who mouthed the word *kittens* in a question.
They both stifled smiles.

"What's on *your* sampler, Genevieve? You've been
so secretive about it. Come, let us see."

She sighed. "Oh, very well."

Ironically, she'd been working on it for some time.
But she finally felt ready to show it.

Millicent took it in her hands and studied it.

Hers featured an enormous urn stuffed full of
astonishing flowers in a profusion of oranges and
crimsons. She'd *invented* those flowers. They were

roselike but not roses, and chrysanthemum-like but not chrysanthemums. No flowers quite like them had grown anywhere on the planet except in her imagination.

She had, in fact, been working on it for some weeks. She'd chosen her finest silk threads for it and the piece glowed.

Millicent ran an admiring thumb over them. "Oh, you've embroidered Olivia's flowers."

Genevieve looked long and expressionlessly at her.

"I'm not quite finished," was all she said, and took the sampler back to do just that.

But then came time to retire for the evening.

This is how Damocles felt, Genevieve thought dismally.

Flat on her back, wide awake, blankets up to her chin, a hot brick at her feet, she ought to feel cozy and sleepy. She'd all but memorized her ceiling since Harry had informed her he intended to propose to Millicent. The fire burned at a medium height.

There was no point in attempting sleep while her mind was crowded, and so she allowed whichever thought was most compelling to crowd through.

And it was this:

Harry had spoken of Millicent in terms of qualities of character. But he never rhapsodized about her lips, or her eyes, or her hair, or her smile. Beyond "you look lovely," Harry had never gone into specifics.

And each and every compliment issued by the duke had been just singular enough to kindle her imagination. Calculated to intrigue, to imply that he saw her in detail, that touching her was a pleasure.

Unconscionably, he'd said. As though being soft

was something she did specifically to torment him. It had almost been an accusation, a dare. She'd received more than her share of compliments in her life. But for some reason the duke made her feel very much like a . . .

Like a *woman*.

Purely and simply.

It had nothing to do with love. Or with marriage. He was thinking of her in terms of . . . of sensual pleasure. And in concluding this, she was overtaken by that raw, awkward feeling again, a restlessness she wanted to surrender to and to escape.

And her restlessness evolved, shifted distinctly into curiosity, which, she discovered, was a remarkable palliative for pain.

Regardless, there was no point in attempting sleep. No matter how she courted it, it wouldn't come. She thought she'd read a book, something pleasantly dull, but this required a trip downstairs to the library.

So she slid from her bed and padded across the carpet.

Then hesitated. And almost tiptoed to the window, and tentatively parted the curtain an inch and peered out.

But there was no one in the garden.

She lit the candle next to her bed and brought it down with her to the library. Likely there would be just enough of a fire left burning to help her find the book she wanted. She raced down the marble steps, quickly and on tiptoe, as they were blocks of ice by this time of night, and as she crept across the foyer toward the library she saw a tall shadowy figure standing in the green salon, pointed toward the window.

Dear God!

Her heart leaped into her throat. Motionless, as riveted as a statue, her spine was suddenly as icy as the floor beneath her feet, she tried to shriek, but no sound emerged.

It was about time an Eversea ghost made itself known, but that didn't necessarily mean she wanted to be the first one to see it.

But her senses settled. A moment later she knew it was the Duke of Falconbridge.

Her breath caught.

And her heart began to hammer in her throat, and this time it was from a peculiar excitement.

His back was to her. His arm was upraised, holding the drawn curtain away from the window, and he was looking intently out, but she couldn't imagine what he might see. That full moon, a sky full of stars. He was still dressed, or mostly dressed. Trousers and boots, a white shirt rolled up at the sleeves. A candle no taller than a thumb was lit and pressed into a dish on the table next to him, and it illuminated a small crystal glass in which glowed what appeared to be brandy. Likely poured from the library decanter.

Which meant he'd likely wandered from room to room.

So she *had* seen him in the garden. Why did he haunt the house every night after midnight? Were all those things said of him true, and did his conscience dog him? *When* precisely did he sleep?

He picked up the brandy and sipped at it, then

lowered it again. The dying fire in the salon illuminated half of him. He appeared to have been dipped in gold.

She stared longer than she ought to. As he was coatless, she could clearly see the outline of his body. He was lean and spare, dangerous as a whip.

She saw his shoulders move in a breath, perhaps a sigh.

And then he released the curtain, and it shimmied back into place.

He turned slowly away from the window, seemingly resigned to needing to return to his room. He began to reach for the candle.

Then he went still.

Something must have caught his eye, because he spun so quickly she jumped.

He straightened slowly to his full height . . . and stared.

Perhaps he thinks I'm *a ghost.*

But no. She was certain he knew at precisely whom he stared.

Riveted, silent, mutually breathless, they regarded each other across a gulf of marble and carpet. His cravat was looped 'round his neck, undone. His shirt was open, revealing a vee of skin burnished by low firelight and fascinating curling dark hair.

She couldn't at all see his expression.

But she could *feel* his eyes on her. And from the distance he managed once again to make her acutely aware of her good mouth. Her naiad hair. Her unconscionably soft hands. And every inch of her skin was suddenly alive, restless, and even the night rail she wore was a sensual disturbance, reminding her that she was a creature that could touch and be touched.

What would happen now, she wondered . . .

. . . if I went to him?

His reputation as a man who took the women he wanted preceded him. He wasn't known to be a despoiler of virgins. Or a cuckolder of married men. And everyone had been shocked when he'd courted Lady Abigail in more or less traditional fashion.

He was absolutely motionless. She entertained for another brief disorienting moment the notion that he was in fact a dream. Her heart slammed in her chest.

She decided to back away.

She took a step forward.

She could have sworn his breath caught.

And then she whirled abruptly, her night rail whipping at her legs, and dashed up the stairs again.

Chapter 13

The following morning dawned a bit cloudy, but the kitchen was warm and bustling as usual, and Moncrieffe was surprised to discover he was in fact rather pleased to be there. He took the seat he took yesterday, and noticed that everyone else had done the same thing.

"Good morning, Lady Millicent. What will you be sketching today?"

He'd decided to be a devil.

"Kittens!" she said happily. "I found a nest of them in the barn. I should also like to sketch some ducks. Perhaps we can all walk out again."

Harry looked less happy about that, the duke noticed. He was decidedly subdued this morning.

"Never gamble with the duke, son," Jacob said from his end of the table, bluntly reading his glum face. "He never loses."

The duke gave a shrug; Harry produced a wan smile, Ian had laid down his silverware because his appetite deserted him in the presence of the duke.

The duke was hungry. He took a bite of egg and stabbed at his ham with a fork, while the housekeeper and a trio of maids bustled about clucking and spying and filling his cup with steaming black coffee fresh off the fire.

He watched Genevieve Eversea incise her egg again. The idiosyncrasy fascinated him unduly. It was as precise and singular as she was.

It was interesting to discover she haunted the house at night, too. He had lulled himself to sleep with that image: her dashing up the stairs, her long black hair sailing out behind her, her nightdress billowing.

Running away from him.

Running away from *herself*. Miss Eversea did that very well.

He anticipated a time when that would no longer be true.

"Waterfowl are handsome subjects," the duke agreed gravely with Millicent.

"I like to shoot them when they're grown," Jacob Eversea said.

"Papa!" Olivia and Genevieve reproached in unison.

But Millicent wasn't offended. She was diverted by the marmalade when it was passed beneath her nose on its way to Harry, who sat next to her, and she intercepted it with a charming wrinkle of her nose.

"What?" Jacob Eversea said mildly. "They're not downy and adorable when they're older, but they *are* delicious," he said amiably and tore off half of his bread in his teeth. "Harriet knows how to do marvelous things with waterfowl and the like and your mother makes a mint jelly . . ."

Isolde Eversea glanced up at her husband with an expression of almost . . . it was almost entreaty.

But then Jacob stopped talking and he never quite met his wife's eyes.

Moncrieffe wondered again what it was about. Some secret marital discord. Perhaps not terminal. The duke remembered a bit of marital discord with his wife along with . . . along with everything else.

"What shall we shoot today, lads?" Jacob continued as if shooting was a given. "Grouse? Pheasant? Duck?" He said wickedly, "The ladies can get their portraits first, and then we'll shoot them." He winked.

"I wouldn't mind shooting a thing or two," the duke offered.

Ian paused mid-chew. He gulped noisily, and then, "I believe we're expecting rain," he said firmly.

The remaining clouds slid away then, and a brilliant celestial ray came crashing through the window.

"My musket is always clean," the duke almost purred.

"And you always were a crack shot," Jacob commented idly.

"Still am," the duke agreed cheerily.

He caught Genevieve's eyes, glinting wickedly at him from across the table. She ducked her head again.

At some point they all noticed Harriet the cook standing silently in the kitchen doorway.

She'd gone pale, and she'd knotted her hands in her apron.

"What is it, Harriet?" Jacob Eversea asked sharply.

"Summat . . . well, summat has arrived, sir." Her hands twisted in her apron.

"Judging from your expression, it's a ransom note of some sort," Mr. Eversea said dryly.

"No, sir. It's . . . they . . ." She abandoned her effort

to explain. "Well, I think you ought to see them," she said darkly.

She vanished from the dining room and returned to the kitchen. The Everseas and their guests heard a good deal of muttered discussion, then some shuffling and jostling ensued.

And then two footmen staggered forth.

They were bearing between them a flower arrangement so brilliant it was nearly *sentient*. A profusion of roses, the heads of which were nearly as pulsatingly crimson and large as actual hearts sprung from a luxurious froth of ferny greenery and minuscule lacy white flowers. It was magnificently intimidating and almost indecently sensual.

The whole thing was the height of a three-year-old child.

Everyone stared at it uneasily, as though it might pull a chair up to the table and help itself to kippers.

Even Olivia was nonplussed.

And then she looked resigned. "I wonder who on earth . . . It's the same after every ball, isn't it? Perhaps we can find a place for them in—"

"They're for Miss *Genevieve*." Harriet seemed as troubled by this as by their very presence in the house.

Genevieve would never forget the stunned silence that followed. Or the sight of every head at the table swiveling toward her. She gained an immediate and very funny impression of being surrounded by *O*s: mouths dropped open, eyes gone wide.

All the eyes beamed such potent curiosity at her she thought little singed holes might appear in her gown.

"Only an outrageously wealthy man would be

able to afford flowers such as those," her mother finally said archly.

And at that, the room was resoundingly silent. Everyone seemed to be vibrating with the effort not to look at the duke.

"Oh, Mama." Genevieve was careful to say this with an eye-roll. Her voice only shook a little. Her heart was flinging herself at the walls of her chest. "That, or a man who just happens to possess or has access to a thriving greenhouse, and that describes most of our acquaintances. I haven't the faintest idea who sent them. Will you kindly bring them to me?"

The footmen shuffled over and settled them down near her with a grunt.

And she reached out with trembling fingers and touched one of the roses. It was, unsurprisingly . . . unconscionably soft.

"A message was sent along with it, Miss Genevieve." Harriet handed over the sheet of folded foolscap, closed with a blob of wax. No seal was pressed into it.

Genevieve slid her finger beneath it to break the seal.

My esteemed Venus—

> *These reminded me of you. In my dreams, your lips are just this soft.*

> > —*Your devoted servant,*
> > *Mars*

Her breath was officially lost.

Her eyes blurred. Instantly she burned, burned

with the scandalous pleasure and shock and . . . *hi-larity* of it.

As usual, the duke had done far too much and precisely the right thing.

She looked up a moment later. She, too, refused to meet his eyes.

He'd accused her of being a poor actress. She would need to prove otherwise, despite the fact that she was certain her complexion was forty shades pinker than it had been when she arrived at breakfast this morning. Because these flowers were both for her benefit and for the benefit of . . . Harry's education. She shouldn't like to waste the duke's efforts.

"They're perfect," she said almost offhandedly. As though she received such things every day.

"We can find a place for them in . . ." Mrs. Eversea stared, her teeth in her bottom lip. She was clearly having difficulty imagining the roses in any of her lower rooms.

The *duke* had no compunctions about staring at Genevieve.

A throat was cleared. She looked across to see Millicent, wide-eyed and wondering, face aglow with wicked but not at all resentful speculation, and Harry, whose face was, once again, unreadable.

Though it was considerably tense about the jaw.

It was Harry who had cleared his throat.

"I say, Genevieve," Harry's voice was cheery, but pitched about an octave higher than usual. "Do you know who sent them?"

"Mars," Genevieve replied laconically. "Or so the message is signed."

This caused another silence, while gazes ricocheted about the table frantically.

"Who is Mars?" Ian demanded suddenly. He shot a quick dark look at the duke.

"The god of war, as I understand it. It's also a planet. A red one, I'm given to understand." Genevieve was enjoying herself.

Not the least because of the expressions on the faces of her family. Her parents wore identically watchful expressions, bemused, eyebrows poised in mid-mast position, prepared to dive or hike as the situation evolved. Their offspring provided endless opportunities for them to test their flexibility and ingenuity. But never had Genevieve tested it.

"Who *is* the mysterious Mars? I think I might swoon!" Millicent placed the back of her hand against her forehead.

"I'll catch you, Millicent," Harry said flatly. The promise rather lacked conviction.

Everyone was clearly waiting for Genevieve to say something.

"Why don't you take them up to my bedchamber, if you would?" she suggested softly to the footmen.

And as though those roses were instead a coronet and she'd been crowned Queen of the Morning, whose commands were not to be countermanded, no one suggested otherwise.

With grunts and knee cracks, the footmen hoisted them again, and stoically prepared to shuffle the long journey up the stairs to her bedchamber.

They needed to pause for a rest and a cool drink on the second landing.

"Do *you* know who sent them?" Harry whispered to Millicent.

"No. But she asked me just the other day if I'd ever kissed a man!" Millicent murmured to Harry.

* * *

The arrival of the roses effectively put an end to breakfast, as it was far too disturbing and exciting an occurrence. Silverware was abandoned, napkins folded, and Harriet ceased pouring the coffee. She wanted to shoo the family from the kitchen, obviously, so she and the rest of the kitchen servants could have a good gossip about the roses.

The duke, sensing this, and sensing no one would depart until *he* pushed his chair back, folded his napkin and did just that.

"I'd love to take you up on your offer of a shoot," he said to Jacob. "Birds or . . . targets."

He glanced over at Ian. Allowed his gaze to linger.

Ian glared helplessly—and darkly—back at him, before trying to find a more comfortable place for his own gaze. It turned out to be his lap.

"Splendid, Moncrieffe." Jacob pushed back his chair. "We'll all go!" It was clear this part was an order to all the young men present, and he directed this to Ian, in particular. "Apart from the ladies, of course. I'll have the muskets fetched and horses saddled. Let's convene in the drive in an hour."

The first thing Genevieve wanted to do was rush upstairs to visit her roses, but Ian intercepted her on the landing.

"Genny . . ."

Her brothers were the only people who got away with calling her Genny.

She looked up at him.

"Good heavens, Ian. It looks as though you haven't been sleeping."

She said this innocently, but the intent was

wicked, and it was etched faintly in censure. She wondered if he'd even notice.

She looked up at her brother, knowing he was considered handsome by everyone female in a position to judge. She saw him anew. She recalled the duke's bleak, inscrutable gaze out over the green as he made his sordid confession. Picturing her naked brother, for a lark, crawling in and out of Lady Abigail Beasley's window and bed simply because he could.

"Genevieve . . . the duke . . ."

"Yes?"

"He isn't . . ." Ian was clearly in a bit of a torment over choosing the next word ". . . troubling you?" He almost mumbled it.

"*Troubling* me? Troubling *me*?" She was amused. He wasn't. "Yes, inflected in every way. Is he troubling you?"

"Why do you think the duke would consider *troubling* me?" She gave him the widest-eyed innocence she was capable of giving.

"He's been known for . . . troubling women."

"If that's a euphemism for seducing women, Ian, for heaven's sake, say it. I can hardly live beneath this roof with all of you without absorbing some of your conversation. And no. He has not *troubled* me."

Ian was laughing now.

"You know I love you, Genevieve . . ." he began.

She rolled her eyes. "For God's sake, *Ian*, I just ate breakfast."

He grinned at her, unable not to. And despite their transgressions it was always rewarding to make her witty brothers grin.

"The duke has been all that is correct and polite, I

assure you. I wonder that you're not more concerned about Mars and the flowers."

"Should I be?" he asked sharply and rather dangerously. The grin vanished.

"Oh, Ian. Please. I am a woman *grown*. And everyone knows I am not the one in the family who involves herself in mischief. I'm the sensible one."

Perversely she hoped he'd disagree. Or perhaps open the matter for discussion, at least.

He didn't. He just sighed.

She put a hand on his arm. "I *promise* I shall send for you the moment I need any manner of protection from overzealous suitors and the like."

Her poor brother did look as though he was losing sleep. She wondered how soon it would be before he was climbing in another woman's window. She suspected "never" might be the answer.

"So the duke *isn't* courting you?"

"Such a preoccupation with the duke! To my knowledge, the duke isn't courting me. His conversation is hardly loverlike. Though he did seem to take an inordinate interest in legal matters. Matters of inheritance, specifically."

"Legal matters?"

"Yes." She darted up the stairs and called over her shoulder. ". . . Specifically he was curious whether or not you'd made a will."

She turned and bolted all the way up the stairs wearing an enormous, wicked grin that her brother couldn't see.

Ian said nothing. She didn't hear him move at all.

Doubtless he was frozen in place.

Chapter 14

Moncrieffe decided to spend the hour before he was due to go shooting—one of the advantages of a visit to the country, firing enormous weapons long distance, and mucking about with dogs—in the Eversea library.

He was buoyant with the triumph of the roses. He'd bestowed pearls upon women he'd courted before, he'd indulgently paid lengthy bills for all manner of folderol presented to him by modistes and run up by mistresses, he'd given jewels to his wife, but never, never had he enjoyed giving a gift as much as he'd had this morning, regardless of its strategic purpose. He'd enjoyed the giving as much as Genevieve clearly had enjoyed the getting, judging from the colors she'd turned and that glow in her eyes. A man could grow almost too accustomed to seeking that response to a gift, the way one grew to love opium (not that *he* was familiar with that particular vice) or drink. He could spend sleepless nights imagining how to go about getting it again.

Harry's response had been almost as much of a pleasure.

Every bit of the large library had been given over

to shelves and books that had been kept passionately dusted, and many of which had even been read, judging from the faint creases along the spines. Most were sturdily bound in leather and stamped in gold lettering, and a quick perusal told him the collection was neatly organized, impressively comprehensive, and startlingly eclectic. He'd expected something more haphazard, given the predilections of the Everseas.

And so he roamed the brown, caramel, and cream-colored wool carpet before the shelves, orienting himself. He liked reading about science and nature and geography, he liked reading about guns and sports and adventures of the sort written about by Mr. Miles Redmond—he'd very little patience for poetry or fiction, as real life, he found, was vivid enough when lived properly, and was best confronted directly, rather than obliquely approached through words strung together by dreams and fancies, á la Byron. Who was represented on the shelves, along with a respectable selection of his poetic brethren.

His eyes toured the spines of the science books en route to his goal. Notably—unsurprisingly—missing were the important volumes about the South American land of Lacao written by explorer Miles Redmond, the works that had made him famous and in demand as a dinner guest and speaker.

One might even say they were as missing as *Lyon* Redmond was.

If one possessed a dark sense of humor.

In a row of books about the natural sciences his eyes were arrested by a title on one slim spine. It wasn't what he'd come to find, but he smiled, and slid it from the shelf. He rifled idly through pages for a moment.

He tucked it under one arm. Likely it would become useful.

He strolled onward. After a few more moments of perusal he found the kind of book he'd in fact been looking for. He pulled it from the shelf, and opened it.

He heard the footfall on marble in the hall outside of the library, and looked up. He wasn't surprised to see Lord Osborne standing in the library doorway. His expression when the roses had arrived had almost been as priceless as Genevieve's.

He suspected Osborne had, in fact, gone in search of him.

He cast his gaze up, but not his entire head. "Oh, good morning again, Osborne."

He dropped his gaze again to the page of the book.

Harry ventured deeper into the room. "I hope I'm not disturbing you, Lord Moncrieffe."

Alex looked up, gazed at him for one, two seconds with a mild, faint, disinterested smile. And then looked down again at the book.

Harry didn't interpret this as an invitation to leave.

"A fine volume there on sixteenth-century Italian painters. The one you're holding."

"Indeed it is," he agreed sagely, though he could have been holding a volume of French erotica, for all he truly knew the difference between fine and not fine. It *was* a volume of sixteenth-century Italian painters. That much he knew. And that's why he was reviewing it. It was like taking a peek into the mind of Genevieve Eversea.

"I recognized the binding. That's how I knew which book you were reading."

"Did you?" His words were so faint they were barely words. As though the book was absorbing his attention so thoroughly none could be spared for conversation.

Harry came forward, pretended to stand before the shelves. Something was on his mind. His whole being fair vibrated with distraction.

"Genevieve—" Ah, and there it was. Harry let her name ring alone, surrounding it with significant little cushions of silence. Essentially throwing his privilege to use her first name down like a gauntlet. "Miss Eversea, that is—is an admirer of Italian painters."

"Yes," the duke confirmed decisively.

Yes was clearly not the word that Harry wanted to hear.

He instantly set to meandering restlessly. He poked up the lid of a humidor and peered in at the cigars; he drew a finger across a collection of liquor in carafes as though strumming a harp, he sat briefly in a heavy brown velvet high-backed chair; he rose again, wandered over to the hearth and stood near the fire, which had been lit and was burning healthily. An extravagance, but then it was a well-used room and the Everseas could afford to burn wood profligately. He craned his head up and peered at the gigantic Eversea ancestor peering down from over the fire. Someone in a ruff, possessing that handsome face stamped on the Eversea men, attended by a skinny, long-nosed dog.

"I've always loved this room," Harry finally proclaimed, with exaggerated—and pointed—affection.

The duke decided to play.

He hoisted his head from his book. "You've spent much time in it?"

"As much time here as in my own father's library, it seems." He presented this triumphantly.

"I hope to spend a good deal of time here as well," the duke allowed cryptically. He returned his eye to the page of the book.

A blessed second of quiet passed as Harry attempted to decipher this.

"Genevieve and I have read that very volume you're holding . . . *together*. I remember one spring picnic we brought it along and had a *cracking* discussion of Veronese as we turned the pages. Together."

"Did you?" What Moncrieffe was thinking: You had an *entire* discussion about one painter? What could be said about *one* painter? He was pleased to not have to attend that particular picnic.

Finally his thumbing rewarded him with what he was seeking.

Veronese . . . Veronese . . . of course! As he'd told Genevieve, he'd seen a Veronese painting when he'd visited Italy. Memorably because he'd found it erotic: Venus and Mars again, and this time Venus was wearing not a shred, and Mars was kneeling, getting ready to, as he'd inappropriately shared with Genevieve, give Venus a pleasuring.

"Genevieve loves a particular *kind* of painter . . ." Harry began in a lecturing tone.

"She likes light and a grace of line, mythological subjects rich in subtext. She believes Botticelli is not rated highly enough as a painter. I happen to agree. I've seen his *Venus and Mars* and I am quite moved by his use of mythological subjects. Very sensual."

Harry looked thunderstruck.

Hmm. The duke didn't know why he should feel authentically pleased by the fact that Genevieve had entrusted him with a confidence she hadn't yet confided in Harry.

"She hadn't shared that particular insight with you about Boticelli, Osborne? Perhaps it's a new one. One she's had only recently."

"I suppose I shall need to reconsider his work," he stammered. "I know very little of it can be found outside of Italy."

"Perhaps you ought to hie off to Italy straightaway to have a look at it. Ha-ha!"

Harry was now frozen in place. He was staring at the duke, and was that . . . oh yes it was! *Temper* actually narrowed his eyes. It was clearly a relatively new condition for him.

"Ha-ha!" Harry laughed unconvincingly. "Perhaps I *should*. Perhaps I should. Italy is a beautiful country. But I should hate to miss the merriment here at Eversea House, so . . . I think I shall stay."

After a moment Moncrieffe allowed himself a faint, faint puzzled frown, as if this was all the same to him.

He returned his attention to the book, of which he'd read only about five or six words. He'd also changed his mind about house parties. Tormenting young lords was proving to be far more entertaining than he'd ever anticipated.

Harry was clearly unprepared to leave the library just yet, as though he thought leaving the duke alone with that volume on sixteenth-century artists was akin to leaving him alone with Genevieve.

Instead he strolled over to the window and

pushed away a sable-colored velvet curtain and peered out. His profile was quite nobly abstracted and troubled.

"We may have rain soon," he said uselessly.

The elephant in the room, of course, was the bouquet of hothouse flowers the height of a three-year-old child the duke had sent to Genevieve anonymously.

"Well," he said brightly, turning around, having made a valiant effort to. "Perhaps we can have a good chin-wagging about art sometime, as I fancy myself something of an expert."

A predictable tactic: befriending one's rival.

Unless this was strictly a display of possessiveness from someone accustomed to basking in unilateral admiration.

"If I could count the number of times I've discussed it with Miss Eversea . . ." Harry said driftingly.

"You've discussed it many times with her?" the duke said thoughtfully.

"Yes," Harry said triumphantly.

"And yet in not one of those discussions did she mention Botticelli and his . . . *Venus and Mars*?"

And the duke casually lifted his head and looked Osborne evenly in the eye.

You're outmatched, Osborne.

Harry stared. He breathed in and out, audibly. He likely agreed with the duke's silent assessment. And wasn't at all happy about it.

Moncrieffe thumbed through the pages to the *T*s and there it was. He studied the engraving to see if he could determine anything "magical" from it. He saw a nude woman. He approved of nude women.

". . . I understand Lady Blenkenship is a lover of art, as well."

"She is!" Harry agreed hurriedly.

"She shared with me her sketches of kittens. I found them very affecting."

There was a hesitation.

"She does love kittens." Harry sounded a bit despondent.

"Who doesn't love a kitten?" the duke murmured, flipping a page.

He in truth wanted to be alone again. He couldn't say he was any more passionate about art today than he was yesterday, but he *did* want to actually *read* a page or two.

"She didn't seem to know much about Botticelli. Or Veronese. Or Titian, Lady Blenkenship. Then again, not one of those artists has ever painted a kitten, to my knowledge."

A hesitation.

"Quite so," Harry acknowledged, a bit glumly.

"In fact, she's a delightful girl, Lady Millicent. So lively and pleasant."

And she was a lush thing, too, with hips a man would be happy to clutch, but that was a conversation for men who were less sober than they were.

"She certainly is." Harry brightened a little. But then frowned and looked uncertain again. He wrapped his hand around the cord of the curtains and twisted the soft thing absently.

The duke studied Harry again objectively. He was a little puzzled. He could see why Genevieve Eversea's head was filled with dreams of the man in front of him. And even twenty years ago Moncrieffe doubted anyone would consider him a handsomer choice than Harry.

And doubtless Harry had never dreamed the duke was a serious rival for Genevieve's affections.

What Moncrieffe had always possessed was *presence*. Like iron filings to a magnet he'd always drawn eyes to him when he entered the room with a gust of certainty and arrogance, comfortable in his rank, his intelligence. He'd never been a weathervane. Rather the opposite, in fact: he could be perversely unmovable for someone who thought and moved rather quickly.

But for a man who intended to set in motion an engagement to Lady Millicent Blenkenship during this very house party, Lord Harry Osborne was showing signs of ambivalence rather quickly.

He knew what to say next. He had an obligation to Genevieve to say it.

"My own art collection is in want of someone who will show me how to love it even more than I do," he said offhandedly.

Those words were potent weapons, he knew. My. Own. Art. Collection.

The unspoken words were of course: Who better than Genevieve Eversea to preside over my art collection?

Harry was deciding what to say. "How fortunate you are to have an art collection," he finally chose. Harry was struggling mightily to contain a note of bitterness.

"Oh, it's ancestors, primarily," he said, all but yawning, and flipped a page of the book despite the fact that he hadn't yet read it. "Row upon row of men and women who resemble me. And some ancient Italian paintings I know nothing about but I'm confident Miss Eversea would be able to identify and appreciate."

He glanced up long enough to reassure himself that Harry was motionless and struggling to prevent his features from arranging themselves in a stricken expression.

And then he returned his attention to his book.

They both swiveled their heads when brisk boot heels echoed on the marble outside the door.

"Ho, Osborne, Millicent said she'd thought you'd gone into the library. We're getting ready to set out for—"

Ian Eversea came to an abrupt halt at the library entrance. The sight of the duke fairly guillotined his sentence.

Moncrieffe straightened lazily to his full height, rather like a puma roused from a nap, and greeted Ian with a steady, inscrutable, very black stare.

Ian was helpless not to stare back.

There were dark purple crescents under Ian's eyes, as though he hadn't slept since . . . oh, since the duke had arrived, likely. Likely had pushed a chair beneath his doorknob. Perhaps slept surrounded by loaded pistols and knives.

Moncrieffe smiled.

Ian flinched.

Harry probably interpreted the startling silence as the usual reaction to Moncrieffe.

"I was discussing Italian art with the duke. It was a pleasure to discover we share a common interest," he said politely. What lovely manners the boy had.

With a rich and heady subtext that the common interest might very well be Genevieve Eversea.

"Your family should be proud of the comprehensiveness of your library, Eversea," the duke said gravely.

"Thank you," Ian said reflexively.

The duke pondered again the manners of the Everseas. Breeding wasn't something that could ever be vanquished entirely, he supposed.

"I'll just go and quickly get into my hunting clothes and meet you in the courtyard. I'll come back to finish my reading later this evening."

"Splendid," Ian lied. The word sounded gargled.

Moncrieffe nodded at the two young men. He idly stacked the books he'd pulled from the shelf on the table next to the settee and strode off down the hallway.

"I thought I'd settle in for a read of this later."

And when Moncrieffe had left the room, Ian took a few steps into the library and read the title:

Poisonous Plants Native to Sussex.

Chapter 15

"I'm not certain I approve of the duke."

This startling confession came from her mother, who was, like Genevieve, Olivia, and Millicent, embroidering. Stabbing needles with skilled precision in and out of various projects stretched over hoops. They'd congregated in the green salon, arranged on the settee and cross-legged on the carpet, firelight warming their skin.

The men had taken out guns and horses today, leaving the women to their own devices, and coming home with a brace of birds each. All apart from Ian.

"Would have thought the boy had drunk his breakfast," his father complained. "He couldn't get off a single decent shot. As though he'd suddenly acquired the palsy. I was *embarrassed* for the boy. The duke, however. I've never seen such fine shooting. Told Ian he ought to take a lesson or two."

The result of that fine shooting had been artfully prepared by Harriet and had served as dinner.

Of which Ian fed bites to a cat beneath the table before he fed bites to himself.

And then they had somehow found the lure of the company of other men more appealing than an evening around the fire with the ladies.

All in all, from Genevieve's point of view, the day had been a respite from wondering whether Harry had proposed to Millicent. She was almost in a giddy mood, as time for sleeping was nigh and another day would have passed without anyone being proposed to. And she'd been with Millicent for most of the day, reading, writing letters, gossiping. Harry's name had scarcely been mentioned, though each time it passed Millicent's lips her stomach knotted painfully.

"Well, that makes you and everyone else in London, Mama. No one approves of the duke. Though I scarcely think it matters to him." She hadn't quite finished her vase of flowers. She considered whether there was room for yet another color in the vase.

"Oh, it's not that. I don't believe a word of any of the gossip—I shouldn't take it as gospel, anyhow—and I'm hardly in a position to judge a man for his transgressions." Which was such a fascinating thing for her mother to say that Genevieve looked up sharply, but her mother was sailing on blithely. "But for heaven's sake, I thought the men were smoking cigars and playing billiards and talking about horses and other relatively harmless pastimes every night. I've left them to it. It was the housekeeper who saw fit to tell me that instead they're playing five-card loo for money. And this came about because she informs me your father has put in an order for more brandy and port. We've emptied more decanters this week than we have in the past year. They've turned our withdrawing room into a veritable gaming hell. And apparently it was the Duke of Falconbridge's idea."

Genevieve and Olivia exchanged smiles.

"Is Papa winning?"

"Only occasionally."

"Is the *duke* winning?"

She already knew the answer, since his reputation preceded him, so she wasn't surprised when her mother said dryly, "Nearly all the time, apparently."

"If Papa *were*, you might think more kindly upon it."

Olivia snorted a laugh.

"Your papa is hardly wanting for money, Genevieve. It's the principle of the thing," her mother reproved, but not without humor. "I shouldn't like our home to be the place where all the neighbors from miles around lose their inheritances. Wives and mothers will descend upon us with pitchforks and flaming torches."

"Olivia will simply stand up and give a speech about abolition and frighten them all away."

"Genevieve Marie Eversea!" Her mother was shocked. And she was difficult to shock.

Genevieve was surprised. Hmm. It really *was* rather a heretical thing to say; it violated one of the unwritten rules of the Eversea household, which was that Olivia's causes were to be endured. She wondered that it had popped from her mouth. Her family didn't regard her as humorless but it most certainly wasn't her role to foment any more . . . events.

As the duke had so astutely pointed out . . . when one's family is so eventful, it was restful to regard something as static as a painting. Or a sampler of a vase of the sort of flowers that . . . awaited her in her room upstairs.

And look where kindness had got her.

She glanced across at Millicent, who was no more forthcoming about matrimony than she was yesterday.

"It's true, Mama. I should welcome the opportunity to lecture angry villagers," Olivia said complacently, with a glint in her eye. "You're just angry that I abandoned you to the duke, Gen."

"Nonsense." Though life might have been a good deal simpler at the moment if she'd been able to dilute the duke's presence with Olivia's. Though he'd had an objective, and when that man undertook something, resistance was futile.

"Are you *ever* going to tell us who sent the flowers to you, Genevieve?" This came from Millicent.

"I did tell you. Mars," she said lightly.

"She *claims* the duke isn't courting her," Millicent teased, directing this to the entire room. "But he smiles a good deal around her."

It was still unbearable to be teased by Millicent about *courting*. And what a thing for Millicent to notice.

"Because he *isn't* courting me." Not strictly speaking, anyhow.

"Isn't he?" Her mother sounded a bit disappointed. *And she'd believed me just a little too quickly*, Genevieve thought, perversely.

"Who's courting *you*, Millicent?"

Oh God. Olivia had asked the question. She'd been teasing. Probably. But Genevieve froze. Because any moment could be the moment Millicent finally said, "Well, I hadn't wanted to *talk* about it just yet as I was savoring the happy news, but Harry and I . . ."

And then the sword of Damocles overhead would drop and cleave Genevieve in two.

But Millicent simply said complacently, "Oh, everyone, to some degree, judging from my dance card the other night. But no one in particular."

Not for the first time did Genevieve wonder whether Millicent was going to be surprised when—*if*—Harry actually issued a proposal. It was grotesquely unfair.

"It isn't like you to be so cryptic about the flowers, Genevieve," her mother noted correctly. "You may trust us, you know. Unless you're ashamed? They're not from Simon Mustlethwaite, are they?"

Simon Mustlethwaite had yearned futilely for Genevieve for years. He had spots and a stammer and a title and a fortune. He possessed little conversation. She was kind, but her kindness knew limits.

She sighed. "Oh, in all likelihood they were sent by someone who danced with both Olivia and I and simply confused our names. Because why else would anyone send a bouquet quite like that to *me*?"

It was the sort of sarcasm the duke would have enjoyed.

"Oh, that sounds reasonable." Her mother sounded both relieved and resigned. "Of course that's what happened."

She stared at her mother. Searching for a sign of doubt, for . . . anything that indicated a shred of suspicion that such flowers might have been directed at her. And as for Olivia, she hadn't even bothered to look up, let alone disagree.

And no one had noticed her sarcasm. Because doubtless no one wanted to see anything but what they *wanted* to see. What they'd always seen.

For God's *sake*.

She couldn't breathe suddenly. The anger built slowly, but inexorably, burning hotter and hotter, and it drove her involuntarily to her feet as surely as if she were powered by steam. She was angry at herself as she was at them, though she could not have said why.

She stood in the middle of the carpet, foolishly holding her embroidery of the enormous vase of lividly brilliant flowers. When she did *that*, mildly curious faces turned toward her. Mildly. For if Genevieve was standing she meant to do something *ordinary*.

And if she'd been Olivia, she would likely have given a speech about how she was *not* only kind and gentle and clever. About how she was weary of being the one her parents needn't worry over.

But she still wasn't given to speeches. And she wasn't certain she wanted them to know the depths of her passion.

Some things were too precious and ought to be protected.

But she was very tempted to give them something to worry over.

"I think I will go to bed. The bright colors on my embroidery are making my eyes ache a little."

This was sarcasm, too, but it, too, seemed to be received literally.

"Sweet dreams," they chorused at her as she abandoned her embroidery to the floor and left the room.

She huffed her way up the stairs, and almost but not quite slammed her chamber door.

She gave a start when she saw the roses in her bedchamber.

They were another entire presence in the room. And not an entirely benign one.

Despite herself, she smiled slowly. They really were *outlandish*, the product of a devilish sense of humor, and of someone who listened, and who . . . she dared believe . . . actually *saw* her for who she felt she was.

She savored again the shock of the morning as she stared at him, and a glow lightly touched her skin, an echo of this morning's blaze of emotion.

A pity about him being Lucifer's spawn.

She was sardonic even in her own thoughts. Lucifer's spawn wouldn't have sent those roses.

She'd stormed off, in her quiet way, but now she was committed to staying in her bedchamber and she wasn't tired. Or rather, she was, but she had no faith that sleep would come easily, given the condition of her emotions.

She pulled pins from her hair to let it down— *you've stars in your hair*—and rubbed at her grateful scalp, and combed the satiny length of it out with her fingers. She would brush it properly later.

For now, she curled up in a chair in front of the fire, kicked off her slippers and tucked her feet beneath her and attempted to read a novel. A Horrid Novel, about an orphaned aristocratic girl wandering the dark corridors of an ancient manor house and encountering a ghost.

Ironic, that.

She lowered the book into her lap and looked toward her window, pensively.

The curtains were drawn. She pictured the duke pacing the garden, his greatcoat whipping out behind him like a dark mist. She recalled him staring out the salon window at nothing, the very personification of loneliness, she realized now. She pictured him turning, slowly turning, half burnished in gold, to watch her watch him.

One ghost recognizing another. He'd been calling her—she was almost certain he had—with his eyes.

And that was the last thought she had until she woke with a start sometime later. She'd dozed off in her chair. The fire was low; the chill was what had penetrated her shallow sleep.

She glanced at the clock. Just past midnight.

She shoved her hair away from her eyes, and when she did those roses glowed at her from the corner of the room. And just like that, the respite from the drama her life had become was over, and all the memories locked into place again.

Motionless, weary, but knowing sleep would continue to elude her, she looked past the bed, which was suddenly her enemy. To her dressing table, where her brushes gleamed, ready to put her hair to rights.

To the window.

And that's where her restlessness sent her. A moment's hesitation, and she parted the curtains . . . and looked out. Idly, she told herself.

Nobody was in the garden.

So she ought to unlace her dress and slip into her comfortable night rail and slide beneath her blankets. She fetched her book and her candle from near the hearth . . . and pushed her feet back into her slippers.

And before she really knew she was doing it, she found herself, like the girl in the Horrid Novel, carrying a candle down the stairs, in search of a ghost.

* * *

When she reached the foyer, she headed decisively for the library. Because she wanted to find a particular book, as the one she was reading wasn't lulling her to sleep.

This was the story she told herself to drown out the truth.

The embers in the library hearth had burned low and the room, she could tell in an instant, was empty. Of humans, anyway. Though when she waved the stub of her candle in quick inspection she saw that the library decanter of brandy was half-emptied. As were, apparently, all the other decanters in the house, if her mama had it right.

Well, then.

The next story she told herself was she ought to bring her embroidery silks upstairs, and that's why she took herself into the green salon. Which was also empty. Apart from Olivia's exotic blooms— significantly smaller than hers, she thought with an unworthy frisson of pleasure—which still sat in the corner, throwing odd spiky shadows across the ceiling.

She hesitated, and admitted to herself she could find no excuse to go into the gray salon.

She went anyway.

He was in the gray salon.

He was standing at the window, looking out at nothing again. Arm upraised to hold the curtain aside. The line of him was eloquent, fine as any sculpture. Perfectly shaped, from shoulder to waist to thigh.

She halted in the doorway. Her heart skipped painfully.

And as if he could actually hear it beating, he turned. Very slowly.

And he didn't look at all surprised. He looked as though he'd been expecting her.

Good heavens. The front of him was in disarray. His slightly-too-long hair was every which way. His sleeves were rolled up to the elbow. His cravat was untied and hung unevenly. His shirt seemed to have been unbuttoned and then rebuttoned crookedly, exposing a good deal of burnished bare skin and curling dark hair at the throat. His whiskers had got a good start on a beard.

"Good heavens," she blurted on a whisper. "What *have* you been doing this evening?"

Moncrieffe stared.

The muscles of his stomach tightened, and his lungs tightened, too. Her hair was down. She had miles and miles of it, all shining like dark water. Her face was small and delicate and white amongst all of it. She'd never undressed for sleep; her dress was rumpled.

"Rescuing baby orphans," he said softly. "What does it *look* like I've been doing?"

"It looks like you've been set upon by thieves."

He winced. "No need to *scream*, Miss Eversea. I *was* set upon by thieves, euphemistically speaking. I prevailed. I generally prevail over five-card loo." He grinned crookedly.

"I spoke in a perfectly ordinary conversational tone. Mother says you've turned the withdrawing room into a Den of Iniquity."

She was teasing him. And she was whispering now to protect his sensitivities, which he suddenly found unbearably touching. She was always so *thoughtful*.

He also found the soft voice unbearably sensual. It was another texture of her, like that silken hair, and her luminous skin, and her hands that hinted she was everywhere soft. Whispers were the proper language for the dark, after all.

"I divested a group of gentlemen of a good deal of money in five-card loo. Harry included," he said with a certain mildly cruel satisfaction. "He's a surprisingly determined and bold player, and I would warrant he oughtn't be playing at all, given what you've told me of his straightened finances, but that could be the reason he does play. He does lose as often as he wins. We're in the country, for God's sake. Outside of shooting and walking about, what is there to do besides playing cards?"

He was half-serious.

A thought slipped through his brandy-weakened defenses: She was the reason he was staying in the country at all. That, and ensuring Ian Eversea went pale every time he saw him and flinched at every loud noise.

He became aware that she was smiling.

"We *might* have had a good deal to drink throughout the game," he conceded. "And a good deal to smoke."

He won so frequently it had almost become dull. But then all the men present were able to go home with a story about how the Duke of Falconbridge bet chillingly large amounts and raked in astonishing winnings. Fearless, they'd called him. Ruthless. Cold. And etcetera.

She took a step closer and was about to take another one when she paused with her slipper hovering off the ground. Then stopped abruptly and moved the candle pointedly away from him.

"If I come closer you'll ignite. I shouldn't like you to become Duke Flambé. Did you *drink* the brandy, or bathe in it?"

He gazed at her. "You're so *solicitous* of my welfare." He was again touched that she didn't want to set him alight.

"I'm more concerned about my mother's curtains. That particular shade of velvet cost a fortune and I shouldn't like to tell her I used a duke for kindling."

He smiled broadly at her.

She smiled in return.

And all at once it felt like a bright light had entered the room, though illumination was provided only by her candle and the gray light that managed to push its way through the window.

And after a moment she settled the candle down on a tiny table.

It was a tiny, fraught gesture.

It meant she intended to stay. For a moment or two, anyhow.

Suddenly his heart was beating rapidly. He was cautious of moving too quickly, lest he frighten the moment away.

"What makes you so certain it's brandy?" He was genuinely curious. "Can you truly identify it just by the smell?"

"You've met my brothers."

The word "brothers" was unfortunate in his weakened state, when he was less capable of filtering feelings. His hand twitched as though it would still have loved to close around Ian Eversea's throat. The very room seemed to tighten around them like a steel band, such was the new tension.

"They really *did*, you know," he said softly, suddenly.

"Did?" She was puzzled.

"The roses. Remind me of you. They're precisely the sort of flowers you ought to have."

Those spectacular, throbbing, lush blooms that now stood guard over her bed.

With petals unconscionably soft.

Something almost like pain or joy flickered over her face. His words had penetrated deeply. And for a moment all either of them heard was the soft, soft sound of swift breathing.

"Well, I wish you an easy night of it, though there seems little hope of that," she said quickly, suddenly. "I'll ring for a footman and send him down to . . . help you. Good ni—"

"Please don't go."

Words as unbidden as her presence, and shaken loose by brandy.

And the hand he would have used to choke Ian Eversea reached out and landed just above her elbow and closed.

Firmly stopping her from leaving him.

Motionless, they stared at each other, and then they both stared down at his hand, as though it belonged to someone else, had naught to do with them.

And then his hand slid slowly up her arm as if it were a road he had no choice but to follow. Up the slim, soft bare skin of her arm. It was so cool, such a silken, heartbreakingly soft path.

She tensed beneath his hand.

And when it touched her hair lying draped over her shoulder, he exhaled softly. He sank his fingers into it, then drew them slowly, slowly out, in aching wonder.

"It's what this night would feel like if I could seize hold of it."

More words let loose by brandy and darkness and foolishness. He wasn't sober enough to feel embarrassed by their lyricism or to wonder how that sort of poetry got inside of *him* and kept emerging around her. They merely struck him as accurate.

She gave a breathless, astonished laugh.

The laugh excited him. And he knew very well what short breath meant.

He knew that Genevieve Eversea was excited.

Her eyes were shadows in her pale face, but he didn't sense fear, only fascination. Her breath came swiftly through parted lips. She didn't move to test whether he'd release her.

He wondered if he *would* release her if she tugged.

He decided he wouldn't.

But she didn't tug.

"Genevieve," he murmured speculatively, landing hard on that first syllable, gliding over the next, as though they were soft rolling Sussex hills, as though each syllable had its very own character and deserved equal attention.

He wound more of her hair in his fist, again, and again. So soft. And this manner he reeled her absurdly closer to him.

And she came to him.

She was so close her breath landed softly on his chin.

She looked up at him. Their gazes fused.

"What did you *think* would happen, Miss Eversea, if you ever encountered me alone in the dark?" he murmured.

And then he eased her head back with a final tug on her hair, and brought his mouth down to hers.

He didn't savor or coax or indulge or finesse. He invaded. With a hint of mockery, a hint of self-indulgent cruelty, his sinewy tongue got between her lips and set to work plundering with the same skillful, carnal recklessness he'd kiss a greedy, experienced lover. To show this clever girl how much she didn't know. To breach her defenses before they had a chance to stir.

Her body was rigid with surprise. Her mouth was hot and soft and sweet as cognac. Her lips were a wonder of give. He knew he had but a second or two before whatever animal instinct lived strongest in her recovered from shock and either kneed him in the baubles; or discovered she actually enjoyed kissing, and surrendered, like any proper wanton.

He hadn't counted on a third option.

Stealthily as a liqueur or an excellent drug, in much the way she'd been doing for days now, Genevieve Eversea—her heat, her scent, her generosity and kindness, her devastating sensuality, entered his bloodstream. Beneath his hand, the lush, lithe give of her body just barely brushing against his chest, the hum of that passion she kept so tamped, burned through him.

The invader becoming the invaded—that was the third option.

He was hers now.

He loosened his hand in her hair and cradled her head, tenderly, tenderly, as though it was made of porcelain. His mouth eased, softened, and surrendered to properly discovering the wonders of hers. Inconceivable that her blossom lips should be so soft, and yet so demanding, and yes, she had begun to demand. She had an instinct for this.

It would be his undoing.

He drew in a shuddering breath and closed his eyes. Paused for an instant, resting his mouth delicately against hers, loath to relinquish the feel of her even for the moment it took to breathe.

Her hands slid up his chest, lingering over where his heart thumped. The cool, soft fingers landed on the vee of skin left bare by his unbuttoned shirt and loosened cravat, her touch at first tentative and cool, then more confident when her curiosity became courage. It slipped deeper inside his shirt, slid against his hot skin, over his hard chest, and he heard himself murmur and sigh, "Dear *God*," as it slid over him, raked lightly into the hair there.

He was shaking.

And so was she.

His big hand fanned and slid over the blades of her shoulders, settling in that sweet space between them, where it fit as though it had been carved just for him. Then slid down the eloquent line of her spine, to the small dip of her back, to cup the sweet curve of her arse.

And then he pressed her hard, closer to the hard swell of his cock.

A shock of pleasure for both of them, and she made a small primal sound in her throat. And she pushed herself against him.

The fit of their bodies was sublime. Unexpectedly right. Their lips nipped, clung, slid; his tongue plunged to taste her again, her head bending back against this sensual assault even as she took as much as he gave. He felt the floor opening up beneath him, and gravity release its hold. Surely he was flying.

He could *taste* the wildness in her, the wildness he'd sensed the way one could taste an approaching storm in a breeze. It felt infinite; it shocked him. He knew she struggled against it, was buffeted by it, but for the moment was utterly in command of it. As she was in command of herself at all times.

Her control excited him almost unbearably. He would steal it from her. He wanted it unleashed. He wanted to be over her and inside when the storm finally broke.

And this is why he ended the kiss.

Not abruptly. He eased it to a close with the grace of an excellent actor ending a scene. He held her close to him, one hand resting on the curve of her arse, the other still wound in her hair, and for a moment their chests rose and fell against each other. Her breasts were crushed against him. Her breath fell softly through parted lips against his chin.

And just as slowly as he'd wound her hair, he unspooled it. It fell from his fist as though it was a yard of silk he'd spun all on his own.

Now that he'd unleashed her, he stood back.

Neither of them spoke. He could hear the roar of his own breath but felt as removed from the sound as though he were listening to the wind blowing down the chimney. And yet he was acutely aware of the surface of his skin; it was feverish, aching from the need to contain the tide of . . . *want* . . . that swelled in him. He was acutely aware of the insistence of his swollen cock and the nausea he recognized as thwarted desire fluttering in the pit of his stomach. Of the quivering tension in his limbs, and the sweat cooling on his back now, all evidence of how fiercely ramped his desire had become with just one brief kiss.

He'd been reduced to heat and ache . . . and astonishment.

He could not recall the last time he'd felt *astonished*.

Disconcertingly, as it turned out, *she* could speak. "So did it?"

She whispered it. But it was a surprisingly bold question.

He opened his mouth. Then shut it again.

He knew precisely what she meant: Did that kiss nearly destroy the memory of all other kisses, and become the benchmark against which all future kisses would be measured? Did it live up to his pompous, purple rhetoric, designed to inflame her dreams and get her bosom heaving and to remind her how very little she knew of kissing?

It was a second before he knew precisely the right answer.

"Almost."

He wouldn't be the Duke of Falconbridge if strategy wasn't as second nature as breathing, and this was far too important to botch.

Her head jerked a little. She went utterly still.

She had the advantage; the dim light of the room framed him, and she remained mostly shadowed as she studied him. He doubted she had the lovelier view.

"You should see your expression," she said softly.

"The duel one?"

"No. It's more like . . . when a snarling dog is swatted across the nose by a kitten. Surprised and affronted. As though the natural order of things has been subverted."

He blinked. Bloody hell, but he was charmed speechless by the analogy.

A second later he was ferociously indignant to be the subject of it.

"Snarling . . . dog . . . ?"

He said it quietly, but his tone suggested he was considering whether to call her out.

The corners of her mouth went up in a quick smile.

It delighted and unnerved him that she wasn't afraid of him. She very much ought to be afraid of him. Perhaps she was, and was simply testing him over and over.

Testing herself, over and over.

And even though he knew who was bound to win and how this would end, he wanted to applaud her.

She was still all pale, blurred, shadowed softness. Her hair was a tumbled and almost comical mess now. She sported a slight halo of fuzz because of his rummaging hands. He knew his own hair was in disarray. He deliberately refrained from fussing with it.

It struck him as unfair that she could read his expression and he couldn't see hers. It was as disorienting as though he'd been deprived of the use of all of his own senses. In so short a time he'd grown accustomed to gauging his own emotions by whatever hers happened to be.

The fire was still low; he likely still stank of brandy and cigar smoke; dawn through the window was still just a suggestion in the form of pale light on the far horizon. Everything was exactly the same. And yet everything was completely unfamiliar. Just like that blessed second after waking from a vivid dream, when the full weight of the life he'd lived hadn't yet seeped in, and he was new as a baby.

Genevieve had ducked her head and was brushing her knuckles across her lips. Back and forth. Back and forth. He watched, irritated, wondering if her lips were swollen. He recognized his irritation as guilt's more tolerable cousin.

"I'm *drunk*," he pointed out.

It was an inane thing to say. It was also no longer entirely true. He'd kissed himself almost all the way to the other side of sobriety.

Her knuckle stilled on her lips and her brows dove to meet in a frown. She brought her hand deliberately down to entwine with her other one and held both of them still against her thighs, and stared back at him. And for a moment, she seemed to actually *consider* his ridiculous words.

"Of *course* you are," she humored, finally, and so very, very gently. "I'm certain that's all it was."

Was that tremble he heard in her voice *laughter*?

A little of it might have been fear.

Of him, or of what she'd just done?

Or of what she *wanted* to do?

Well, she *ought* to be afraid of what he wanted to do. Or at least possess a healthy sense of self-preservation.

But he had little doubt that he would be able to do it. All it required was strategy.

She was backing away from him now.

Don't go, was his first panicked thought.

Followed by: *Hurry up*.

"Shall I send a servant down to look after you?" she said as she backed away.

She couldn't help it, of course. The looking after him. The looking after of people. He thought of her again gently replacing, retying Millicent's bonnet. She *breathed* kindness. He surged toward it hungrily and just as quickly surged away.

"No. I'll see myself up," he said curtly.

See what she'd reduced him to? *Simplicity.* Perish the thought.

She paused, perhaps waiting for the acerbic twist to his words.

He didn't have it in him at the moment.

So she really did leave.

Chapter 16

~~~ ∞ ~~~

S he raced back up the stairs, and closed the door and leaned against it momentarily, as if locking all untoward desires out.

But there the roses were, standing guard like a sentry. Announcing to the world who Genevieve Eversea *really* was.

They really do. Remind me of you.

Her very good mouth stung from that very good kiss. And she remembered his words, as though they'd been a spell that had lured her downstairs and into his arms in the first place. *It should make you want to do things you'd never dreamed you'd want to do, and in that moment all of those things will make perfect sense.*

Almost, he'd said.

He was lying. She smiled half to herself.

Unless . . . he wasn't. Her smile faded.

Because the notion that a kiss could be better than *that* . . . it was nearly inconceivable. Surely if one kissed someone one loved it would lift her right from her body.

It should herald, or at least promise, the most intense physical pleasure you've ever known, regardless of whether that promise is ever, ever fulfilled.

She drew in a shuddering breath. She sat down hard on the edge of the bed.

She rested the backs of her fingers gingerly against her thoroughly kissed mouth, and regarded herself in the mirror.

Promise. It had been exactly that.

And then she pulled her hand away from her mouth and studied it. The hand that Harry had kissed.

That the duke had pinned with his fingers to the grass just the other day.

That she had slid into the duke's shirt this evening as his tongue tangled with hers.

Memories of textures came back to her, all out of order: his tongue, sinewy and hot and sweet with brandy and how the touch of it to hers had sent hot quicksilver through her veins. The skin of his chest, smooth and taut and covered in crisp dark hair she'd actually tangled in her fingers. Hard thighs, hard cock, firm hands, all pressed with conviction and extremely confident knowledge against her body, and how her body knew just how to blend into his. Her body had been *designed* for this.

Ah, but he'd also wound his hands into her hair. That, for him, had been indulgence. A grace note, a tender savoring.

He'd been shaking with desire for her.

The power of all of this was extraordinary, and really, she ought not to summon memories of it any more than she ought to summon spirits during a séance.

She stood up abruptly and approached the roses instinctively. She stroked the velvety softness of one again. Then cupped one of them in her hands. And imagined the duke's hand sliding beneath her arse, pressing her up hard against his cock.

She closed her eyes against the shock of pleasure that stormed her at the memory.

She imagined him heading up to his bed. Was he reliving the kiss? Would he sleep? Or were such kisses a common occurrence for him, the man who knew about . . . horses.

She was afraid.

She dropped her face into her hands, breathing hard.

And she wasn't afraid for the reasons she ought to be. It was the last part of his recitation that worried her most.

Regardless of whether that promise is ever, ever fulfilled.

Because truthfully, given how she felt when she relived the kiss . . . she thought she might *die* if that promise wasn't fulfilled.

Autumn was a rectangle of brilliant blue through the kitchen window and a line, as far as the eye could see, at least from that particular window, of bare trees. Another clear day, another hearty breakfast.

Mrs. Eversea touched Mr. Eversea on the arm ever so slightly. A signal. The sort of thing married people did. A universe of meaning could be conveyed with a minute twitch of a brow. Because if anyone else had regarded Genevieve Eversea so directly and at such length over breakfast it might have been considered untoward. But their guest was doing it, and he was a duke.

But perhaps he was simply weary, and had been captivated by his reflection in the silver coffeepot directly across at an angle.

And this is what Jacob Eversea conveyed to his wife with a tip of an eyebrow. A sort of shrug.

All of the men sitting around the table looked significantly more disreputable this morning. They'd managed to dress and button themselves up correctly, but those who weren't serviced by a valet had missed a few whiskers on their faces when they attempted shaving with hungover hands. And every single pair of male eyes was red.

Ian Eversea inadvertently intercepted the duke's gaze. The duke took his knife and slid it with slow precision across his plate, bisecting a slice of ham the way a brigand might slice a throat.

Ian swallowed noisily.

"Ian, your appetite seems a bit off," his mother accused. "Perhaps you ought to drink less."

The duke chewed slowly. Swallowed.

And smiled.

He wasn't admiring himself in the coffeepot.

Genevieve Eversea was her usual composed self, weary and lovely in some sort of soft shade of blue, and the hair which had poured like a dark waterfall over her shoulders last night was magically coiled and pinned up and tamed. Women did like to show their hair who was in charge.

His hand hummed with the memory of its feel. He would have it down again before the week was out.

"The day is so fine I thought we could take a journey to Rosemont," he announced to the table. "My estate here in Sussex. I spend so much time in London that I seldom have a chance to see it. 'Tis but an hour's journey from here, and rain hasn't yet made an unholy mess of the roads."

"Why, Moncrieffe, that's downright sociable of you."

The duke rewarded Jacob Eversea's wryness with a very dry look.

And all of a sudden Jacob pushed the silver coffeepot over to him.

Isolde Eversea glanced at her husband and bit back a smile.

"Oh, now, sir." Harriet the cook was irritated at having her role usurped. She swooped down and bustled over and poured the duke another cup of coffee, lest he sprain a wrist waiting upon himself.

"I didn't know you had an estate in Sussex, Moncrieffe."

This from Lord Harry Osborne, who attempted a smile along with it.

"I do," the duke said easily. "And I've a few paintings that could benefit from the eye of an expert. I inherited the paintings. I should like to know more about them."

Faint blue rings arced beneath Genevieve's eyes. She hadn't slept much, either.

She wasn't meeting his eyes directly yet. She would.

"Perhaps Genevieve and I can be of some assistance to you there," Harry volunteered hurriedly.

Moncrieffe ignored Harry. "I also think I might have a painting of a kitten somewhere in the house . . . but it's been so long since I've visited . . ."

Millicent smiled at this. She wasn't so simple that she didn't know when she was being both humored and teased. But she didn't mind.

"Remember the swans?" Genevieve said suddenly, almost enthusiastically. "Do you remember our first visit to Rosemont, Millicent? We went on a whim when the duke was away."

"They were splendid," Millicent agreed.

"But is the house open, Moncrieffe?" Jacob Eversea wanted to know.

"I sent word ahead a few days ago that I might spend a day or two there, and the staff no doubt has made it ready for visitors."

Harry's head jerked up suddenly. His fork froze midway to his mouth. His knuckles had gone white on it.

And then he gingerly laid it down on his plate. He cleared his throat.

"Do you . . ." He stopped. The tension around his jaw made it seem even more eloquently square. "I say, Lord Moncrieffe, do you . . ."

Everyone turned to Harry.

Handsome Lord Harry Osborne looked a little worse for wear after losing more than he could afford to lose to the duke at five-card loo. His eyes sagged a bit, from a poor night's sleep. Was it simply too much brandy? Or was he, too, tossing and turning over Genevieve Eversea? Or over Lady Millicent Blenkenship? Was he running amuck, kissing Millicent's hand after midnight?

He *ought* to toss and turn over Genevieve Eversea, the duke thought.

The duke had done precisely that last night.

The duke favored him with his attention. "Yes, Osborne?"

". . . do you have a greenhouse at Rosemont?"

Harry fixed him with a surprisingly intense gaze. A curious hush fell over the room.

Genevieve looked at Harry, eyes wide, fascinated

at this turn of events. Then she flicked her eyes to the duke, and then studiously back down at her plate, admiring the pattern of roses about the edge, and her neatly eviscerated egg.

Harry was officially *jealous*. Or so it would seem.

The duke allowed that silence to settle in, to become significant. And then he smiled faintly, and said almost disinterestedly, "Doesn't everybody have a greenhouse?"

He could practically hear the whirring minds of everyone at the table attempting to extract meaning from the statement.

Everyone hopped a little, startled, when Harriet dropped a fork.

"It's lovely, Harry," Genevieve said gently. "Rosemont is. It will be a nice short trip and diversion today. And think of the gallery. You'll enjoy it."

She smiled at him, and Harry smiled weakly in return.

A rogue surge of jealousy swept up over Moncrieffe. She was trying to ease the young fool's disquiet. Because she was so damned *thoughtful*.

"Won't it be amusing, Harry!" Millicent enthused. "Swans! Oh yes! Let's all go."

"I've other plans," Ian said quickly.

"Perhaps you ought to go have a talk with your cousin Adam, Ian," his mother suggested.

The implication being that Adam the vicar might be able to help Ian unburden his conscience or regain his appetite.

"And be certain to bring your sketchbook, Lady Millicent," the duke urged somberly. "Because everywhere you look . . . it's beautiful."

He was looking now at Genevieve.

Genevieve stared back at him with those cool blue eyes. She knew his words were part of a game, and yet she suspected it wasn't entirely a game.

And it was perhaps this confusion that put the color in her cheeks.

Or perhaps she was thinking of where his hands had been the night before.

A man could hope.

A picnic was got up, cold fowl and cakes and dates and half of a wheel of cheese packed hastily in a basket, so they needn't feel a twinge of hunger for the few hours they would be away, and so they wouldn't startle the duke's staff with a need to feed a sudden small invasion of aristocrats.

Installed in the duke's barouche, the final party, consisting of the Duke of Falconbridge, Harry, Millicent, and Genevieve (slippery Olivia had begged a previous commitment) and attending footmen, they rolled through Pennyroyal Green past Miss Marietta Endicott's academy, past the Pig & Thistle, past the vicarage, where Adam stood outside talking to Ian and lifted an arm to wave while Ian glowered; past the two enormous oaks entwined in the town square, said to be so entwined that one could no longer stand without the other, though they battled with each other for their share of light and air and earth. And this, it was said, represented the Everseas and Redmonds.

Nearly an hour into their journey, over more rolling Sussex hills, every now and then a glimpse of the sea winking on the horizon, the duke said, "Ah. And so we're here. On Rosemont land."

"And how did you come to own Rosemont, Moncrieffe?" Harry wanted to know. Perhaps hoping he'd won it in a card game and could win an estate of his own one day.

"It was part of my wife's dowry," he said, his face turned toward the window.

The duke smiled mordantly to himself at the sudden silence. No one ever knew quite what to say when he mentioned his dead wife. It was a useful ploy when he wanted a conversation to end.

Which wasn't necessarily the case at the moment.

"And now it's mine." He turned back to them brightly. "You'll find the house isn't grand, not like Eversea House or some of my other properties, but it is snug and the gardens are fine. Women seem to like the garden best of all. That, and the dolphin pool."

"Satyr," Genevieve corrected swiftly.

And then she smiled, realizing he'd said it purposely.

Moncrieffe bit his lip against a smile.

"Do you recall Vaccario's engraving, Genevieve?" Harry added hurriedly. "The satyr watching a sleeping girl? We found it in the bookshop in London."

"I recall it." She looked across at Harry. He sat next to the duke.

"Winter and Summer" she would have called any engraving of the two of them.

Except that she'd had a taste of winter, and winter, as it turned out, was incendiary.

Millicent sat next to her, and she wondered if Harry and the duke were making similar comparisons among the two women in their own heads.

"Charming bit of baroque art," Harry pressed on, almost desperately. "Vaccario's engraving."

Normally Genevieve would have taken this up eagerly. "It is, indeed," she agreed politely. She was distracted by thoughts of . . . tasting Winter.

"Oh, the two of you always talk so much about what things *are*. Baroque and medieval and so forth. Why don't you simply look at them and enjoy them?"

Millicent said this good-humoredly.

They all stared at her. And this was the key to Millicent's charm, and why, no doubt, Harry had thought he wanted to marry her. Everyone needed a reminder to simply look at things and enjoy them, without labeling them.

The house was at the end of a long road lined with bare, long, long aspens and birches, which would meet in an arch when leafed out in spring. The hills undulated like a green blanket tucked carelessly about the house, which sat on the highest of them. The vista showed them sheep and cows grazing in fields neatly bisected by hedges serving as walls.

"It's quite lovely, Moncrieffe," Harry said, earnestly, a bit despondently, when a jewel box of a simple redbrick house, surrounded by a circular drive, came into view.

The satyr was busy spitting water in the center of it.

"My wife did love it," the duke told them.

Everyone suddenly wondered if that was the reason he never visited.

But he'd said it strategically. And he wasn't patient. Moncrieffe hadn't undertaken the trip to be sociable, truly, or to do more meandering about green Sussex land. He'd undertaken the trip for selfish reasons.

So though he didn't quite rush them through the

house when they entered—he was greeted with genuine delight by the small staff—he did set the pace for the tour, and his pace was generally always a swift one. He pointed out the marble in the foyer was Carrera, that the chairs in the sitting room were Chippendale, that the carpets had been purchased in Turkey by his wife's father.

And then he brought them to the gallery.

"It's this one."

He watched Genevieve breathlessly as her eyes fell on the painting.

And then she went still. And as he watched it was if the sun itself rose inside her.

He caught his breath and turned, wonderingly, following her eyes.

What *he* saw was an appealing image of a nude woman stretched on a chaise. The woman's gaze was very direct—almost as direct as the gazes his friend Wyndham painted on the women sprawled on his canvases destined for bordellos—and her breasts were bare. It was perhaps not the sort of painting mixed company ought to be staring at in a concentrated fashion. Still, the bosom, as bosoms went, was modest, and the woman's hand rested modestly over her mons.

His wife had loved this painting.

To Moncrieffe, it was decorative and nude; it was an asset on his books.

His staff kept it dusted.

He knew what it was to Genevieve.

"It's . . . *Titian*," Genevieve breathed. "I'm sure of it."

A slow, awestruck, disbelieving smile took over her face. Stunned pleasure shone from her eyes. And he was certain her heart was racing with the sheer delight of being in the *presence* of the thing.

Because his heart was racing at simply watching her love it.

She turned to look at him as if he himself had painted it. Her radiance rendered him absolutely silent. He could only bask.

One was either moved by something or one was not, he knew. Certain tastes—for fine wine or teas, for instance—could be acquired. *Skill* could be acquired, but talent could not. And passion was either innate . . . or it was not.

He still in truth didn't care to know much about the painting.

He only cared about what it did to Genevieve Eversea.

And it was *this* that gave it its value in his eyes. Not the name of the artist, or the pigments he had used.

He felt her joy as his own.

"Venus," he finally said.

She laughed at the obviousness of that. "Yes!"

"You can touch it." He laughed softly. "Gently now."

She flicked her eyes toward him, and by the slight lowering of her eyelids knew she'd heard the innuendo precisely as he'd meant her to.

"Oh, I cannot. It's priceless."

"Oh, it has a price. Ask my bailiff what the current valuation is. Everything has a price," the duke said unsentimentally.

She simply quirked the corner of her mouth.

"It's Titian, all right." Harry peered at it critically. He said it quickly and almost nervously. He clearly wanted his voice heard, because all at once it was apparent that he and Millicent were somewhat forgotten. "Look at the pearly skin on the girl, Genevieve, and the little dog sleeping next to her. . . . That red of its hair is so singularly Titian. The dog in the painting typically represents fidelity. And you'll notice that it's asleep."

The duke saw a dog sleeping next to a naked woman.

He only cared whether Genevieve cared. He liked to listen to her talk about art.

"And I believe Veronese was Titian's assistant at one time," Harry continued, speaking almost too quickly.

"Venus and Mars," Genevieve and the duke said in unison.

Harry fell abruptly silent.

Millicent was staring at the painting, too. The image actually looked rather like Millicent, with the wide doe eyes and open face, but since the painting was of a nude, no one was going to say it.

In front of two women, anyway.

"It's very pretty, but how can she just sprawl there, uncovered, for everyone to see?"

Millicent wrinkled her brow. She didn't sound as though she were condemning it, necessarily. She sounded authentically curious and a little amused and just a bit repelled.

Millicent was perhaps the most literal young woman the duke had ever met.

Harry was looking at her incredulously. Undecided as to whether to smile or smack a hand over his forehead.

"Quite so, Lady Blenkenship," the duke agreed

somberly. "She is rather brazen. Perhaps a bit too exposed. I like a Venus one can uncover a bit at a time."

And this was so obviously, obviously an innuendo that everyone stirred a little, disconcerted.

Genevieve went very still, as if that particular innuendo had drifted over her like gliding hands. He awaited a scorching blush, a sideways scolding look.

Genevieve suddenly turned to Harry and said hurriedly, "And look, Harry, the young ladies in the painting in the back . . . her servants. They are rummaging about in the clothes trunk."

Harry looked very directly at her. "Perhaps they're in a hurry to cover her. To protect her virtue." He made it sound like an admonishment.

The implication was as bald as the woman on the painting was naked.

"I thought you loved Titian, Harry."

He hesitated. "I *do*." The words were almost—not quite, but almost—a moan.

A short, awkward, confusing silence followed. The duke decided to call a halt to this particular portion of the tour.

"You asked about the greenhouse, Osborne. Would you like to see it?"

It, too, was a gauntlet laid down. A very, very subtle one.

"Perhaps a visit to the greenhouse can wait until after we have a bit of a picnic," Genevieve said brightly and too quickly.

She knew exactly what they would find in the greenhouse.

"I should like to see it now." Harry was uncharacteristically firm.

"I should like to see it, too," Millicent said in solidarity with Harry. "I like flowers! I should like to sketch any interesting flowers you may have."

"*I'm* feeling a bit peckish," the duke said.

And as he was a duke, he won. And so they went off to enjoy their picnic, and Genevieve won a greenhouse reprieve.

Chapter 17

⌒◯◯⌒

The footmen and Harry carried the picnic hamper down to the grass near the lake, on which a half dozen or so enormous, irritable, gorgeous white swans floated. The willows had lost most of their leaves, otherwise they would have wept all over the banks very picturesquely. Millicent followed after Harry and the footmen, whipping out her sketchbook the way one whips out a sword, as though she couldn't face another moment without capturing the idyllic scene.

And surely Harry wouldn't propose to Millicent surrounded by footmen. Though now Genevieve was a bit worried he would be sorely tempted to trot off and do it in this lovely little place. She would love to receive a proposal here.

Genevieve was walking and thinking about the strained expression on Harry's face in the gallery. His distressed rush of words. Some suspicion had just been subtly acknowledged and he disapproved.

Harry was *jealous*.

Or Harry was concerned about her.

She preferred to think of it as *jealous*.

But why should this make her unhappy? Because she only felt truly at peace when he was happy.

Which, she had to admit, had been nearly all the time until the arrival of the duke.

"I could imagine being very happy here," she said aloud. "It's so lovely. Serene without being dull. Snug and welcoming."

Oh, God. Please don't say that describes me.

But the duke never did take up obvious temptations. "We never lived here long. But it was one of her favorite homes."

We. Her. His wife.

What had she been like? What had become of his first duchess? She still didn't feel free to ask the question. Still, she thought the house she loved said a good deal about her.

Genevieve hoped he'd been loved by his wife. She was certain he hadn't made it easy for her to do it, however.

In the absence of banal conversation, last night's kiss echoed in her. Today he was every inch a duke; last night he'd felt very human, vulnerable and alone. His clothes askew, his skin warm, his lips . . . she had to stop to take in a breath at the rush of pleasure that shot through her body at just the thought of his lips. She'd felt a right to him; she'd taken as much as given in that kiss.

But in truth, the Titian had made her feel shy again. She of course knew he was wealthy and powerful and influential, but for some reason the possession of that small wonder of a painting delineated this even more sharply.

She knew he'd wanted to show it to her because he'd known she would love it.

She was uncertain how she felt about that.

He said nothing else for so long she wondered if

he was in fact at a loss over what to say. She'd never once during their short acquaintance heard him clear his throat or stammer. She'd never seen him fidget or blush. But she had no doubt he suffered doubts of his own. He composed himself *inwardly*. Sparing the world his awkwardness, hiding vulner-ability. Preserving his pride.

"Well, Miss Eversea, I think our plan is working a treat," he said finally. "Did you see Harry's face when he saw the Titian?"

"Yes. But he's suffering."

"Oh, for heaven's sake. Of course he's suffering. It's precisely the point." He was half amused, half irritated.

"But . . . he's my friend. And I . . ." She didn't know how to put into words what it was she felt.

"Yes, yes. You love him. And etcetera. Though he has *entirely* taken you for granted."

She bristled. "He hasn't, you know. He cares for me, I know it. And please don't allow him to gamble anymore! He'll lose his inheritance."

"Your concern for the man who hasn't a clue whether or not he loves you or another woman is touching. But he's a grown man and I am neither his father nor mother, and it is not my place to stop him from gambling if he wishes to do it." The duke was curt.

"But you *don't* have to take his money."

"And he doesn't have to gamble," he said simply.

He was right, of course. She sighed a short frus-trated sigh.

"He's either suffering pangs of pure jealousy simply because he's used to your slavish devotion, Genevieve, or *my* attentions to you have cast you in an entirely new light and his heart has been swung 'round like a weathervane. And if that's the sort of man you want, that's the sort of man you will have, if our plan works. Has he said a word to you about me?"

She said nothing. Of course he hadn't.

"But he looks unhappy." She was wretchedly torn. She had never been able to bear seeing Harry unhappy. Even while he was making her miserable.

"Wait until he sees the greenhouse," the duke said with ghoulish glee.

"I think we ought not look at the greenhouse," Genevieve said firmly.

"What do you suppose you'll find there?"

"Roses the size of baby heads."

"They all were sent to you. He'll see nothing."

"Then we don't need to see it."

"Very good. If I refuse to allow him to see it, then the mystery will deepen. *Imagine* the torment."

He was right, of course, about everything, and this shut her up. Strategy was indeed the answer, and it seemed to be working.

"Though he could even now be proposing to Millicent."

He *would* have to add that. He did have a sadistic streak.

The two of them paused a moment. The duke shaded his eyes.

"Though she's getting too close to the swans, and they might snap off one of her limbs. I think those swans are carnivorous. That one in particular. Lucifer."

Millicent was indeed trying to lure one closer with a crust of bread. Genevieve bit back a smile.

Millicent's bonnet was of course already precariously askew.

Genevieve looked up at the duke again to discover him watching her so peculiarly, so intently, her heart leaped.

"Genevieve."

"Yes?"

"I should like to kiss you again soon."

Oh.

Her breath left her in a gust. Not a word-mincer, the duke.

He smiled faintly. "You thought I would pretend it didn't take place?"

"I knew you would never allow me to forget it took place."

The smile became something else, and that's when she saw how and when he deployed that enveloping, wicked smile. "Well?"

She breathed in deeply, nervously, her hands burrowing into the fabric of her skirt. "I . . . I don't think I should allow it."

He actually laughed. "Let's stop pretending, shall we, that you're someone who approves or disapproves of things, or allows or doesn't allow them or what have you. You and I, at least, know that isn't true. Allow me to phrase it differently: I think we ought to kiss again. Soon." She could tell by the way he said "soon" that he was amusing himself by tormenting her.

"It's not archery or a picnic or a casual pastime." The calm discussion of something that had turned her inside out was spinning her head. She heard the taut beginning of hysteria in her own voice. "You might at least try a different tone."

"You prefer me to sound ardent?" He sounded dubious. "I can certainly *try*."

"Please don't!" That would be worse.

She walked on quickly.

He caught up easily.

Up ahead of them, Harry was assisting the footmen in unpacking the hamper. She saw the half wheel of cheese emerge. He looked toward them and smiled, white teeth flashing. Lest she forget how it felt to be smiled at by Harry.

And here she was striding next to a man whose erection had pressed against her last night, with her complicity.

"I just don't think it's wise," she said again nervously. *Damn, damn, damn.*

"Wise!" The duke was amused. "Of course it isn't *wise*. We wouldn't be doing it for the *wisdom* of the thing."

She gave a short, breathless, incredulous laugh. "But . . . *listen* to yourself. It's just that you sound so . . . as though I should meet you again in some specific location and we should set to it? Like a shooting party?"

"I'm so glad to hear you making the arrangements—"

"I'm *not* making *arrange*—"

"—as I'm not a gifted planner."

"You plan *everything*," she said irritably, which made him smile again. She did like his smile. "And besides, what can you possibly *gain* from another . . . kiss?"

Crunch, crunch, crunch. Footsteps over leaves on the path as they walked. He seemed to be considering his reply.

"I enjoy it. I enjoyed kissing you. You enjoyed kissing me. What more reason do we need to do anything?"

Heat rushed over her limbs. *I enjoy kissing you.*

"We are not in love."

He sighed, and the sigh evolved into a short exasperated laugh. "For heaven's *sake*, Miss Eversea. Last night alone should have taught you that love and desire do not necessarily go hand in hand, and one can indulge one without . . . enduring the other. It wasn't virtuous, what we did. And I shall not believe you if you claim virtue as a reason for not wanting to kiss me, for I'm very certain you are not the sort."

He was so darkly wry.

"But you *know* that *we* won't ever . . . that I'll never entirely . . ." Her voice was choked and faint. She couldn't say it. *That you'll never see me stretched out nude like Venus on the chaise in your gallery.*

He stopped abruptly.

She stopped abruptly, too. Like a bloody pet called to heel.

Infuriatingly, the duke got one eyebrow slowly, sardonically up. "You won't ever *what*, Miss Eversea? Make love to me?"

She was scarlet again, judging by the temperature of her face. But the *things* he felt free to say . . . !

If she'd had any sense at all, she'd run as fast as her legs could carry her to join Harry and Millicent. But safety was hardly available there, either.

Harry glanced back then, sensing . . . *something*. As he always seemed to. He shaded his eyes, watching the two of them.

Clearly his equilibrium had been disturbed. *Oh, Harry.* He does care for me, he *does* know me.

Oh, bloody, bloody hell.

"I don't want to kiss you again," she said faintly. Emphatically.

She wasn't certain whether it was true, but it was certainly the right thing to say.

He rolled his eyes. "Of *course* you don't," he soothed insincerely. And continued walking swiftly.

The swans seemed to have massed and were advancing on Millicent, who still appeared to be cooing and holding out a slice of bread.

"And I think we ought not," she called to him firmly and conclusively.

"Of course you do," he called back with mocking equanimity.

She made an exasperated sound. She should have stalked in the opposite direction.

She hurried to catch up to him.

"Unless your plan is to . . . inveigle an indiscretion and compromise me in order to . . ."

He paused again and mulled, head tilted.

So she paused again. She'd begun to feel like his shadow.

"Ah. I see what you're saying. A trap? Clever! But now, now, Miss Eversea, now what did I just say about planning? And how it isn't my forte? I hardly lured you like a spider into a web last night. *You* arrived and accosted me with your irresistibility, and in my drunken helplessness, what choice had I but to kiss you? I'm a creature of instinct. You really ought to have known better."

She snorted inelegantly. "You plan your every *breath*."

He smiled at that, tipping his head back, and she saw that double set of dimples at the corners of his mouth made by his smile, like a stone skipped across water. The wind ruffled and lifted his black hair.

And her heart skipped, too.

Black, that was, apart from a frost of gray at each temple.

He was old. He was almost forty.

"I did *not* plan . . . last night." And now he was sincere. She could tell by the falter. He was almost bemused. And the way he said "last night" made the words seem like a euphemism for splendor. They encompassed a world of sensations and memories, those words.

It was one of the most terrifying, exhilarating conversations she'd ever had.

She felt buoyant and helpless, like a leaf that could be borne away on the wind and end up anywhere at all. Someplace marvelous, higher and higher still. Heaven.

Or crushed beneath a foot.

She felt sickly nervous.

"And speaking of traps, one might be tempted to believe the *trap* was all for me," he continued on an air of feigned injured indignation. "Can you imagine what would have happened had your father happened upon our tableau? Of the two of us, I'*m* the one with the title. He'd shoot me on the spot or hold me at gunpoint until a special license could be obtained."

She didn't like the reference to marriage. She cut her eyes nervously to Harry and Millicent again.

Only to discover that Millicent was quite a distance away now because she was fleeing a swan, her skirts clutched up in her hands to free her ankles. The swan made shockingly good time on its webbed feet, long neck outthrust as it tried at intervals to take snaps out of her. They were trailed by a footman who fruitlessly pelted it with bread, and by Harry, who was waving his hat madly and shouting.

The footman's wig flew off and smacked Harry full in the face. He stopped to claw it off.

The duke shrugged. "Lucifer has a temper. He'll get bored in a moment."

"But I'm the one with the fortune. I needn't trap anyone," Genevieve said, believing him about the swan.

"Touché," he said almost happily. "No, you are a prize. You're no *Olivia*, of course," he reiterated, mocking her again. "But you're hardly a consolation prize."

"Is this a trick? Do you plan to seduce and abandon me to punish Ian?"

This brought him up short. He was genuinely surprised. "Genevieve, listen to me. We will both be agreed on the beginning and end of it. I will never, ever willingly hurt you. Do you believe me?"

She stared at him, biting her lip.

"I swear it on all that I hold dear," he added.

She looked at him skeptically.

"I hold some things dear, believe it or not."

"Don't swear it at all. You don't need to. I believe you."

He nodded once. "Very good."

"But don't you see? I *can't*. It's simply very wrong."

He took three more long strides away from her. And then stopped. He actually sighed a long-suffering sigh. She was surprised he didn't extract his watch from his pocket, because he had the air of a man who was done negotiating and had tired of the topic.

He looked around at the landscape, but apparently his eyes found nothing they wanted to light on.

His mouth quirked in resignation. And he turned to her.

God. He'd eyes like mirrors. A changeable dark green splashed through with gold shavings. Hazel, she supposed she'd call it. His lashes were so black and thick. She stared at him now. There was a powder mark beneath his skin. A tiny scar beneath his chin. He was almost ugly, when viewed as a set of amplified details and features.

Taken together, those details were devastating. She could not have designed a more thoroughly *desirable* man if God had assigned the task strictly to her.

Though it seemed more the sort of task the devil would delegate.

It could also have a little something to do with the fact that she knew what it was like to kiss him.

And when he spoke he spoke quietly, quite seriously. He didn't look at her.

She followed his gaze.

Millicent was growing more and more distant. One of her slippers had flown off and arced through the air. It landed, bounced, and began to tumble down the green.

Harry and the footman were far behind her, both doubled over, hands on their knees, wheezing.

The swan stopped at last, apparently bored. He waddled back to the pond and waded in. He glided majestically, serenely back over the water.

"Genevieve, I saw something in you Lord Harry didn't see, *can't* see, because it isn't in him to see it. Ask yourself why this is so. Ask yourself whether this might be rather an essential oversight on his part. Ask yourself if you've just discovered something about yourself that you may otherwise never have known. Ask yourself why you came looking for me last night, and whether you want to know more."

He turned to look at her now. "Because . . . I'm the one who can show you. And you may never have another chance to learn it in *just this way*. With someone you can trust. And who wants it as badly as you do."

She stared at him. She scarcely heard him, because she was panicked and furious with this new realization:

She thought his eyes were beautiful.

"Two members of the same species always recognize each other, no matter how unlikely that might seem, Genevieve. That Redmond fellow, Miles, he would be able to tell you a thing or two about that."

"I'm not a member of your *species*. And please don't speak of the Redmonds to me."

He grinned because he'd made her say something ridiculous. The grin was wicked, white and tilted.

She panicked, because she thought of sun-shot ponds and sunlight coming down through trees when she looked in his eyes now, and judging from the temperature of her cheeks he was a devil sent up from Hades, not a bloody poem.

She might be turning any number of colors, from scarlet to parchment to all those shades of rose in-between, but he regarded her evenly.

He was older, bolder. He knew of whores and wars, violence and vendettas. He knew precisely what he wanted, always.

He wanted her.

For a disconcerting few moments he didn't speak. And she had the strangest notion he was studying her the same way she'd been studying him just moments before. Reassessing. Entertaining impressions about her and rejecting them (her eyes are beautiful!), only to have them float insistently back before his mind's eye.

He didn't seem to care that she wasn't speaking.

"You'll kiss me again." His low-voiced, arrogant confidence made her wish she had something clutched in her hand to throw at him. "The advantage of being a member of *our* species, Miss Eversea . . ." very deliberate, that, and he waited for her face to go thunderous ". . . is one that does whatever one wants because they want to and because they *like* it. And you both *want* to and you *liked* it. Not every woman does. Ponder that."

She glared at him.

"But liking it has more than a little to do with *who* you're kissing. And when you kiss me again it will have naught to do with *wisdom*. It will be because you will be unable to think of anything *else* until you do. Find me after midnight."

He strolled onward, whistling what sounded like *The Ballad of Colin Eversea*.

Chapter 18

I t was of course all she thought about the following day.

The duke had sent Genevieve, Harry, and Millicent back to Pennyroyal Green in his barouche, and stayed behind at Rosemont to take care of some estate business. During the journey, Millicent shared with Genevieve a new collection of sketches she'd made.

"I call it *Angry Swans*," she announced.

One sketch showed a swan rising up out of the water, enormous span of wings upraised menacingly, neck outthrust.

"This is what I saw just before it came after me," she explained.

Millicent was still a trifle put out that such beautiful animals should have been so unwelcoming, so as proof she'd captured their behavior in charcoal.

"They're wonderful," Genevieve said very sincerely. "Very convincing. It's a new direction for you, though, isn't it? Menacing waterfowl?"

"I think I prefer the kittens," Harry said. He'd been silent until then.

"You dislike moody animals, even if they're beautiful, Harry?" Genevieve teased.

"I dislike believing things are one way when they're really another way entirely."

And if that wasn't an innuendo, Genevieve didn't know what one was.

She just didn't know if he was referring to his own heart, or to *her*, in general.

But that could very well be her conscience interpreting it.

She sighed. She felt a certain kinship with that swan. Everyone thought Genevieve Eversea was serenity and purity itself. When she really was capable of . . . alarmingly original behavior.

And something else, something slightly traitorous, crept into her thoughts. What kept Harry from just saying what he thought? When the duke never seemed afraid to do it?

It was an unfair comparison. The duke was an older, wiser, more confident man.

And the duke couldn't possibly break her heart if he said precisely what he thought.

He could, however, keep her body restless.

The duke hadn't returned to Pennyroyal Green by dinner.

There was a moment of indefinable terror when Genevieve knew, *knew* he was gone for good. That he'd been toying with her. That he'd remained behind at Rosemont and from there had decided to return to London in pursuit of *horses*. This was followed by a great swoop of relief she wouldn't have to make a decision about kissing him again, then furious *indignation* that she wouldn't have to make a decision, all of which was very ironic considering the women had devoted the evening to the quietest of pastimes, reading and embroidery and mercifully benign gossip about the neighbors. Not the barbed sort that permeated London ballrooms. The soothing sort about who had a new horse or baby niece.

Harry and Ian had taken themselves off to the Pig & Thistle for darts, which meant for the duration no proposals were being issued to anyone.

"Is aught amiss, Genevieve?" Her mother had asked her once, peering at her as she stabbed with an excess of vigor into her embroidery.

The flowers on her sampler were growing everlusher, crowding the vase as though clamoring for escape. Tonight, with uncharacteristic whimsicality, she impulsively decided to stitch a flower outside the vase, as though heretically, it had escaped the bouquet altogether. There was a pleasing asymmetry and messiness to it.

"Aught, Mama," Genevieve lied a little too easily.

She looked up with innocently widened eyes when her mother said nothing for a long time. Merely fixed her with an unreadable look.

But she went motionless with an unseemly relief and an uncertainty that made her nearly nauseous when carriages began rolling up to the drive. Neighbor gentlemen spilled out. Much laughter echoed in the foyer, the footmen took coat after coat, and then the men disappeared into the room behind the ballroom.

The game of five-card loo would get under way.

Which obviously meant the duke had returned.

Long, long after the ladies had abandoned their embroidery and repaired to their bedchambers, Genevieve remained awake. She didn't undress for her bed. She kicked off her slippers and curled up in a chair and attempted to give her attention to the orphan in the Horrid Novel, but when the orphan met a mysterious handsome stranger she stared at the book incredulously, then frowned at it punitively and laid it down with a sigh. She listened instead to carriages departing now, carrying away men whose pockets were doubtless lighter now than when they'd arrived this evening.

The roses in the corner looked as fresh as the day they'd arrived. They seemed everywhere in her peripheral vision, and they drove her to the curtain.

She parted the curtains of her bedroom window and looked out onto the back garden. The sky was blue-black and glass-smooth; stars had been flung in reckless handfuls over it. Between two trees was the dull gray outline of a stone bench.

And moonlight glanced from the polished toes of a pair of Hessians.

The duke was lounging upon the bench, looking as much a part of it as any gargoyle carved into a medieval edifice. He casually stretched. He looked up to the window.

And raised one hand. She thought she saw a flash of teeth. A grin.

Bloody man.

She dropped the curtain, but stood staring at it as if she could stare right through it. Her heart had started up a thudding that sent blood ringing through her ears, but she moved as quickly as if she were fleeing war drums.

She slid her arms through the deep brown, fur-lined pelisse and turned to stare. This time her eyes were on the clock.

And it was after midnight.

She flew down the back stairs, slippers in her hands until she reached the back door.

Her breath announced her approach with little white puffs, but the cold was certainly bearable. She stopped right before him, suddenly at a loss as to what to do next.

"Good evening, Miss Eversea. Why don't you sit beside me? The stars are particularly spectacular tonight, don't you think? Dazzling. As if they've all had a good rinsing from the storm."

His voice was appropriately low for someone lurking in a garden at midnight. But there wasn't a shred of triumph in it.

She hesitated.

He gave the bench an encouraging pat.

She settled down next to him. The cement chilled right through to her bum, even through her pelisse. She pulled her fists into the belled sleeves of her pelisse to warm her hands. She ducked her chin, and looked down at their feet in disobedience of when the invitation had been to look at the stars.

She looked up suddenly, as though she'd heard a sharp sound.

As it turned out, it was the force of his gaze that had brought her head up. He was staring at her fixedly. He didn't flinch or pretend he was doing anything other than baldly admiring her. One might even say *devouring* her. Imagining what he would like to do to her.

Finally one corner his mouth tilted with a sort of lazy satisfaction.

Devil. She thought she could see the constellations reflected in his eyes. A girl could forget her precise location in the universe when a man looked at her with eyes like those. She could forget where he began and she ended.

"Aren't you going to gloat?" she whispered peevishly.

He blinked. "Gloat? About what? I thought you came out to admire the stars," he reproved gravely. "I welcomed the company. For we're here in your garden, in your father's house, beneath a window where anyone craning their head properly could see."

Was he really toying with her?

She was speechless with disappointment and embarrassment.

He laughed softly, ruefully shaking his head. "You should see how *disappointed* you look. *Honestly*, Miss Eversea."

Bastard! Very well, then, she'd look at the bloody *stars*.

"Ha-ha!" she laughed unconvincingly, tilting her head up. "Don't be silly. You're quite right, of course. I thought it a beautiful night. Who could be disappointed in these stars—"

At some point as she spoke, in a motion as natural as an exhale or a stretch, he'd begun sliding his hands up her thighs.

She stopped talking.

And thinking.

And breathing.

She resumed breathing on a shuddery exhale.

And as her thighs were bare apart from the garters holding up her stockings; his hands heated all the way through the fine silk of her dress to her skin. Every tiny hair on her body stood erect, as if craving his attention. She felt spangled with heat, cinders everywhere on her body. "Molten" rather described how she felt between her legs.

He strummed his thumbs softly, softly, back and forth, back and forth, against her thighs.

Oh God. She opened her mouth to reiterate: *Only kissing.*

"*Guh*," surprisingly, was what emerged instead. A sort of hybrid gasp-sigh.

"'Guh,' indeed," he agreed, softly.

She would have laughed. But the sensation was too new and too total, and desire gathered with a distracting, heavy intensity beneath the weight of his hands, coaxed by those feathery stroking thumbs, and her entire body, brain included, was invested in enjoying *that*, not in making coherent sounds. She fought to keep her thighs from falling open like a trap door, inviting him deeper in. Was it cold? Were they outdoors? She knew only his touch.

"I would never *dream* of disappointing you, Genevieve," he reassured her on a rough-silk whisper that dragged against her imagination the way his fingers dragged along her thighs, stirring possibilities into life.

But he proceeded to do exactly that when his hands arrived at the top of her thighs and stopped. The sweet spot at the juncture of her legs gave a great breath-stealing throb of protest.

He was closer now, so close she could feel the heat of his body, wear it like a second pelisse. And now that her very bones were molten—she had the presence of mind to consider that this had certainly been almost too easily accomplished—she had no choice but to flow right toward him.

She tipped up her head as his mouth was coming down.

You would have thought they'd done this dozens of times, rather than just once before, that it was more natural to her than breathing, judging from her sigh of relief. But he of course dictated how she would be kissed. And the kiss, too, was devastating, his mouth landing soft as moth wings, then sliding gently enough to show her how a universe of sensation and want could be coaxed from her lips. How the slide of his lips over hers could create craving everywhere in her body.

"Fur," he approved on a murmur against her mouth, because the backs of his hands encountered the lining of the pelisse as his hands journeyed up her thighs, along her hips, her waist, taking such savoring pleasure in her womanly curves it was like he was pointing them out to her deliberately, persuasively: *You're a woman. Don't you see? You're made for this.*

It was a decidedly dangerous way to think.

She knew what to do. Or rather her body did. She wrapped her hands around his head, threaded her fingers into his hair, which was soft and cold, and slid down around his ears, which were chilled, and which she strangely wanted to warm for him.

He sighed as her fingers dragged along his throat. She loved the sound savagely.

His body was so hard. And so large. He was clearly so much stronger than she was, and she liked the fear of him and the sense of being enclosed and protected.

It should have been awkward, the two of them twisting toward each other on the bench, but it felt effortless; she'd gone pliant with desire and heat. She loved the feel of his large, warm hands spread over the blades of her shoulders, and then the shivery light strokes of his fingers against the rectangle of bare skin above where her dress laced, dancing there, tantalizing her with the possibility that he might open the laces. The contrasts drugged her: his hard male body and his delicate touch; the scrape of whiskers against her own smooth cheek; his chilled skin and his hot, hot, velvety, savagely demanding mouth.

He growled low in his throat.

"Bit like a badger," she murmured aloud, without intending to.

"Pet names, my squirrel?" he murmured.

She laughed.

"*Shhh,*" he admonished. "No man enjoys being laughed at while he's kissing."

His mouth abandoned hers but was traveling from her lips to her ear, down, down to the silky hidden place beneath her jaw. Every place his lips touched fired quicksilver communications to the far reaches of her body, until she was alight, shivering like a flame.

And suddenly nothing was funny, and everything was urgent.

She heard herself utter a word: *please.*

And here, she knew, is when he began to lose his grip on control. Tension vibrating in his big body, desire tightly reined, his hands tightening on her, becoming less careful and purposeful and strategic, more demanding, which told her more about what he truly wanted. She sensed they were on the precipice of something dangerous.

Good.

His head dipped; his tongue drew a leisurely path to the base of her throat and his lips opened hotly there.

It was her turn to make an animal sound: a low moan she hadn't known she was capable of, the very sound of want. And his mouth opened on a slow, hot caress over the thump of her heart, beneath the soft swell of her breast.

"*Sweet,*" he whispered.

With a certain amount of effort he swept her onto his lap. She looped her arms around his neck. And he eased her around until, shockingly, she straddled him. His hands slid up her thighs again, beyond the tops of her silk stockings this time, to cup her buttocks, and to slide her closer.

The bulge of his cock was seated hard beneath at the join of her legs.

"*God, Genevieve,*" he swore.

The contact sent a bolt of pleasure through her that made her gasp. She was suddenly afraid, and suddenly greatly in need. She might have said something, but his mouth was on hers again, drinking, capturing her tongue with his. His hands tense and trembling with want, fumbled at the laces at the back of her dress.

And God help her, she helped him. She nearly dislocated an arm to reach back there. He spread them wide, and he tugged until he'd freed her breasts.

Wait. They'd said they'd *kiss* again. This was something entirely different.

The cold air was a shock against her skin, but he immediately cupped her breasts in his hands, which were miraculously warm. She closed her eyes. The pleasure was astonishing, unexpected, and she closed her eyes against the wondering expression in his as much as against the force of the pleasure.

His thumbs stroked her peaked nipples, and each stroke was a sweet bolt of lightning through her body.

She threw her head back at the exquisite shock of sensation and knew, somewhere in the distant reaches of her senses, that she'd gone mad.

And also that she didn't care.

"*Alex*." Her voice was threaded from her rushed breath.

His arms slid behind her and he tipped her backward and closed his lips over her nipple.

She jerked from the exquisite pleasure of it.

He traced a hard filigree shape with his tongue, and her hands clutched his shoulders as the pleasure fired through her.

And he slid his hands beneath her buttocks and pulled her abruptly tightly against him. His cock was so hard it hurt as she ground down against it.

But she loved it. She trembled from whatever it was she wanted.

He was so bold. He explained nothing, offered no clues, made no assumptions about her delicate senses. Her mind sought to keep up but her senses were overwhelmed and then in command and they managed to convince her mind it could sit this session out. A faint, faint echo of panic sounded within her, knowing this could be out of her control rather quickly.

But he'd said she could trust him.

He was arching up against her, and again she felt the desire pooling.

"Alex . . ."

She could feel his body quaking beneath her hands. And then his hand was gone and he was fumbling with the buttons of his trousers and suddenly his cock was against her, hot, velvety, thick against the vulnerable skin left bare above the tops of her stocking.

She was afraid. But her skin felt as though cinders were falling everywhere on it, lightly, lightly, and a pressure welled, an exquisite need drove her.

"I can't . . ."

"Christ, Genevieve . . ." He gasped it. He sounded astonished.

"I want . . . need . . ."

But she couldn't speak anymore in complete sentences. Her breath was hot against his throat, and she could taste the salt and musk of him when she licked the cord of his neck.

He stopped suddenly. Held her fast. Motionless. With arms like iron bands.

His breathing was bellows; she could feel the sway of it against her torso.

Why? What?

And then cruelly he scooped her from his lap and stood her upright as surely as if she was a ragdoll.

"No," he said.

She stared at him, abashed, and sick with disappointment. The air was icy now that she was away from his body; she felt it drying the sweat on her skin.

"Control is rated too highly, Miss Eversea. I will not grind against you like a boy grinding a parlor maid. I will not spill in my trousers. And I was very close to doing exactly that."

Oh dear God. She was scarlet with embarrassment.

"But I . . . we can't . . . I won't . . . I'm sorry . . ."

He held up a hand.

"I said that we ought to kiss again, and we have. Do not be sorry. Because I am not."

The words were rushed. Surely he hadn't had a fit of conscience?

And why should she feel affronted or abandoned if he wanted to preserve her virtue?

She brought her hands up to her face, about to cover them with shame.

And impatiently he swept them down again. He held them fast in his own for a moment.

As it turned out, he hadn't had a fit of conscience. Quite the opposite.

His voice was still low, his breathing still ragged and short. He sounded peculiarly angry as he held her hands in his.

"I want you badly. You want me badly. I want to make love to you. No more . . . juvenile fumblings. I want you naked beneath me. The decision is entirely in your hands."

And almost symbolically, he released her hands then. Gave them back to her.

And to think she'd once *enjoyed* his honesty.

As her body adjusted to its usual temperature, she pulled her pelisse more tightly around her. Shivering now from thwarted arousal and the loss of his heat. Shivering in fact a little from fear. She'd been on the verge of something remarkable. Of something irrevocable. Her ability to think was returning to her only in fragments.

"And Genevieve . . . if you think this was good

. . . if you sensed it could be incredible . . . you know only a fraction of what I can give to you. Think Boticelli. Think Veronese. Allow your imagination to run free. And you still won't come close to the pleasure available to your body. It's yours to take."

Bastard to leave her with kindling for her imagination.

"Find me at midnight again if you want to know more, Genevieve. But those are the rules."

They stared a moment at each other in the dark.

The stars stared down at them.

"Why are *you* allowed to make the rules?" she whispered crossly after a moment. When really she ought to have been scandalized by the "naked and underneath me" portion of the conversation.

He grinned at her. "Now, tell me. Is that something you would have dared say to *anyone* before you met me?"

And as right as he was, it didn't mean she should simply take what she wanted.

He brushed the backs of his fingers against her cheek. His hand lingered there. She turned her face into it, almost involuntarily. Then he took his hand away quickly, as if he was afraid it would be the last time he touched her and he'd enjoyed it too much.

And he backed away one foot, two feet, watching her, as if memorizing how she looked standing there in the shadows beneath the moon and stars.

And then, because it wouldn't do for the both of them to creep back into the house up the stairs, he vanished around the corner of the house.

Chapter 19

A nd thus her days and nights were divided neatly: the day was for a torment of anticipation regarding whether Harry was finally going to propose to Millicent alleviated by the wicked, delicious, staggering memory of what she'd been getting up to at night, and the nights seemed to be for a torment of anticipation regarding . . . what she'd be getting up to at night.

Truly, there was no rest for the wicked.

But if anyone noticed anything was amiss with her, they said naught. Apart from her mother, who noticed the faint shadows beneath her eyes and promptly ordered her to drink another of Harriet's simples. Harriet's simples were probably effective in that the mere threat of them frightened one away from allowing illness to take hold.

But if Harry had issued a proposal—and the opportunities to do it were legion for a resourceful man—he hadn't announced it. Millicent wasn't glowing unduly. There were no hushed reverent whispers between them. Harry didn't have that clubbed-in-the-head-by-happiness look her brothers walked about wearing when they'd married.

Genevieve concluded no proposal had taken place.

Then again, he'd nearly expired from the effort it had taken to break her heart with the news that he intended to propose to Millicent. She could only imagine how difficult issuing an actual proposal would prove for him.

Perhaps she ought to order him one of Harriet's simples.

And so that evening, because Mrs. Eversea informed Jacob Eversea that she longed for his company and the company of her sons, which was really her way of interrupting the blatant gambling for a night, they were sitting about in the parlor. And the men were clearly restless.

It was Millicent—spontaneous, cheerful Millicent, who wasn't the least *sensible*—who introduced the notion of playing blindman's buff after dinner.

It was greeted with wariness.

"We're to put on blindfolds and crash about the parlor?" Genevieve had never wanted to do anything less. If she put on a blindfold, Harry might seize the opportunity to propose to Millicent while she wasn't watching.

"The objective is not to *crash*, silly. But to seize upon and identify each other. We'll move the breakable things out of the way," Millicent explained.

"I can hardly move my *bones* out of the way and all of them are breakable as far as I know." Olivia was being obstreperous.

"We shan't knock you to the floor, Olivia. I'll seize you carefully," Ian assured her.

The men thought this was hilarious.

"With *blindfolds* on?" Genevieve was nervous about the notion. The crashing about was one thing;

the blindfolds were quite another. She'd never been enthusiastic about relinquishing control.

"And we seize . . . each other?" Harry said, as though he almost didn't dare to hope. Because the girls were eligible for this, too.

All of the men were snickering into their fists.

And Genevieve had a sudden image of him seizing Millicent and Millicent seizing him.

"I think we ought to play cards," she suggested firmly.

"We can go one entire evening without playing cards," her mother countermanded immediately.

The duke was sitting silently in the corner, long legs casually outstretched, arms loosely crossed over him, surveying the room with ironic eyes.

They lingered on her; he gave her the faintest of smiles.

It was almost impossible to believe that this was the man who had said to her *I want you naked beneath me*.

Apart from the rush of blood to various places in her body when she thought it, she could almost imagine it hadn't happened at all.

He seemed so cool, so elegantly removed, distantly amused, a monarch for which the world conducted its amusements. He seemed entertained by the very notion of blindman's buff.

She could not for an instant imagine him consenting to totter about in a blindfold.

It was clear the rest of the *men* thought this was a marvelous idea.

Almost too good to be true, in fact.

"Silly!" Millicent corrected patiently. "One person

at a time wears the blindfold. And then he or she tries to tag the rest of us whilst we scatter out of the way and even tease and taunt the blindfolded person. And if we happen to be seized upon, the blindfolded person has to identify us."

"I think you can pay for something like this at the Velvet Glove," Colin volunteered. "You wear a blindfold while one of the girls there seizes your *mmmmph!*"

His wife, Madeline, also present, had reached over to pinch him hard.

It was the most peculiar sensation to be surrounded by people she'd known her entire life, knowing not one of them—certainly not her brothers or her parents, and she was certain not Harry, not Millicent, would ever have dreamed for an instant that Genevieve Eversea had sat astride the duke in the garden last night, and that she'd helped him unlace her gown so he could take her nipple into his mouth.

She ducked her head to hide her face. Perhaps a blindfold *would* help disguise the flushing, if she were in fact coerced into playing blindman's buff and she continued to have such thoughts.

She studiously avoided looking at him. She would not be sitting astride him again. Or beneath him. Or in any other place other than opposite him, preferably surrounded by other people as witnesses and deterrents.

She knew he had no such compunctions about avoiding looking at her, and he was doing it now.

Even as all the while the men, being men, were negotiating changes to the game amongst themselves to make it less tedious and more of a man's game, and suggestions flew thickly.

"This is the sort of game that would be vastly improved if we were all very, very drunk."

"Or if a wager is involved."

"Or if one of us volunteered to place an apple on his head and invited others to shoot it off."

The duke happened to address this directly to Ian.

It quelled momentarily the spirited negotiation.

"I'm not wearing the blindfold," Ian said very quickly.

Genevieve stifled a smile. She wondered if her brother's nerves would ever be the same after this week.

After a discussion as heated and orderly as a parliamentary debate, it was agreed that every time someone was tagged and incorrectly identified by the blind man he or she would be allowed to take a drink. The blindfolded person would *also* have to take a drink, because it was unanimously agreed that a drunken person staggering about blindfolded would be amusing. But the successfully identified people would be removed from the game, and therefore not allowed to drink at all, thereby solving the problem of cheating, and every identified person would need to give the blind man a shilling.

The clutching of clothing was to be permitted as a means of guessing identity; after a brief heated discussion, so was the feeling of faces. The feeling of anything else was deemed not cricket, after a giggled discussion.

And now that the game had been modified to the men's satisfaction, the first "blind man" was chosen: Millicent, by default.

Within an hour, the parlor was a giggling drunken melee.

Millicent was hopeless at guessing, but everyone enjoyed putting themselves in her way to be grabbed and released. So she won no shillings, but she failed at the guessing so many times that she was rapidly woozy from sherry and staggered into the corner and found herself unable to back out of it again, and had to be rescued and comforted and fed hot coffee by Mrs. Eversea.

Colin was next, and he cracked his knuckles, submitted to being blindfolded, and promptly proved to be an excellent and ruthless player. He knew the lay of the land (the parlor) well, he had long legs and a long reach, and an excellent sense of smell.

He caught hold of Ian's coat just as he tried to flee and gripped hard.

He leaned in for a sniff. "Smells like a horse's arse! I've got Ian!"

"No sniffing aloud! We never discussed sniffing! I cry foul!" Ian was outraged. "I'm not giving you a shilling!"

"Give him a shilling! It's not his fault you smell like a horse's arse!" Olivia leaped into the fray, loving a debate, any sort of debate.

"Are you confusing the word *smells* with the word *behaves*?" the duke asked from the sidelines, in all seriousness.

"*Smells!*" everyone chorused.

A heated vote later it was decided that whether or not Ian actually smelled like a horse's arse, Colin had indeed guessed correctly, so Ian handed over a shilling and shook hands with his brother.

It seemed Moncrieffe was simply biding his time,

watching the proceedings with Mr. and Mrs. Eversea, who refereed from the sidelines.

"I can hardly avoid smelling you. You're right in my face!" Colin explained by way of pacifying Ian.

When Colin was done, Harry took a turn being the blind man.

The blindfold, really a cravat, was wound 'round his eyes and he was spun 'round a half dozen times by an overzealous Ian and set free amongst the players. Genevieve reached out to touch him, realizing she had never done quite that before: held onto his arm outside of a waltz. Touched, let alone tasted, his skin. Clung to his coat, or slid a hand inside his shirt to touch his chest.

But he'd kissed her *hand*.

But before she knew it, Harry seized hold of Genevieve's arm.

"He's got one!" The enthusiastic cry went up.

She went silent.

Harry's face was flushed and merry beneath the blindfold. And for one breathless moment she held very still as Harry's fingers fumbled at the silk of her skirt, then glanced across her elbow, and decorously ventured no farther, though the rules, as such, would have allowed him to touch her face. Doubtless he knew he had a female in his clutches. It felt odd to feel his hand gripping her, the heat of it impersonal, questioning. She *ought* to feel breathless to be touched by him.

She looked down at his hand and wondered whether he'd touched a woman the way Moncrieffe had touched her.

She glanced over at Moncrieffe then.

But Moncrieffe's eyes were fixed to Harry's hand

with a cold, riveted fascination. As though it were a poisonous snake. He was so still he called to mind a big animal about to spring.

And so she stared at the duke, while Harry fumbled at her wrist.

"It's Olivia!" Harry guessed at last.

"Aww, Harry, you've gone and botched it, and now you have to give Genevieve a shilling. And she has to drink, and she's a raucous drunk!" Colin winked at her.

"I am nothing of the sort!" she denied as she laughed, pretending to be appalled.

"She can't even finish a dark at the Pig & Thistle," Harry defended proprietarily, with a swift glance at the duke. Abashed, perhaps, that he'd gotten it wrong.

"You should have sniffed her, Osborne!" Ian suggested.

Harry went scarlet. Thrust his hands into his coat pockets.

"I never thought you'd be slow enough to be caught by me," Harry explained to her, almost by way of apology.

You ought to have known me, she couldn't help but think. By the very temperature of my skin. By the texture of it. By my mere *presence.* You ought to have known.

"I'll give you a shilling later," he added, glumly.

"I forfeit my shilling," she forgave him gallantly. "And you can have my drink."

And then everyone turned when it was clear the duke had risen slowly to his feet portentously.

"I'll take the blindfold, Harry."

The amazement lasted a full second.

A second later, everyone was foxed enough to tease him, and a chorus went up. "Ooooooooooh, Your Grace, catch me if you can!"

Genevieve watched in fascination as they bound his eyes, which remained fixed on her until they disappeared from view behind the cravat blindfold.

To his credit, he was surprisingly game. He taunted the others back when they taunted him. He made sweeping snatches and missed as the others dodged his grasp.

She, like the others, circled and wove about him.

And with an unerring instinct that surprised her not in the least, his hand whipped out and deftly closed over her arm.

"He's got one of us!" Colin bellowed in mock-alarm.

She froze the moment his fingers landed on her.

His fingers traced the sleeve of her gown, to and fro, and he frowned as though genuinely puzzling out who might be wearing lutestring silk this evening.

And from the silk of her sleeves they skimmed the silk of her warm, bare arm. It was scarcely a touch, but it was as though he'd stroked her entire being awake. As though it were spring, for God's sake, gooseflesh bloomed everywhere on her skin. She wondered that the whole room couldn't see her nipples rise beneath the silk of her gown.

She was certain he already knew who it was and was merely prolonging it for the sheer devilish pleasure of it. She was half amused, half scandalized, and wholly aroused.

And casually, with every appearance of fumbling,

he had the sleeve between his fingers, then let his hand wander. He frowned in concentration as his fingers skimmed, lightly, lightly along the edge of her bodice, tantalizingly just above the swell of her bosom, tracing the satiny skin of collarbone, up to her throat, where her heart beat.

Lingered there, where it thump, thump, thumped.

And then, quite gratuitously, slid beneath her jaw, across her lips, and hovered.

I want you naked beneath me.

And lest she should harbor any doubts about whether that was what she wanted, too, he was showing her, with the most casual of touches, that her body now only felt truly alive when he was touching her, and reminding her of the promise of pleasure that lived in every cell of her.

Dear God.

"Why, it's Miss Genevieve Eversea," the duke said softly.

It was only then that the two of them noticed that the entire room had gone utterly silent. All those foxed eyes watched the duke and Genevieve, puzzled over whether they were actually seeing something untoward, or whether the duke was just being particularly, solicitously careful of Miss Eversea's person.

"Give him a shilling, Genny!" Millicent demanded cheerfully.

The duke untied his own blindfold and relinquished it to the next volunteer, which was Olivia.

He resumed his seat at the edge of the proceedings.

They both knew he'd won more than a game of blindman's buff.

* * *

And when Genevieve went up to her bedchamber later, it wasn't to sleep. It was to pace the carpet and to watch the clock. Out of spite, time slowed.

But it could not defy the turning of the earth, and midnight arrived.

And down the stairs she went.

She found him in the library this time. But he wasn't standing at the window gazing out into the darkness. He was standing near the doorway, watching the foyer for her, which made him almost too easy to see.

"Were you looking for me, Miss Eversea?" he asked softly.

She found she was so nervous she couldn't reply. She simply bit her lip.

He smiled at her. "Were you perhaps looking for scintillating conversation? A discussion about art? Of which I know a little more now than I did when I first arrived, I'll have you know."

"Do you?" She was too astonished to be irritated by his teasing.

"I spent an hour or so in here the other day. Quite a collection you have. I wanted to investigate it."

"Why?"

"Why did I spend time in the library? My curiosity was . . . aroused."

Something about the way he said "aroused" looped around her as surely as a warm arm around her waist. She was desperately nervous. But she was curiously thrilled to suspect he'd done it to learn more about her.

"Why was your curiosity aroused? What did you learn?"

"I read that Boticelli painted something called *Venus and Mars* in which Mars, poor devil, is nearly naked and flattened as though Venus has just thoroughly had her way with him, and that Veronese painted one in which, ironically, Venus is entirely naked and Mars is clothed. I prefer to imagine the latter."

"But you knew that already. Do you even *like* art?"

A hesitation. "I like cricket."

"And that's all?" She was smiling now.

"I like dogs. I like horses and hunting and fine wines. I like traveling. I like books about the natural sciences. I like chess and fishing and I like making money hand over fist and I enjoy making love to beautiful women. I like speaking with you. And looking at you. And I read a book about art and I tried to become interested in light and form and the like. I think I prefer to imagine the firelight playing about your form."

Genevieve had never heard a list she'd liked as much, though she could hardly say why. He was more of an artist in some ways than people who professed to enjoy it were, people like Harry—and even herself—who could not see without analyzing. It was in the things he saw and the words he chose to describe them and in how he touched . . . as he was touching her now.

Because almost before she realized it, the backs of his fingers were sliding against her throat. Where the skin was satiny smooth and pale.

"And so. Do you intend to have your way with me, Venus?" he murmured.

She still didn't have the vocabulary for this sort of sensual encounter. Her entire being seemed to rush the surface of her skin, greedily savoring his touch.

"I've told you what I want. How much do you want to know, Genevieve?" It sounded like a serious question. Also a fairly fraught one.

"How can I answer that honestly when I don't know how much there is to know?"

"You're not entirely naïve about . . . the process."

Very romantic. *The process.*

"It's impossible to remain naïve when I live with my brothers who will go on talking and surrounded by animals that will go on mating in front of one."

"You may be reassured to learn there's more to it than horses and dogs would have you believe."

"Given that my brothers have more than once risked their lives over it, I gleaned as much."

He was smiling at her. His hand never stopped moving over her skin, but he smiled. She'd noticed that he seemed to find her infinitely amusing, even, dare she say it, *enchanting*.

He liked *talking* to her.

This amused her.

"Oh, I can assure you women have risked their lives for it, too."

Her heart was walloping away in her throat, and she was certain he could feel it, as his fingers lingered there. Nearly everything on her body that could stand erect was erect now, clamoring for his touch. The hair on the back of her neck, her arms. Her nipples.

"Are you afraid, Genevieve?"

"No. You do enjoy saying my name."

"It has a lilt."

"I see." Her voice was faint.

"Because you should consider being a little afraid."

And now she was, just a little, despite the fact that his tone sounded entirely reasonable.

"Why?" she whispered.

"Once we've made love, you might find you won't be able to do without me."

Made love. Christ, but she was in over her head, but in the moment it seemed there was nothing she could do to extricate herself. She didn't want to extricate herself, and therein was an important clue to the fact that she'd lost her sanity. Or handed it over to him.

"Difficult to imagine." She'd meant to sound sarcastic. But her voice had begun to make a liar of her, because it had gone lulled, soft, trembling.

His turn to smile in the dark.

"I meant what I said in the garden," he gently warned.

"Have I been coy so far?"

"No," he said shortly.

Well, then. What next?

And there was a moment where she thought *he* might be at a loss. His hand paused against her throat. A moment passed where she was tempted to suggest, *Perhaps you're the one who's afraid*. But it wasn't the sort of thing one said to him, even in jest.

But she was wrong. He did know where to begin, and as usual, it seemed as natural as breathing, as an exhale. He'd *already* begun; as they'd spoken he'd drifted nearer and nearer, and now he brushed his lips between her eyes. Surprisingly tender, devastatingly sensual, light as a breath. And just like that she turned into smoke; she was indistinguishable from the night; she was only sensation.

She knew only relief that he was kissing her.

She closed her eyes, the better to savor the filaments of pleasure that shivered through her when his lips dragged to her temple, when his tongue delicately traced her ear, when his breath blew softly there, lips and tongue landed velvety hot on that vulnerable place hidden beneath her jaw, that place where her heart thumped madly, betraying everything she felt. She turned her face into his kisses, asking for and seeking pleasure as though it was her due, as though it was her natural place in the universe to accept it from him, as though she was made for only this. And his hands slid down, down, down, possessively over her breasts, over the curve of her waist, tracing lightly, lightly, the seam of her buttocks.

And when she was thoroughly sensually drugged, at last his mouth reached hers.

The kiss was rough.

His lips crushed hers; he took it deep instantly, his tongue sinewy and searching. Her tongue dueled with his as his arms wrapped 'round her back, one beneath her arse, and held her hard against him as her head bent from the force of it. As if he'd transferred the force of his passion to her she was now feverish, shaking. His body hummed with tension; she felt it in him, in how his ragged breath shook his body, when her hands landed on shirt, then slid down his hard body to claim the power over him she knew she possessed. She dragged her hands hard over his hard cock.

He hissed in a breath, and ducked his head. He

pressed his hips into her hands, grinding against her. She stroked him hard, feeling the enormous contours of him, growing harder, swelling beneath her touch. He took her face in his fingers and the words were gasps in her ear:

"Not here. Your bedchamber."

Chapter 20

A silent journey. Almost a dash. Short in duration, but long enough to allow her to change
her mind and call a halt to all of it. But she fumbled
at the doorknob with clumsy fingers, opened it, and
led him inside.

And even as she turned to lock it, he stood behind
her, his fingers deftly unlaced her, demonstrating
an unnerving facility with undressing women. He
spread the laces wide, and pushed her hair aside
to place a soft kiss at the nape of her neck, before
he urged the dress from her shoulders and gave
it a helpful downward tug to ensure it was soon a
rustling wad at her feet. She inhaled a shuddering
breath as the air of the room struck her bare skin
and gooseflesh rose over her. With trembling fingers, before she could think otherwise, she unfas-
tened her stays and dropped them to the floor. She'd,
in a fit of practicality, removed her stockings earlier.
They were silk and easily shredded.

"Turn. I want to look at you," he ordered.

"Why?"

"Because you are beautiful and I want you."

Dear God. He spoke like he moved: quick, purposeful. His delivery made everything sound true

and right and . . . *sensible*. Which was dangerous indeed, as the last thing this was meant to be was sensible. He'd undressed with startling alacrity while she was facing her door, and she hardly knew where to look first. She knew he meant it, because she could see in his fierce eyes and the swift rise and fall of his shoulders, and his hard cock, thick and large and curving up toward his belly, how much he did want her.

And he stared, drinking her in, and dear God, her knees went weaker still at the look in his eyes.

She wanted to tell him, too, that he was beautiful, but it wasn't quite the right word. It seemed inadequate and perhaps not exactly true. He was overwhelmingly new to her, alien, and astoundingly . . . *male* . . . his skin very fair, his body spare, all hard, lean muscle, his chest furred with dark hair, a trail of it following the seam of his ribs to where his cock curved upward against his belly up from its nest of curling hair. His small, hard buttocks were almost comically white and muscular. She saw a few scars scattered over him.

He saved her from the onslaught of sensations and impressions and from having to make a statement when he pulled her against his bare body.

The feeling of his skin against hers, her hard nipples brushing his, was extraordinary; his skin was hot; he smelled wonderful and strange, of smoke and musk and something she was sure was uniquely his.

He didn't want coy. She'd claimed she wasn't. And yet it was counter to her nature to let momentum take her, to surrender. She struggled with it, and he felt the tension in her body.

"It's all right," he murmured into her ear, his breath, his voice, erotic, so persuasive, the voice of ultimate safety and ultimate danger. "I have you. *Shhh*, now, Genevieve."

He teased her breasts with his fingers, savoring their softness, watching her head tip back when he was at first gentle with them, then demandingly palming her nipples. He placed a kiss at the base of her throat, and began to slide down the length of her body, stopping to nip, then suck at, each nipple, and she twined her fingers in his hair.

But he had a destination. He was dragging kisses down the length of her body, down the seam between her ribs, his hot hands fanning over her back, to cup her buttocks, to drag up the downy fine hairs along her thighs, gently stroking the tender skin between them, urging them, she realized, apart, apart, apart. And she had no time for shock or shame before his tongue delved between her legs, where she was hot and slick and aching.

She jerked. It was a lightning strike of unadulterated bliss through her body.

"Oh, God . . . it's . . ."

"It's Veronese."

She gave a choked laugh. He *would* be witty now.

"Never say I'm not a lover of art." He blew softly, and then his tongue stroked again.

She swore a word she wasn't even certain she'd known.

"Tell me, is it good?" he murmured.

Was it *good*? She'd no words for what it was, and she didn't want to narrate.

"Tell me." He sucked gently, his hands stroking, stroking her thighs.

"Oh God. *Too* good . . . harder . . ."

How did she know she wanted "harder"? But she knew. She gripped his shoulders. Hard, strong, solid, necessary when the world around her was dissolving into spangled heat. She found herself arching against him as his tongue, like hot, muscular satin, stroked hard where she was slick and aching, and his fingers followed with deft and skillful strokes.

"*Oh, God . . . Help me . . .*"

Help me? That seemed absurd. But she was afraid; she was hurtling toward a precipice over which lurked something extraordinary. She was comprised only of need.

He knew. "Soon," he reassured her.

But what did that *mean*?

Salvation was not too strong a word for what she needed. It built in urgency, until she was shamelessly rippling into his caress, her body abetting him. The universe narrowed to a single point of pleasure.

Suddenly she felt the edge of the bed against the back of her knees; his hands eased her backward in his arms. She tipped. Her eyes were closed. The counterpane scratched against her bare back. He pressed her thighs far, far apart. She was wide open to him now, and his muscular, brilliant tongue delved deeper, found an indescribable rhythm and stroked her, and her body colluded until they found precisely the rhythm she needed. Her fists knotted the counterpane, and she arched into him, rippling with the untenable pleasure. She hissed her breath through her teeth. She was hot or she was cold or there was some other word that meant both; all she knew was that her skin stung as if every cell of it was alive and singing hallelujah, and that pleasure was a river roaring through her, threatening the very seams of her being. Building, building.

And bliss crashed over with a white burst behind her eyes.

It whipped her body upward and tore a silent scream from her, and her skin was all over stars. She shook and shook beneath him.

"Alex. . . ."

"Hold on to me, love."

Love?

Her body was limp and heaving from the extraordinary release, but he was brisk. She opened her eyes to find his hands propping him up on either side of her. He raised his long body up, and with one hand he positioned his cock and guided himself in.

No preamble. She gasped. There was a bite of quick pain. And he thrust past her resistance, into her snug heat, deeply, inexorably joining himself to her.

"Genevieve." His voice was a ragged prayer. His chest swayed shallowly. "I . . ."

He'd lost his words.

She understood.

He hovered on strong arms over her, his eyes burning into hers, allowing her to adjust to the feel of him inside her. Extraordinary to be joined like this with him, to be so dominated, and yet to possess the power. She slid her hands wonderingly over his hard chest, and he closed his eyes to her touch. He was slick with perspiration, and she touched her tongue to his nipple. His lungs bellowed in and out. She watched his lashes shiver on his cheeks.

He opened his eyes again. The muscles of his

back, his arms, quivered. His breath shuddered hotly over her.

"I want to go slow for you. I don't think I can."

She dragged a hand over his cheek and said all she knew. "I want you."

And it was these words that loosed the tether on his control.

This. This is what my body is made for.

It was languid at first. He'd tried, at least, for a measure of finesse. He sank into her and pulled slowly back, allowing her to feel every inch of him again, and then again. She grew accustomed to the remarkable feel of him, and she felt, extraordinarily, an echo of the need he'd banked earlier rising, rising in her.

"*Alex . . .*" she whispered. A question. A plea.

He groaned softly and swore.

"The way you feel, Genevieve . . . Mother of God . . ."

His pleasure was hers, the power she had to give him pleasure excited her unbearably. Instinctively she enfolded him, locked her legs around his back, inviting him deeper still, arching up to meet him as he sank into her again.

The cords of his neck were taut. He dipped to kiss her; she parted her lips and took his tongue to twine it with hers; their mouths melded, carnal and savage and sweet. Their teeth clashed. And as he thrust she found her head thrashing from him, because she knew she would come again.

And this made him wild.

And then she felt it when it was no longer within his control. His white hips drummed, the tempo grew ever swifter. She arched to meet him, drawing hot breaths in. She clutched his shoulders, her nails dragging over his biceps, and whimpered his name, for as their bodies clashed hard another release came from nowhere and she growled like a feral thing, thumping his back with her fists as the rush of pleasure crashed through her, bucking from it, and he pounded into her until he swore hoarsely and pulled from her body with a ragged groan.

His release wracked him, shook his big body like a rag hard as he spilled over her belly.

He lowered himself over her gently like one killed.

She held on to him, and he to her, until their breathing steadied.

She stroked his hair, realizing this was the first time she'd ever seen him truly peaceful, and wondering why his peace was hers.

"Well," he murmured, finally. "Well, well, well."

That's exactly how she felt. Very, very well.

She was still on a cloud somewhere, except that the cloud was her bed, and the only thing anchoring her to earth was the body of the warm, sweaty man next to her, upon whose muscular arm her head now rested, and whose heavy thigh was now covering hers. He was so fair. His calves were slim and hard and elegantly muscled and she knew an impulse to nibble on one. She traced a finger around his nipple, just because it was a small round thing, a leathery little coin. It ruched like her own did.

"That's excellent," he murmured huskily, "what you're doing, but I can't possibly accommodate you again yet. Give me at least a minute or two. I'm not a man of twenty years."

"Does it matter? Your age?"

"It does indeed. A bit." He didn't sound at all rueful about it.

Which meant Harry would be hard within minutes of such a romp, apparently. The things she was learning . . .

"I'll wait," she allowed magnanimously.

He laughed softly, and his chest jumped beneath her cheek.

"Genevieve . . ." he drawled after a moment.

And said nothing else.

She turned to him quizzically.

He lifted his head up a bit to look at her. "Oh. That's all. Just 'Genevieve.' I just think from now on I'll use your name as an exclamation of extreme satisfaction. When things are going very well I'll shout '*Genevieve!*' In lieu of hallelujah. Or if someone says, 'Finally we should have fine weather after days of rain,' I'll say, 'Well, Genevieve!' "

He laughed, and she was blushing.

For heaven's sake, *now* she was blushing?

She'd been divested of her virginity officially, though she knew vigorous horseback riding and the like could occasionally do that rather *unofficially* to a woman. She'd thought it would be profound. She hadn't considered how natural it might feel. She'd never suspected what splendid humor a bout of lovemaking would leave her in, or that lying with a naked man in its wake would seem entirely reasonable. She'd heard other women complain euphemistically about it.

She had no complaints.

Pleasure for the sake of pleasure. Passion for passion's sake.

A relinquishing of control in order to gain control and power.

How right he had been. She'd thought it had been the talk of the seducer. Of course it had been, but he hadn't lied.

"Moncrieffe . . ."

"Alex."

"Alex then . . ." She paused. "What truly became of your wife?"

"Are you wondering whether I poisoned her? Don't you think I did?"

"Of course you didn't. But the rumor didn't spring from nowhere."

"You *are* clever." He sighed contentedly.

"Yes."

He was quiet a moment, perhaps pondering where to begin, or remembering the moment of his wife's death. Perhaps she oughtn't have asked.

"She died eating oysters. The doctor said her body reacted badly to them. It was the first time she'd eaten any, and it happens in that way for very few people. There was naught we could do . . . she rather suffocated, I suppose you could say. It interfered with her breathing, until she no longer could. It happened quickly, and it was horrible."

Oh, dear God.

He must have felt her tense. "Are you sorry you asked?"

"I'm sorry it happened," she said, her throat thick with the truth of those words.

He was quiet for a very long time.

"So am I."

Which she sensed didn't begin to encompass how he felt, but he'd always managed to convey a universe of meaning in whatever few words he chose to use.

She didn't want to know more, and yet she did. Was he still sorry? Was that what had made him . . . well, the man everyone saw today?

"I didn't know what was happening to her at the time," he said softly, suddenly.

"Were you afraid?"

He thought about this, too. She liked this. The talking, the thoughtfulness, the carefulness with which he entrusted her with his memories.

"I will say this to you: I have been shot in war and in duels. I have been cornered by knife-wielding thugs. I've been kicked by angry horses and I've had vases hurled at me by angry mistresses. But I . . ." He inhaled a sound, then exhaled one, ruefully almost defeated. But his fingers trailed over her spine, as if he found comfort in the warm reality of her. ". . . I had never, never been more afraid."

What she felt was a peculiar anger that the world should ever have treated him thus.

"You were afraid because there was naught you could do for her. And you could only watch her suffer."

She thought his silence was her answer.

Until he confirmed, "Naught."

The darkest, bleakest syllable she had perhaps ever heard in her life.

"It was like the day we waited for word of Colin's death. We did everything we could to save him, to defend him, and still we knew he was going to die.

One never feels more like a speck upon the breast of the universe in those moments."

She felt his finger still on her a moment, as if he was taking it in. She didn't want him to stop stroking.

"It was the worst day of my life. Worse than the day my son died."

Chapter 21

S he thought for a moment he hadn't meant to say it. Because he stilled again, as though he'd surprised himself.

"You had a son?" she said softly.

He spoke to the ceiling, but he stroked her arm, finding comfort in the aliveness of her.

"He was just a baby. He was about . . . this big." He curved his arm in the shape of a baby, and all at once she could see him holding the tiny thing in one arm, and looking down at it, and imagine how he must have felt to be a father.

It knocked the breath from her completely.

"Could fit him in the crook of an arm. He lived a few months. A fever took him."

His voice was even, very contained. The tone drew boundaries around the words and topic and urged caution: *This is all I will say.* It was a perilous thing to be a baby in their times; nearly every family she knew had buried a little one too soon. Her own included. There was a gravestone in the churchyard over a brother she'd never known.

"What was his name?" she asked, careful not to ask too gently.

"Gilles. A rather ambitious name for a baby, don't

you think? Gillyflower, she'd called him." He smiled
faintly. His beard was starting up, she noticed. This
seemed intolerably poignant, the rakishly disreputable shadow of his whiskers juxtaposed with talk
of losing a baby. "He died just a few months before
she did."

She thought her own heart would break. *Gillyflower*. He'd lost a wife and a baby in the space of a
few months.

"What did *you* call him?"

He looked at her. "Gilles," he said sternly.

"Of course," she said. No Gillyflower nonsense
for him.

But then he noticed she was studying him.

"Don't think I don't know what you're thinking.
Your eyes have gone all limpid and terribly kind."

Had they? "What am I thinking?"

"That I've gone off the notion of love altogether
due to an irretrievably broken heart, and that it has
made me a bitter hard man out for vengeance. That
I've been nursing devastation all this time. But it isn't
like that, you know. Not altogether."

Drat. She *had* been rather thinking that. "Everyone thinks you poisoned her."

"I doubt anyone really thinks that. They just enjoy
saying it. People like to be frightened and they like
to make myths. Who am I to deprive them of that
pleasure?"

"Don't you mind? Couldn't you put a stop to it?"
She was indignant on his behalf.

"What could I have done? It's absurd to defend
something that cannot be proven. I've never been a
merry sort though I'm hardly truly dour. And after

she died I quite simply wanted to be alone. I grieved. The gossip suited me, and it suited me to be fearsome, because then a path was cleared away from me. No one bothered me which meant I didn't need to deflect pity, which I can't abide. And then . . . well, I quite grew to like it, frankly. I can see from your expression you were hoping for a different answer."

He, as usual, had laid waste to preconceived notions.

"I have a certain mystique. I've a good deal of influence and money. One or two friends who aren't servants." He smiled again, dryly.

"But nobody likes you." She meant nobody in the *ton*, she supposed. This was the accepted wisdom.

"Oh, 'nobody' is an exaggeration. You do."

She smiled slowly. This amused her. As if *she* was enough. The Everseas were astonishingly wealthy and possessed significant influence, as well. But they weren't dukes, and she was a youngest daughter.

Though the King did like to proffer titles to the Everseas and Redmonds and then snatch them away, as he'd just done when he'd styled the new Earl of Ardmay. The King derived perverse entertainment from watching the Everseas and Redmonds genteelly battle for prestige the way two cats danced for a dangled kipper.

"Not everyone is you, Genevieve. And *needs* to be liked. Or to be tremendously careful about what they say or do. Controlling yourself isn't going to control the world around you."

This turned her smile into a frown.

"Is *this* careful?" She swept a hand over their nude abandon.

"No, but you've me to thank for it. It isn't something *you* would have considered . . . fomenting, shall we say. From a kiss on the hand."

Good heavens, but she was sorry she'd ever told him about the kiss on the hand.

"But I came to find *you*."

He smiled a slow, lazy, satisfied smile. "So you did."

They were quiet for a moment.

"Do you think me cold?" he asked suddenly. It sounded like a serious question.

Did he really care? How could a man who turned her into flame be cold? But she did give it some thought. She found his unapologetic honesty compelling, intimidating, hard. Like breathing the cleanest cold air. Tremendously, strangely freeing.

She laid her hand flat over his chest. Crisp curling hair, warm skin stretched over hard muscle, a few scars where war and life had got to him, a heart that thumped beneath her hand, a body that stirred and fiercely demanded when she touched him, a heart that had loved unequivocally, had been battered by loss. He did everything passionately, with single-minded intent. He was a man one could trust with one's life if he was loyal to you. A man to fear if he was not.

"No. Not cold at all."

He surprised her. Gently, he laid his hand over hers.

Your hand is unconscionably soft, Miss Eversea.

For a moment, his chest rose and fell beneath her hand. It felt almost more intimate than the lovemaking itself, and she was uncertain whether to take it away, or whether she wanted to. It was this push-

and-pull she'd felt from the moment she'd met him.

What was he thinking?

Had he lain just like this alongside his wife?

"And I didn't turn to stone overnight. I've always been rather stubborn and I'm unlikely to change. There's naught wrong with money, with power, or with a little fear inspired by respect or respect inspired by fear. I'm not a very nice man, but I don't care. I don't have to care." He stretched luxuriously, taking his hand away from hers. "I'm a duke."

This made her smile. And shake her head.

"As for everything else said about you . . . have you dueled?"

"Yes."

She propped herself on her elbow and looked down, aghast.

"Oh, now. One can hardly reach adulthood without fighting a duel!"

"One *can*," she objected. "Harry can."

"Oh, *Harry* can," he repeated, rolling his eyes.

More silence.

She wondered at the etiquette of mentioning Harry while she was stretched alongside another man. But somehow she didn't suppose this lovemaking was a betrayal of Harry, given that Harry intended to betroth himself to another woman.

Until he came to his senses, of course. Which he seemed to be doing. As the man next to her was helping Harry to see her in the necessary light.

And in this she fancied herself very modern. It wasn't a notion she would ever have entertained before the appearance of the duke. Love and desire do not necessarily always coincide, he'd said, and as it turned out, it was true.

"Was she beautiful?" She meant his wife.

"Was she *beautiful*?" He repeated this question almost scornfully, sounding amused. As though he'd expected it. He shook his head. "How like a woman to ask that question! I don't know."

"You don't know! But you were married to her!"

He shifted away from her, very, very subtly. "That is to say, I suppose she was. Of course she was. Ah, Miss Eversea." He was laughing at her again when he glanced up and saw her expression. "So sorry to disappoint you, but you want to know the color of her eyes and hair and all about her ruby lips and the like and because you're a woman you want to know whether you are more beautiful. *I* found her beautiful, and that's all that matters. And it's less about how she appeared. Because that's all a bit misty for me now, and her miniature doesn't do her justice. Does anyone's miniature do them justice?"

She shook her head somberly.

"It's everything she . . . well, everything she was."

He said it evenly, but his voice went quieter and he turned over onto his back. He didn't want to look at her when he said these things, apparently.

And she was coming to know that when things were important he didn't trust his eyes not to reveal it. He looked away instead.

Control, indeed.

She would honor it.

"Beauty has so much less to do with that than women know. With curly hair and the like," he said suddenly. He glanced sideways at her; the corner of his mouth twitched wickedly, and he got hold of one strand of her stubbornly straight hair and drew it out, pensively. "The greatest pleasure of my life was knowing I kept her safe and happy while she lived. I looked at her and thought 'beautiful,' and likely I would have thought the very same thing when we were seventy. But it's all quite distant now."

He interpreted her silence as confusion or skepticism. She was, in fact, mulling what he'd said.

"Truly," he insisted.

She reflected on men. "Did you love her?"

"I wonder if Harry enjoys being interrogated. He is welcome to you, if so. *Yes.* I loved her."

"Did you know straightaway?"

A curious hesitation. "Yes."

"And Lady Abigail . . ."

"Well, yes. If you're going to ask all of the same questions, I do believe she's beautiful. I'd planned to do my best to love her. And that's all one can really do. I shall find someone else," he said on a yawn. "Oh, perhaps Millicent, once Harry comes to his senses and discovers his devotion is all to you."

She was aghast on his behalf.

"That's all you can really *do*? Love selects you, Moncrieffe, not the other way around. Harry is my best friend, and I've loved him for as long as I've known the meaning of love, from the moment we've met. I cannot imagine life without him. What more can I ask from happiness?"

"As long as you've known the meaning of love," he repeated slowly, as if she amused him. "What more can you ask, indeed. Since you're an expert on what it is to love. I don't imagine *passion* ought to play a role in a marriage." He was mocking her. He drew a gently, possessive, also somewhat mocking finger down the inside of her arm, along the faintest blue vein, just to watch the gooseflesh rise.

"I'm certain he's passionate. He definitely expresses himself passionately with regards to art and poetry."

"And you know all of that from a kiss on the *hand*. And vehement conversations about Italian artists."

"It was an excellent kiss." It was barely a kiss, she now knew. Still, she'd cherished it for a very long time and wasn't about to relinquish the notion now.

"How do you know you didn't like that kiss simply because you like to be kissed?"

Well. Another excellent question.

"I thought all men arrived in the world with . . . this sort of knowledge." She swept a hand about their bodies again. "Or perhaps . . . oh, learned it at White's."

His expression was comically aghast.

"My dear, you're the beneficiary of much of *my* knowledge, and I can assure you that you do not want to know how I arrived by it, as it was hardly remotely as genteel as White's. Not all of my teachers, shall we say, would be accepted into polite society. Harry is far too decent a lad to have . . . availed himself of the same teachers."

He was talking about whores, she was certain. Or actresses.

Shocking.

Intriguing.

But his voice had become promisingly low and pensive, and on the word "teachers" he tipped on his side. Their faces were inches apart now, and he traced her lips with one finger, lightly, lightly, then placed his lips there as if he'd drawn them into being. Softly his fingers skimmed up her rib cage to her breasts. He cupped each of them in his hands, and ducked his head to close his lips over her nipple, and gently, gently suck.

"*God*," she murmured.

"Do you want me again, Genevieve?"

She couldn't speak. Of course she did. She just didn't want to *discuss* it.

"You will," he promised on a whisper.

She wrapped her arms around him the better to hold him close as he came for a kiss. All the textures of his mouth were compelling; he knew so many ways to kiss, and each of them ultimately devastated her. She felt his cock swelling and growing harder, nestling against her belly, and this gratified and excited her, because he'd had various exotic teachers and yet he wanted *her* very, very much. She threw a leg over him to press her body against him. She was already wet with wanting.

Yes, she wanted him. She was a wanton, apparently.

"Wait." He tipped her over onto her back, rose up over her, and she watched as his beautiful body rose up and covered her. She arched up, opened her legs to accommodate him, as he guided himself into her. So thick and hard and shockingly masculine.

She gasped when he was deeply seated.

But then he lowered himself over her and with languid, graceful ease rolled the two of them so that they faced each other. And side by side, legs entangled, he moved inside her. His hips rocked almost languorously; they rippled together like a flame. Their eyes locked. Their mouths met and parted, caressed and left each other in distraction, as pleasure banked in each.

"I want to watch you come," he whispered

against her mouth. "I want you to watch me come."

It was so coarse and shockingly intimate, and it ought to have appalled her, she supposed, but it was frantically erotic.

She understood his temptation to turn away when he revealed something important, for she felt—she knew—he could see right through her, had penetrated her body and her mind if not her heart. She felt exposed, raw. But she bravely kept her eyes open; she was both lost and found in the soft, burning depths of his eyes. But their mingled breath became a low roar as release came upon them. His eyes became brilliant and intent and inwardly focused; he was lost to her. She closed hers as her head thrashed back, because she only wanted to feel what was coming upon her, not see, not think. An impulse entirely new. And she was keening from the urgent press of her release, which came from everywhere in her body, roared toward escape like a molten river. He knew his was upon him, too. She was arching against him, shattering into bliss and he drew himself from her body with a gasp.

He came against her belly, his release wracking him almost brutally, her name—his new hallelujah—on his lips.

The hands of the clock were on the one and the six. His eyes were closed. Hers were open. She watched his eyelashes shuddering. He looked a decade younger and limp with bliss.

"The thing is, now you expect it to be like this always," he said suddenly.

Like "this." Like exiting your body prematurely for Heaven and crashing back to the earth like a falling star, brilliant and spent.

The clock face was neatly divided by the gold hands now. He would leave soon.

And she thought she didn't need to ask what time of night his wife and baby had died. She was almost certain she knew the answer.

"Isn't it?" she whispered.

She was suddenly afraid.

He inhaled and folded his arms behind his head, and pressed it into the pillow, and sighed out a breath. She looked into his furry armpit, that achingly splendid curve of his bicep, and marveled at herself for the intimate knowledge she now possessed of him, and how little shame she felt about it. He was quiet, eyes open now and aimed at the ceiling, where the shadows of the fire fitfully danced.

And then he tipped over on his side and looked down at her, frowning slightly, as though she were an arithmetic problem.

She was tempted to reach out and gently smooth out the lines around his eyes, wondering if sadness or squinting into the sun or just the inevitable process of growing older had caused them.

She pictured his arm bent in the shape of a baby.

She felt the pain of his loss inside her like a savage hook. She wanted to reach into him and take it out, as though it were shrapnel. But the pain was old to him, and somehow it had become a part of him. He could bear it and speak of it. It had shaped him; he had accommodated it. He had loved and he had lost and it had made him who he was.

But it was new to her. She wanted to cry for him, because she was truly sorry he'd known any pain at all, and she was angry, too, and didn't know why. Life was, quite simply, unfair. It killed wives and babies, it made young men long to propose to the wrong women.

A line for his wife, a line for his baby, and a line for . . .

Pure contrariness.

The ones that appeared about his mouth when he smiled she liked very much.

She would never say this to him aloud. At least not yet. But she suspected he was wrong about love. Very wrong. He had loved truly and he had suffered pain. In deciding to marry Lady Abigail he'd been protecting himself against that sort of pain again, for he hadn't loved her. And in making love to someone he desired but didn't love, someone who in fact loved someone else, he was doing precisely the same thing.

They found forgetfulness together. Passion had its uses.

Would she become like him, she wondered, should Harry in fact propose to Millicent? Avoiding love in order to avoid pain?

"No," he said finally. He was almost whispering, too. "It *isn't* always like this."

He wasn't smiling now.

"You're telling me the truth?"

A *little* smile now. And the lines. "I'm telling you the truth."

Her turn to turn over and cross her hands behind her head. "Hmm."

"Hmm, indeed."

"And this is good?"

"Can you imagine it ever being better?"

This was a very unnerving question, indeed. She

could not. She mulled it, troubled, but didn't answer. She was too drowsy and thoughtful.

"I can assure you it . . . it has never been like this," she thought she heard him say, as sleep closed in on her.

And at some point it claimed her fully, because she awoke before dawn in a chilled room beneath the blankets, and he was of course gone.

And on his way back to his bedchamber, Moncrieffe quietly passed Ian's room. He paused.

And out of pure deviltry, he gave the door one hard thump with his fist.

He heard a tremendous crashing sound and a great thud, as though Ian had leaped out of his skin and fallen out of bed.

But Alex was back in his room even before Ian reached the doorknob of his.

But when he got there, he stared at the bed, and found he couldn't yet get into it.

He ought to have been exhausted by the lovemaking. He ought to have lost consciousness the moment his head pressed against his pillow. But he was enervated and stunningly alive and afraid. He wanted a cigar, because he was in need of the obscuring comfort of a cloud of smoke, and he wanted to think, and he needed something to do with his hands.

So he wandered back down to the library, poured himself a drink, clipped a cigar and lit it.

He sucked it into life, settled onto the settee, sorted through the variety emotions that paraded by for his consideration, and admitted something to himself. The most compelling of them was fear.

He was afraid.

Again.

He breathed in, and sighed out, but that didn't help.

He *was* afraid of very little, as he'd explained to Genevieve. Men confident in their skills with weaponry and with women had very little to fear. He possessed wealth and power and security. He'd known loss and lived through it, though it had turned him into a sort of sentry, patrolling the perimeters of whatever small world he happened to be visiting at the moment until the hour of midnight, the hour when things were taken from him, passed. Every night.

And he could still scarcely believe he'd told her about his wife, about Gilles, both of whom were secrets and yet not really. But then one's defenses tend to get pummeled during lovemaking. And he was glad he had told her.

But here was the thing he feared: he wanted to talk to her every day. He wanted to make love to her every night. He wanted to know every curve and angle of her body, every hollow, every freckle, every scar. He'd never known a more clawing hunger for a woman's body, and it shocked him, and he was clever enough to know it had only a little to do with her body. An incinerating, honest passion, the equal of his, was only the expression of who she truly was.

He wanted to know all of her thoughts. He wanted to tell her . . . well, most of his. He would ask nothing else from life if he would be allowed to protect and cherish her for the rest of his.

And yet he knew she hadn't a clue, really, about

what he felt. She was still deciding what she thought love meant. She was convinced it meant Harry. And thinking it meant Harry and believing it amounted to the same thing.

The irony was exquisite.

He blew a perfect ring of smoke and closed his eyes. *Beautiful.*

He snorted. He wished for access to all the world's languages at once, for then he would have a better word for how he felt and what she was. But he re-lived again the feel of her falling apart in his arms, the feel of her body welcoming his into it, and how he felt like a simpleton, entirely new and blessed, and he knew *beautiful* would have to do.

How about that? He'd been mastered at his own game. He was man enough to admit it. Men truly were simpletons.

How had it happened?

Like the measles, love is most dangerous when it comes late in life.

George Gordon, Lord Byron, had said that, and it was a dire day indeed when he found wisdom in the words of that bloody fool. But he understood. Before he'd been too young to really understand; he'd loved and he'd married as a young man will. But now he understood why someone would write things like "she walked in beauty like the night" and so forth. Because poetry was a barrier against raw emotions. It distilled them into bearable music, allowed one to accommodate them a little at a time.

Because he'd known the sort of loss that sent a man spiraling into nothingness as surely as if he'd been dropped out of the sky. He'd felt the wind of the abyss whistling behind him.

And so of course he was afraid.

Because he was staring down yet another loss.

But that didn't mean he was a coward.

When he returned to his room he still didn't sleep. For he knew what he would do next, and soon.

And no man slept the night before that sort of thing.

Chapter 22

Today the group of them were to walk out to the ruins for sketching. The day obliged them with sunny skies dotted all over with cottony clouds, but shawls were tugged closer and the wind whipped at coattails and once even took away Harry's hat, which he'd had to chase nearly a mile, and which made everyone guffaw.

"Shoot it, Harry! It wants to get away!" Millicent called.

Genevieve pondered the internal chaos of everyone present. Apart, that was, from Millicent, who was strolling as innocently as usual alongside Harry once he caught his hat. She was excited about an opportunity to draw waterfowl, for she now embraced the opportunity to capture what she saw as the darker side of nature.

The duke had managed to subtly separate Genevieve from the rest of the crowd by striding on a little too rapidly, as usual, as though reaching the ruins were a matter of great urgency. She suspected he could not care in the least about the ruins.

She watched his seven-league legs cover the ground, and imagined him over her last night, his legs wrapped 'round hers, his lean hips plunging himself into her again and again—

She needed to stop as the blood rushed to her head, and then she'd realized she was all but dashing to catch him, as though she'd become an extension of him.

The soreness between her legs was a delicious reminder of the wildness, and try as she might—she thought she should at least try—she could not regret it.

Or feel guilty about it. She'd done it for herself; she had not been seduced, so much as she'd participated in a new world of pleasure.

And she should feel wicked. But she felt powerful. That she should know such pleasure, do something so *incredible*, made it perversely seem not only entirely possible, but likely, that Harry would realize he loved her and muster the courage to do what was right, which was, of course, propose to her.

She realized the duke hadn't said a thing for a few minutes.

And that's when she was worried *he'd* regretted everything.

She spent a few moments worrying so deeply about this that when he did speak he was startling as a thunderclap. As though the words had broken the surface of the day.

"Here is what I am thinking, Genevieve."

He stopped abruptly and turned and stood.

So she stopped, too.

But . . . something was different about him. A stillness. A carefulness. Was he . . . Was he *nervous*? Surely not. Was he *angry*? Perhaps.

He looked as though he hadn't slept. He had faint

gray shadows beneath his eyes, whereas she had slept deeper and more dreamlessly than ever before.

"Are you unwell?" she tried.

"Un—" This for some reason seemed to astonish him. He blinked. "No." He frowned.

"But . . . is something amiss?"

"No."

"But you look so—"

"Hush," he said.

She was startled to be shushed by him, and not a little affronted. Confused, she obediently pressed her lips closed and folded her hands in a parody of schoolgirl obedience and waited. Glowering.

But it was a few seconds more before he finally spoke. He seemed to be listening to a rush of thoughts in his head.

"We could marry," were the words he finally produced.

Oh.

The breath went out of her in a gust.

"Each other," he clarified, when it seemed she would never say anything. Would just stare.

He watched her intently. The morning sun landed directly on his face. He looked his age this morning, weary.

She darted a look up the road, as though she wished she could flee in that direction. Perhaps it was an idle suggestion, a sudden inspiration, his words. Not an actual proposal. Her hands folded and unfolded as she studied him.

"I should like to marry *you*, Genevieve," he clarified then.

And yet she still couldn't read his face.

Oh dear God. Now she feared it *was* a proposal.

Though he'd more expressed a preference than asked for her hand in marriage.

Her first thought immediately thereafter was: *I will never, ever receive a proper marriage proposal.*

The second was a terrible feeling that every time a man spoke of marriage she would be rendered mute.

"Do you need me to say it in yet another way?" Tersely and a bit ironic now.

But of course he was as dignified as ever. No blotchy blushing or stammering for him. No fussing with leaves or buttons. But he was watching her carefully. And he was so motionless. All the fierceness was in his eyes. And because now she knew that when tempests of emotion moved inside him he held very still, she wanted to touch him to soothe him.

And she didn't want to touch him this way because she was suddenly afraid.

I don't love him.

He doesn't love me.

Ah, but that was likely why he'd proposed. She'd come to that realization last night.

He saw in her protection from the ultimate hurt, the ultimate risk.

"But . . . we don't love each other," she pointed out. Practically, she thought.

His head went a little. Perhaps acknowledging this.

"And I love Harry, as you know."

There was a moment of silence.

"Of course," he said.

"And I'm not your sort, as you mentioned before. Too clever."

Another hesitation. She was terribly worried he

was hurt, and yet this seemed unlikely. Possibly his *pride* was hurt.

"Not my sort," he repeated slowly, privately amused at something. "Answer me this, Genevieve. Do you suppose you *felt* like my sort the night before last?"

Felt. Last night. Nude, sweat, sucking, tasting, clawing, kissing. Oh God. Just thinking of it made her glance at his hands and lips and he knew, knew what she was thinking, and his pupils flared hotly. He seemed almost angry.

"That's different," she said faintly.

"Oh?" Eyebrow up. Why, why, *why* didn't he ever blush?

"You said as much yourself," she protested breathlessly, confused now, and panicking a little, her face warm. Why had she thought she understood men? She knew nothing, nothing at all about them.

Why did he have to *ruin* it?

"So I did," he humored, softly. His voice was strangely frayed. "Nevertheless, we could do worse than each other."

Flattering.

She hesitated. Frantically searching his face for a clue to what he was *truly* thinking or feeling. Odd, she'd gone from feeling intimacy, from feeling known and possessed, to feeling utterly at sea. She hadn't the faintest idea what to say.

"Of course we could do worse," she soothed.

A warning flicker crossed his face. He was, as usual, intolerant of being pacified.

"But don't you want better for yourself, Moncrieffe? Shouldn't you want to be in love?"

He didn't quite scowl. But she could see the tightening of his jaw, the tightening of his lips, and oh, *splendid*, now he was getting angry.

"What is the primary objection? Would you prefer that I'd kissed your *hand*?"

She understood why one would restrict kissing to the hand. Perhaps Harry was simply far more sensible. Kissing lips led to boundless indiscretions and complexities.

"No! You know that I . . . You *know* what I want. It's still possible. And . . . Well . . . I . . ."

What she wanted was for things to remain precisely as they had been. She wanted their plan to remain intact and unchanged. She wanted to make love to him at night and pursue Harry during the day.

"I like things the way they are."

He turned and began walking onward. One step, two steps, three steps.

She followed. At first.

Until she realized she was doing what amounted to running in order to catch up with him. He blazed down the lane, and no matter how she tried she would never reach him unless she ran, frantically. She would *not* chase him. She would *not* indulge his childishness. But watching him, she had a strange panicky sense that he would keep moving and moving and eventually disappear. Like a terrible dream, in which no matter how close she came he would forever be just out of reach.

And then she wondered if he was in fact running *away* from her. The dangerous duke. Away from *her*? She halted.

"I'd rather not run or shout at your back, if it's all the same to you. If we're to have a conversation."

Admirable sarcasm. It was his siren song, sarcasm. Odd, but she so seldom spoke acerbically to anyone until he'd come along. He did bring out all of her finer qualities.

He stopped abruptly. Then turned around, and she thought she saw bemusement flash over his face when he realized how far behind him she now was.

She remained dutifully motionless and waited for him to come all the way back to her.

And so he did. She was relieved. But he stopped at a distance greater than the length of his tall body from her. As if he didn't trust himself to come closer, or was depriving her of the physical closeness of his company.

Still, the sun nicked glints from his green eyes. It was like staring at coins at the bottom of a wishing well.

What did he really wish for? Would he ever really know?

"Alex . . ." She tried his name, tentatively. Softly. Luring a frightened pet. Worried he would hate the softness again.

But she saw him soften, perhaps remembering the first time she'd used his given name.

And she saw him exhale roughly, exasperated.

She was terribly worried, and yet she could not have said why. "You're not . . ." What word should she choose? ". . . disappointed?"

She'd chosen that word very, very carefully.

"About . . . ?"

Damn him. His voice was even. Almost insouciant. "Your proposal?"

"My . . . Of course not. As it wasn't a proposal so much as it was a suggestion."

Ah. Well, very good he'd clarified *that*.

"Good. I should very much dislike losing your friendship."

"Should you?"

The irony in his voice made her nervous. "And you ought to be loved."

His eyes widened again in what she feared was incredulity.

"Ought to be loved . . ." He repeated each word wonderingly, as if it was the quaintest, most naïve thing he'd ever heard.

How about that. She *also* disliked feeling mocked.

"I don't want to marry you," she explained conclusively then, irritably. A little desperately.

A sense of déjà vu reared: She'd also said she didn't want to kiss him again, and look where that had got her.

"You don't want to be the Duchess of Falconbridge?"

Was he genuinely astonished, or was the astonishment sarcastic? Argh! Her mind was a snarl of impressions and her stomach was in knots and while her impulse was to leave him straightaway— why was that always the impulse around him, and why did she always instead ricochet right toward him instead, and why did it always lead to being naked?—she wanted him to *feel* and not bat things back at her with irony.

"It has naught to do with being Duchess of Falconbridge."

Was *that* it? His pride was wounded? For of course who wouldn't *want* to be a duchess?

She yearned for the days when she'd been able to address one emotion at a time. When she knew precisely what emotion she felt and why and for whom. It had been forever since she felt that way.

Forever. In other words, just last week.

"You don't mind, do you?" she asked. "That I do not wish to marry you?"

And then the sound of Harry's laughter floated back to them from up the road, and she turned toward the sound, then lingered, helpless not to. Something in her was soothed by it, and she wanted to chase it like a butterfly. Safety. Familiarity.

"You can't say it often enough," the duke said with a cold, cold irony. He shook his head, as if he was amused by something.

He kept walking. And she stopped and waited while Harry hurried toward her.

"Genevieve, Millicent was just reminding me of the most amusing thing you said at Farnsworth's house . . ."

She walked with Harry between her and Millicent. She said nothing. She felt clubbed and confused, and she was happy to be with them.

The duke walked on a few steps ahead, alone.

Chapter 23

A nd that evening the duke, true to his role as a bad influence, lured all the men present into playing another game of five-card loo, leaving the ladies to talk amongst themselves.

Millicent showed her a sketch of a nest of little kittens she'd found sleeping piled up together in the barn, her true nature drawn right back to her true calling.

She's right, Genevieve thought. She was *right* to sketch kittens. They *were* soothing. And perhaps this was key to Millicent's nature: she drew soothing things, things grounded in reality and possibility. Ordinary things. Adorable things. She didn't trouble herself with complicated Italian art of nude mythological beings or poetry or become entangled with difficult, fascinating men. It was probably why she liked Millicent.

Which came first, Millicent's temperament or the kittens?

"I think you should continue with the kittens," she encouraged. "I do believe they are your forte. Though I do admire the angry swans."

She *thought* she was soothed, except for at intervals she glanced toward the doorway. Grateful neither the duke nor Harry entered the room.

And then later, much later, Genevieve lay in bed, thrashing as though the sheets were her enemy, as they'd become since the beginning of the house party. She sat up, and wrapped her arms around her knees, and watched the fire avidly as though it had secrets to reveal.

When it was clear no secrets could be found there, she turned her attention to the clock.

Midnight had never before been so powerfully significant.

She'd never been more aware of her own skin, which was alert, expectant, restless as any other creature that typically found sustenance after dark. Or of the texture of her sheets, which suddenly slid with unbearable sensuality over every part of her that was bare. Or the silence inside and outside of the house, the echoing dark, all of which seemed to be waiting, even yearning, for her footsteps, in search of him.

But everything was *wrong* now.

And since she didn't know why it was, and she didn't know how to make it better, and because she was tired of confusion, it was wisest, it was best, to stay where she was. They had partaken of each other as a means to forget. And as it could go no farther, it was best to stop altogether.

She was glad to have made at least that decision.

Which was, of course, why she flung herself out of bed and padded to the window to part the curtains and peer out. Because as usual, whenever she'd decided to stay away from him she found herself heading straight *to* him instead.

She wondered what law of physics was involved in this peculiar effect.

And then decided that physics couldn't possibly have anything to do with lust.

He wasn't in the garden, at least where she could see him.

Indecisively, she seized her candle, and turned her doorknob, and peered down the hall. The faint smell of the candles doused in their sconces lingered.

She took four steps. But then her feet felt the chill of the marble and burned from the cold, and she rationalized that if she moved quickly onto carpet she would be warmer. So she dashed on tiptoe down the staircase, her hand flat and sliding on the mercifully polished and gleaming banister as she went.

And she tiptoed across the foyer and began with the library. The fire had burnt down to embers. The chairs were empty.

She stood, foolishly indecisive.

"Moncrieffe?" She whispered it.

The word virtually echoed back at her. Almost as though he were gone forever.

An absurd fancy.

She crept from the library, made the icy journey across the chilled marble of the foyer again, her hastily seized stub of a candle scarcely lighting inches in front of her, but she knew the way so well it was scarcely necessary.

She wandered into the green room. She recognized the feel of the carpet on her bare toes. Olivia's exotic blooms towered menacingly in the corner.

He wasn't behind them. She knew because she looked.

She abandoned the green room in favor of the parlor, where they had stumbled about in blindman's buff, and he had identified her from her heartbeat and the texture of her skin.

And she paced like a frantic ghost, growing reckless now. "Alex . . ." she called softly in the room where she'd first kissed him. As though the word was a conjuring spell.

But he wasn't there.

She'd stopped feeling the cold.

And now panic drove her. Down the servant's stairs, out through the kitchen, where a fire did burn and a kitchen boy stirred on the hearth restlessly but never opened an eye. Her bare feet were mercifully numb with the cold now.

She ventured out the kitchen door, and stood in the frigid dark for an instant.

And in that moment she accepted failure.

The grounds seemed as vast as the sky, inscrutable, and if he wanted to hide from her, if he was out there, she would call for him forever and her voice would echo mockingly back to her.

And if he didn't want to be found, he would not be found.

She wanted to howl to the sky.

Damn him.

For *ruining* things. For changing the rules, such as they were. For being the one to decide what the rules were. For introducing her to the hunger in her, and for making it clear he was the only one who could assuage it.

Why had she agreed to any of it?

Because she'd wanted him. Because they were the same *species*.

She was the girl of enormous crimson roses and savage kisses, and only he knew it.

She would be shameless, desperate if she knocked on his door during the journey back to her room. She wasn't *that* desperate.

She paused before it. Oh, bloody hell.

She tapped.

Apparently she *was* that desperate.

She pressed her ear against the door and heard nothing, nothing at all.

Was he ill? Was he sleeping?

Was he gone altogether?

She carried that notion like a new burden back to her own bedchamber. Only to confront those roses, standing in the corner, mocking her now. Oh God. What would become of the girl who'd earned those roses if she didn't marry Lord Harry Osborne?

She closed the door behind her, pressing her back against it, closing her eyes.

If the duke had departed Pennyroyal Green, surely her father or mother would have mentioned it? Surely a man like the duke wouldn't slink away out of disappointment from Eversea House in the dark of night?

Perhaps one more little look around the house.

She opened her door again to bolt out, but her path was blocked by a large wall of a chest.

Her heart flew into her throat and mercifully stopped her from shrieking. She could have stumbled, but he casually stretched out a hand and touched her shoulder. Righting her.

Simultaneous fury and a silent vehement *hosanna* almost lifted her clean out of her body.

"You *frightened* me," she hissed.

"I doubt that." He was almost but not quite whispering. "How long have you been looking for me, Genevieve? In vain?"

How *dare*—

"I haven't looked at all for you," she lied. "I thought I heard a sound in the hall, and so I opened the door just now. And now that I know it's you I can close it again."

She began to do just that.

He stretched out that hand again and pressed it against the door. He was too strong. She abandoned her efforts to close it.

"Is that *so*," he drawled on a whisper. "Funny, by the firelight it looks like your cheeks are flushed. Almost as though . . . well, *almost* as though you've been dashing all over the house for an hour. And you're breathing *almost* as though you've just had a brisk run up the stairs."

Bloody man.

"The breathing is because you frightened me," she maintained stiffly.

But why wasn't he inviting himself into her bedchamber? The fire was burning in there, illuminating him just a little. It wasn't safe to stand on the threshold of her room after midnight chatting with a duke.

Any more than it was safe to dash all over the house silently calling his name in various rooms, of course.

"I see. It's not because you darted to peer out into

the garden. And then took a circuitous lap about the library while you were at it. And from there, toured the green parlor, and the gray parlor, though you didn't take a peek behind the settee. And then all but bolted outside my chamber door and hovered an instant before stalking back to your own bedchamber. Nothing at all like that."

With every sentence her temper increased ten degrees.

"You *spied* on me?" she hissed.

"I simply wondered what you were doing, dashing all over the house like that. Since you weren't . . . *looking* . . . for me." He was diabolically amused. "Perhaps you'd left something in one of the rooms? A book of some sort? Although I did wonder why . . . you called my name."

She was speechless with fury now.

"I would in fact call it a *desperate* search," he goaded on a cruel, cruel drawl. "You're *perspiring* from the search."

He reached a finger beneath a chin, where a bead of sweat traveled, and drew his fingertip up her throat.

She slapped his hand away.

He froze.

His eyes flared. A warning.

She doubted anyone ever slapped him. And lived very long thereafter.

She didn't regret it.

Her hand stung. It was worth death to her in that moment to slap him.

And then she watched as he leisurely touched his fingertip to his tongue and sucked her sweat from it.

And now something else sizzled along her spine.

He might as well have been sucking her . . . elsewhere. She watched the lift and fall, lift and fall of his chest. He was breathing faster now.

"I was concerned about you." Her voice was hoarse on the heels of that thought. It was hoarse from wanting him, and from the relief, and the fury, and fear, from darting about in the cold, and the pure joy of seeing him standing there. "You seemed in an odd mood after . . . after our conversation today. And I know you don't sleep well."

It wasn't untrue. She *had* been unable to stop thinking about him. In that sense she was unbearably concerned about him.

"Ah. I see. You thought perhaps I was devastated on the heels of your refusal. Once again, you oughtn't trouble yourself, Genevieve. It was really more of a suggestion. Nothing more."

And now *he* was lying. But she wouldn't accuse him of it. Not when he was at last standing before her.

Not when she might be able to lure him into her bedchamber.

"I think you were more concerned about *you* and what you wanted. From me."

So that was his theory? she thought indignantly.

He was exactly right.

It infuriated her. And frightened her. What had she become? He roamed after midnight. And now she knew of a certainty *her* doom was to roam halls after midnight, searching for him, once he was gone.

Once he was gone?

One day he would be, of course. But the notion was unthinkable.

"You're mad." Her voice was faint.

"Well, of course I am. But I'm not wrong, am I? Remember when I warned you might not be able to do without me?"

She was panicked that he was correct. "You should go. Now."

Now, now, now. It all needed to stop now.

He was utterly unmoved by this suggestion.

"Here is what I wonder, Genevieve. You can go searching for me to ask for what you want from me. To *demand* what you want from me. And yet you cannot seem to tell Harry what you want and how you feel. Why do you think that is? What, pray tell, is the difference?"

It was as though he'd slapped her.

Bastard.

She didn't want to think of that. "I want you to go," she whispered.

"After you answer my question."

She put her hands to her face. Brought them down. "You're my friend." She was panicking. "I was worried about you. I was so afraid I would lose . . . I would lose . . ."

"The pleasures of my body."

Argh! "The pleasures of your company. Your friendship. Surely you see me that way, too. We are friends, you and I."

"Friends," he repeated thoughtfully. Rolling the word about in his mouth as though investigating the bouquet. "Do you know, Genevieve . . ."

He sounded as though he'd had a useful revelation.

"Yes?" she prompted gently.

"I can see your nipples *right* through your night rail."

She whipped her arms into a bandolier shape over her chest.

"*Don't* look through my *night rail!*" she whispered with absurd vehemence.

They stared at each other furiously. She could hear his breath sawing in and out. Was he angry? Aroused? Some combination thereof?

In a startlingly deft motion, he seized hold of the night rail at her hips and yanked it off over her head.

She didn't even have time to gasp. So surprised was she that she all but assisted him, as her arms shot up high.

She was entirely nude.

He looked at his hand, filled with bunched fine muslin, almost in surprise.

"There. I'm no longer looking through your night rail. And oh, look. It's just like the Veronese."

They glared at each other in fury for a ridiculous moment.

Rather like Venus and Mars. Boticelli's version.

And then he swore under his breath and came at her.

She backed away swiftly until she was in the center of her bedchamber, and he closed the door behind him, sliding the bolt.

And she backed swiftly away while he stood just inside the door.

They stood at a safe wary distance from each other on the carpet, like two stalking animals.

And then suddenly they weren't.

He'd reached out and pulled her to him or she'd all but flown to him, it was all the same; regardless, the meeting was violent and sudden.

He lifted her up; she nearly climbed him. Her arms locked 'round his head, pulling his mouth to hers; their lips met, tongues tangled and teeth clashed before the kiss became settled, became a battle, a celebration, a point proven: no kiss had ever been deeper, sweeter, more melting, more seductive, more of a relief.

He scooped his hands beneath her arse, lifting her higher, so he could bury his head against her throat, and he groaned, uttered a filthy and thoroughly erotic epithet. His mouth was so hot and insistent on the soft flesh of her throat there she feared, half hoped, it would leave marks, a brand. And his hands seemed everywhere on her; she was clothed in his heat, protected and ravished. Utterly exposed.

He slid her down the length of him to the floor, down over the swollen cock straining behind his trousers, and she moaned. She was shockingly close to her release. Trembling on the brink.

He got her by her shoulders and turned her abruptly to face the dressing table.

"Look at yourself," he demanded, the words hoarse. "Look at us."

He lifted her hair away from her face. It slid down one of her shoulders, a caress against her bare skin, colluding with him to give her pleasure. She saw in the mirror a girl with a heart-shaped face that was hers, and yet not: it was wickedly flushed and languid-lidded from lust and glinty-eyed with desperation for it to be sated. Her skin was all over rose from heat, her mouth was kiss-swollen; her own sensual beauty, viewed this way, shocked her. She sensed she saw what he saw in her, the white curving girl with full breasts and long neck and a body that craved his, and this was why he wanted her to look. Who *wouldn't* want this girl?

The realization was disorienting. Embarrassing. A gift.

"Watch," he ordered into her ear, and his rough, ragged breath was a caress, too, raising gooseflesh along her arms, her throat.

And so she did. She watched as his hands covered her breasts, roughly thumbing her nipples to peaks; she watched herself ask for more of that by arching back against him. She saw her mouth part, her rib cage jump on a helpless gasp of intense pleasure, as she writhed beneath his touch. Their eyes met in the mirror; his were dark and luminous and fiercely intent, his mouth unsmiling, jaw tense, as his big hands slid down over her ribs, the curve of her waist, the seam between her ribs, sliding, sliding down to cover the triangle of hair between her legs.

Lamplight glanced from the gold signet ring and one of his fingers slipped between her dark curls and expertly stroked. Hard. Just once.

But her white body arched as the bolt of pleasure cleaved her.

He did it again.

"Please."

"You feel incredible to me. So wet." His voice was hoarse, drugged-sounding, wondering. She was beyond shame. She wanted him; her body made that clear. His hands disappeared from the mirror, from her body, and she was about to protest when she realized he was unbuttoning his trousers. He got them down as far as his hips, springing his cock. He dragged his hands down her narrow back and pushed her inexorably forward. Not knowing what else to do, she tipped and gripped the edge of her dressing table. His hand slipped swiftly between her legs, stroking, lulling, and then his knee urged her legs farther apart, then she felt his cock nudging against her, and she moaned softly as she gave a throb of anticipation.

He impaled her with one swift, deep thrust.

She saw the wanton in the mirror thrown forward by the force of his invasion, then toss her head back and bite down on her lower lip from the exquisite primal shock of the joining. He pulled slowly, slowly back, and brought a hand around to stroke her.

He pulled back and thrust forward again, hissing out his pleasure, his fingers moving against her with the rhythm of his body.

But he wanted to take, and he did. He cared more about his pleasure in the moment than hers. Selfish, demanding, primal, male, he took, she was helpless against it and she loved it. He gripped her hips and pulled them back against his as he drummed into her, each thrust taking him as deeply into her as he could go, and she felt him everywhere in her body, in the soles of her feet, at the outer reaches of her being. Her hair dropped down over her eyes, blinding her with silky tangled darkness as they rocked hard together, their bodies slamming rhythmically, and then she could feel it soaring toward her. So soon. So soon.

"Alex . . . I. . . ."

But his breath was a rapid savage rasp behind her. He plunged and plunged again.

Her release was surprising and total, a nova of pleasure exploding with her inside it. It bowed her body with its force. His name was her silent scream;

her knees buckled, but he held her fast 'round her waist and in the mirror he was nearly a blur as he drove himself to his own release. A ragged groan tore from him, as though he'd been ripped from his own body.

He never came inside her.

He kept her from falling. His arms were steel bands 'round her waist. She could have crumpled to the floor just like her night rail.

He scooped his arms beneath her and lifted her as though she were made of down, and gently, gently, settled her on the bed.

She'd never felt more precious. And she covered her eyes with her arm at the rush of feelings, too many to sort, all of them bigger than she was, most of them new.

She *was* abashed.

He stretched out next to her and gently but firmly lifted her arm away from her face. He wanted to see her, apparently. She still didn't want to open her eyes. It felt safer, somehow, to keep them closed. Through the cloud she floated upon she felt his lips, soft, soft, achingly tender, brushing over her eyelids, her cheek, her forehead, her throat, her lips. So soothing. A tender inventory. He murmured things that may have been endearments.

"Your feet are ice," he murmured. And his hands matter-of-factly rubbed heat into them, then slid up her calves. He gently, gently combed them through her hair, smoothing it gently, efficiently away from her face. He strummed them over her forehead softly, softly, softly.

She sighed and opened her eyes. And met his.

And in her weakened state she simply allowed

herself to surrender to their beauty and to the expression in them, which was one of such undisguised tenderness it ought to have unnerved her.

She smoothed his hair from his face, pushed it back. It stayed. It was soaked with sweat. He was still entirely clothed.

He lay down alongside her.

Both were in excellent humor now. Spent, limp, pensive, too magnanimous in their satiety to feel anything but pleased with the world. Other inconvenient emotions could wait. Nothing was confusing or frustrating. It was all about recovery.

They didn't speak at all.

Until she did. "It isn't a *terrible* idea."

She was certain he knew what she meant.

She'd expected him to snort. Instead he stiffened next to her.

"Are you perchance describing my suggestion of marriage?"

Suggestion. She was never going to get a proposal. She lifted one shoulder in a nonchalant answer.

"Tell me again it isn't a terrible idea when you're *not* addled from sex."

Hmm. She supposed she *was* rather addled from it. How odd that this existence could feel more vibrant than the one she lived during the day, but it wasn't at all real and it was entirely temporary. No proper life could be made from the pursuit of blinding pleasure followed by limp exhaustion. All of this had been the most reckless, satisfying, terrifying thing she'd done in all her born days. She supposed she was due for something of the sort, given her bloodline.

She had the uneasy sense that she'd only just

begun discovering the magnitude of what her body demanded.

"Very well, Genevieve. If Harry proposes to Millicent before the week is out, then I will marry you. I will consent to be your consolation prize."

Something about his tone was a bit wrong, but she was still . . . addled. And she couldn't put her finger precisely on it.

If Harry proposes to Millicent.

With those words, reality intruded unpleasantly, and once it made inroads, she noticed that the fire was lower now, the wick on the oil lamp was burning down, sweat was drying on her body and she was now cold, the soreness between her legs made itself known.

And the notion of Harry marrying anyone but her was painful enough to penetrate the haze of it all. She sighed gustily. Remembering how all of this that had come to pass had begun with Harry.

The duke had become her means of forgetting. Her brandy, her opium.

"Shouldn't at least one of us marry for love?"

"I thought you loved only Harry and would *only* love Harry until the mountains crumble into the sea, and so forth. And are you telling me now you wouldn't mind being a duchess should your love for Harry not come to fruition? You can live with that?"

There was a taut note in his voice. It wasn't his usual dryness. She couldn't read his mood, and when she couldn't it made her uneasy.

"If you can," she added.

Silence.

"Anyone would be honored to be your duchess," she tried softly.

The softness just made him smile some sort of secret, rueful, dark, and private smile and shake his head. *Kind*, she suspected he was thinking, and not kindly, either. Disparagingly.

"It isn't a weakness to accept kindness," she told him tartly, which was ironic, as this was hardly a kind thing to say. "It isn't a weakness to allow yourself to be cared for."

"It is if the kindness is given out of pity. If it is, then it's not called being kind. It's called being *patronizing*."

"I simply cannot bear seeing you unhappy."

The admission was an intimate one, and so fierce and almost anguished it startled both of them into stillness and silence.

"You cannot bear to see *me* unhappy, or *anyone*, Genevieve?" he said ironically.

She wouldn't answer. She knew the answer.

You, you, you.

But what did this mean? How had this come to pass?

Tension was drum-taut between them.

"This will be the last time we make love," he said, almost conversationally.

She scrambled upright. *Last*. Not a word she enjoyed.

The fire had burned very low, and she was thoroughly chilled now. Her night rail was . . . She scanned the room.

". . . Over near the wardrobe, where I dropped it."

She wasn't about to press up against him for warmth. He didn't offer, either. She didn't quite leap off the bed to retrieve it yet, either.

He was in fact holding himself still in what appeared to be a finite amount of space on the bed, and she sensed that if she held her hands up she'd encounter walls up around him, invisible ones but present nonetheless.

"Are you punishing me?"

She'd blurted it. Two measures of how she'd changed in a few short days. She blurted things—if only to him—and considered being denied the pleasures of his body a punishment. She sounded like a child.

She hoped it sounded a bit like a jest. It wasn't. She, once again, was panicked.

He still wouldn't look at her. He was watching the ceiling as though it were a crystal ball. He'd rested his forearm across his forehead, as if checking for fever.

"Mmm . . . consider it a latent attack of honor. Harry is sleeping under this roof, after all. I'm not getting any younger, you know. I'm in danger of being used up by you entirely and if I marry I imagine my wife would object to a spent and useless man. And I've *so* much more I haven't yet shown you . . ."

And with that taunt, he rolled from the bed. He'd only to rearrange his clothing and button his trousers, which he did while staring down at her. It was the first time she'd felt a bit of a trollop.

She watched, going hot in the face. He hadn't even truly removed any clothes, they couldn't even wait for that, and they'd gone at it as fiercely as ferrets.

She'd *seen* ferrets go at it, so she knew.

Genevieve wanted to keep him with her and wanted him to go so she could be alone with whatever emotions were buffeting her.

He stood back and gazed at her. She felt his eyes

on her, soft and thorough as his fingers. He inhaled. She watched his fine furred chest rise and fall, and she thought she saw a little mark on it where she'd nipped or clawed him.

"If this is the last time, oughtn't there be a farewell?" She sounded so desperate. She wanted a kiss. Because she knew if she kissed him she could make him stay.

"This *was* farewell, Genevieve. Couldn't you tell?"

And with that he was gone, as quickly as he did most things.

Chapter 24

BAM. BAM. BAM.

Alex had just managed to drift into a shallow fitful sleep when he became aware that the thumping wasn't his heart, getting ready to explode, nor was it his head, as he hadn't had all that much to drink tonight for a change. He'd left Genevieve only an hour before.

BAM. BAM. BAM.

He opened one eye and with an extraordinary effort tipped his head to one side on the pillow to squint at the clock. He could just make out that the hands of it were positioned at two and twelve. He dragged his palms up punishingly hard over his face, as if trying to wake himself up one body part at a time, beginning with his features. He pushed his hair back, and rolled over, reluctant to do more than that, and waited for his brain to make sense of the pounding.

In seconds he realized it was the door. Someone was rhythmically pounding at his chamber door.

BAM BAM BAM!

A fire in the house? Was somebody ill? An angry husband? Wait—no, that was a guess rooted in his past; it had been years since he'd seduced a married woman. Jacob Eversea with a pistol prepared to shoot him for making love to his daughter under his roof? Or hammering the door shut to keep him prisoner until he did? Ian Eversea desperately demanding he meet him at dawn over pistols?

He was awake now. As none of the possibilities were pleasant he slid from bed, reflexively seized his pistol from the table next to his bed—always clean, always loaded, powder always dry, such was his trusting nature and so beloved was he by the *ton*—and unlocked and cocked it. He seized his trousers and shoved his legs in, and with another stride was at the door.

BAM! BAM!—

He slid the bolt abruptly and opened the door about two inches.

Someone nearly fell in. He shoved the door hard back to keep them from landing on top of him.

The hall was dark; all the candles in the sconces long since doused. And yet the damned golden hair still gleamed.

"I need to talk to you, Moncrieffe."

Good grief. The man had slurred an entire sentence into a single multisyllabic word.

He pushed open the door a few more inches, and Osborne all but poured through the opening.

"Osborne, what the *devil*—"

He was in shirtsleeves, floppy hair a scrambled mop, his eyes ringed in red. From fatigue? Weeping?

"Do you love her?" he slurred.

Moncrieffe was instantly alert for danger. He flicked his eyes over the man, searching for weapons. He shifted his pistol in his hand.

What did Osborne know?

"Osborne, I want you to leave *now*," he managed coldly.

"DO YOU *LOVE* HER?"

Harry lunged forward and tried to seize Moncrieffe by the lapels and stopped short, confused, when he realized Moncrieffe wasn't wearing a shirt.

The stopping short nearly toppled him.

He righted himself with some effort. Moncrieffe stood back, pistol lowered surreptitiously at his hip.

Good God, the boy was *foxed*.

Harry immediately looked sincere and apologetic and frantic.

"Here ish the thing, Moncrieffe. It hash all gone badly, badly wrong. *Badly* wrong. Badly . . ." Harry stopped, and frowned, displeased that his chain of thought had slipped his grip.

"Wrong?" Moncrieffe suggested darkly.

"Yesh!" Harry agreed in almost angry surprise. "That's preshisely it. You see it, too!"

Oh, for God's sake. "I'm not certain I do. What have you been at, Osborne? Whiskey, brandy?"

Harry waved impatiently, vaguely, and the gesture nearly swung him off his feet. "Whatever was in all the bottles in the library. For the pain."

"Well, naturally. It's why liquor was invented. 'For the pain.' There were quite a few bottles in the library."

"None now," Harry announced with glum satisfaction.

Wonderful.

"Have you come to . . . hurt me, Osborne?" He managed to make this sentence sound amused.

Harry eyed the pistol balefully.

"Oh, I'm afraid of you, I'll admit, Falconbridge.

But you can put your pistol away. I'm not the sort. I cannot see you've done anything *wrong*."

The relief was profound. The intensity of it was a potent reminder that what he'd been doing was not only foolish . . . he'd allowed it to get out of control.

It was far more in command of him than he was of it.

"But here ish the thing, Moncrieffe. I had a plan. I did. You weren't meant to be here at this house party. You weren't meant to court her, she wasn't meant to care for you, you weren't meant to . . ."

He shoved his hands through his hair as his despair escalated until his words rushed from him in angry, tormented, bursts.

He paused.

"I. Love. *Her. I* do."

The words were anguished gasps.

Moncrieffe stood back. As much from the fumes as from the pure force of the terror of first heartbreak.

Something was amiss here.

Osborne took a noncommittal step, then paused and frowned at the ground, puzzled. Wondering perhaps whether one of his boot heels had suddenly grown higher than the other, or whether the carpet was laid over water.

Moncrieffe hooked his boot around the rungs of the chair at the writing desks and shoved it over to Harry with his foot.

Osborne sat down in stages: bum hard on chair, elbows hard on thighs, head dropped hard into his hands, breath rushing out of him in a great exhale.

And for a while he just breathed.

Everything has a rhythm, Moncrieffe couldn't help but think, watching. The sea, our breathing, our anguish, our love. We couldn't endure the force of any of it all at once. It *has* to ebb and flow.

Moncrieffe sat down opposite Harry, almost gingerly. The emotion in the room was too volatile and uncertain; he didn't know what might disturb it. The hour was late, he was weary, and in his vulnerability an image crossed the membrane of his memory then: it was midnight, the clock his wife had loved chimed out the hour with obscenely merry chimes. He was hunched over in a chair, and another man, a doctor, stood near him, having delivered his news. She was dead in the next room.

Agony. Emptiness.

He watched Harry. He tried to ignore the creeping contempt he felt for himself. Oh, he'd been so clever. With his games and strategy. He'd nearly had for himself what he wanted. He would have punished Ian Eversea beautifully.

Instead he'd managed to build for himself a brilliant trap with nasty teeth, and no matter how he turned, they tore at him.

Then again, with the arrival of Harry, he may have just been presented with a brilliant opportunity.

What a man he'd become to have such a thought in such a moment. He was not wealthy by accident.

Harry sighed. His voice was steadier, but still muffled with emotion.

"My whole life I've loved her. Genevieve."

"Your whole life." Moncrieffe repeated the words, stalling to give his mind space in which to unravel what was happening here. He didn't think he was witnessing his plan, Genevieve's plan, coming to fruition. The plan where they showed Harry his heart because he didn't know it.

I had a plan, Osborne had said.

They'd *all* had a "plan," apparently. Not one of those plans seemed to be unfolding as . . . planned.

It was almost funny.

He sighed and reached behind him for the shirt he'd abandoned next to his bed when he'd fallen into it. He slid his arms into it, but didn't bother to button it. He seized the poker to poke at the fire, but the fire wasn't interested in giving off more heat.

"She's . . . oh, but she's beautiful. Don't you think? For heaven's sake, don't answer that," Harry added hurriedly. "I don't want to know. I know I will do anything to make her smile. She has a dimple *here.*" He pointed. "Have you *seen* her shmile, Moncrieffe? What am I saying? Of course you have. She smiles for *you* . . . all the time."

He drifted momentarily on a satisfying tide of self-pity.

Alex said nothing.

"And by God . . . she's . . . she's so funny and clever and very, *very* funny and . . ." He sighed, and stared into the fire.

"She's clever, too," Moncrieffe suggested diabolically.

"She *ish,*" Harry agreed vehemently, shocked at their accord. "So you noticed all of it, too."

A pause, as in his weary state all of the things that Harry had said, all the things Genevieve was, settled over him, beat inside him.

"Yes." With an effort he said it in a voice of infinite, implacable patience and reason. A steady voice, that gave away nothing. "I've seen it, too."

"From the first?" Harry demanded.

As if he would answer such a question. From the first he'd wanted to ruin her, abandon her to punish someone who had yet again taken something from him too soon.

He didn't care at all about Ian Eversea anymore.

He was standing once again on the precipice of losing her. When there was a hairsbreadth of a chance, after tonight, he could have her forever, simply because her body wanted him.

All he said was, "You ought to choose fewer words that contain *S* for the time being. You are spitting all over me."

Harry inhaled deeply, as if hoping to suck a little of Moncrieffe's own patience from the air. "Likely you are right," Harry agreed gloomily. "I shall try."

"Why are you here? Why have you so rudely interrupted my sleep?"

"I need to tell you this, Moncrieffe. It's my only hope. For as long as I've known her I've loved her. From the start I knew. I don't know if *you've* ever felt such a thing, Moncrieffe, but I shaw her . . . saw her . . . and it was like I could . . . I could see . . ." He glanced up, sheepishly, then turned his face back toward the fire, mouth tilted wryly, abashed at his own hyperbole. "I could see what forever would be like. I liked it." His voice grew pensive again.

The muscles of Alex's stomach tensed. *Forever.* He could see what forever would be like. And forever was what he was about to lose.

Again.

He couldn't allow it again.

Harry looked up. "And then *you* came along." He was back to the self-pity now. "They say you plan to marry her."

Moncrieffe neither confirmed nor denied this. Because he was, at heart, a strategist. He wasn't in the habit of enjoying bosom chats with anyone, let alone drunken lordlings, and he sensed he might learn something that could get him precisely what he wanted.

"Many a life has been made or broken on a misfortune of timing. I cannot be responsible for yours."

"The timing was perfect until you arrived. I had a plan. I needed a plan, because I'm not a bloody duke," Harry pointed out bitterly. "I cannot simply buy her with money and a title."

"Have a care, Osborne. You're enjoying my hospitality on sufferance at the moment. I do hope you'll arrive at a point soon."

Harry jerked his head up in surprise at the tone, sobered. And then he looked about him as though he found the "hospitality" bafflingly wanting.

"I thank you for hearing me out, then, Moncrieffe," he managed with sodden dignity, even if it was an afterthought. "As I said, I had a plan. For you see, I never could quite read her heart. I thought . . . I *thought* she loved me, too. But I never dared propose because I hadn't enough money to suit her father. I'll inherit a title but I've no home to give to a wife. Not yet. I've tried to earn money on my own, but I thought, well, if she loves me I might very well chance it; if I knew for certain that she loved me her parents might be persuaded to allow us to marry. And how I want her in my . . ."

He was stopped from finishing that sentence by something dark and dangerous glinting in the duke's eyes. Because that last word was going to be *bed*.

"But I didn't know whether she did. You see, she never showed it in a way that convinced me. I had to be certain. And sho . . . so . . ." He sighed. "I told her I intended to propose to Millicent. To see what she would say or do. To watch her face. To force her hand."

Moncrieffe was difficult to shock. But the potent cruelty Osborne had perpetuated in the name of *love* speared him motionless.

He leaned slowly back in his chair, and then froze, staring at the young man. He looked at handsome Harry and saw Genevieve's white, hunted face, sick with misery; saw her entire being aglow at the very *idea* of Harry, and because *he* knew—*he* alone knew, of all the people in the world, not her family, not this idiot before him—the depths of her passion, her feeling, and ability to love. . . . He knew this boy had nearly killed her.

Out of *cowardice.*

He'd never known such purifying rage. It was a sour, metallic taste in his throat. He could scarcely speak.

He stared at Osborne so long and so silently that Harry finally turned his head. He flinched at the black, scathing glare he intercepted.

"Just to be very clear . . ." Alex managed slowly, his voice thrumming with suppressed violence. " . . . in order to force a confession of love from her, you thought you might *frighten* her into showing her feelings? You thought you might *break* her heart in order to *win* her heart?"

Osborne met his gaze. Chin up, his own eyes suddenly ablaze.

"What the hell kind of man are you?"

"You can't understand, Moncrieffe. How would I know? How would I *know* if she did? She's so . . . serene. So self-contained and so kind. To *everyone.* I knew we were special friends. And yet I couldn't be certain she felt more than that for me."

Serene. He thought of the nude girl flying at him, of savage kisses that rocked him to his viscera, of her body submitting to his, of her quickness in putting him in his place.

He wouldn't curl his hands into fists. But he did press them flat against his knees. He had not invented this part of her, her passion. It was already a part of her.

But Harry . . . peace and conversation and friendship. That was part of her, too.

"And I have naught to offer her but myself. I would simply propose this *instant* if I had property. And this is why I know you can't understand. Haven't you ever been *afraid*? Haven't you ever wanted something so badly you can't imagine your life without it, but you *can* imagine the devastation and *pity* that will follow if you spill your heart and she has to tell you, oh so kindly—because she's kind—that she doesn't love you *in that way*?"

Fear. Alex knew he was a fine one to pontificate about fear. He'd issued the world's most tepid, careful marriage proposal. Because he'd been afraid to tell Genevieve he loved her.

Not that it would have made much of a difference.

She loved Harry.

Harry in his youthful innocence had put his finger right on it. And Moncrieffe pushed the realization away. He took in a sharp breath.

Harry took Moncrieffe's silence as a reason to go on.

"God help me, it was only because I was afraid of losing her. And I honestly didn't feel I deserved her, for I had nothing to give her. I simply needed to know whether she loved me. I'm not proud of it, but I have never loved anyone more."

Moncrieffe could still scarcely get the words out.

"I just can't believe you would *do* such a thing to someone you . . . loved."

Osborne was very, very drunk, but he wasn't stupid. "But I couldn't hurt her, could I, if she didn't love me?"

And now Harry's blue eyes fixed on him almost searchingly.

Moncrieffe couldn't believe he had almost shown his hand.

"You just said you weren't certain whether she did love you. And if she does love you anywhere near as much as you claim to love her, imagine the pain you may have caused her with your whole charade."

Harry looked up at him and blinked. And as he thought about it, his face slowly went white.

After a moment he swallowed.

"*Gallant* of you," Moncrieffe drawled, twisting the knife.

Moncrieffe knew a surge of hatred for himself for saying it. But he wanted Harry to feel what he'd done to Genevieve.

Haven't you ever been afraid? The words still echoed in his ears. He remembered taunting Genevieve: *You can demand from me what you want but you can't tell Harry what you want.*

He knew Genevieve felt safe enough to be honest with him, to be real with him, to be abandoned with him . . . because she wasn't afraid of losing him. And she wasn't afraid of losing him . . .

Because she didn't love him.

In other words, she could imagine forever without him.

Stupid. How *stupid* men were. He, and Osborne, and bloody Ian Eversea . . . the *havoc* they caused. To themselves and to others.

He was momentarily paralyzed by the rush of realizations.

"And so that's what I came to ask. Do you love her, Moncrieffe? Does she love you?"

He should not allow silence to go by.

He could have answered in any number of ways. He was, in some ways, no braver than Harry. Because if he was he would have encouraged Harry to tell Genevieve the truth about what he'd done and get a proposal over with, just to see what transpired. It would be the honorable thing to do. May the better man win, and all that.

He was still the stronger man. The wiser man. He was not a kind man.

And he was *definitely* not a martyr.

What he said was:

"And what do my answers matter to you?"

"Because if you don't love her, you should step aside. Because I do love her. And I will make her happy."

And Alex's senses tingled. Naïve Osborne had spilled into his hands unimaginably valuable currency: his trust. And he could tell him anything at all: Yes, Genevieve had agreed to marry him. Yes, she loved him. He could send Osborne on his way, call a carriage for him. Perhaps he'd go off to fight a foreign war to forget his heartbreak.

In all likelihood he wouldn't go mad from grief and attempt to shoot him. The poor young devil possessed honor.

But he doubted Harry would ever quite be the same.

He recalled the look on Genevieve Eversea's face that first morning he'd walked with her. Pale, lightless. A shell of herself.

Genevieve loves this person, he thought. Which—and this was the most perverse realization of all—made him want to protect Osborne, if only a little. So what he said was, "I must advise you against telling me what I should do, Osborne. It has never ended well for anyone who has attempted it."

Harry's head jerked up. He stared at Moncrieffe, searching for some better answer in his face.

Moncrieffe met his gaze evenly. He felt the weight of the hour, of his years, of his own damn nature, of, in truth, the last hour's worth of lovemaking, because taking the woman in question in a standing position wreaked havoc on a man's thighs, regardless of years of horseback riding.

Harry at last sighed and sank his head in a nod. He got to his feet—soberer now than he'd been when he arrived, though it was doubtful he'd achieve true sobriety until he'd slept until noon. He shuffled a little to find his balance when he was upright. And the first shadows of desolation showed in his face. Imagining what was to come.

He already looked older.

Then again, it was three o'clock in the morning. He might in fact be growing a beard. Unlikely as it seemed.

"They say you've no heart," is what he said.

To Alex's shock, the barb landed. Brutal as a wasp's sting straight to the organ in question.

It took a tick of the clock to compose himself, because it had stolen his breath.

"Believe what you will," he said calmly.

"You won't tell her I was here?"

He shook his head. "You have my word."

Harry was at the door when he paused and asked, "What *do* you plan to do, Moncrieffe?"

Alex almost smiled, albeit decidedly bitterly. Echoes of Ian Eversea, speaking to him from beneath the sheets of his erstwhile fiancée's bed. Another man who had deprived Alex of what he'd wanted. *What do you intend to do, Moncrieffe?*

When it came to love, everyone became brand-new and stupid and lost, he supposed. Including him.

Nevertheless, he still planned to get what he wanted. But first he had to do what was right, for there was no other way to get it.

"I plan to bid you good night, Osborne."

This, at least, was one plan that didn't fail.

Chapter 25

L ater, when they spoke of the grand convening of
the men of Sussex that Saturday over five-card
loo at the Eversea house, they spoke of it in shocked,
gleeful, rueful tones. No one could recall just how
the play had got so deep, except that the Duke of
Falconbridge was present and everybody wanted to
impress him and he kept winning.

Nobody *set out* to lose thousands of pounds.

But it happened.

Eversea knew to invite only men who could afford
to lose, but inevitably others who simply wanted to
win joined the game. The instructions were to bring
only cash and things you wished to wager.

The women of the house were all but ordered
to stay away, and they did so mostly gratefully, if
nervously. They played the pianoforte. They embroidered. They tried to ignore the gleeful shouts
and the opening and closing again and again of the
great main doors as all the wealthiest men within
fifty miles arrived. Some even came in from London.

Coats came off. Sleeves were rolled up. They'd
said three footmen hovered near with decanters,
and the glasses were never empty. Cigar after cigar
was lit and smoked and lit and smoked; smoke

formed a second ceiling, and eyes reddened from it, and the servants would complain for weeks after of the futility of ridding the curtains and carpets of the stink and entreat Mrs. Eversea to replace them. She did, because Jacob won as much as he'd lost, so it was almost as though he hadn't played at all.

Though his nerves took some time to recover.

The atmosphere went from bonhomie to intensity to something . . . less friendly.

And one by one men lost their nerve and their money and pushed away from the table in blustering, nervous good humor and backed up to line the walls and watch, seek out the billiard table, anything to find safety away from the game, which seemed to have acquired an unstoppable momentum.

Until only a few remained.

Falconbridge was one of them, of course.

Falconbridge was doing more than his share of winning. Again and again his hand raked the shillings and pound notes toward him. He began accepting vowels for a time from sweating men, and then politely, regretfully refused them with a hike of a brow that indicated he knew more about their finances than they ever dreamed. Ice in his veins, they'd said. But this was why he was wealthy.

The cards were too afraid of him to do anything other than align in winning configurations, they said.

But Falconbridge was simply observant and clever and a good deal more sober than anyone present.

Harry had lost nearly everything, only to win half of it back.

And Moncrieffe had taken the lad's money.

"I could use a partner in billiards, Osborne," Ian said pointedly, nervously.

But Harry wouldn't push himself away from the table.

And at last, with a face as solemn as any vicar presiding over a funeral, he bet every last penny he had.

The duke's head went back, impressed. Then came down hard.

He was silent for a moment. He sucked at his cigar, thoughtfully, before speaking.

"Well, Osborne," he drawled. "I'm near out of loose blunt here at the moment. I'll take everything you have, no doubt. So, if you're set on doing this . . . I'll put up the deed to Rosemont. I own it outright. I can spare it."

They thought the boy would faint, witnesses said afterward. Though ultimately he held up admirably. It was something about the greenish tinge his pallor took on at the duke's words, and the beads of sweat dotting his hairline.

Silence came and lay over the room like another layer of smoke.

And then through it they heard the rustle of prayers by men who weren't religious. The ruination of a young man was never a pretty thing to witness.

One of Harry's fists formed a white knot against the table. The other held his cards as though it were a pistol that may or may not have a ball in the chamber.

Handkerchiefs came out to mop brows until the room looked white with surrender flags.

All the Eversea men made a mental note to lock up all the firearms out of fear of what a ruined Harry might do to himself.

And then Falconbridge sighed, and all of the faces followed, slowly, slowly, in astonishment and rank disbelief, as time slowed, and with one sweeping motion the duke turned his cards . . .

. . . facedown.

And the breeze from the collective exhales in the room nearly served to clear the cigar smoke.

"I fold, Osborne," Moncrieffe said quietly. "You've got me. I've no choice but to cede the deed of Rosemont to you."

Harry was frozen. He stared, a faint frown on his face, at the hand of cards facedown. The words hadn't seemed to register yet.

"I regret its loss. But I trust you'll put it to good use."

The duke watched him carefully, his own hands flat against the table.

Harry closed his eyes and his head fell back limply, as one killed. His sigh gusted up his blond hair.

The room erupted in roars and cheers. Everywhere were hands jostling him, slapping him in masculine congratulations.

The duke was still a moment longer, watching. His expression inscrutable. His eyes red-rimmed with smoke, sagging with fatigue. Cigar dead between his fingers.

And as the crowd massed around Harry, no one noticed when he slipped from the room.

That night it rained. Hard.

Pity it couldn't have rained in the game room, the maids thought the next day, as they encountered the morning-after stink.

All the Eversea men seemed to have stayed in

bed, because none of them appeared at the breakfast table at the usual breakfast hour. Nor did the duke.

But Harry did.

He intercepted Genevieve near the kippers on the sideboard. And Genevieve's eyes were ringed in red, too, but it was because she hadn't slept at all.

She would never tell a soul it was because she'd spent a futile two hours roaming the house, from room to room in search of the duke.

And she'd never found him.

"How was the game, Harry?" she asked dully. "When did it end?"

"God knows. I think the sun was coming up, but that could have just been the light from all the cigars. The game was . . . remarkable."

So perhaps the duke hadn't even gone up to bed. And then she spent a moment wondering how on earth cards could surpass the pleasures of her body.

And Harry looked downright disreputable this morning, she noticed on second glance. But he seemed to be nervous again. Almost . . . no, not *diffident*. There was something determined about him along with the nervousness.

"I've something I wish to discuss with you, Genevieve," he said suddenly. "Will you go for a stroll with me?"

She stared at him. *Surely* he hadn't just said what she thought he'd said. She was whipsawed by a very unpleasant sense of déjà vu.

"No," she was tempted to say emphatically. Alternatively: "Beg me." Or "Where's Millicent?"

She regarded him contemplatively. He must have seen doubt and resistance in her eyes.

"Please . . . Genevieve."

So he *was* begging. Interesting.

And yet . . . What now did he intend to tell her? That he'd gotten Millicent with child and he wanted *her* to be the godmother? she thought sardonically.

He was sweating, just a little. She saw the sheen of it on his face. And it wasn't warm in the kitchen. His fingers were curled into his palms. Nerves. But his jaw was resolute. He looked . . . older.

It struck her that Harry had undergone a thorough emotional buffeting this week, too. His jaw was likely weary from clenching and tensing more this week than he'd clenched it in an entire lifetime.

"It just rained. There might be mud," she pointed out.

She realized she'd acquired a layer of protective ambivalence, and she was afraid, loath to let him through it. This is what he had done to *her* this week.

But her heart was beating a little faster now in a peculiar recognition, as though Harry was a soldier coming home from a long war and it was becoming reacquainted with how it felt to love him.

For surely she did. He was Harry. Familiar, beloved, the architect of her greatest misery. The keeper of her greatest happiness.

"You've never been frightened of a little mud before." He smiled a little at this.

Still difficult to resist his smile, especially when it was all for her.

And so because the duke was nowhere near, she didn't resist. She smiled, too. They basked in each other's smiles for an instant.

"I might even lay down a cloak for you to walk over puddles. Like Sir Walter Raleigh."

"Well, if you insist on muddying your clothing, who could resist an invitation?"

And so they went for a walk.

It *was* muddy.

Not everywhere, but the grass squished beneath her boots, and all the fallen leaves were now plastered like wallpaper to the road in the lane.

"I don't know where we'll walk, Harry. We shall need a gondola."

He didn't laugh. He in fact said nothing at all. She turned to look at him, and saw he'd gone white in the face.

"Harry, do you need to cast your accounts?" After all, she could only imagine what kind of debauchery had taken place over the game table last night.

"For heaven's sake." He sounded pained. "*No.*"

She thought of the duke, how still he'd held himself when he'd issued his . . . *suggestion* of marriage. And then she knew.

The thought had only detonated in her mind when Harry impulsively seized her hand.

"Genevieve . . . Oh God. I'll just say it. It's you I've loved. It's you I've always loved. I love you."

Oh.

She stared at him as she had the first time. As though she surely must have heard him incorrectly. For she'd heard those words in her dreams and in her imagination in his voice countless times, and the possibility remained she was still dreaming.

And yet:

"As your dearest friend?"

Well. She'd surprised herself. Where had that sarcasm come from? For it was unmistakably that, and it had been reflexive.

He did flinch. But he didn't relinquish her hand. For a moment when she glanced down at it she was confused, for he wasn't wearing a signet ring, and then she reminded herself it was *Harry's* hand.

"As a woman," he said firmly.

They stared at each other.

Well, then.

The words reverberated through her. She wasn't certain anymore whether they were thrilling . . . or whether what she felt was the echo of an old thrill.

"I wish you would say something." He smiled faintly.

His smile faded when she remained silent.

"Are you finished saying what you wanted to say, Harry?"

This clearly wasn't what he'd wanted her to say. He stared at her, smile gone.

Surely she oughtn't be so cool? Where was the Genevieve Eversea who would have thrown herself into Harry's arms?

"I suppose not," he allowed. "I could go on and say I've been a fool. And a coward, Genevieve. I know nothing about love, you see, only that I've loved you."

"But I thought you intended to propose to Millicent?"

"Millicent hasn't a clue I ever intended to propose to her."

Millicent never really did have a clue about many things, bless her heart.

"Given my financial position, I never thought you would accept me and I didn't dare trouble you with a proposal. And now . . . well, things have changed and I thought I'd risk it. Do you care for me?"

Trouble her with a proposal? Dear God, had he no idea what he'd done to her with the news he'd wanted to marry Millicent?

But of course she cared for him. Of course she did. For everything was the same. *He* was the same. Same blue eyes. The sun did the same things to his hair: set all the colors in it gleaming. Same hairs in his nose and eloquent planes in his face and the same fine mouth that had kissed the hand he was now gripping so tightly.

To think she'd extrapolated from one kiss on her hand a world of pleasure. She'd never dreamed of the universe of pleasure that lay beyond that.

Moncrieffe had still never kissed her hand.

But *something* was different. She'd expected her heart to stop, and then leap skyward. It *did* skip. But she wasn't certain whether it was joy or surprise. Or . . . trepidation?

That was wrong. It was an entirely different word from anticipation.

More déjà vu: She was once again staring at him without speaking, and entangled in emotions she could never hope to sort. They chased each other 'round and 'round, and she couldn't grasp any of them to begin sorting them out.

If he doesn't issue a proposal . . . she thought.

Never mind; he would do the speaking, as he had before. He continued into her silence.

"And I hoped . . . I hoped against hope . . . you would consent to spend the rest of your life with me."

"As your friend?" *Why* was she bedeviling him?

He was crimson now, and blotchy. "As my wife." He said it almost defensively.

She'd launched a "yes" at him before. "Yes" had been in her heart every time she looked at him.

But now it seemed she'd forgotten how to form the word.

"Genevieve, please. You *must* tell me. Do you love me?"

She'd never seen Harry . . . wretched before. It was fascinating. And she of course, as always, wanted to save him from suffering.

"I love you." The words were hesitant. They didn't feel untrue. But they felt strange in her mouth. Not like the words to a song she'd sung for ages, which is how they'd once felt. Like words to a song she was remembering.

But relief and joy suffused his face with light and relief that was almost holy, and she watched it with awe. She wondered how her own face looked to him.

"And will you be my wife?"

She would be choosing the rest of her life with the next sentence. She'd dreamed of this day her entire life. Or perhaps it was just the rest of her life had just chosen her, as she'd once told the duke. *Love chooses you.*

"I will be your wife."

He held her face in his hands and looked into her eyes. In her mind's eye she saw another man's arms curled in the shape of a baby. She allowed Harry to hold her face. She saw him too clearly in a moment when she ought not be seeing or thinking at all, but feeling. And there was a flailing moment of dread— surely only nerves—that she already knew all there was to know about him. That he would never surprise her, that he would never teach her anything, that she already knew him too well, that he was too safe, that they were too alike, that he was simply wrong.

Nerves, surely. She'd got what she'd wanted, and naturally it was impossible to believe. She'd *wanted* safety and certainty.

She'd wanted Harry.

"Genevieve," he breathed.

She didn't so much kiss him back as allow herself to be kissed. At first. For he was good at it, and she'd learned about herself that so was she and that she liked being kissed, though she had the presence of mind not to let this on. She also realized her mind oughtn't be involved at all in a moment where she was being kissed for the first time by the man she loved—certainly she'd done very little thinking when she was in the arms of the duke—but there it was, whirring away, assessing. It was . . . different. Where had Harry learned to kiss? *Stop thinking at once*, she told herself. And once again she was thinking when she ought to be surrendering to the moment. He took her lips softly with his, and parted them with his own, and spent a moment in soft kissing before he got his tongue between them, and her tongue met his warily, and so their mouths meshed.

It was a good kiss, and she indulged her curiosity: his mouth was different than the duke's, his . . . approach was different. His arms went around her and hers around him, though this felt strange and new, and she felt the thrumming tension of desire for her in him, and she could feel the start of his erection, which pressed against her belly.

But nothing was stirring in *her*.

Yet. If nothing else during the past week she'd learned she was human. It might simply be only a matter of time.

He loved her and wanted her and she would be cherished and safe her life through.

He released her, and he gazed upon her, flushed with happiness.

She gazed back at him with fascination, a detachment that lifted her up out of her body and watched the two of them. He was utterly familiar, very dear . . . and had become a total stranger. She moved her eyes to the buttons on his shirt—no nacre buttons for him—and imagined unfastening them with unseemly haste, sliding her hand inside his shirt. Imagined Harry nude and avid and sweating and plunging again and again into her body and—

Heat stormed her face. She was certain she'd gone scarlet. Was it desire or mortification? Surely one could become the other fairly easily.

Harry stood back from her, in all likelihood assuming his erection was unnerving her.

"I will be gentle, Genevieve," he said to her softly, interpreting her embarrassment and apparently satisfied with the success of the kiss.

"Gentle" sounded dull.

His face was radiant with joy and relief. He'd gotten through the proposal. His life, as far as he was concerned, was complete. Now that he had her, and always would.

She would be Lady Osborne.

There was relief in knowing the endless tangle of confusion and uncertainty of the preceding days was now over. She inhaled her first peaceful breath in days: her future was now certain. She allowed the rays of his joy to wash over her, until she almost couldn't distinguish his happiness from her own, because she was always happiest when he was happy, too.

She smiled at him. There was a symmetry, an inevitability to their union that her artistic eye appreciated. She *would* be happy. Why shouldn't she be happy when she was marrying her dearest friend?

"Of course we will."

"Will we go share the news with everyone now? Oh!" He stopped. "And before I forget . . ."

He fished in his pocket and emerged with a fistful of daisies.

"Flowers for you." He beamed. "The sort you *like*."

Chapter 26

⌒◯◯⌒

Everyone seemed surprised, judging from the silence that greeted Harry's breathless announcement (had *no one* ever suspected?), and yet willing to be delighted by the news of their engagement. Her brothers, all looking much worse for wear after the previous night's debauchery over the card table, and even Millicent, professed delight. Her parents even more so now that Harry had property and a title and a nice pile of winnings to start off their married life, thanks to the duke.

"We're used to you, Osborne," was what Jacob Eversea said by way of a blessing, with a clap on the back and a kiss on the cheek for his daughter. Still, he had a faint frown between his brows, even as his lips were smiling. He seemed a bit puzzled.

"What's that in your hand, Genevieve?" her mother asked, after kissing her on the cheek and giving her a hearty squeeze.

Genevieve proffered the daisies. "Harry gave them to me right after he proposed."

"Nothing like those flowers on your sampler," her mother commented lightly, but it was accompanied by the sort of penetrating look that usually resulted in Harriet being ordered to prepare a simple for her.

Genevieve was startled. "No."

Her mother's mouth parted as if she meant to say something. And then she closed it again.

"I think you'll make him very happy," is what she finally said.

An odd way to put it, Genevieve thought.

"Speaking of the duke," her mother said, though no one had. "He left something behind for you. Wrapped in paper in the green salon."

"'Left' something . . . *behind* for me?" Genevieve said faintly.

But when she saw how cheerful Ian was, she knew no other event could have made his face so fulsome. Certainly it wasn't only her engagement.

"Oh yes. Falconbridge departed outrageously early this morning," her father told her. "Almost as though he didn't sleep at all last night after the card game. But then I suppose has to see the little matter of what he lost." He winked at Harry.

Genevieve was frozen in place. *He was gone.*

"Well, go see what he left for you," her mother urged.

Harry followed her into the green salon. The rectangular parcel in question was propped against the settee. She knew what it was before she knelt to unwrap it.

She tore off the paper with trembling hands while Harry silently watched.

And they both dropped to their knees in reverent silence when Titian's *Venus* was revealed.

She read the message attached.

*With felicitations for your every happiness in
your wedded life, and with much gratitude for showing me the true beauty in it.*

> *Your humble servant,*
> *A.M.*

Humble. She almost snorted.

Harry was silent.

She read the message again and again. But no
matter how often she read those few words, it never
said anything else, never revealed anything more
to her. She didn't know why she thought it ought
to. She held it tightly, but it didn't burn her skin, the
way his kisses had.

She didn't know why suddenly things were
blurry. And her heart was pounding sickeningly. It
wasn't pounding because she'd become engaged to
the man she loved.

It was pounding as though she'd been *betrayed.*

He'd *known.* Somehow he'd *known* Harry was
going to propose. But how?

She licked dry lips. "Harry . . . what's the thing
that decided you? That made you propose to me this
morning of all mornings?"

Harry was as surprised by the question as he was
by the gift.

"I hesitate to tell you but you may as well know
as I vow to never keep a secret from you. I won an
estate in the card game."

She sat down hard on the carpet. "You did *what*?"

"For *you*," he reiterated mischievously, laughing
at her shock. "I won it for *you*. And it unnerved me
so thoroughly I promise I shall never gamble again."

She stared at him.

"I suppose I should say . . . well done," she began cautiously.

Which made him laugh.

"But . . . from *whom* did you win the estate?"

"From Falconbridge, if you can countenance it."

Oh God. Just saying his name was almost as good as conjuring him. She wanted to hear his name again and again. The hollow howling in her gut was surely wrong. As were her clammy hands.

Something was terribly awry. The back of her neck prickled in portent.

"I can't countenance it, as a matter of fact. How did it come about?" Her voice came to her distantly. Her breathing was a little rough.

"It's a bit of a blur. But I will tell you this: His heart is not so black as one might think."

Heart. The word *heart* chimed in her head. The portent only amplified. *No. His heart is precious. His heart is worth having.*

"What makes you say that?" she heard herself say calmly.

"I will never tell another soul what I'm about to tell you. But during the last hand of the evening, he called my bluff, and I showed him my hand—I had an excellent hand, by the way. I wasn't simply being reckless. And he took one look and *folded* after my final wager. He claimed I had the better hand, and he'd lost. I'm a grown man, Genevieve, but I nearly fell right out of my chair, for I had wagered every last shilling I had. And he'd put up his property in Sussex. Rosemont. So I won it. It's mine."

Her heart stopped then. She gripped the note until the edges crushed in her fingers.

Harry continued on, obliviously cheerful.

"Well, everything after that was a bit of a blur. Everyone had rather scattered after that hand, including the duke. I never had a chance to shake his hand or say good-bye. I lingered, savoring my victory a bit, as God knows that room has been the sight of defeats this week. And the servants began to enter to tidy everything. Well, when all the guests were clear of the room, I took a peek at the duke's cards, out of curiosity. His hand was still lying there, all of it, facedown. And . . . Genevieve, he'd *won*. He had the best flush. He would have *ruined* me if he hadn't folded."

She couldn't feel her limbs. "You're saying he lost to you . . . purposely?"

"I cannot say whether it was purposefully. But it made it possible for me to propose to you. And so I did."

But we don't love each other. She'd said that to the duke. When he'd *suggested* they marry. He'd never said any such thing to her. He'd never agreed. He'd merely absorbed her words, like a blow.

He'd made it possible for Harry to propose to her. He'd given her everything he thought she'd wanted because he *loved* her. And it was all he could do for her, because he thought she loved Harry.

The greatest pleasure in my life was making sure she was happy and safe, he'd said about his wife.

"Perhaps we can name a child for him. Our first son."

She didn't precisely recoil. But she looked at Harry in rank astonishment. Dear God, he truly was oblivious.

He misread her. "Very well. Alexandra if it's a

girl. If you prefer a girl. Anything at all as long as he or she looks like you."

He loves me. Harry really does love me.

And she found herself thinking a violently heretical thought:

But what does he really know of love?

"Genevieve, what do you think?"

She looked at Harry for a silent moment. She touched a hand to his cheek briefly. The first time she'd done anything of the sort.

He gazed back at her warmly.

"That *bastard*," she said vehemently.

And then she bolted.

She dashed past her astonished family out of the house at a run and learned from a shaken stable boy, who was paralyzed by the sight of the furious Miss Genevieve Eversea advancing upon him—she was the quiet one, the sweet one!—and who would have nightmares for a week about it, that the Duke of Falconbridge had told his driver to take him to Rosemont.

Genevieve promptly turned to the head groom.

"Take me to Rosemont now," she ordered him. "Harness the team and have the driver take me there *now*."

"Now, Miss Genevieve . . ."

"*Now.*"

If she'd had a whip she would have cracked it. He took a step back as surely as if she had and put up an arm to do it, as if in defense of her lightning-bolt gaze.

Her family and Harry were astounded a short time later when the Eversea barouche hurtled down the drive.

* * *

She found him, after demanding his where-abouts from the footman who'd so kindly received them the other day, in an office, sorting through the papers that would make it possible for Harry to take Rosemont.

She paused in the doorway to watch him for a moment.

She said it quietly. "You *bastard*."

Moncrieffe turned slowly. When he saw her he went motionless. If anyone could drink with eyes, he did it. He drank her in.

Not that there wasn't a particle of *trepidation* in his gaze, too. Because there was.

It was a long while before he could speak. "It was 'badger' . . . before."

She *wouldn't* smile.

"You would have let me *go*. You would have allowed me to marry him."

"I did let you go. I did allow you to marry him. Did he propose?"

He said it so coolly she nearly struck him. Her hand actually raised, she dropped it down again. She was shaking with fury. So much this man had unleashed in her. Laughter and truth and depth and passion, and oh yes, temper.

He eyed that hand warily.

"Yes. He proposed."

"And did you accept him?"

"Yes. I accepted him."

There was a beat of silence.

"Ah." He stood watching her, a frown between his eyes. She could feel him beginning to retreat into himself. "That *is* a dilemma."

He thought this was amusing? *She* was in hell.

"You *love* me," she accused softly.

He didn't admit it. He didn't deny it.

He *was* breathing rather more quickly.

"Are you here for a reason, Genevieve?" His voice was growing colder. His way of imposing distance.

Her frustration howled from her. "You helped me show Harry's heart to him. But you couldn't show mine to *me*?"

"Listen to yourself, Genevieve. You sound like a child stomping her feet. How spoiled and greedy you've become. I can only teach you so much. You're a grown woman. I can attest to that." He raked a look over her that took in the wine red walking dress that yes, suited her beautifully and wouldn't clash with her complexion should she go scarlet with a blush or anger. "And some things you have to learn entirely on your own."

"But . . . you left. And you *gave* him Rosemont. You lost to him *deliberately*."

"Genevieve . . . I swear to you. It wasn't meant to hurt you. Or Harry. But tell me, how would you ever have seen it otherwise? And isn't it better to know?"

"It" being her heart.

"It" being how she truly felt.

Damn him. He was right.

It didn't mean she was any less furious with him.

"I couldn't see it because *you are* my *heart*, damn you! And *how* can I see my own heart if it's beating in my own chest?" She was practically raging at him.

He had no answer to that apparently. But something fierce and thrilling flashed in his eyes, and stayed there and the devil . . . he smiled slowly, as though a dim pupil had finally come around.

"And so you see now." He was demanding clarification.

She still wasn't ready to say it. "And now, because of you, I have to break Harry's heart."

"Do you?" he said softly, swiftly. He took a step toward her.

She took a step back. "I don't want to do it."

"*Everything* has a cost, Genevieve," he said softly, stepping closer.

She took a step back. She put her hands up to her face. And yes. Of *course* it was hot. It always seemed to be around him.

"It's a *terrible* cost. He loves me . . . so *much*." Her voice cracked. She made it sound like his fault.

"You cannot get through life unscathed, Genevieve."

"Stop lecturing me. I don't *want* to hurt anyone."

"Then what a pity it is that you love only me," he retorted.

Silence was absolute.

They stared at each other, astonished to hear that word for perhaps the first time between them.

And then wary.

She inhaled, and sighed out the breath, and closed her eyes.

"Bastard," she murmured. This time it sounded very like "I love you."

His mouth twitched at the corner. He may have released a breath.

They continued to regard each other warily from a distance beyond the reach of their fingertips.

"Have you stopped loving me?" she whispered.

Astonishing what she now had the courage to ask. "Because of how stupid I've been?"

"Tell me first what you came here to say and then I'll tell you whether I ever did."

His idea of humor. And she noticed he didn't rush to her defense when she'd called herself stupid.

It would have been silent, except that her head thudded so hard the blood rang in her ears. Nobody spoke, until:

"Bastard," he whispered mockingly right along with her.

She was going to say it. It was welling in her. Her head felt as though it might float away from her body from a sort of joyous terror. Vertigo again—everything associated with love seemed to make a person either desperately physically uncomfortable or out of their minds with pleasure—but it was the kind of vertigo that deceived her into thinking she was flying. And all at once she could see forever, but she wasn't entirely certain the forever she wanted would be hers. That she would ever reach it.

It was up to the man she had all but sent away.

And she had to say it anyway.

And though she could scarcely even feel them, her lips formed the words, and sound emerged, sounding frayed, and small and cracked, forged in her somehow before she was born, since before time, words meant only for him.

"I love you."

Three of the most powerful words in the world offered to one of the most powerful men in London in such a small voice.

And at first she thought nothing at all had happened. He didn't blink. But then she realized she'd somehow set him . . . softly ablaze. Emotion burned from him, and his eyes . . . she would never forget his eyes in this moment.

His hands remained at his sides.

Which is when she noticed they were trembling.

God help her, that's when she felt tears begin to burn at the back of her eyes.

One got away. And she brushed her hand roughly against it.

And the man who never cleared his throat . . . cleared his throat. And his voice, in truth, wasn't a good deal louder than hers.

"Then it's just as well that I love you, Genevieve."

Very, very softly he said it, as though the two of them were in church, or as if he were reciting a spell. With that way he had of making everything he said sound true and right. Then again, they'd become so used to speaking to each other softly, as so much of their conversation took place in the dark.

And she doubted *he'd* been anywhere near a church in a very long time.

"Well, good," she sniffed.

"And I would be honored if you would consent to be my wife," he added.

Finally a proper proposal!

"Once you've jilted Harry."

Oh God, but he was a devil. Who in their right mind would marry this man? She'd have to be mad. It was wicked and awful. But she was laughing and crying all at once.

"Yes, please, I will marry you."

"Yes please?" he mocked gently, and as quickly

as he always moved she was enfolded in his arms.

And this was when she could feel him at last surrender his calm, and his whole body was shaking.

Oh God. So he'd been *afraid*. He'd taken an enormous risk. He'd come so close to losing her. But he was a gambler, and the legend still held true: the Duke of Falconbridge always won, even when he lost.

She held him fast, and soothed him as he'd comforted her the other night, when she'd frantically searched the house for him and then erupted in a storm of love for him, though she hadn't seen it for what it was.

He'd known.

He kissed her hair, her forehead, and then her lips, and that's where his lips lingered.

"But I will have to tell everyone now. I have to break Harry's heart. It will cause such distress. Or at least an uproar."

"Blame me. Everyone thinks I'm an evil bastard anyway."

"I will kill anyone who dares say it aloud."

"Then you'll be very, very busy shedding blood."

She laughed.

"Hush," he said. "In exchange for causing an uproar, I will dedicate myself to making you happy for the rest of your life."

"Then you only need live for a good long time, for you are everything I need to be happy."

He gave a short wondering laugh at this. She felt his shoulders jump beneath her hands, and suddenly this seemed fascinating and precious. She felt shy and desperately protective and it was almost more than she could bear, but then he was always a little ahead of her in terms of realizing and bearing things. She would bear it happily.

And then gently he extricated himself from her, and stood back. He lifted her up onto the desk and leaned toward her. "Genevieve . . . there is something I need to do *now* . . ."

"Yes?" She was breathless with anticipation.

He took her hand . . . and brought it up to his lips . . . and kissed it.

"Something for you to cherish forever," he said.

She had no doubt that she would.

Epilogue

While the duke took care of obtaining a special license, Genevieve set out to do one of the hardest things she'd ever done. She invited Harry out for a walk along the lane to do it, because . . . well, why not? She was beginning to associate that walk with being marched before a firing squad, and perhaps it was a ceremonial part of every life change from now on. He paused to pick up a leaf, one of the few that hadn't yet been trampled or disintegrated by rain.

Harry was silent for a long time after she told him. In as few sentences as possible, that she could not marry him and would be marrying the duke instead.

"I cannot say I'm surprised," he finally said.

She didn't want him to expound on that, and so she only said, "I'm sorry to hurt you."

He sucked in a breath. And then he dropped head in a nod. And then he pressed his lips together and kept nodding. She had a terrible suspicion this was the way men fought off tears.

He took another breath. He crumbled the leaf into powder. She wondered if he considered it symbolism.

"Did you ever love me?" he finally asked.

"Of course," she said softly, astonished. "I love you still, Harry."

He gave a short laugh. "As a *dearest friend*."

She didn't correct him. He was quoting himself with considerable bemusement, perhaps for the first time hearing it the way she'd heard it that day he'd told her he intended to propose to Millicent. How absurd and hurtful such warm-sounding words could be.

He thrust his hands into his pockets and stared at her as though seeing her for the first time, assessing, detached, wondering, and a panoply of expressions crossed his face. Doubtless it was very similar to the way she'd looked at him that day he'd finally issued his proposal.

She didn't take any pleasure in it.

They were quiet now. Even though she'd always wanted to spare him unhappiness, always wanted to make things better for him, she didn't ask him what he was thinking. This was something he would need to understand and accept without her help.

"Perhaps I'll proceed to the Continent," he said defiantly. "Go off to fight a foreign war."

"I hope you won't."

"I probably won't," he admitted glumly after a moment. "Though the Continent might do me some good."

She smiled faintly. And so did he.

"Harry . . . the duke is sincere in wanting you to have Rosemont. He forfeited by his hand and followed the rules of the game. It's yours."

"He likely meant it to be *yours*, Genevieve."

She didn't answer that, because it's precisely what the duke had wanted. The duke had intended to make a *statement*. He'd sent a message to Genevieve with it.

He'd certainly succeeded.

"It's yours now."

"As consolation prizes go, it could be worse." Harry smiled crookedly. There was a hint of self-deprecating irony and a new hardness in his voice.

She thought that heartbreak might just give his character the shadows and corners and angles it needed to make it truly *interesting*. To deepen and shape it.

She was sorry she would be the one to help make him truly interesting.

But she'd never apologize for falling in love with a man who already was.

"Well, that's more like it, dear," her mother said with relief, with another hug and a kiss, when she learned that Genevieve would be marrying the duke.

Hmm. Her mother was full of surprises.

"Are you sure you want this one, and you won't keep trying men on and taking them off like hair ribbons? You're sure the duke is the last of the future husbands you'll be producing?" Her father was teasing her, which meant he heartily approved. Doubtless he entertained visions of endless games of five-card loo in his future.

Both of her parents were a bit misty.

"You see," Ian told Colin later at the Pig & Thistle, "I *did* do the man a favor. I found him the *right* wife."

Colin snorted. "You can say that now, but I will forever cherish the look on your face when our Genevieve told us she'd be marrying the duke." Colin promptly imitated that look.

"So I looked like someone who'd been clubbed in the head? Thank you. Fascinating."

Ian had the sinking suspicion Colin would imitate that look frequently and mockingly for the rest of his life.

Colin acknowledged this by raising his tankard to his brother sardonically and then taking a swig of ale. "Do we think he truly intends to marry Genevieve?"

"He sent for a special license. The man is smitten. The wedding is in a few days' time."

"Well, isn't that remarkable."

Colin began to go misty-eyed at the notion of marriage again, so Ian kicked him beneath the table before he could begin rhapsodizing about the matrimonial condition.

"Ow. So have we established that the duke *doesn't* intend to kill you?"

"He doesn't. He said Genevieve would kill him if he harmed a hair on my head, and that he cherishes the things she cherishes so he'll refrain from murdering me." The duke had in fact pulled him aside to say this. Ian left off the part where Moncrieffe had said, "Even if the things she cherishes are feckless."

He suspected that he and the duke might, eventually, one day, dare he think it . . . be friends.

"Who knew our Genevieve could be so surprisingly strict?" Colin mused.

"I would never have guessed it."

They toasted to their sister's happiness.

And as for Genevieve and Moncrieffe, they were married in the church at Pennyroyal Green by her cousin Adam Sylvaine, the vicar, and by the time the clock struck midnight on their wedding day, they were both fast asleep in each other's arms.

They didn't wake until the sun was high in the sky the next day.

At Avon Books, we know your passion for romance—once you finish one of our novels, you find yourself wanting more.

May we tempt you with . . .

- **Excerpts** from our upcoming releases.

- Entertaining **extras**, including authors' personal photo albums and book lists.

- Behind-the-scenes **scoop** on your favorite characters and series.

- **Sweepstakes** for the chance to win free books, romantic getaways, and other fun prizes.

- Writing **tips** from our authors and editors.

- **Blog** with our authors and find out why they love to write romance.

- **Exclusive content** that's not contained within the pages of our novels.

Join us at
www.avonbooks.com